本书是国家社科基金一般项目
"评价学取向的典籍英译批评研究"（编号:18BYY034）
阶段性研究成果

价值论观照下的文学翻译批评研究

Axiological Approach to Criticism of Literary Translation

张志强 刘国兵 著

中国社会科学出版社

图书在版编目（CIP）数据

价值论观照下的文学翻译批评研究：英文/张志强，刘国兵著. —北京：中国社会科学出版社，2023.3
ISBN 978-7-5227-1741-8

Ⅰ.①价… Ⅱ.①张… ②刘… Ⅲ.①文学翻译－翻译理论－研究－英文 Ⅳ.①I046

中国国家版本馆CIP数据核字（2023）第060758号

出 版 人	赵剑英
责任编辑	夏　侠
责任校对	李　姐
责任印制	王　超

出　　版	中国社会科学出版社
社　　址	北京鼓楼西大街甲 158 号
邮　　编	100720
网　　址	http://www.csspw.cn
发 行 部	010－84083685
门 市 部	010－84029450
经　　销	新华书店及其他书店

印　　刷	北京君升印刷有限公司
装　　订	廊坊市广阳区广增装订厂
版　　次	2023年3月第1版
印　　次	2023年3月第1次印刷

开　　本	710×1000　1/16
印　　张	18.75
字　　数	307千字
定　　价	99.00元

凡购买中国社会科学出版社图书，如有质量问题请与本社营销中心联系调换
电话：010－84083683

"The healthy development of the course of translation of our country cannot be guaranteed without translation criticism. We are quite short of translation criticism nowadays. The practice of translation criticism should be greatly strengthened." (Ji Xianlin, qtd. in Xu Jun 2003: 396)

Preface

Ever since the 1980s postmodernism has greatly influenced the field of Translation Studies. As a result, traditional philologist and structuralist paradigms were marginalized. Various cultural approaches offered various, sometimes conflicting, criteria for criticizing literary translation, and some of them with radical individual constructivism and deconstructionism as their philosophical foundations have almost made "translation criteria" a meaningless term. Translation has thus been made a "free play" of translators and readers as meaning has become indeterminate and "anything goes". The plurality of criteria has brought forth people's doubt about the scientificity and objectivity of any criticism of literary translation. It has put the study of criticism of literary translation at stake, making us rethink about our previous approaches. Inspired by Lv Jun's axiological-oriented approach to translation criticism, the authors of this book turn to evaluation theories and axiology in general in order to get more insights into criticism of literary translation.

The authors first gave a detailed review of the previous studies of translation criticism and criticism of literary translation in light of paradigm and system theories, finding that difference among the existing paradigms and sub-paradigms mainly stems from people's different understandings of the nature of translation, the essence of literariness and different outlooks of value.

Based on their introduction and discussion of evaluation theories and axiology in general and in light of evaluation theories of social constructivism, the authors gave a detailed analysis of those main factors of criticism of literary translation, including the nature of criticism of literary translation, the objectives, the classification, the properties, the principles, the criteria, the methodology and so on.

Our studies show that the essence of criticism is evaluation and literary translation and criticism of literary translation are forms of human practice to create values. The object of our criticism of literary translation is the value relationship between the subject and the object. Criticism of literary translation cannot be separated from epistemology as to pass on reasonable value judgment, we have to know the subject and the object and their relationship. Axiological approach to criticism of literary translation holds a dialectical view on the subjectivity and objectivity. It does not deny there is subjectivity and relativity in criticism, but is strongly against the dogma of "anything goes" and absolute relativism. Though criteria for criticism are context dependent, they are nevertheless fixed in a specific context. Though criteria are pluralistic, there is still objectivity in them as they are determined by the needs of the subject which are both subjective and objective. The objectivity lies in the constraints of the objective laws of things (texts) and the objective laws of social development on the subject. Axiological-oriented criticism of literary translation is practical-oriented, reflexive and constructive. It is not confined to the judgment of what Is, but rather, emphasizes the judgment of what Ought to be, seeking a proper combination of description and prescription. This book discusses in detail issues such as translation criteria, criteria for translation criticism, the maximal criteria, the minimal criteria, judgment of ethic and politic values, intellectual value and aesthetic value of literary translation etc. offering a fairly systematic framework for criticism of literary translation and expounding the significance of meta-criticism for the development of studies on criticism of literary translation. It is hoped that this book can attract readers majoring or interested in foreign languages, Translation Studies, literature and comparative literature alike, offering them some new ideas concerning literature and criticism of literary translation.

Contents

Chapter 3　Studies on Criticism of Literary Translation: Status Quo and Problems

Chapter 4　Axiology and Evaluation: Theoretical Foundation

Introduction

Katharina Reiss in her "Author's Foreword" of her *Translation Criticism: The Potentials and Limitations* (2004: xi) says that "[t]he sheer bulk and undeniable significance of translations in today's world require that the quality of translations be a matter of special attention". Study of translation criticism has both theoretical and practical significance as "[u]ndeniably many poor translations have been made and even published" while "[t]he standards most often observed by critics are generally arbitrary" (ibid). More than fifty years ago, Reiss thought "a careful study of the potential and limitations of translation criticism" necessary "because the present state of the art is inadequate" (ibid).

0.1 Research Background

A survey of the practice of translation criticism tells us that the situation described by Reiss has not changed much during the past decades. Criticisms were made either according to a certain moral code or a certain aesthetic standard. They were either based on critic's own experience, impression or on a certain criterion relying largely on a certain translation theory. Some of them focus on the appreciation of a translation, others on finding faults. Some are quantitative while others qualitative. Some stay at the technique level, others at textual or cultural levels. Theoretical studies on translation criticism are inadequate as well compared with the large number of translated texts and practice of translation criticism. Though with the development of Translation Studies at home and abroad, more systematic studies on translation criticism concerning its basic theories is underway (Yang Xiaorong 2005), so far as criticism of literary translation is concerned, it remains a subject that has not been established (Wang Hongyin 2006; Lv Jun & Hou Xiangqun 2009; Liu Yunhong & Xu Jun 2014). Criticism of literary translation is even more underdeveloped compared with the large number of translations of literary works and criticisms of non-literary translation generally known as translation quality assessment (TQA). Due to partly the short history of Translation Studies as an independent discipline, and partly to the complexity of literary translation itself, study of criticism of literary translation is far from systematic and is still in its infancy. On the one hand, in the net-era and the current context of globalization there have been more and more cultural exchanges and more and more literary translations. On the other hand, excellent translations and criticisms are in a small number. Ever since the 1980s postmodernism has greatly influenced the field of Translation Studies. As post-structuralism and deconstructionism became prevailing, traditional philologist and structuralist paradigms were marginalized and there appeared various cultural approaches which view translation as a cultural and political event rather than a linguistic activity. Polysystem theory and the manipulation school analyze the mechanisms of canonization, and reveal the manipulation to which the foreign texts may be submitted in the process of their entering the target cultural system. Feminist approach carries out a rereading and rewriting of the existing translation to recover women's works "lost" in the patriarchic canon, to call people's attention to the subjectivity of the translator, especially the female translator for the purpose of achieving political visibility. Postcolonialist theories view translation both as a tool for the maintenance of colonialism, reinforcing the hegemony of the colonizer and for dehegemonizing the cultural hegemony and any form of ethno-centrism. The Brazilian "cannibalism" encourages translators to devour the language of the colonizers to produce "a new purified and energized form that is appropriate to the needs of the native peoples" (Munday 2001: 136;). Thus, translation is seen "as the battleground and exemplification of the postcolonial context"(Munday, Pinto & Blakesley 2022: 178). These approaches offer various, sometimes conflicting, criteria for criticizing literary translation, and some of them with radical individual constructivism and deconstructionism as their philosophical foundation have almost made "translation criteria" a meaningless term, dethroning the "author" and the "original text" on which the traditional criteria are based. Translation has thus been made a "free play" of translators and readers as meaning has become inderterminate and "anything goes". The plurality of criteria has brought forth people's doubt about the scientificity and objectivity of any criticism of literary translation. Public readers, translation students and some translation studies scholars can not help feeling perplexed and puzzled over the issue of translation criteria and criteria for criticism. This has obviously put the study of criticism of literary translation at stake and makes us rethink about our previous approaches.

0.1.1 Translation studies in the West

Translation Studies has witnessed a great progress in the 20th century. Snell-Hornby (2006: preface) in her *The Turns of Translation Studies: New Paradigms or Shifting Viewpoints?* offers us a critical assessment of the development of translation studies, concentrating, as she herself says, "on the last twenty years and focusing on what have turned out to be ground-breaking contributions (new paradigms) as against what may be seen in retrospect to have been only a change in position on already established territory (shifting viewpoints)". Actually, Snell-Hornby gives a tentative assessment of the development of Translation Studies over the past thirty years. For she talks about the "pragmatic turn" in linguistics and in translation theories owing to the development of text-linguistics in the 1970s, the "cultural turn" in the 1980s, the empirical and cognitive turn in interpreting studies, and the globalization turn in the 1990s. She also gives a review of the state of Translation Studies at the turn of the millennium. She observes a tendency of "back to linguistics" shown by the "resurrecting the age old debate on the concept of equivalence" and the use of computer corpora "with the themes of 'translation universals'" (ibid: 151-152). She comments that "[i]t seems that Translation Studies, after the 'cultural turn' of the 1980s, the 'historical curve' and the 'cognitive twist' of the 1990s (see Chesterman 2002), seems at the beginning of the new century to be facing a globalized, hence anglophile levelling off" (ibid: 155). In recent years, some scholars also speak of an "ideological turn" (Matthew Wing-Kwong Leung) or a "sociological turn" (Michaela Wolf), but in Snell-Hornby's opinion, they are not new paradigms and can be embodied in the "cultural turn" in its broad sense (ibid: 172).

From the above-mentioned development in Translation Studies, we can see that the discipline at present is becoming more and more interdisciplinary and approaches are becoming more and more pluralistic. Different cultural approaches and linguistic approaches are still underway. Translation scholars are seeking breakthroughs by means of borrowing theories and findings from other fields such as philosophy, psychology, neurophysiology, sociology etc. Mona Baker, for example, introduces narrative theory (the typology of narrative proposed by Somers and Gibson) to the study of translation and interpretation and published her *Translation and Conflict: A Narrative Account* providing "an original and coherent model of analysis that pays equal attention to micro-and macro aspects of the circulation of narration in translation, to translation and interpretation, and to questions of dominance and resistance" especially in times of war (Baker, 2006:

back cover). She also wrote a series of articles on corpus-based translation studies. Meanwhile, there is also a tendency to combine literary and linguistic approaches with cultural approaches. Some achievements have been made in this respect both at home and abroad.

0.1.2 Translation studies in China

In China, the 20th century also witnessed a flourish of Translation Studies. Numerous articles appeared in various journals and attempts have been made to make translation studies a discipline of its own right. Huang Long published his *Translatology* in 1988, a pioneering book in Translation Studies in China, discussing not only written translation, but also oral interpretation and machine translation. Liu Miqing published his *Modern Translation Theories* in 1990, another pioneering book trying to give a comprehensive theoretical account of translation. Chen Fukang published his *A Chronicle of Chinese Translation Theories* in 1992, an early attempt at a systematic reflection on Chinese translation theories.

Yet, with the ongoing process of globalization, translation studies scholars in China were, for quite a while, engaged more in "listening" to the whistling of the West wind from the field of Translation Studies than "thinking" in their own way. Xu Jun and Mu Lei (2009) point out that many researches on translation studies in China, are just the introduction, justification and application of the Western translation theories, short of critical inquiry into those foreign theories. This is largely because we have been greatly influenced by foreign translation theories. Earlier in 1984, we read *Nida On Translation* by Tan Zaixi, books of Peter Newmark in photograph and so on. Then there were Jin Di and Nida's *On Translation* and articles introducing the Western linguistic theories of translation. At the turn of the century, we read Liao Qiyi's *Studies on Contemporary Western Translation Theories* (2000), mainly introductory, and Shen Yuping's *Selected Western Translation Theories* (2002). Publishing houses such as Shanghai Foreign Language and Education Press and Foreign Language Teaching and Research Press published series of works in Translation Studies abroad helping the publicity of the Western translation theories.

However, with the coming of the new epoch and especially with the rapid development of China's society and economy, translation studies scholars in China began to gain more and more cultural confidence. The new century ushered a new stage featured by digesting and critical thinking of those foreign theories of translation and establishing our own theories. There were efforts made to compare traditional Chinese translation theories with those in the West, to rethink and reinterpret plenty of our traditional translation theories and even try to establish schools of our own. Collections of essays in Translation Studies were published and monographs came out at a speed much faster than one can follow. And the last two decades actually witnessed a wake of the awareness of not losing our voices in the circle of Translation Studies worldwide with the implementation of the initiative "going global of the Chinese culture". Liu Zhongde published his *Studies on Western Translation Theories* in 2002. Zhang Boran and Xu Jun (2002) complied a memoir entitled *Translation Studies Facing the New Century* which contains a number of articles comparing the Western theories with the Chinese ones. In 2003, Xun Jun published his *On Translation* making a fairly comprehensive discussion on almost every aspect of translation. Liu Miqing (2005) published his *A Comparative Study of Chinese and Western Translation Theories* giving a systematic comparison between the two and criticizing some of the tendency to underestimate Chinese translation theories. Chang Nam Fung (2004) published his *A Critical Study of Chinese and Western Translation Theories*, offering us some insightful comments on the functionalist approach and the cultural approaches in the West, pointing out not only some of our misunderstanding of the related theories but also some shortcomings of the discussed theories and some improvements that can be made. Tan Zaixi (2005) published his *Translation Studies*, with one of its chapters focusing on the comparison of Western and Chinese translation theories. Lv Jun and Hou Xiangqun (2006) published their *Translatology—A Constructivist Perspective of Translation Study* carrying out a paradigmatic approach to Translation Studies and trying to establish a new paradigm featured by social constructivism. To be more exact, it is Lv Jun (2001) who has pioneered the constructivist translatology in light of Thomas Kuhn's paradigm theory and with Jurgen Habermas' Universal Pragmatics as the philosophical foundation of his study. In the following years, Hou Xiangqun joined Lv Jun's study in illustrating the constructivist paradigm based on a critical review of the previous paradigms. As this paradigmatic approach can give us a better understanding of the overall Translation Studies, the authors think it necessary to introduce it here.

According to Lv Jun and Hou Xiangqun (2006), there have been some paradigmatic changes in Translation Studies in China. The first is labeled "philologist" paradigm. In this paradigm, the intention of "the author" is absolutely authoritative and divine, and can be traced and obtained by the reader. Translators as well as critics turn to every clue of the author, everything concerning the author, the autobiography, the life experience, the historical background and even the author's correspondence with his or her friends, should be studied to ensure a sound translation. The second paradigm is closely associated with structuralism in linguistics and therefore can be called the "structuralist" paradigm, with analytic philosophy as its philosophical basis. In this paradigm, the authoritative position of "the author" gives way to "the text" and "language" which is the material of a text. Rules of language shift or transfer and the interior laws of the text become the foundation of interpretation, translation and criticism alike. Translation and criticism of this paradigm seems more convincing and more objective compared with the first paradigm as "the text", unlike "the author", is always "there" as a substantial object. It seems that all those problems in translation can be solved through linguistic analyses: structural analysis, semantic analysis and contrastive analysis.

The third paradigm appears with another trend of the "linguistic turn" in the field of philosophy, taking an ontological view of language rather than an instrumental view. What more directly influences and makes the third paradigm dominant is modern hermeneutic philosophy which argues that meaning and understanding or interpreting can only come from the dialogue between the reader and the text. Modern hermeneutics not only overthrows the monarchy position of "the author", but that of "the text" by deconstructing language which is traditionally regarded as an effective tool for the production, interpretation and analysis of meaning. Gadmer's concept of "fusion of horizons" undermines the "indeterminacy" of meaning. The neographism "Différance" coined by Derrida indicates that language generates meaning through the "play of Différance". Meaning cannot precede différance, and therefore, there does not exist any pure, totally unified origin of meaning. From a deconstructive point of view, meaning is not a prior presence expressed in language. It therefore cannot be extracted from one language and transferred into another. Pursuing meaning is not a matter of "revealing" some hidden presence that is already "there" in "the text" or with "the author". The traditional theory of meaning has failed to capture this crucial point (Davis 2004). Those different approaches to translation with the "cultural turn" all belong to this third paradigm as they share the same theoretical foundation—poststructuralism and deconstructionism and question the notion of "originality" and reverse the traditional hierarchical relation between the source text (ST) and the target text (TT). They do not believe there is the "original" meaning and hold that the term "equivalence" in translation is problematic and even, should be discarded.

In the last two decades, we could find some of the translation theories put forward by Chinese scholars were gaining international influence. For instance, the Eco-translatology proposed by Hu Gengshen at the turn of the century has proved to be a multidisciplinary and interdisciplinary eco-paradigm, which has attracted many scholars from different countries, providing "a new epistemological perspective and methodological path for the study of translation theories and translation practice" (Hu Gengshen 2021:1-6).

Speaking of Translation Studies in China, we must not forget that some large-scale parallel corpora have been built enabling us to carry out researches which were impossible before. Translation Studies is also becoming more and more interdisciplinary with socio-cultural approaches as the dominant trend.

Though many scholars in China are familiar with Western translation theories, and some of them even proposed their own approaches, for example, the "translator behaviour criticism" by Zhou Lingshun, yet, there has not been enough dialogue between Chinese scholars and their Western colleagues because many of their researches are written in Chinese and published in China.

The above-mentioned works are only a small part of the achievements made by Chinese scholars. There are, needless to say, many other scholars who have made their contribution to the development of Chinese Translation Studies.

0.1.3 Studies of translation criticism and criticism of literary translation

As far as translation criticism is concerned, the study on it is quite insufficient. Translation criticism, according to James Holmes (1988), belongs to the Applied Translation Studies. "Applied Translation Studies" distinguishes itself from the "Pure Translation Studies", referring mainly to the application of translation theories to translator training and translation criticism, translation policy etc. Translation criticism is thus supposed to be practical-oriented and depends largely on the development of translation theories as the latter are supposed to provide the former with principles and criteria. Holmes believes that descriptive and theoretical translation studies provide the scholarly findings for translation criticism and that "[t] he level of such criticism is today still frequently very low, and in many countries still quite uninfluenced by the developments within the field of translation studies" (Holmes 1988: 79).

In the West, the practical orientation of translation criticism has a far-reaching influence on the development of the study on translation criticism. Most of the relevant works are concerned with, actually, the assessment of translation quality. The underdevelopment of translation criticism can be easily seen as one cannot find the term "translation criticism" in all the influential dictionaries of Translation Studies published in the West. Most of the researches and writings on criticism of literary translation in the West are unsystematic too, as underdeveloped as translation criticism as a whole.

In China, there are many articles and books on or touching upon translation criticism, including criticism of literary translation. However, most of them are not systematized. There are only three monographs concentrating on translation criticism: Yang Xiaorong's *Introduction to Translation Criticism* in 2005, Wen Jun's *Introduction to Criticism of Technical Translation* in 2006, and Lv Jun and Hou Xiangqun's *An Introduction to the Science of Translation Criticism* in 2009. And two monographs on criticism of literary translation are *Studies on Criticism of Literary Translation* written by Xu Jun in 1992 and *On the Criticism of Literary Translation* by Wang Hongyin in 2006. Nevertheless, as is Richards' often-quoted words, translation "is probably the most complex type of event in the history of the cosmos" (Nida 1993: 1), and so far as translation criticism is concerned, especially criticism of literary translation, things become even more complicated. Compared with numerous translation of literary works there exist in the world, we can say that our study on criticism of literary translation is rather inadequate around the world.

0.2 Research Motivations

Complex as translation and translation criticism are, people have never stopped their studies on them. Just as great efforts are being made to seek breakthroughs in Translation Studies as a whole, there are also efforts to pave the way for the establishment of a discipline of translation criticism. Toury (1995/2001: 18) points out rightly the applied extensions (translator training, translation aids, translation criticism etc.) have no direct relationship with theoretical and descriptive translation theories. For the application of the theoretical and descriptive translation theories to any of the applied extensions, we need some "bridging rules" and "at any rate, none of them can draw on Translation Studies alone" and each of them "can become an object of study too". Translation criticism should no longer be confined to the application of translation theories to the measurement of the quality of a translated text, but rather, it should include our critical reflection on translation events and translation theories. "In a broad sense, translation criticism is an overall evaluation of the process and product of a translation in accordance with certain criteria" (Lin Huangtian 1997: 184). "It is a mental activity based on a certain value, an intellectual activity involving the analyses and evaluation of a certain translation phenomenon (including translated works and translation theories) and an integrity of aesthetic evaluation and scientific judgments" (Fang Mengzhi 2004: 346). The study of translation criticism differentiates itself from the practice of translation criticism in that the latter is the "object" of the former and the former has a nature of meta-cognition and meta-criticism as Lv Jun (2006; 2009) points out in one of his articles and in the book *An Introduction to the Science of Translation Criticism*. It calls for the guidance of axiology, especially the evaluation theories in axiology instead of translation theories.

The study of value or axiology in the West has a long history and theories of evaluation are well developed. Though in China axiology has a much shorter history, it has been developing very fast and is quite fruitful. Tremendous findings in axiology have drawn the attention of some scholars in the field of Translation Studies in China. Xu Jun (1992) once pointed out that in studying criticism of literary translation we need the help of axiology and Lv Jun (2006; 2007) wrote several articles analyzing the relationship between axiology and study on translation criticism, seeking to establish a subject of translation criticism of its own right.

According to Karl Popper, any scientific research undergoes the process of P1 → TS → EE → P2 (P1 refers to the problem we are facing, TS refers to our tentative solution, EE is the abbreviation for error elimination, a stage of hypothesis testing and P2, the new problem) (Zhao Dunhua 2006: 40). While we are fully aware there is no easy solution to problems such as translation criticism, it is, nevertheless, our desire to crack the hard nut that has lent us different approaches. Seeing the insufficiency and necessity of in-depth study of criticism of literary translation, viewing criticism essentially as a kind of value judgment and inspired by the above-mentioned scholars, especially by Lv Jun's axiological-oriented approach to translation criticism, the authors of this book turn to evaluation theories and axiology in general in order to get more insights into criticism of literary translation. It is also hoped that the current research will make due contribution to the establishment of a subject of criticism of literary translation of its own right.

0.3 Research Questions and Objectives

As is stated above, we are short of systematic studies on translation criticism around the world and studies on criticism of literary translation are even more inadequate. In this book, the authors choose to make criticism of literary translation as the object of their study. In order to get more insight into the research object, they intend first to examine the following questions: 1), what do we mean by "translation" and "literary translation"? 2), what are the essences of "criticism", "translation criticism", "literary criticism" and "criticism of literary translation"? 3), where we are in the studies of translation criticism and criticism of literary translation? 4), what are the main factors that have led to the current crisis of criticism of literary translation? They then intend to investigate how we can resolve the crisis and better our study of criticism of literary translation in light of evaluation theories and axiology in general. And this again leads them to investigate into the objectives, the principles, the criteria and the methodology and the properties of criticism of literary translation in light of evaluation theories and axiology in general. This research aims at making the study of criticism of literary translation more systematic and scientific by finding answers to the above-raised questions and by offering an axiological approach to criticism of literary translation. It is meant as an endeavor to make some contribution to the establishment of a subject of meta-criticism of literary translation.

0.4 Research Significance

This study is quite different from the previous studies in that it views translation criticism as a special kind of evaluation. It is not based on any translation theory, but rather mainly on evaluation theories and axiology in general, and findings of epistemology are also borrowed. According to axiology, any social activity is value-oriented or value-driven; the activity of translation is therefore also value-creation. Criticism of a translation is on the one hand actually to judge its values and on the other hand, also to create value and for greater value. As evaluation theories in axiology can offer us a broader vision, we can expect a more comprehensive understanding about the nature and features of criticism of literary translation. It is hoped that such a study will benefit not only the practice of criticism of literary translation, but also the theoretical research of criticism of literary translation. It is also the authors' hope that this study will be a further step towards the establishment of the subject of translation criticism. That is to say, the current research potentially possesses both the theoretical and practical significance for the criticism of literary translation and for translation criticism as a whole.

0.5 Research Methodology

The current study is mainly a qualitative and evaluative one. The methods adopted are mainly literature analysis and interpretation. As criticism of literary translation is closely connected with one's views on translation and especially literary translation, the authors will first give a survey of definitions of translation and literary translation. A review of the practice and theoretical study of criticism of literary translation is then given to find out what is the current situation of criticism of literary translation in China and in the West. To get a clear picture of the previous studies on criticism of literary translation, the authors adopt a paradigmatic approach in light of paradigm theory and system theory. They then introduce some theories of axiology which offer the theoretical foundation for investigating into the nature, objectives, different types, principles, criteria and the methods of criticism of literary translation, giving a detailed analysis of some of the main factors and issues involved in the study of criticism of literary translation. In order to know the research object more clearly, they will use both the method of description and that of comparison. In brief, to fulfill the objectives stated in section 0.3, the authors will adopt methods such as description, inductive reasoning, and comparison and dialectic analyses of the relevant documents. The nature of this study therefore will be descriptive, explanatory, explorative, and theoretical in general, with a bright tinge of meta-criticism, featured by concept interpreting and evaluating as often is in the field of humanities.

0.6 Organization of the Book

This book consists of seven parts. The first part is an introduction to the whole book, stating the research background, research motivations, objectives, significance, methodologies and the structure of the book. In the first chapter, natures of translation and literary translation are discussed in detail. The second chapter gives a review of previous studies of theories and practice of criticism, literary criticism and translation criticism in China and in the West in order to know better their essences. The third chapter is a detailed review and discussion of criticism of literary translation at the practical and theoretical levels. The fourth chapter serves as a theoretical foundation offering an introduction and discussion of axiology and the related evaluation theories. Chapter 5 is the authors' detailed discussion about the value of literary works, values of literary translation and main factors concerning criticism of literary translation. Chapter 6 is the summary and conclusion of the research, pointing out the major findings of the present study and offering some suggestions for further studies at the same time.

Chapter 1
Translation and Literary Translation

"What translation is? I am afraid that none of those engaged in studying translation theories can avoid asking and answering this question. Personally, I think there are at least two reasons for this: one is that it seems the starting point of all the scientific researches to ask what X is and the other is that we have to know first what translation is to discuss the other related important questions in translation studies". (Xu Jun 2001: 5)

The earliest monograph on criticism of literary translation *Studies on Criticism of Literary Translation* by Xu Jun (1992) begins with the definition and the essence of translation. Following Xu, the authors of the present book will first of all come to the discussion about the definition of translation as people's ideas about translation criticism are often related with and can often be inferred from their definitions of translation. Actually, the authors find it a common way for many writers doing scientific researches to begin with the definition. Alexander Fraser Tytler once said (at the beginning of his *Essays on the Principles of Translation*), "if it were possible, accurately to define, or, perhaps more properly, to describe what is meant by *a good Translation*, it is evident that a considerable progress would be made towards establishing the Rules of the *Art*, for theses Rules would flow naturally from that definition or description" (qtd. in Shen Yuping 2002: 166). And Tytler's three principles, or "laws of translation" in his own words (ibid: 167), are simply the result of his analysis of what *a good Translation* is. Actually, We can further Tytler's statement by saying that if we know what a translation is or should be, then it is easier for us to know, and to agree upon, how to criticize a translation or how to evaluate a translation as Yang Xiaorong (2005: 8) says to the effect that one's idea about translation determines one's views on how to evaluate a translation. "Before attempting to develop a model for translation quality assessment, we first have to be more precise about what we mean by translation" (House 1981: 25). House's words are to the point. However, the fact is that it is hard to give a definition of translation to everyone's satisfaction as Tytler further mentioned "[b]ut there is no subject of criticism where there has been so much difference of opinion" (qtd. in Shen Yuping 2002: 166). Hartmann (2006) reviewing *An International Encyclopedia of Translation Studies* published in Berlin in 2004, says that "I looked in vain for a secure definition of translation, in terms of proposed theoretical models and empirical observations of the process".

Things are made even more complex as the word "translation" can refer to the result of translating and the process of translating itself. In the fields of physics, chemistry, computer science and medical science, people use the term "translation" to refer to quite different things. And in China, the term *fanyi* also refers to a person who does written translation or oral interpretation. The authors of this book do not want to discuss all those definitions since it is on the one hand impossible and on the other hand unnecessary. Only part of them will be discussed to meet the demand of the present research of getting to know those representative ideas about translation in the field of Translation Studies. And to meet our demand, the definitions to be discussed include those of the ancient times and the present day in China and in the West.

1.1 Definitions of Translation in China

China is a country with a long history of translation activity and naturally quite a number of definitions of translation have been given. Martha P. Y. Cheung (2005) speaks of the importance of our views on translation for developing a general theory of translation and comments that "[w]e really have too little knowledge of the thinking of different peoples about 'translation', and what we do know about the topic is so patchy it would be premature to talk about integration". He lists five definitions of translation in ancient China. The first is offered by the first Chinese dictionary *Shuo Wen Jie Zi*, compiled by Xu Shen, a famous scholar in the Eastern Han Dynasty: "those who transmit the words of tribes in the four directions". The second by the book *Li Ji · Zheng Yi* or *Corrected Meanings of Book of Rites*: "'yi' means 'to state in an orderly manner and be conversant in the words of the country and those outside the country'". The third is provided by the 7th century annotator Jia Gongyan: "'to translate' means 'to exchange', that is to say, to change and replace the words of one language by another to achieve mutual understanding". The fourth is from the Buddhist monk Zan Ning in the Northern Song Dynasty: "'to translate' means 'to exchange', that is to say, take what one has in exchange for what one does not have". The fifth comes from Fa Yun (a Buddhist monk too in the Song Dynasty):

"By 'fanyi' (translating) we mean taking the Sanskrit language and rendering it into the language of China. The original and the translation may sound different when read out, but their meaning is largely the same" (Cheung 2005).

From the above definitions we can see that people in China in ancient times viewed translation as a way of communication with the purpose of making the communicators who speak different languages understand each other.

In modern China, more definitions are given and from these definitions we can see people's changing views on translation.

Lin Yutang holds that translation is an art and a creation. Those engaged in literary translation must first try to capture the style and spirit of the original and then give the fullest play of their subjectivity to reproduce the artistic beauty of the original (Chen Fukang 1992: 332-333).

Yu Guangzhong (2002: 37) has the same idea as Lin Yutang. He also considers translation as "an art, especially literary translation". In one of his articles entitled "The Art of Transformation", he says, "translation is just like marriage, it is an art of compromise between the two" (ibid: 55).

The above idea about translation is quite typical in China before the linguistic theory of translation was introduced. It is also popular among literary translators as can be seen from Xu Jun's interviews with those famous literary translators in China. Xu Yuanzhong (often mispronounced as Xu Yuanchong in China) regards translation as "the art of beautification", Xiao Qian and Wen Jieruo think it as "artistic creation" and "recreation", and Ye Junjian holds that translation is "a kind of literary creation" as it is featured by "recreation" (Xu Jun 2001).

In a course-book compiled by Zhang Peiji *et al.* (1986: 1) translation is defined as "a linguistic activity in which the content expressed in one language is re-expressed in another language accurately and completely".

Fan Cunzhong's definition is almost the same as the above one: "translation is to express what has been expressed in one language in another language, accurately and completely" (Fan Cunzhong 1985: 80).

Feng Qinghua (1997) defines translation as a linguistic practice in which content expressed in one language is expressed in another language.

Huang Zhonglian (2000) gives two definitions and both of them regard translation as cognitive and linguistic activity involving the transfer of cultural information from one language to another.

The above definitions can all be said to refer to the ideal state of translation in that the set tasks for translation are simply impossible to fulfill, especially for literary translation. Another common feature of these definitions is that they all view translation as mainly linguistic transfer.

Wang Kefei (1997) holds that translation is a cultural activity in which translators express the meanings contained in one language in another. This definition is representative in that it regards translation as a cultural activity.

A definition recommended by Fang Mengzhi (1999: 4-5) is that "translation is a process of message transfer between different semiotic system with different rules in accordance with social needs" and the message to be transferred include not only the semantic and stylistic but also the cultural message. The merit of this definition, according to Fang himself, lies in its higher degree of generalization. It includes both interlingual and intersemiotic translations.

Tan Zaixi (2005: 7) defines translation also as "a process in which the meaning contained in one language is expressed in another" and regards translation "mainly a craft with many artistic features".

According to Zhang Jin (1987: 8), "[t]ranslation is the process and the instrument of communication between two language-communities. Its aim is to promote the political, economical and / or cultural progress of the target language-community. Its task is to transfer intactly the logical or artistic representation of the reality embodied in the ST to the TT". This definition, though fairly comprehensive, is but quite idealistic.

The above three definitions, as we can see, have something in common. All of them view translation as a process and each focuses on different aspects and features of the process.

Xu Jun (2001: 5-6) once gave a comparatively comprehensive discussion on the definition of translation: ontologically, the definition should tell the nature of the activity; functionally, it should tell the purposes or tasks; and formally, the types of it. He further pointed out that in terms of form, it is a language transfer; in terms of nature, it is a message transfer and exchange; and in terms of its fundamental purpose, it is to overcome language barrier aiming at readers' understanding. We should therefore regard translation as a cultural exchange. In another book *On Translation*, he offers us his more penetrating thoughts on the essence of translation and defines translation as "an intercultural communication by means of code transferring (or changing of linguistic signs) and with the purpose of reproducing the meaning of the original" (qtd. in Lv Jun 2004). This definition, according to Lv Jun (2004), though brief, entails not only the essence of translation, but also the means and purposes of the activity, and at the same time touching upon the main factors of translation: language code, meaning and culture. It tells of, therefore, the more essential nature of translation as an object.

Lv Jun and Hou Xiangqun (2001: 2) hold that translation is a special form of communication. They view translation as a communicative action involving message transfer between two languages and two cultures, and in principle, trying to maintain the original message and function in the process. In their *Translatology—A Constructivist Perspective of Translation Study*, they again define it as an intercultural communication via signs, involving a complicated process of message receiving, interpreting, processing and re-expressing (Lv Jun & Hou Xiangqun 2006: 30).

The above three share the same view that translation is an interlingual and intercultural communicative action.

He Lin (1984), a famous philosopher in China, once gave his philosophical thinking on translation and regarded translation as a communication action between the interpreter and the original text, involving many stages such as reading, understanding, interpreting, translating and so on. The objectification or the result of this mental activity is translation. Translation is thus the crystallization and completion of such a communication action.

In order to define translation, some people make distinctions between its marrow sense and wider sense. Gu Zhengkun, for instance, in his discussion of meta-translatology, defines translation in the broad sense as "a transfer of a certain form and its meaning in general sense" and as "one way of the existence of life". He defines translation in the narrow sense as "translation action with language as medium and object" (Gu Zhengkun 2003: 305). Readers can see that here translation in the broad sense and translation in the narrow sense as well are not well defined as there is obscurity in the former and circularity in the latter. Nevertheless, Gu's definitions bring us some philosophical (metaphysical) thinking on translation. Gu's further comments and discussion on the definition of translation show more clearly his philosophical concern about translation: "[t]here are hundreds of definitions of translation, each possessing to a certain degree validity. ... It (translation, the author) is not merely an interlingual behavior; rather, it is, as far as its essential nature is concerned, a matter-spirit communication closely related to many other disciplines" (ibid: 311). On the following page Gu says again that "[t]ranslating is just such a behavior of understanding as making possible the communication not only between human beings themselves but also between human beings and the substantial world" (ibid: 312).

Huang Long (1988: 18-21), in his book *Translatology*, says that we can define translation from different perspectives and viewed in light of message equivalence and materialist dialectics, "[t]ranslation is the unity of opposites wherein an equivalent and aesthetic intercommunication of bilateral alien languages (letter language, semiotic language, animal language) in social science (including theology in a broad sense) and physical science is performed theoretically and practically through oral interpretation and written translation by the agency of human brain or electronic brain". This definition sounds a thorough description of the meaning of the term "translation" as it tells us of the extension of the term "translation". But, it also has the shortcoming of circularity and is not quite concise.

The above three definitions are put together because these scholars, Gu Zhengkun in particular, are thinking about translation at the more metaphysical level or at both levels.

At the pure metaphysical level, we take translation as an abstract entity. In his *An Ontological Study of Translation* published in 2005, Cai Xinle talks about "meta-translation" and says that ontologically, "translation exists (is born) in the self-generation of the human beings". Translation is logically prior to culture and beyond the logic of language (Cai Xinle 2005: 198). Cai points out that to define translation is to tell our perception of it based on a judgment which has a certain degree of logic. Translation is translation itself and when we use the pattern "translation is…" to define it any other words than "translation" that follow "translation is" will not tell what translation is in its purely ontological sense (ibid: 239). Cai's discussion here indicates that he is not only talking about translation metaphysically but also thinking about language metaphysically. This reminds us of discussion on translation by Derrida who thinks it impossible to define translation by language (Munday 2001: 162-174). In spite of this, in another place of the book by Cai (2005: 244), he tries to give us a definition, saying that "translation is the imitation of the 'existence' or the imitation of the 'form' of existence".

From all the above-mentioned definitions we can see that people's definitions of translation are from different perspectives and at different levels. There have been some changes as can be perceived if we take a diachronic look at these definitions—from static to dynamic, from idealistic to realistic, from the artistic view to the linguistic view, from linguistic to cultural and lingual-cultural, from product to process, and from one-sided to more comprehensive, from physical level to metaphysical level. And synchronically, we find the existence of almost all of them—translation as an art, as mere language transfer, as cultural exchange and then, as a process of interlingual and intercultural communication action and then again, as one of the ways of human existence. Some of the definitions sound formal while others informal. We will return to the formality of definitions in our later discussion.

1.2 Definitions of Translation in the West

The domain of translation has always been the site of a curious contradiction. On the one hand, translation is considered to be a purely intuitive practice—in part technical, in part literary—which, at bottom, does not require any specific theory or form of reflection. On the other hand, there has been—at least since Cicero, Horace, and Saint Jerome—an abundance of writings on translation of a religious, philosophical, literary, methodological or, more recently, scientific nature. (Berman 1992: 1)

According to Berman, though numerous translators have written on translation, it is undeniable that most of the definitions are from non-translators, from theologians, philosophers, linguists, or critics. And as they are not professional translators, they tend to "assimilate it to something else: (sub-)literature, (sub-)criticism, 'applied linguistics'" (ibid).

Actually, we can not find as many formal definitions of translation as one would imagine, especially in ancient times, from sourcebooks such as Douglas Robinson's *Western Translation Theory: from Herodotus to Nietzsche*, Lefevere's *Translation/History/Culture: A Sourcebook* and other dictionaries of Translation Studies.

Lefevere (2004: Introduction; 86) for his purpose specifies the definition of one of the two kinds translations proposed by Petrus Danielus Huetius (1630-1721), French bishop and educator, "a text written in a well-known language which refers to, and represents a text in a language which is not as well known". He thinks this definition "the most productive" and quotes it at the very beginning of his book.

There are two more definitions in Lefevere's book. One is by Juan Luis Vives (1492-1540), Spanish humanist: "A version is the transfer of words from one language into another in such a way that the sense is preserved" (ibid: 50). The other is from Jacques Pelletier du Mans (1517-1582), French poet and grammarian: "Translation is the truest kind of imitation" (ibid: 52).

In modern times we find more definitions and the following are some of them:

G. R. Gachechiladze regards translation an art, and a special form of artistic creation, observing the general law of art, just like creation in one's mother tongue (Du Jianhui 1998). And to achieve the artistic equivalent, Gachechiladze thinks that the translator has to be creative.

Malcolm Cowley (1898-1989), an American novelist, poet, literary critic, and journalist, defines translation as "an art that involves the re-creation of a work in another language for readers with a different background" (Cowley 1978: 831). The above two definitions can be regarded as the representatives of the artistic or aesthetic view on translation abroad, featured by the use of the terms such as "creation" and "re-creation".

Leonid Barkhudarov defines translation as "the process of transformation of a speech (or text) produced in one language into a speech (or text) in another language" and "[d]uring this process of transformation the level of content should remain unchanged" (Zlateva & Lefevere 1993: 40).

J. C. Catford (1965: 20) views translation as "the replacement of textual material in one language (SL) by equivalent textual material in another language (TL)" and thinks that the theory of translation is "a branch of Comparative Linguistics".

Wolfram Wilss (2001: 112) defines translation as "a procedure which leads from a written SLT to an optimally equivalent TLT and requires the syntactic, semantic, stylistic and text-pragmatic comprehension by the translator of the original text".

According to Peter Newmark (2001: 7), "[t]ranslation is a craft consisting in the attempt to replace a written message and/or statement in one language by the same message and/or statement in another language".

Nida and Taber (1969/ 2004:12) say that: "translation consists of reproducing in the receptor language the closest natural equivalent of the source language message, first in terms of meaning and secondly in terms of style".

Hatim and Mason (1997:1) consider translation as "an act of communication which attempts to relay, across cultural and linguistic boundaries, another act of communication."

In *Translation Terminology* complied by Jean Delisle, Hannelore Lee-Jahnke and Monique C. Cormier (2004: 272-273), translation is defined as "an interlinguistic transfer procedure comprising the <interpretation> of the <sense> of a <source text> and the production of a <target text> with the intention of establishing a relationship of <equivalence> between the two <texts>, while at the same time observing both the inherent communication parameters and the <constrains> imposed on the

<translator>".

The above seven definitions stand for the linguistic view, and indeed, the seemingly ever-lasting appeal of the linguistic view on translation.

The linguistic view on translation is featured by its implicit or explicit source-text-orientation and the use of terms such as "equivalence", "same", "reproduce" or "relay". It is usually more prescriptive than descriptive, as it not only tells of what translation or translating is, but also what it normally should be.

There is, besides the artistic and linguistic views, a lingua-artistic or lingual-aesthetic view on translation. The Czech translation theorist Jiri Levý says in his *The Art of Translation* that: "A translation is not a monistic composition, but an interpenetration and conglomerate of two structures. On the one hand there are the semantic content and the formal contour of the original, on the other hand the entire system of aesthetic features bound up with the language of the translation" (Bassnett, 2004: 15). He sees literary translation as "both a reproductive and a creative labour with the goal of equivalent aesthetic effect" (Munday 2001: 62). Snell-Horny (2006: 22) also comments that "Levý went beyond the role of precursor and proved to be one of the pioneers of modern Translation Studies….For Levý literary translation is a form of art in its own right, and has a position somewhere between creative and 'reproductive' art".

A lingual-cultural view on translation is to be found in Christiane Nord' definition: "Translation is the production of a functional target text maintaining a relationship with a given source text that is specified according to the intended or demanded function of the target text" (Shuttleworth & Cowie 1997/2004: 182). This definition shows that while translation is a linguistic activity, it is mainly influenced and determined by the system of the target culture.

Different from the above-mentioned views, Gideon Toury (1995/2001: 26) considers translation as "cultural facts" and proposes that a translation is "taken to be any target-language utterance which is presented or regarded as such within the target culture, on whatever grounds" (Shuttleworth & Cowie 1997/2004: 182).

Andrew Chesterman (1997: 59) holds the same view. When talking about what counts as translation, he says that "[i]n brief, a translation is any text that is accepted in the target culture as being a translation". Alternatively, we might say that a translation is any text which falls within the accepted range of deviance defined by the target-culture product norm "translation".

Bassnett and Lefevere (2004) in their "general editors' preface" of *Translation,*

Rewriting and the Manipulation of Literary Fame claim, "[t]ranslation is, of course, a rewriting of an original text". According to Lefevere (ibid: 9), translation, historiography, anthologisation, criticism, and editing are all forms of rewriting and "translation is the most obviously recognizable type of rewriting", and "potentially the most influential because it is able to project the image of an author and/or those works beyond the boundaries of their culture of origin".

Anthony Pym regards translation a process of generating and selecting between alternative texts. "Translating can be seen as a problem-solving activity in which a source element may be rendered by one or more elements in the target language" (Pym 2007: 44). This definition indicates that translation is not pure linguistic, it involves the selection of the socially or politically correct words, phrases and texts. In other words, a translation is a translation when it is accepted as a translation and only as a translation.

The above four definitions look at translation mainly as socio-cultural activity. They are more descriptive than prescriptive. Scholars viewing translation as mainly socio-cultural activity offer many different loose definitions of translation as "manipulation", "collusion", "rewriting" and "palimpsest", etc.

Still, we have some other different definitions. Jean Sager, for example, gives the following definition: "[t]ranslation is an externally motivated industrial activity, supported by information technology, which is diversified in response to the particular needs of this form of communication" (Shuttleworth & Cowie 2004: 182). This definition, unlike the above-mentioned ones, speaks of translation from the angle of a social profession.

And there are formal or informal definitions and descriptions of translation in a metaphysical manner. Munday (2001:162-174) gives one chapter to the philosophical theories of translation in *Introducing Translation Studies: Theories and Applications* which introduces "modern philosophical approaches to translation that have sought out the essence of (generally literary) translation". Among them, one finds George Steiner's "hermeneutic motion", thinking "real understanding and translation occur at the point where languages diffuse into each other". Walter Benjamin holds that translation "does not exist to give readers an understanding of the 'meaning' or information content of the original. Translation exists separately but in conjunction with the original, coming after it, emerging from its 'afterlife' but also giving the original 'continued life'". Translation "both contributes to the growth of its own language (by the appearance in the TL of the new text) and pursues the goal of a 'pure' and higher language. This 'pure language' is released by the co-existence and complementation of the translation with the original". Jaques Derrida, with his rereading of Walter Benjamin, "interrogates Jakobson's division of interlingual, intralingual and intersemiotic translation, pointing out the illogicality of Jakobson's definition of 'interligual translation or translation proper', with the word translation being used as a translation itself" and his remarks on translating indicate "the impossibility of fully describing and explaining the translation process by language". Derrida "deconstructs the distinction between source and target texts, seeing not only that the commentary is a translation of a translation, but also that original and translation owe a debt to each other".

Nord once made her comments on Derrida, saying that for Derrida, "translation somehow extracts and transports something which would then have to be imagined as existing beyond language" (Nord 2001:52). Bassnett also commented on Derrida's rereading of Walter Benjamin and his idea about translation being something that "ensures the survival of a text" and "becomes the after-life of a text, a new 'original' in another language" (Bassnett 2004: 9).

Here, translation as we can see, in the eyes of the above-discussed scholars thinking at the metaphysical level about the essence of translation, is either "understanding" or "after-life of the original" or something that is "beyond language" and has not an independent status.

Undoubtedly, each of these definitions has captured a particular aspect of translation and translating, yet, each of them is, in one way or another, missing some of the essence of translation.

1.3 Problems of Definition of Translation

We speak of and make brief comments on many different definitions of translation both in China and in the West in the above two sections. We are not, as has been said, trying to know how many different definitions there exist in the world, what we want to know is what translation or translating really means for the purpose of specifying our study object. We come to the definition of translation, simply because it is normally assumed that a definition is supposed to tell of the nature of an object. But, as we have already noticed, the definitions we talked in the above two sections are not all formal and all satisfactory. In other words, not all of them meet the requirement of a formal definition.

According to *Modern Chinese Dictionary*, "definition is a brief and concise description of the essential features of an object or that of the connotation and denotation of a concept". Usually, a definition consists of the genus (the family) of thing to which the defined thing belongs, and the distinguishing feature which marks it off from other members of the same family. The requirements for a formal definition, therefore, are the following: first, a definition must set out the essential attributes, i.e. the central features of the nature of the thing defined; secondly, a definition should avoid circularity; thirdly, a definition must not be too wide or too narrow; then, a definition must not be obscure, except for some scientific and philosophical terms difficult to define without obscurity; and last, a definition should not be negative where it can be positive.

In light of these requirements, we have excluded some definitions in the last two sections which are nevertheless also enlightening, such as those stating what translation is NOT.

> Ways of processing texts that fail to meet the criteria regarded as pertinent to translation in a given community may result in the product being called paraphrase, imitation or pastiche, but not translation. In this sense norms police the boundaries of what a culture regards as 'legitimate' translation. Moreover, norms embody social and ideological values. The implication is that translation is not an immanent but a relative concept, culturally constructed and therefore historically contingent. (Hermans 2007: 88)

According to Hermans, the definition of translation is culture-bound and culture-determined. Thus, we have to ask what culture we are in before we can ask the question "what translation is".

Susan Bassnett goes further than Hermans as to deconstruct and discard the term "translation". In Bassnett and Lefevere's *Constructing Culture: Essays on Literary Translation*, Bassnett has an essay entitled "When is a Translation Not a Translation?" In this essay, she asks that: "But can we always be certain that we know what a translation is? And is the object we call a translation always the same kind of text?" (2001: 27). She then goes on to talk about several kinds of translation and one of them is Toury's concept of "pseudotranslation", referring to "the text that claims falsely to be a translaiton". "Some writers, Toury points out, resort to the term 'translation' to describe a text that they have created from scratch themselves. He argues that the use of what he calls 'fictitious translations' is often a convenient way of introducing innovations into a literary system" (Bassnett & Lefevere 2001: 27-28).

Besides "pseudotranslation", Bassnett also discusses "self-translation" and "fictitious translation" etc. She gives example of Samuel Beckett who "famously wrote in both French and English, claiming at times to have translated his own texts" (ibid: 30) and expresses her dissatisfaction and discomfort with "definitions of translation, and in particular with the moralizing discourse of faithfulness and unfaithfulness". She concludes that "[i]t is probably more helpful to think of translation not so much as a category in its own right, but rather as a set of textual practices with which the writer and the reader collude" (ibid: 39). Translation has thus become a kind of "collusion".

Bassnett and other scholars of various cultural studies, like Toury, though more descriptive in their approaches, yet, as Munday points out, "have their own ideology and agendas…to move translation studies closer to a cultural studies framework" (Munday 2001: 138). We can not say the cultural view on translation is not right, but the problem is that, as Snell-Hornby (2006: 157) says, "[t]he major question arising here is what exactly is a 'translated text'…For the purposes of objective scientific data, Toury's definition of translation as quoted above will not suffice".

It seems that we are lingering too long on the socio-cultural-oriented definitions of translation. The reason for it is that these definitions are trendy both in China and in the West at present. Yet, from the above discussion we can see that if we want to find the essence of translation and translating, we cannot depend totally on the cultural approaches which are actually featured by their anti-essentialism and diversity— with a trend of deconstructing translation. Translation will be nothing if translation is everything and everything is translation. What is more, we must be aware that while the cultural approaches share some ideas about translation, there exist divergences and even conflicts among them as Munday (2001: 139) pointed out "these new cultural approaches have widened the horizons of translation studies with a wealth of new insights, but there is also a strong element of conflict and competition between them". To get a clear picture of it, one can refer to examples given by Munday (ibid). One can also go to Toury (1995/2001). In Toury's *Descriptive Translation Studies and Beyond*, one reads:

> To be sure, even now, there is at least one major difference between the interest of the two target-oriented paradigms, which also accounts for the different assumptions each of them proceeds from: whereas mainstream Skopos-theorists still see the ultimate justification of their frame of reference in the more 'realistic' way it can deal with problems of an applied nature, the main object being to 'improve' (i.e., change!) the world of our experience, my own endeavors have always been geared primarily towards the descriptive-explanatory goal of supplying exhaustive accounts of whatever has been regarded as translational

within a target culture, on the way to the formulation of some theoretical laws. (Toury 2001: 25)

If we take an overview of all the above-mentioned definitions, it is not hard for us to find the problems. Theo Hermans' comments on previous definitions of translation is that "[n]early all traditional definitions of translation, whether formal or informal, appeal to some notion of invariance or equivalence" (Hermans 1999/2004: 47). He explains that it is the way we intuitively think about translation: "surely translation means saying the same thing, or something which amounts to the same thing, in a different language" (ibid: 47). While our traditional view of translation is the replacement or substitution of one language by another, modern views on translation are quite different from the old and some of them, such as Hans J. Vermeer and Justa Holz-Manttari etc., view translation as "a form of translational action based on a source text" and others radically counter that of the old. Gideon Toury holds that "a translation is what is regarded as a translation" (ibid: 49). This of course, does not serve as a good definition, but it tells a change of people's attitude toward translation, from prescriptive to descriptive. Here, we must say that Hermans' comments and analyses are objective, but it dose not mean that "descriptive" is better than "prescriptive". A definition, after all, is to tell us about the nature of something and the essence of things can only be told by means of our verbal expression which may be a description of the meaning that a term bears in general use and the meaning that the speaker intends to impose upon it.

The problem of the existing definitions, as the authors see it, is not whether they are accurate or not, or descriptive or not, in capturing the essence of translation, but rather that some of them are quite one-sided. They either fail to tell the distinguishing features that make translation a translation, lack of the proper degree of width, or are too absolute, going to an extreme often. For example, if we say translation is rewriting, we are being too wide, as many forms of rewriting do not obviously fall into the family of translation. If we say translation is an art, we should also state what quality or qualities it has that distinguishes it from other things bearing the name of an art. And if we want to tell of the requirement for the task of translation, we should make it reasonably obtainable.

Actually, few definitions in the fields of social science and humanity meet the requirements. There might be mainly three reasons. The first is that the objects to be defined are often complicated and people's understandings about them are difficult, different and dynamic. The second is that people do not quite observe the rules of making a formal definition. The third is that some of the terms referring to these objects are too well established in the common lexicon to be defined for scholarly use. Littelejohn and Foss once mentioned the difficulty to define "communication": "Theodore Clevenger has noted that 'the continuing problem in defining communication for scholarly or scientific purposes stems from the fact that the verb 'to communicate' is well established in the common lexicon and therefore is not easily captured for scientific use" (Littelejohn & Foss 2005: 6). The problem of definition of translation is, to a great extent, quite like that of the communication, almost of the same nature.

Ideally, to give a thorough definition of an object or concept, people can entail both the intentional (connotative) definition, trying to specify the necessary and sufficient conditions for a thing being a member of a specific family, attempting to set out the essence of the object, and the extensional (denotative) definition, specifying the extension of the object. For our purpose of specifying the object of translation for translation criticism, we are more concerned with the intentional (connotative) definition of "translation".

To understand the essence of translation, we have first to know what is essential. In philosophy, Essence is the attribute or set of attributes that make an object or substance what it fundamentally is, and which it has by necessity, and without which it loses its identity. Traditionally, or in an Aristotlelian sense, we can expect to know the essence of an object from its definition, for a definition is supposed to be a statement of the essential attributes of the object. However, as has been stated above, partly owing to the extreme subtlety and complexity of translation, and partly owing to the limitedness of people's perception and their not observing strictly the rules of defining objects, it is hard for us to get a definition to our satisfaction from all kinds of the definitions discussed here.

In fact, the question "what translation is" is something ontological, and directly or indirectly, something epistemological and closely connected with linguistics. Ontology, according to Aristotle, is a systematic account of Existence or Being, concerning specifically a series of questions such as what categories of being are fundamental and in what sense the items in those categories can be said to "be", what is a physical object, what features are the essential, as opposed to merely accidental, attributes of a given object, what constitutes the identity of an object, how many levels of existence or ontological levels are there, can we explain the meaning of saying a physical object or a non-physical entity exists etc.

From the above list of questions, we know that existence has levels. So does essence. Therefore, we can have essence of translation at its different levels. According to Roger T. Bell (2001), the term "translation" has three meanings: (1), translating, referring to the process; (2), a translation, referring to the product; and (3), translation, an abstract concept. That is to say, translation can at least have three levels and each level has its own essence. Looking back at people's definitions of translation, we can say that they are actually talking about the essence of translation at its different levels and from its different aspects. This can be seen more clearly from the following discussions:

"In the scientific examination of the translation process, it should be remembered that three of its characteristics are defining properties: its interlinguality, its uni-directionary, and its irreversibility" (Wilss 2001: 60).

"The essence of translation lies in the preservation of 'meaning' across two different languages. There are three basic aspects to this 'meaning': a semantic aspect, a pragmatic aspect, and a textual aspect of meaning" (House 1981: 25).

According to M. Lederer, the nature of translation process is something universal. "No matter what language and what article it is, the translation procedures of excellent translators are all the same. They share the same features: discriminating the meaning and re-expressing the meaning" (Xu Jun & Yuan Xiaoyi 2001: 152).

Lv Jun and Hou Xiangqun (1999) make it clear in their article "Meta-translatology and Plural Approaches in Translation Studies" that meta-translatology is the theoretical study of the essence of translation and the scientific analyses of the inherent relations between different factors involved in translation. They give us a detailed illustration to the essence of translation as a special form of communication with its intercultural and interlingual features to distinguish it from other forms of communication. For any translation, in any way, is a process of message transfer.

Tan Zaixi (2007) posits that translation is governed by two types of properties, properties that are defined in both "absolute" and "relative" terms. On the one hand, "transfer/change" and "equivalence" are absolutely needed for a text to qualify as a translation, and on the other hand, "transfer/change" and "equivalence" should never be measured in the absolute as the total "transfer/change" and "equivalence" is not the essence of translation. This view of the essence of translation reminds us of the words of M. Lederer. They two bear some resemblance but Tan's is more dialectical and hence more reasonable.

1.4 Towards a Working Definition

As can be seen from the above discussion, some of the definitions are more descriptive, others more prescriptive or stipulative; some of them are aesthetic-oriented, others linguistic-oriented; some are socio-cultural-oriented and still others philosophical-oriented. Comparatively speaking, those lingual-aesthetic-oriented and those lingual-cultural-oriented definitions are preferable as they are more comprehensive, capturing more of the essence of translation and those with a dialectical view are preferable as they have avoided going to the extremes.

While we are fully aware that there will not be a single definition of translation that can tell of all the essential features of translation it is the requirement of our study to specify translation for the criticism of it. What is more, as Lv Jun (2004) says, "[h] ow to define translation involves one's perception of the essence of translation and at the same time, it determines the point of departure of his scientific research" . Based on the critical review of the definitions of translation, we will set out to propose a working definition hereafter in this section. The authors think it necessary to have a working definition of translation simply because we are facing so many different definitions of translation and it is quite possible that when we come to our discussion about translation, though we use the same term "translation", actually the "translation" in Tom's mind is quite different from that in the mind of Dick.

Xu Jun (2003) once gave a fairly comprehensive summary to the characteristics of translation saying that the activity of translation is social, cultural, interlingual, creative and historical. As Lv Jun (2004) once commented, this is a comparatively thorough description of the essential features of translation. On the basis of all the above-discussed definitions, especially following Xu Jun and Lv Jun's ideas and in light of the famous sociolinguist Dell (Hathaway) Hymes' sociolinguistic framework for the analyses of "communicative event" or "speech event", the authors of this book will make an attempt to define translation in a sociolinguistic way.

"Sociolinguists believe that the study of language must go beyond the sentences that are the principal focus of descriptive and theoretical linguistics. It must go beyond language and bring in social context…The focus of attention shifts from the sentence to the act of communication, the speech event" (Spolsky 2000: 14). Hymes first proposed the notion of "speech event" in his article "Ethnography of Speaking" (1962), which he later changed to "Ethnography of Communication" (1964) to reflect the broadening from instances of language production to the ways in which communication (including oral and written) is conventionalized in a certain speech community, calling for a new area of study, a kind of linguistics that explores language not just as a formal system of vocabulary and grammar, but as something culturally shaped in the contexts of social life, and a kind of anthropology that takes speaking, and communication in a broad sense, as its primary subject matter. This actually has brought about a new discipline, featured by the combination of a kind of linguistic study grounded in the social life and a kind of cultural study focused on speaking and verbal and non-verbal communication in a general sense. Hymes introduces several concepts as basic units for the ethnographic study of communication. "Speech event" is one of them (the other concepts are chiefly communication act, communication situation, and speech community etc.) This notion of "speech event" is coined by Hymes to be used as the unit of analysis of contrasting patterns of language use across cultures or speech communities. This term shows his dissatisfaction with the previous approach which focused on ostensibly distinct "languages" as an ideal construction covering up complexities within and "across" linguistic boundaries. It obviously indicates a pragmatic turn, focusing on language in use.

A speech event is also called a communicative event which normally consists of several communicative act or speech act (Zhu Wanjin 1992: 182). It involves actions of many kinds that are socio-culturally bounded with a beginning and ending and can be understood by formulating norms or rules about it. A communicative act is a specific social interaction, most typically parts of larger sequences of integral aspects of a communication event and of a social action (Carbaugh 2007).

Hymes developed a model to assist the identification of components of a speech event in the context. Actually, as Brown and Yule (1983/2000: 38) once commented, Hymes "sets about specifying the features of context which may be relevant to the identification of a type of speech event in a way reminiscent of Firth's".

Hymes' model lists many components or contextual features that can be applied to the analysis of speech events: message form; message content; setting; scene; speaker/sender; addressor; hearer/receiver/audience; addressee; purposes (outcomes); purposes (goals); key; channels; code; forms of speech; norms of interaction; norms of interpretation; and genres (Hymes 1974: 53-62).

The authors of this book hold that translation is an intercultural and interlingual speech event involving the translator's expressing in the target language his/her understanding and interpreting of the source language discourse in a specific socio-cultural context. This is intended to be a working definition of translation in this study. Such a definition can meet, to a great extent, the requirements for a formal definition and the need to specify the study object of this research. First, it is brief and concise as required by a formal definition. Second, it tells of the family to which translation belongs. Thirdly, it tells of the distinguishing features of translation as a speech event that distinguish it from other forms of speech events. Fourthly, as a speech event has a beginning and ending, this definition includes both the process and product of translation. The word "intercultural" indicates that this kind of speech event (translation) involves at least two cultures and is therefore not a pure linguistic transfer between two languages. There are many culturally-bounded norms to be observed in the transfer. Of course, some other merits of this definition can be mentioned. The term "speech event" is in a broad sense, social action and therefore translation is embedded in the social life and calls for different approaches, including of course, a sociolinguistic approach. As a social action, translation has its purposes or in Hymes' term, "Ends", including the various intended goals and the actual outcomes. And as a social action, it may sometimes involves intralingual and intersemiotic translation as a speech event may involve different codes or signs. The word "speech" also tells of the nature of historicity of translation as it indicates the dynamic use of language instead of language as a static system. Besides, it is easier for us to put different types of linguistic transfer, including oral interpretation and abridged translation, into this definition and potentially excludes machine translation from this study. In brief, to take a sociolinguistic view on translation and define translation as an intercultural and interlingual speech event in a specific context has, in a sense and in a way, captured the changing feature of translation as a speech event is always an event in a specific context. The concept of translation as a speech event is, to a certain extent, just like the concept "field" used by quantum physicists—treating translation as something between the physical and metaphysical planes. Last, but not least, dialectically, this proposed working definition, can be said to be both descriptive and prescriptive as when describing what translation is, it simultaneously tells us what should not be regarded as translation.

1.5 Classification of Translation

We all know that language is a very complicated phenomenon and Catford once said that "[t]he concept of 'a whole language is so vast and heterogeneous that it is not operationally useful for many linguistic purposes, descriptive, comparative and pedagogical. It is, therefore, desirable to have a framework of categories for the classification of 'sub-languages', or 'varieties' within a total language" (qtd. inShen Yuping 2002: 338). The same is true for translation and translation studies. Compared with language, translation is even more complicated as it involves at least two languages and cultures. Translation takes many different forms and is such a complex event that many scholars in translation studies tend to classify translation into different types and to study the "varieties" of translation. Williams and Chesterman (2004: 89) in their *The Map: A Beginner's Guide to Doing Research in Translation Studies* said that "translations are always unique, up to a point. The exciting thing is to discover a pattern within this variation. People are pattern-seeking animals, after all". Actually, we are not seeking patterns for excitement; it is out of the requirement of our scientific research and for the purpose of knowing the nature of translation better.

Almost every mature discipline has its own taxonomy. A well-established taxonomy is a necessary for the study of a subject and for the classification of knowledge of the subject (discipline). It is significant for the studying of the specific aspects of the discipline. However, in translation studies, such taxonomy has not been established so far. Though many books and articles on translation have touched upon this topic and actually efforts have been made to establish a typology of translation by many translation scholars just as that by linguists to establish language types and text types in general, it seems that none of the existing typologies are well-established. The authors of the present book has no attempt at arriving at an exhaustive typology of translation, but for the coming discussion on the literary text, they will first give a brief review of some chosen existing typologies and try to find a more acceptable one.

The existing classifications are quite different. Scholars distinguish types of translation according to quite diverse parameters: direction of translating (into or out of the mother tongue), medium of translation (written or oral), degree of modification in the process of translating by translators or methods (literal or free), function of the ST or the TT (expressive, informative, vocative or pragmatic, literary etc.), integrality of translation (partial or full), content or subject-matter of the ST (scientific-technological, institutional-cultural, or literary), genre of the ST (letter, notice, report, textbook, advertisement) etc.

Schleiermacher is a remarkable precursor in this aspect and the first one to distinguish oral interpretation from written translation:

We shall be able to distinguish two different fields [in translation] as well. They are not totally distinct, of course, since this is very rarely the case, but they are separated by boundaries that overlap and yet are clear enough to the observer who does not lose sight of the goal pursued in each field. The interpreter plies his trades in the field of commerce; the translator operates mainly in the fields of art and scholarship. (qtd. in Lefevere 2004:142)

Today we can see that Schleiermacher's classification is quite a rough one, but it is historically significant as his is the first move to call people's attention to the different features between the two forms of translation. Though we do have oral interpretation of literary works, it is certainly not the concern of this book; therefore we will not go into details about it, confining our discussion only to written translation, and to be more specific, literary translation.

It is noticed that most of the contemporary typologies are functional. That is to say, they classify translations according to the function of language and the aims or purposes of the translations. House (1977/1981: 188) distinguishes between covert and overt translations. The former is trying to keep the function of the source text and to assume the translation the status of an original in the target culture; the latter is a translation to make the receiver aware that it is a translation. In her essay "Translation Quality Assessment", House has some explanation to her own approach based on the distinction between ideational and interpersonal language functions developed by Halliday. "The suggested basic requirement for equivalence of a given textual pair (SL and TT) is that TT should have a function—consisting of two functional components, the ideational and interpersonal—which is equivalent to ST's function, and that TT should employ equivalent pragmatic means for achieving that function" (Chesterman 1989:158).

Reiss (2000/2004) distinguishes four types of translation: content-focused, form-focused, appeal-focused and the audio-medial type. The first three types are obviously based on the function of language as is shown by the table below:

Table 1.1

Language function	Representation	Expression	Persuasion
Language dimension	Logic	Esthetics	Dialogue
Text type	Content-focused (informative)	Form-focused (expressive)	Appeal-focused (operative)

(Reiss 2004: 26)

For the fourth type, Reiss holds that it can have any of the function of the above three text types.

Nord (2001: 47-51) tries to combine the considerations brought forward by House and Reiss, distinguishes between "documentary" and "instrumental" translations. She holds that the former aims at "producing in the target language a kind of document of (certain aspects of) a communicative interaction in which a source-culture sender communicates with a source-culture audience via the source text under source-culture conditions". And the latter aims at "producing in the target language an instrument for a new communicative interaction between the source-culture sender and a target-culture audience, using (certain aspects of) the source text as a model". Under the category (type) of "documentary translation", one can find "comparative linguistics", "Greek and Latin classics" and "modern literary prose"; under the category (type) of "instrumental translation", one can find "instructions for use", "Gulliver's Travels' for children" and "poetry translated by poet".

Newmark (1988/2001: 39-40) in his *A Textbook of Translation* gives one chapter (Chapter 4: Language Functions, Text-categories and Text-types) to the discussion of text types. Based on Buhler, he identifies three functions of language: expressive, informative or vocative. He thinks that a text can hardly be purely expressive, informative or vocative; most texts include all three functions, with an emphasis on one of them. Under the type of texts with expressive function, Newmark lists serious imaginative literature, authoritative statements, autobiography and personal correspondence; under text types of vocative, he lists notices, instructions, propaganda, publicity and popular fiction. Thus, literary texts such as "serious imaginative literature" and "popular fiction" belong to different text types.

Obviously, the above classification of text types and types of translation do not meet our current demands. For if you turn to them to look for a separate "literary text", you will get a loss or confused and do not know what a "literary text" is as they either do not offer a type of "literary text" or put those, to our common sense, belonging to "literary text" under quite different text types.

In their "Types of Translations", Barbara Snell and Partricia Crampton classified translations into (1) non-commercial translation (as an exercise or for pleasure); (2) professional translation (literary and book translation including scientific and technical books, translation of fiction, drama and opera); (3) promotional and instructional materials including all other texts translated for publication, considered as the highest level of non-literary translation, including advertising copy or slogans, instruction leaflet, service manuals, instruction on forms, commodity and sales literature, captions, signs and notices, legal and official documents, contracts and tenders, scientific papers and technical articles etc.(Picken 1983: 109-120). Here, the classification is made in terms of the materials to be translated and literary translation is classified into professional translation. Such a classification is acceptable in the current context as we are discussing criticism of literary translation and most of our criticisms are on the professional literary translators and their published translations.

We are happy to see that in 1991, Newmark published his *About Translation*, in which he offers a five-fold classification and saying that according to the translation approach used in producing the target text, we can differentiate semantic translation from communicative and that according to the content or subject-matter of the ST, scientific-technological, institutional-cultural, or literary translations. This is of course a step taken further toward a category of separate literary translation.

What interests us is that in 2004, in an article entitled "Non-literary in the Light of Literary Translation", Newmark (2004) said in his "Abstract" that "[t]he purpose of this article is to contrast non-literary with literary translation. … They differ essentially through intention (literary texts belong to the world of imagination whereas non-literary ones belong to the world of facts) and through the fact literary texts are about persons while non-literary ones are about objects". Though Newmark is not talking about the problem of classification, actually he seems to mean that translation can be divided into two types: non-literary and literary.

Juan C. Sager is another scholar who has shown great concern about the classification of translation. As early as 1983, in his article "Quality and Standards: The Evaluation of Translations", he made distinction between literary and non-literary translation in accordance with the "content or function of the source text" (Picken 1983: 125). But in 1998, in another article entitled "What Distinguishes Major Types of Translation?", he again made a distinction between literary translation, Bible translation and non-literary translation on the basis of a number of parameters including the purpose of the target document, the relative status of the target document in relation to the source document etc (Sager 1998). The inconsistency of his classification is obvious.

In an article devoted to Pierre Klossowski's translation of the *Aeneid*, Michel Foucault said that: "It is quite necessary to admit that two kinds of translations exist; they do not have the same function or the same nature" (Berman 2000: 277). Foucault does not explicitly distinguish literary translation from non-literary translation. Berman explains that "literary" translations (in the broad sense) are concerned with *works*, and texts are so bound to their language that the translating act inevitably becomes a manipulation of signifiers, while "non-literary" translations (technical, scientific, advertising, etc.) perform only a semantic transfer and deal with texts that entertain a relation of exteriority or instrumentality to their language (ibid).

In China, many scholars have also tried to give their classification. The one given by Gu Zhengkun (2003: 305) seems best fit in with the current context: "Translation in its narrow sense can be divided into oral interpretation and written translation and they are both the transfer of the meanings and forms of languages. Written translation can again be divided into literary and non-literary translations. In terms of the forms or genre, literary translation can be classified into poetry translation, prose translation, drama translation, novel translation and specialized transformational translation (such as film subtitling calling for the considerations on the length of wordings and the movement of the actor's lips)".

From the above discussions we can see that it is not easy to mark a clear demarcation between different types of translation and to give an all-round classification. But as far as the current study is concerned, it is practical to accept those typologies that make distinctions between literary and non-literary translation. Actually, despite the disagreement as to how to classify translation in the theoretical endeavor, it is quite common for universities to distinguish their courses and even certificates between literary and non-literary translations.

In the following section, the authors will focus on literary translation and our further classification of literary translation.

1.6 Literary Translation

To understand literary translation, we need first to know something about literature. It seems that there is not much to talk about literature, yet, as a matter of fact, it is not as simple as one may think.

1.6.1 Literature and literary texts

In our daily life people usually take it for granted as to what literature is. If you ask people to give a definition of literature, you will either get no answer or hear quite different opinions. In fact, literature is one of the things that are hard to define, almost as difficult as translation. Ever since the ancient times, people have been trying to define literature, thinking it as, as Plato did, imitation, or an imitative art "a long way off the truth", or as Aristotle, imitation plus representation: "Since the objects of imitation are men in action, … it follows that we must represent men either as better than in real life, or as worse, or as they are" (qtd. in Zhang Zhongzai 2000: 13; 42). There are also people who give metaphorical definitions to literature, comparing it to "mirror", for example, and to many other things.

Literature, in its broad sense, refers to all the products, oral or written, with language as the medium; in the narrow sense, it only refers to those verbal products with aesthetic function. Literature is often said to be the art of language. The so-called "literary language" or "literary code" usually refers to the deviant from the norms of everyday communication and the creative use of the potential of the language system. It is assumed to be self-reflexive and to carry a connotative, expressive or aesthetic meaning of its own, carrying or giving hints to the writer's intentions or implications.

Literature and literariness are often associated with a particular choice of subject matter, usually imaginative, fictitious and unpractical, able to produce a particular aesthetic effect on the readers.

For quite a long time in the history of our human beings, people are satisfied with their intuitive and take-it-for-granted definitions of literature. It is in the course of the nineteenth century, according to the book *Text and Experience: New Analytic and Pragmatic Approaches to the Study of Literature*, that the study of literature became professionalized. At that time, "there was a concerted attempt to make the study of literature an academic pursuit, 'a particular branch of learning or science'" (Olsen & Pettersson 2005: 1), and "the arrival of the academic discipline of literary studies not only required a method of study but also a determinate field of study" (Olsen & Pettersson 2005: 1). To delimit such a field, people need a well-defined concept of literature. Those broad, vague, non-theoretical and everyday notions simply cannot meet the demand for the academic research. What scholars needed are well-defined concepts of "literary work", "literary text" and "literature" to be used as theoretical tools.

A number of different concepts of literature emerged in literary studies in the course of the twentieth century. According to the above-mentioned book, there exist roughly six different types of concepts of literature. The first is from the Russian Formalists, taking literature as "fore-grounding", as discourse drawing attention to its own markedly unusual phonological, syntactic, and semantic structures (ibid). The second notion, "gaining wide acceptance from the 1940s onwards, makes fictionality a central element in the concept of literature" (ibid: 1-2). The third emphasizes the concept of "practice" and thinks that "literature has no definite formal characteristics but is language employed in a certain determinable fashion" (ibid: 2). Olsen, honorary professor of literature in University of Bergen, Norway, for instance, has long been one of the main proponents of viewing literature as a practice, arguing that "the writing and reading of literature rest on a system of roles and expectations to which empirical authors and readers are supposed to conform. ... When attempting to specify these roles and expectations we are dealing not with matters extrinsic to literature, but with such key factors in literary transactions as 'the experience of the literary work' and 'the particular value of a work for a reader'" (ibid: 3).

The fourth concept of literature gained prominence in the 1970s. It is the product of post-structuralism and New Historicism. The poststructrualist intellectual revolution of the 1960s and 1970s challenges the older historicism on several grounds and establishes some assumptions. They believe that the word "history" has two meanings: one is "the events of the past" and the other is "telling a story about the events of the past". History is thus textualized. The relations between literature and history, therefore, must be reconsidered. "There is no stable and fixed 'history' which can be treated as the 'background' against which literature can be foregrounded. ... Literary works should not be regarded as sublime and transcendent expressions of the 'human spirit', but as texts among other texts" (Selden, Widdowson & Brooker 2004:188-189). The notion of text was put prior to the concept of literature and consequently any principled distinction between literary works and other genres of texts was removed. As a result, the notion of "literary work" was replaced by the notion of "literary text". And "literary text" is regarded as "just text" that may have no inherent artistic or aesthetic value that endows it with a special status as "works of art" (Olsen & Pettersson 2005: 2).

The fifth notion of literature, according to Olsen and Pettersson (Pettersson is Professor of Swedish and comparative literature in Lund University, Sweden), "arose out of a combination of poststructuralist and deconstructionist theory with certain versions of Marxism and feminism, both of which saw the concept of 'literature' as an ideological tool for imposing certain political and social values on a reading public" (ibid). And the sixth one can be found among those "impressed by the poststructuralist and Marxist/feminist 'critique' of the concept of literature but nevertheless wanted to find a minimally binding reference for the concepts of 'literary work', 'literary text', and 'literature'. This line of reasoning manifests itself in the attempt to make the notion adjectival rather than substantival—not the denotation of a genre or a type of discourse, but rather of a mood, 'the literary', a spirit that may hover more or less perceptibly over a text" (ibid).

Terry Eagleton's *Literary Theory* opens with a chapter "Introduction: What is Literature?" He says that "[t]here have been various attempts to define literature. You can define it, for example, as "imaginative" writing in the sense of diction—writing which is not literally true" (Eagleton 1983: 1). After making comments on people's ideas, especially the Formalist's ideas about literature, he argues that literature can be defined as "highly valued writing" (ibid: 11) and goes on to stress the social and ideological conditioning of values and value judgments, saying that "[t]here is no such thing as a literally work or tradition which is valuable in itself, regardless of what anyone might have said or come to say about it. 'Value' is a transitive term: it means whatever is valued by certain people in specific situations, according to particular criteria and in the light of given purposes" (Eagleton 1983: 11). Eagleton mentions the famous experiment made by I. A. Richards described in Richards' *Practical Criticism* (1929), to illustrate how subjective literary value-judgments can be. Richards once gave his undergraduates a set of poems, withholding from them the titles and authors' names, and asking them to make their comments. The resulting judgments were that time-honored poets were marked down and obscure authors celebrated (ibid: 15).

Facing so many different conceptions of literature, we cannot help feeling a bit puzzled. But for the specific purpose of studying literary translation and criticism of literary translation, we can only agree that literature, though its nature hard to capture, is but something substantive rather than illusive. It is mainly represented in the form of texts which carry unique or prominent features that other texts may not have or are less prominent. Otherwise we cannot distinguish literary texts from other texts. Then, what are those unique or prominent features that distinguish literary texts from others? Torsten Pettersson is Chair Professor of literature in Uppsalu University, Sweden. He is also a poet and novelist. He argues that when we identify a text as being literary, we base our judgment "on a complex interplay between several perceived qualities" (Olsen & Pettersson 2005: 5). Usually, three components or qualities can be perceived. One is the literary work's expressiveness, another is representativity, and the third is form, "the pleasing structures and patterns exhibited by the work" (ibid). Torsten Pettersson holds that "expressiveness, representativity, and form are pivotal in literary experience. Although they do not together define literariness, they are values which readers of Literature are trained to look for and which authors of literary works seek to afford "(ibid).

Torsten Pettersson's idea about the "expressiveness" and "representativity" is somewhat obscure and he does not give much explanation. He regards the former as "the reflection of a literary persona created by the author" and the latter as "the wider significance acquired by a work through the relationships, partly produced by the reader, between its characters and events and real people and phenomena" (ibid). The author of the present dissertation thinks that "expressiveness" is a quality or feature that can be found in almost all the writings, all the texts since the aim of our writing is to say something, to express ourselves. Its Chinese translation can be "*biao da li*". Literary text has no exception, of course. In China, in an ancient book entitled *Shang Shu · Yao Dian*, we can find "*shi yan zhi*" or poetry for expressing feelings and thoughts (Fu Daobin & Yu Fu 2002: 19). Confucious' idea about the function of poetry (literature or in his own terms "*the Book of Songs*") is that poems can teach people to *xin, guan, qun and yuan* (i.e. poems can arouse one's mind, can improve one's ability to observe and judge things; they can teach one how to get along with others and how to express one's resentment). (Wang Fulin 1997: 284). In the Northern Song Dynasty, Zhou Dunyi put forward "*wen yi zai dao*" or writing for expressing and conveying truth (Min Ze & Dang Shengyuan 1999: 58).

When Peter Newmark talks about the expressive function of language, the first text type he mentions is "Serious imaginative literature" (Newmark 2001: 39). In Reiss' discussion of expressive function of language and translation, she mentions only the aesthetical dimension of the language and "the expressive function is restricted to the aesthetic aspects of literary or poetic texts" (Reiss 2004: 26; Nord 2001: 41). From their discussions we can see that expressiveness, though a quality of almost all writings, is certainly a prominent feature of the literary texts.

"Representativity", as the author understands, can be rendered into "*biao xian li*" in Chinese. It embodies two features. One is "typical", indicating that what is depicted can show the most usual characteristics of a particular type of person or thing. The other is "symbolic", indicating that the author's description of one thing (often but not always, fictional object or phenomenon whose relationship with reality is not one-to-one) is actually representing something else, there are symbolic meanings or morals that are conveyed by the author and can be understood or interpreted by the reader.

Literary texts value ways of expression and representation very much. Consequently, the form of the texts becomes an essential element that contributes to the literariness. They often estrange and defamiliarize the ordinary speeches, and in doing so, bring us into a fuller and usually more intimate possession of experience.

Literary utterances or texts are usually those intended primarily by their authors to be capable of affording an aesthetic experience with more or less aesthetic character. The writer may intend also to promote the revolution, to make himself rich and famous, and so on. But he has to write something the reading of which will yield the kind of contemplative rewards the tradition has long associated with aesthetic experience. "There is little doubt that a literary text can produce a particular aesthetic or poetic effect on its readers. This could be referred to as the specific value of its own, affecting the interaction between writer and reader…The reader thus decides to read a text as literature" (Nord 1997/2001: 82).

To sum up, literary texts are those texts with aesthetic values. And our analysis of a literary work is explicitly or implicitly evaluative. The attitude of poststructuralists and the like toward literature is accompanied by their deep-seated mistrust of values and value-judgments. Nevertheless value-judgments about literary works and of works of art in general are unavoidable. And as a matter of fact, one can hardly escape value-judgments in any field, in and outside of aesthetics. Deconstructionists cannot avoid believing that their theoretical approaches are superior to other rival approaches. Whether a text is literary text or not is partly dependent on one's value-judgments. Literature and literariness and literary texts are concepts that are language-bound, culture-bound and value-bound. And to ensure a reasonable value-judgment, we'd better know more about the prominent qualities of literature and literary texts.

1.6.2 Concept of literary translation

What, if anything, is distinctive about literary translation? Few would doubt their intuitive sense that there is a difference between Ted Hughes' rendering of a play by Aeschylus and the English-language label on the packet of white powder in a Greek supermarket identifying the stuff in it, for the tourist's sake and good health, as sugar, salt, detergent or rat poison. But how are they different? Interestingly, Emma Wagner, a translation manager with the European Commission who mentions the Ted Hughes versus rat poison example in a discussion with a translation theorist, refers to the two kinds of translation as the top and bottom ends of the range, respectively. (Chesterman & Wagner 2002: 5)

The above quotation has three implications: one is that people are naturally and intuitively aware of the difference between literary translation and translations of other genres, the second is that people are not quite clear about how they are different from each other, and the third is that it is not simply a matter of identifying a fact, value enters the picture as well. That is to say, when identifying the facts, alue-judgments are involved. And to the author of this dissertation, the third point is what makes most of the controversial criticisms on literary translation.

It is widely accepted that literary translation is a distinctive kind of translating because it is concerned with a distinctive kind of text. But Theo Hermans in his article "Literary Translation" argues that "[t]he fact however that text typologies do not agree on what to contrast literary texts with—technical, pragmatic, ordinary? — suggests that what distinguishes literary from other texts may not be entirely obvious. And if there is no agreement on what makes literature distinctive, it may be equally hard to decide on what grounds literary translation should be awarded its own niche" (Hermans 2007: 77). Katharina Reiss (2004) in her *Translation Criticism: The Potentials & Limitations*, gives a review of various attempts to distinguish different kinds of translation. A.V. Fedorov, Peter Brang, Otto Kade, J. B. Casagrande and Georges Mounin, among others, all include literary translation as a separate kind, but their criteria for doing so are not clearly stated. "[T]he classifications thus far advanced have been inadequate, primarily because they have shown no consistent principles in defining the various types of text, and the reasons given for the distinctions that are drawn (if given at all) have been variable and weak" (Reiss 2004: 23).

Indeed, our study on literary translation and the relevant classification are inadequate. This can be seen also from entries in some famous dictionaries and reference books of translation studies.

Dictionary of Translation Studies has entries for "literal translation", "free translation" and the like but not "literary translation" (Shuttleworth & Cowie 2004).

Routledge Encyclopedia of Translation Studies has entries like "literary translation: practice" and "literary translation: research issues", but neither gives a clear and adequate definition to "literary translation" (Baker, 1998/2004). The former contributed by Peter Bush only states that "[l]iterary translation is the work of literary translators" (Baker, 1998/2004: 127) and the latter by Jose Lambert, in the section "Literary translation: a problem of definition", after saying that "[t]he very use and combination of *literary* and *translation* is symptomatic of the casual way in which the concept of literature and of translation have so far been taken for granted. Neither concept is simple or well defined in most cultures" (ibid: 130), gives an explanation as to why it is so difficult to reach an agreeable definition of "literary translation" while confessing that it is the duty of translation studies scholars to investigate into this type of translation.

In the two-volume *Encyclopedia of Literary Translation into English*, edited by Olive Classe (2000: viii), one also finds a take-it-for-granted way concerning the concept of literary translation. As translation is commonly referred to interlingual translation, and " 'literature' and 'literary' tend to imply 'aesthetic purpose, together with a degree of durability and the presence of intended stylistic effects', so 'literary translation' is read as conventionally distinguished from 'technical translation'" . This is almost as equal as saying those are not non-literary translation are literary translation and offers not much help for our purpose.

Peter France's *Oxford Guide to Literature in English Translation* makes a more determined effort. It speaks of literary translations as translations "designed to be read as literature" and cites with approval Gideon Toury's distinction between "literary translation" and the "translation of literary texts", the latter, non-literary form of translation being described as "informational" (France 2000: xxi). Toury makes a distinction between "translations of literary texts" and "literary translation", arguing that despite some overlap, these texts are produced via different methods and with different aims, and consequently the questions they pose to scholars will necessarily be different. Toury's distinction rests on his view, derived from Roman Jakobson and the Russian Formalists, that literature is characterised by the presence of a secondary, literary code superimposed on a stratum of unmarked language (Toury 2001: 36-37). In Hermans' opinion, "a formal definition of this kind no longer has currency in literary studies and anyway sits uncomfortably with the intentional aspect of accepting as literary any translation designed to be read as literature. The search for a definition of literary translation leads nowhere" (Hermans 2007: 78).

According to Edwin Gentzler (2004: 11), "[l]iterary translation in America is often viewed as a form of close reading".

Rose (1997: 20) holds that "Literary translation is a transfer of distinctive features of a literary work into a language other than that of the work's first composition. But literary translation is also a form of literary criticism".

However, for historical reasons, when we mention literature, and literary translation alike, what come to our mind, often but not always, are texts displaying certain features, notably such things as the foregrounding of language, the alienation from ordinary speeches, the separation from practical contexts, and the perception of texts as both aesthetic objects and self-reflexive constructs. Hermans suggests that we follow a "conceptually sustainable way of modeling literary translation" based on a prototype theory which views the prototypical literary translation as "one perceived, and perhaps also intended, as a literary text, and hence as possessing literary features and qualities; around prototypical texts a host of other texts of more or less questionable membership will cluster, allowing the system to evolve in time" (Hermans 2007: 79).

In China, we are never short of discussions on literary translation. People have also made efforts to clarify the concept of literary translation.

Mao Dun (qtd. in Zhang Jin 1987: 14) once gave a definition of literary translation saying that "literary translation is to express the artistic conception of the original text in the target language for the target readers to get the same enlightenment, the same feeling and the same aesthetic experience as that of the readers of the original text".

The definition of literary translation by Zhang Jin (1987: 13-14)himself is based on his definition of translation: "literary translation is the process and the instrument of communication between two language-communities in the field of literature. Its aim is to promote the political, economical and / or cultural progress of the target language-community. Its task is to transfer intact the artistic conception embodied in the ST to the TT". And for Zhang Jin, literary translation is forever an art.

Guo Moruo once delivered a speech entitled "On Literary Translation" saying that "[t]ranslation is featured by creativity. Good translation is equal to creation… Sometimes translation is more difficult than writing" (qtd. in Liu Zhongde 1991: 8).

Xu Jun (1992) points out that literary translation differs from translation of other types in that it tries to reproduce the aesthetic value of the original text: its beauty of thoughts, beauty of artistic conception and beauty of form. And to best realize the reproduction of the aesthetic value, the translator has to give a full play of his or her subjectivity. But to say literary translation is recreation is not to say that the translator can change the content and form of the original of his or her own will. There must be a certain degree of recreation that makes a recreation an acceptable and preferable translation.

Zheng Hailing (2000: 39) defines literary translation as "artistic translation requiring the translator's aesthetic experience of the contents and styles of the original text and the complete reproduction of the artistic images and styles in another language for the target readers to get the same enlightenment, the same feeling and the same aesthetic experience as that of the readers of the original text". Zheng holds that we can distinguish literary translation from non-literary translation in terms of the language used. All those works translated in literary language (such as novel, prose, poetry, feature report, drama etc.) belong to literary translation. And literary language is featured by its vividness, lyricism, accuracy, precision and musicality etc. (Zheng Hailing 2000: 37-38; 183).

In one of his articles entitled "Translation and Creation", Yu Guangzhong (2002: 30) says "translation, I mean literary translation, poetry translation in particular, is completely an art".

Jin Shenghua (1997: 13) quoted Gao Keyi, a famous literary translator, "literary translation concerns not the question of whether it is 'right or wrong', but rather, the question of whether the translation is 'good, better or worse'". Jin says that "literary translation differs from the other translations in that it should meet a higher standard….A good translated literary work is itself creation".

The above-mentioned scholars and translators view literary translation as creation or recreation. This is quite typical in China and in fact over the world, among literary translators in particular. But there are other voices.

Xu Yuanzhong (2000) holds that "literary translation is a rival between two languages and even two cultures to see which language can better express the content of the original text".

Yang Wu-neng argues that the essence of literary translation is interpreting, a special interpreting different from the general interpreting and the scholarly interpreting (Xu Jun 2001:167).

Based on the theory of communicative action put forth by Jurgen Habermas, Lv Jun (2002) proposes that literary translation is a special kind of communicative action and literary text is a medium of social communication.

Anyway, in the West and in Chin as well, studies on the concept of literary translation are still insufficient. This is partly because the complexity of literature and literary translation themselves, and partly it is because we have not paid enough attention to the ontological study of literature. Literature was for a time marginalized. Fu Daobin and Yu Fu (2002) talk about the neglect of literature, especially modern literature, by the contemporary in their book *What is Literature*, pointing out that on the one hand, literary creation has become more and more commercialized and writers tend to take care too much about their own feelings, and on the other hand, more and more readers turn to other medium than books and are attracted by other forms of amusement. Literary studies, though not marginalized, were largely assimilated by cultural studies, focusing mainly on its social, ideological and political function.

According to Hermans (2007: 79), the development with respect to the study of translation and of literary translation in particular, has undergone the same course. "Questions of definition and demarcation have given way to functional approaches that have been increasingly preoccupied with the roles assigned to and the uses made of translation by a variety of factors in varying contexts".

Just like the discussion on the definition and essence of translation, studies on the definition and essence of literary translation have brought us more understandings of the phenomenon of literary translation, though it is quite difficult for people to come to a single definition of literary translation. The divergence mainly comes from people's understanding of literariness and what makes a literary text. For the purpose of a better discussion of criticism of literary translation in the current context, we would like also to put forward a working definition of literary translation, following the pattern of definition of translation in general: Literary translation is an intercultural and interlingual speech event involving the translator's expressing in the target language his or her understanding and interpreting of a literary text of the source language in a specific socio-cultural context.

1.7 Types of Literary Translation

To investigate into types of literary translation, we need first to probe into types of literary texts.

As is discussed in the above sections, literary texts are primarily the products of writers who have specific expectations for their readers conditioned by their own literary experience, as well as a certain command of the literary codes. This means that readers' involvement is one of the conditions of the completeness of literature and the readers' ability and relevant experience are also requirements to make literary texts and literary activity meaningful. Literary activity actually consists of two parts: one is the creation of the writer and the other the appreciation of the reader. Things are made further complicated as the creation of the writer is often more than one types and the reader may come with different background. As a result, not all literary works of all types can be understood by all the readers. Visual poetry, for example, can only be understood fully by those readers who have some knowledge of visual poetry and have the competence to interpret it, to make it significant for themselves. This ability to interpret literary texts is usually known as "literary competence" on the side of the readers.

Then, how many types of literary texts and types of literary translation do we have?

We have said that it is more acceptable to classify translation into literary and non-literary because we are studying literary translation and criticism of literary translation. Here, we can say it is more practical to classify translation in terms of its materials to be translated than in terms of its function as Newmark and Nord etc. do. For in terms of materials to be translated, it is easier for us to identify the genre of literary works. Though we have to admit that different people in different cultures may have different ideas about what literary works are, it can be safely assumed that different people in different cultures do have something in common as to what literary works are: poetry, fiction, drama—no one will deny they belong to the genre of literature. To be more concrete, we can list various poems, novels, novella, short stories, science fiction, essay in its narrow sense (essays expressing the writer's experiences, feelings and thoughts), autobiographies, fairy tales, folklores etc. according to their content (subject-matter) and their formal structure. And accordingly, there are novel translation, poetry translation, drama translation, essay translation and translation of other texts that are regarded as literary texts in different cultures.

Chapter 2
Previous Studies of Translation Criticism

As is well known, in Holmes' (1988:78) map, translation criticism is a separate area of applied translation studies. However, as to what translation criticism is, Holmes offers us no definition and in fact few translation scholars have ever. This indicates, first, the underdevelopment of, and secondly, an obstacle to the development of the theoretical study of translation criticism and translation studies as a whole. In this chapter, we will have a general review of our understanding of translation criticism and our ways of doing translation criticism in China and in the West.

2.1. Definitions of Translation Criticism in the West

Despite the daily use of the term translation criticism, there has been the short of a definition of translation criticism that satisfy all of us. Katharina Reiss (2000/2004: 3) says that translation criticism is practiced under different names and Hatim and Mason hold that:

> Even within what has been published on the subject of evaluation, one must distinguish between the activities of assessing the quality of translations (e.g. House 1981), translation criticism and translation quality control on the one hand and those of assessing performance (e.g. Nord 1991: 160-3) on the other. But while all of these areas deserve greater attention, it is not helpful to treat them as being the same or even the similar to each other since each has its own specific objectives (and consequences). (Hatim & Mason 1997: 197)

This is quite true and can be seen from the following remarks by House (1997: 1): "[e]valuating the quality of a translation presupposes a theory of translation. Thus different views of translation lead to different concepts of translational quality, and hence different ways of assessing it". And remarks of Nord also serve an example. When talking about "forms and functions of translation criticism", Nord says:

Book reviewers rarely comment on the quality of a translation because normally a translated book is reviewed as if it were an original. If there is any reference to the book being a translation, the assessment is usually based entirely on a rather superficial analysis of the translation in relation to the target-cultural norms of language and literature. (Nord 1991)

Nida and Taber (1969/2004) speak of "Testing the Translation" to refer to translation criticism in various possible ways in their *The Theory and Practice of Translation.*

Wilss also distinguishes testing of translation from translation criticism and does not think the latter a science:

In comparison to L2/L1 error analysis, TC (translation criticism, the author) is in a less favorable starting position. While error analysis is focused on classifying, describing, explaining and evaluation transfer phenomena on the basis of the dichotomy "wrong/ correct", it is the task of TC to make quality assessment of a translation as a whole as objectively as possible, thereby taking into account both positive and negative factors. (Wilss 2001: 216)

Peter Newmark thinks "[t]ranslation criticism is an essential link between translation theory and its practice; it is also an enjoyable and instructive exercise, particularly if you are criticizing someone else's translation or, even better, two or more translations of the same text" (Newmark 2001: 184).

Gerard Mcalester tries to distinguish translation criticism from translation evaluation and translation assessment, regarding translation criticism as statements concerning the appropriateness of a translation, a kind of value-judgment of a translated work:

Translation evaluation is the placing of a value on a translation, i.e. awarding a mark, even if only a binary pass / fail one. Translation criticism consists in stating the appropriateness of a translation; this also implies a value judgment, which need not however be a quantified one, though it should perhaps be explicitly justified for it to be of any value. Translation assessment used as a cover term for the other two procedures. The verbs evaluate, criticize, etc. and the agent nouns evaluator, etc. are used analogously. (Mu Lei 2007)

Louise Brunette (2000) in an article "Towards a Terminology for Translation Quality Assessment" says that "[t]oday, determining and measuring translation quality has come to be known as translation assessment, which is distinct from translation process evaluation according to such standards as DIN 2345 and ISO 9000". This statement indicates that "assessment" is more product-oriented and "evaluation" is more process-oriented. But from the author's discussion of the assessment procedures and the definition given to translation quality assessment, we can infer that while "assessment" is more product-oriented, "evaluation" runs through the whole process including the product: translation quality assessment (TQA) (translation evaluation; quality evaluation) is defined as "[m]anagement term. Determination of the quality of a translated text or a check after the fact for management purposes, i.e. measuring the productivity of translators and the quality/price ratio of translations. A numerical rating is assigned".

According to Munday (2001: 30), translation assessment involves the fact that "a more expert writer (a marker of a translation examination or a reviser of a professional translation) addresses a less expert reader (usually a candidate for an examination or a junior professional translator)".

Snell-Hornby says "...translation critique (evaluation) based on an adequate theoretical model (applied extension) is not only desirable but necessary..." (Snell-Hornby 2006: 109-110). This quotation shows that Snell-Hornby sees translation criticism as a kind of "evaluation".

As has been stated in the "Introduction" of this book, one can not find an exact entry of "translation criticism" in the influential dictionaries in the West. In *Routledge Encyclopedia of Translation Studies* Edited by Mona Baker (1998/2004: 205), there is an entry "Reviewing and criticism" by Carol Maier which says:

Reviewing and criticism are evaluative practices that provide distinct but inseparable response to published literary translations (translations of literature in the broadest sense of not only imaginative writing but also non-fiction and other materials in the humanities). On the one hand, the differences cited conventionally between the two forms of evaluation hold true for translation as well: the reviewer alerts a reader to new books, describing them and passing judgment as to whether they are worth reading and buying; the critic addresses books that may or may not be new, considering them in detail and usually assuming a reader's familiarity with them (Oates 1990; Leonard Woolf 1939: 29; Virginia Woolf 1939: 7). On the other hand, neither the reviewing nor the criticism of literary translations has developed fully as an art—unlike the reviewing and criticism of literature.

This certainly is not a definition of translation criticism and its distinction between "reviewing" and "criticism", as Wen Jun (2006: 9) points out, is not quite meaningful.

To sum up, there has not been a formal and satisfactory definition to the term "translation criticism" in the West.

2.2 Definitions of Translation Criticism in China

In China, people tend to use "translation criticism" instead of "translation quality assessment" as it was in the West. Though there are numerous articles talking about translation criticism, many of these articles do not give definitions to it. In this section, we will only choose some of the representative ones to offer the reader an overview and to come to a definition by the authors of this book.

Two definitions given by dictionaries are as follows: 1), "in a broad sense, translation criticism is an overall evaluation of the process and product of a translation in accordance with certain criteria" (Lin Huangtian 1997: 184); and 2), "it is a mental activity based on a certain value, an intellectual activity involving the analyses and evaluation of a certain translation phenomenon (including translated works and translation theories) and an integrity of aesthetic evaluation and scientific judgments" (Fang Mengzhi 2004: 346).

As to definitions which appear in articles and books, the following are representative:

"Translation criticism is the evaluation of the translated works" (Zhou Yi & Luo Ping 1999: 146).

"Translation criticism refers to the (scientific or artistic) analyzing and evaluating of the translation process and product" (Wen Jun 2000).

"Translation criticism in its normal sense is to make comments on a certain translation in light of a certain criteria and by means of analysis, or it can be comments on a certain phenomenon in translation through the comparison of different versions of one and the same text" (Yang Xiaorong 2005: 3).

"Translation criticism is an empirical, aesthetic and cognitive activity featured by intellectuality" (Wang Hongyin 2006: 46).

"Translation criticism is the practice of the critical study of a translation and other questions related to translation" (Peng Zhen 1997). It is noticeable that Peng Zhen also points out that translation criticism involves value-judgment and evaluation of the translated literary works.

"Translation criticism is a cognitive activity involving the scientific analysis, interpretation and comments on various translation phenomena, translated works and translation theories based on a certain translation theory and theories of translation criticism" (Wen Xiuying 2007: 38).

Xu Jun (2003: 403) gives a detailed discussion of the term of "translation criticism". He says that "in a broad sense, translation criticism is the understanding and evaluation of translation and in a narrow sense, it is the critical reflection and evaluation of the translation activity, including not only the concrete evaluation of certain translation phenomenon and a specific translated text, but also the general evaluation of translation essence, process, techniques, functions and impact"

Si Xianzhu (2004) says that when talking about translation criticism, people both home and abroad tend to use "translation criticism", "translation assessment" and "translation evaluation" alternatively and without being well-defined. His idea is that "translation assessment" is "species" and the other two are "genera", linguistically, the former is super-ordinate, consisting of criticism of the translated texts focusing more on the socio-cultural level, theories of translation criticism and criticism of translation theories, while the latter two are subordinate, basically confined to judgments of the quality of translated texts, focusing more on the textual level.

According to Mu Lei (2007), some well-known English dictionaries such as *Random House Unabridged Dictionary* (2nd edition, 1993), *Webster's Third New International Dictionary* (1993), *Longman Dictionary of English Language and Culture* (1992) and *The Concise Oxford Dictionary of Current English* (ninth edition, 1995), do not make a clear distinction between "assessment" and "evaluation". Both of them can mean "to analyze critically and judge definitively the nature, significance, status, or merit of something; to determine the importance, size, or value of something". Mu quotes Kenneth D. Hopkins' *Educational and Psychological Measurement and Evaluation* to further distinguish "assessment", "evaluation", "measurement" and "testing": "measurement" is the statistic description of an object; "evaluation" is a process of generalization and explanation featured by value-judgments; "assessment" and "evaluation" is non-statistic and not so accurate quantitative description, or a value-judgment while "testing" is the technology to collect information.

To sum up, in most cases, scholars in China tend to use the term "translation criticism", but alternatively they also use "translation review". The two terms make little difference. This reminds us of the two terms "literary criticism" and "literary review" that have long been used in literary studies in China. So far as the content or scope of translation criticism is concerned, some scholars think that the object of our criticism is only the translated text, others hold that the translator, the process, the product, the impact and even the theories of translation should all be included in the criticism; as to the nature of translation criticism, most of the scholars think that it is a kind of evaluation (see Xu Jun 1992; Liu Shushen 1997; Wen Jun 2000, 2003; Zhen Hailing 2000 etc.), with a few of them speaks of value-judgments in particular(see Lin Huangtian, 1997; Peng Zhen 1997; Liu Shushen 1997; Wen Jun 2003; Fang Mengzhi 2004 etc.), others regard it a cognitive and intellectual activity; so far as the methods are concerned, some think that translation criticism should be done in accordance with certain translation theories, others with a certain criterion or a certain theory other than translation theories.

2.3 Essence of Criticism and Translation Criticism as Evaluation

2.3.1 Criticism and literary criticism

The famous literary critic René Wellek defines criticism as "study of concrete works of art", including "describing, interpreting and evaluating the meaning and effect that literary works have for competent but not necessarily academic readers" (qtd. in Zhu Gang 2001: vi-vii).

According to Tang Jun (2005), The English word "criticism" is originated from the Greek words "krĭnō" and "krités", the former means "judgment" and the latter "judge" or "juryman".

Wang Hongyin (2006: 15) gives us a detailed etymological examination of the word "criticism" in his *On the Criticism of Literary Translation* (文学翻译批评论稿). Wang quotes Liang Shiqiu to make clear the exact meaning of criticism. Etymologically, the word "krites" in Greek means discrimination and value-judgment. In *A Dictionary of Modern Critical Terms* by the British critic Roger Fowler, one finds that etymologically, the word "criticism" means "to analyze" and later "to judge" (Ling Chenguang 2001：47). Webster's Online Dictionary says that the word "criticism" can be dated 1607. Longman Dictionary says that the word has the following meanings: 1) the act of criticizing usually unfavorably; 2) a critical observation or remark; 3) the art of evaluating or analyzing works of art or literature; 4) writings expressing such evaluation or analysis and 5) the scientific investigation of literary documents (as the Bible) in regard to such matters as origin, text, composition, or history. The Collins Cobuild Dictionary says criticism can mean the expressing of the disapproval of something or somebody and it can also be a serious examination and judgment of literary works. *Webster's New Dictionary of Synonyms*

(1978) lists "critique, review, blurb and puff" as synonyms of "criticism". It says that,

…criticism is of all these terms the most nearly neutral and the least capable of carrying derogatory connotations. The proper aim and the content of a criticism have never been definitely fixed and are still subjects of controversy, but the term usually implies an author who is expected to have expert knowledge in his field, a clear definition of his standards of judgment, and an intent to evaluate the work under consideration.…critique is sometimes preferred as a designation of a critical essay, especially of one dealing with a literary work; but currently it is often avoided as an affection. Review is now the common designation of a more or less informal critical essay dealing particularly with new or recent books and plays (this reminds us of Maier's distinction between reviewing and criticism. the author). The term is frequently preferred by newspaper and magazine critics as a more modest designation of their articles than criticism or critique and as permitting less profound or exhaustive treatment or as requiring only a personal rather than a final judgment of the merits and faults of the work. …Blurb is applied chiefly to a publisher's description of a work printed usually on the jacket of a book for the purposes of advertisement. Puff, a word once common for any unduly flattering account (as of a book or play), in current use applies especially to a review that seems obviously animated by a desire to promote the sale of a book or the success of a play regardless of its real merits or to one that is markedly uncritical in its flattering comments.

In China, traditionally, people use the term "*ping lun*" (评论, review) to refer to "criticism". In Liu Xie's *Wen Xin Diao Long* (文心雕龙·论说) there appears the words "*ping*" (评) meaning evaluation and judgment, and "*lun*" (论) meaning analyzing and explaining. In *Yan Shi Jia Xun* (颜氏家训) and *Yu Zhong Zhi Sheng Zhi Shu* (狱中致甥侄书)，there appears the term "*ping lun*" (评论, review). As for the term "*pi ping*" (批评, criticism), it is regarded as the abbreviation of "*pi zhu ping shi*" (批注评释) that first appears in the Song Dynasty in the national imperial examination, referring to the annotation and comment on an article, not totally the same as the meaning of "*ping lun*" (评论, review). Some scholars, therefore, think that the correct translation of "literary criticism" into Chinese should be "*wen xue ping lun*" (文学评论). But the current situation is that "*wen xue ping lun*" (文学评论) is more often used in the daily life while "*wen xue pi ping*" (文学批评) is more often used in the books and articles by scholars in the field of literary studies (Li Guohua 1999：16-17).

One thing we should be aware of is that the term "literary criticism" has its broad sense and narrow sense. René Wellek says that in the narrow sense, literary criticism takes a specific literary work as its study object, focusing on the evaluation of the object. In the broad sense, it refers not only to the evaluation of a specific work and a specific writer, but also theories about literature (ibid: 18-19). To avoid misunderstanding and confusion, we should make clear in what sense scholars are using the term. Li Guohua (ibid: 17), for example, defines literary criticism in its broad sense: literary criticism is the analysis and evaluation of literary works and literary phenomena including literary movements and literary schools in accordance with certain criteria. However, some scholars tend not to distinguish the two senses. Cai Yi, for instance, defines literary criticism as study and evaluation of a certain literary phenomenon and a scientific activity associated with and based on appreciation (Huang Shuquan 2001: 3). It seems that this definition makes no distinction between literary criticism in its broad sense and narrow sense. But we can see its focus on specific texts from the latter part of the definition. In a similar way, Ling Chenguang (2001:46-61) defines literary criticism as the aesthetic evaluation of the literary phenomenon in accordance with certain aesthetic standards, stating the moral and aesthetic value of a literary text. He holds that literary criticism falls into the category of evaluation and is both scientific and artistic, both objective and subjective.

From the above discussion we can see that people often have different understandings about literary criticism and often use the term in different senses. But whether in its narrow sense or in its broad sense, or both, literary criticism is commonly regarded as an intellectual practice involving description, interpretation, analyzing and evaluating.

2.3.2 Evaluation, literary criticism and translation criticism

As the word "criticism" is originated in the West and as literary criticism is a well-established discipline already, people tend to turn to literary criticism to seek a better understanding of translation criticism (see Xu Jun, Wang Hongyin). This is quite natural and helpful especially for criticism of literary translation as they two bear some common features.

Yang Xiangrong (2005: 5-7) says that criticism of literary translation and literary criticism are comparable as they share the same key issue of literariness and the artistic value of a text. She also quotes Wang Kefei (1994) to call our attention to the difference between the two: their study objects and purposes are different. While literary criticism deals with evaluation of an original work and aims to not only improve literary creation but also to criticize the societies and cultures, having no direct relation with creation itself, criticism of literary translation, on the other hand, studies the problems existing only in the translated works and with improving the quality of translation as one of its main purposes. Yang further points out that as translation critics are facing two languages and two cultures, criticism of literary translation is more complicated than literary criticism. Methodologically speaking, adopting theories of literary criticism is only one of the approaches of criticism of literary translation which has an interdisciplinary nature.

To ensure a better understanding of translation criticism, we should realize that translation criticism, just like literary criticism, has its broad sense and its narrow sense and people's understanding of it is also different and changing. In its narrowest sense, it is mainly a practice concerned with translated texts—the strategies and methods used, the degree of equivalence, the impact it has on the readers and the value it possesses for truth-seeking, knowledge spreading, aesthetic experience and for social progress. Yet, in its broad sense, translation criticism includes the criticism on any thing concerning translation or having something to do with translation— translation policy, translation environment, translation teaching, translation theories and so on and so forth.

In the end of the above section, we have summed up the prominent features of "literary criticism": intellectual, practical, descriptive, interpretative, analytic and evaluative. Ontologically, the essence of "criticism" is, first and foremost, a human practice or an activity involving mainly description, interpretation, analyzing and evaluating. And the core element among them, then, should be "evaluation". The following explanations serve our reasons for this judgment:

First, according to *Cambridge International Dictionary of English* (2004), the word "evaluate" means "to judge or calculate the quality, importance, amount or value of (something)". "Evaluation" as value-judgment is the closest to the etymological meaning of the word "criticism"; secondly, almost all definitions of literary criticism and translation criticism take "evaluation" as its dominant element; and thirdly, methodologically, the activity of "evaluation" can actually (though not necessarily) entail both description, interpretation, cognition and analysis; fourthly, as Juan C. Sager says "[a]ny evaluation involves both comparison and measurement on a relative or absolute scale" (Sager 1983: 124). "Comparison" is one of the essential features of criticism. Any criticism, in order to tell what is proper and in what way, involves comparison, explicitly or implicitly. "Measurement" is the statistic description of an object. It is very helpful for the judging and calculating of the value of the object criticized and is therefore, very important to get to a convincing criticism. Linn and Gronlund in their *Measurement and Assessment in Teaching* say that evaluation always involves a value-judgment in accordance with the degree of satisfaction that the result of a measurement can meet and a complete evaluation program includes measure and non-measure which can be formulated as: Evaluation = measure (quantitative description) + non-measure (qualitative description) + value-judgment (Mu Lei 2007).

Last but not least, all the practice of the human being is to create values. Marxism holds truth and value are the two yardsticks of all human practice. Evaluation is actually one of the basic ways of human existence and social progress. Feng Ping in her book *On Evaluation* points out that "human cognition has two different orientations: one is to reveal what the world is, the other is to reveal the meaning and the value of the world....The former can be called knowledge, and the latter, evaluation". Feng argues that evaluation can be defined among various human activities "a cognitive action with a purpose of reforming the world (a step further than knowing the world)" (qtd. in Lv Jun 2007d: 262-263). Translation and translation studies are two of the most important social practices. They are also value creation and evaluation can help us know how much or what kind of value they have created. Actually, "evaluation is inescapable. Given the mass of material confronting any member of society, some sort of critical sifting is necessary…and it is precisely evaluative criticism which in large part maintains and modifies them" (France, 2000). When commenting on the practice of translation criticism, Carol Maier says that "[i]n the case of both reviewing and criticism, an interest in and concern for evaluation is leading to the study of past evaluative practices, to discussions about the criteria appropriate for the evaluation of translations, and to the scrutiny of current trends in reviewing and criticism" (Baker 1998/2004: 205).

To sum up, we can say that the most essential feature of criticism is evaluation. Ontologically and methodologically, evaluation covers almost all the essential elements of criticism—both literary criticism and translation criticism: practice, cognition, description, both quantitative and qualitative, interpretation, comparison, truth-seeking, analyzing, discriminating and value-judgment. And these elements speak well of the characteristics of criticism: the co-existence of description and prescription; subjectivity and objectivity; the combination of scientificity and artisticity. Translation criticism in a broad sense can be defined as an evaluative practice involving quantitative and/or qualitative description, interpretation, comparison, discrimination and value-judgment concerning any translational event (including the motivations and purposes of translation, the choice of texts to be translated, translation policies, the implementation of translation, translators, strategies and methods adopted, translation contexts, the outcome of translating, translation theories etc.) in accordance with implicit or explicit criteria. But to define translation criticism this way is facing the danger of enlarging the scope of translation criticism to a too broad field. For once the criticism of translation theories is included in translation criticism, it is inevitable that our analysis will go to the level of discussion about translation theories and such a criticism will be more theoretical-oriented than practical-oriented and have a nature of meta-criticism, entering the field of theoretical study of Translation Studies as a discipline described by Holmes (1988), far away from the practical nature of translation criticism. And according to Gu Zhengkun (2003), criticism of translation theories is more closely related to metatranslatology as the latter is a theory about translation theories, used to explain, evaluate or deconstruct general translation theories, including translation criterion and is meant to establish the norms of the criticism of translation theory. Therefore, in reference to our definition of translation and our understanding of the essence of criticism and that of evaluation, we prefer to give a definition of translation criticism in its narrow sense, but not as narrow as confining it to criticism of translated texts only: **Translation criticism is the evaluation of the process, outcome and impact of an interlingual and intercultural speech event in a specific context in accordance with implicit or explicit criteria, involving quantitative and/or qualitative description, interpretation, comparison, discrimination and value-judgment**.

One thing we need to mention is that to exclude criticism of translation theories from translation criticism in its narrow sense does not mean translation theories have nothing to do with translation criticism. According to James Holmes (1988: 37), translation criticism is different from translation theory in that the former is mainly concerned about the product of translation and subjectivity is hard to avoid, while the latter is concerned about translation principles and models, about the description of existing translations. But in reality, translation theories have been one of the sources of our criteria of translation criticism, just as Newmark says "[t]ranslation criticism is an essential link between translation theory and its practice" (Newmark 2001: 184). Though many criticisms may base upon theories other than translation theories and even without any theoretical foundation, still there are many based on a certain translation theory. It is, therefore, sometimes, inevitable to apply to and discuss on a certain translation theory in translation criticism and such a criticism consequently will be both practical and theoretical as Yang Xiaorong (2005) once pointed out. That is to say, translation criticism can be practical-oriented and it can also be theoretical-oriented. If it is theoretical-oriented, aiming not to mainly evaluate a translation but to discuss and improve or revise a translation theory, it will become mainly the criticism of translation theories and fall into the category of translation criticism in its broad sense. And here we must add immediately that sometimes there is no clear demarcation between the two.

2.4 Translation Criticism in China: An Overview

According to Xu Jun and Mu Lei (2009), from 1978 to 2007, monographs on translation criticism in China came up to 61, occupying 3.9% of the whole monographs on translation studies, and most of them appeared at the turn of the century. The number of articles on translation criticism (criticism on translation activities and specific translated texts, excluding translation quality assessment and testing) came to 685 in 15 key journals of foreign language studies in China, occupying 8.2% of the total. The two scholars think that translation criticism in China has made great progress since 1978, with the expanding of the scope from concrete comments on translated texts, translation phenomena, and translational events to the general evaluation of translation essence, process, techniques, functions and impacts; the vision of translation criticism has also been broadened by putting the criticism in a specific historical context and regarding translation as cultural exchanges; and ways of translation criticism have also been enriched—besides traditional error criticism, translation appreciation, comparison of different versions and quantitative analysis, there hace been criticism from the perspectives of many disciplines or theories such as polysystem, functionalism, feminism, psychology, hermeneutics, pragmatics, relevance theory and communicative action etc. At the same time, translation criticism has become more systematic and theoretical, gradually taking the turn from impressionism judgments to scientific analysis and evaluation. But generally speaking, there still exist many problems such as improper criticism or irresponsible criticism, lack of scientificity of criticism and the ineffectiveness and inefficiency of criticism. Judging from the current situation of symposiums on translation criticism, we can say that the development of translation criticism is not fast enough and remains a field to be improved and strengthened.

Han Shuqin (2021:46-50) reviews the studies of translation criticism in China from 2011 to 2021. She found 349 articles concerning translation criticism from CNKI and 31 monographs on translation criticism from www. nlc. cn, the website of China National Library. Among the 31 books, 24 are theoretical and 7 are practice-oriented. This shows that theoretical studies on translation criticism in China is growing faster than ever. However, studies on the core issues like the criteria for criticism is still inadequate and there is still the shortage of a complete system of discourse concerning translation criticism.

Among all those books on translation criticism in its narrow sense, the influential ones published in the last two decades are *On Translation* by Xu Jun (2003), *Introduction to Translation Criticism* by Yang Xiaorong (2005), *On the Criticism of Literary Translation* by Wang Hongyin (2006), *Introduction to Science Translation Criticism* by Wen Jun (2006), *Translation Criticism and Appreciation* by Li Ming (2006), *Translation Studies: A Functional Linguistics Approach—Constructing a Translation Quality Assessment Model* 2007), *Translation Criticism: From Theory to Practice* by Wen Xiuying (2007), *An Introduction to the Science of Translation Critisim* by Lv Jun and Hou Xiangqun (2009), *Studies on Models of Translation Criticism* by Xiao Weiqing (2010), *Translator Behavior Criticism: A Theoretical Framework* by Zhou Lingshun (2014), *Studies on Translation Criticism* by Liu Yunhong (2015), *Studies on Discourse of Translation Criticism of the 20th Century in China* by Liao Qiyi (2020) and so on. They are all remarkable efforts towards a systematic study of translation criticism. These books make valuable researches on the concept, the principle, the methods, the criteria and other aspects of translation criticism. Xu Jun gives a long chapter to the discussion of translation values and translation criticism, offering some enlightening insights about the theoretical approach and principles of translation criticism. Yang Xiaorong's *Introduction to Translation Criticism* is the first monograph and a great step taken toward a systematic study on translation criticism in China. Yang offers a considerably through survey of the types of translation criticism, classifying translation criticism in terms of the degree of integrity of translation (total, abridged or outlined, translated and edited), in terms of directions of translation (English to Chinese, Chinese to English and back translation), in terms of genre (literary and non-literary), purpose (aesthetic appreciation, error-finding, translation research and technique discussion), subject of criticism (ordinary reader, expert and translator himself or herself) and in terms of the object (the translated works, the translator and other things). She also gives detailed analysis of the subject, object, reference, different levels, methods, criteria and other things concerning translation criticism. All the other books mentioned here are significant in one way or another, making translation studies and translation criticism in China more and more systematic.

In collecting the documents concerning translation criticism in China, the following books are worth mentioning. They are *On Translation Criticism* edited by Jiang Zhiwen and Wen Jun (1999), *A Hundred Year of Translation Criticism in China* edited by Wen Jun (2006), *Studies on Translation Criticism: Theories and Methods* by Liu Yunhong and Xu Jun (2015) and *Criticism of Criticism: Construction and Reflection of Theories of Translation Criticism* by Liu Yunhong (2020). These collections offer us some representative researches on translation criticism in China and help us get a glimpse of the development of China's studies on translation criticism.

Besides the above-mentioned books and anthologies, some journal articles are also very significant toward the establishment of translation criticism as a discipline. Lv Jun, for example, published his "Axiology and the Science of Translation Criticism" in 2006, discussing the necessity of criticism for the disciplines in humanities, and the differences between practical translation criticism and theory of translation criticism and pointing out that the theory of translation criticism is a part of theory of evaluation which should be based on axiology. He further illustrates briefly the relation between axiology and theory of translation criticism and the function of axiology in the theory of translation criticism. Another article by Lv Jun (2007a) "The Crisis of Translation Criticism and the Science of Translation Criticism" points out that since the deconstructivist paradigm of translation studies appeared on the scene, we have encountered a crisis in translation criticism. He analyzes the phenomenon and makes clear that it is not the deconstructivist paradigm that has caused the crisis but rather it is our prejudicial view about criticism that has narrowed down our scope, on the formal level of text, and has expelled value criticism. In fact, it is the deconstructivist paradigm of translation studies that has broadened our view and paved a way to meta-criticism of translation. In another article by Lv Jun (2007b) "An Axiological Reflection on the Criteria of Translation Criticism", he gives an axiological survey of the previous criteria of translation criticism, pointing out that it is a mistake to take translation theories as their theoretical foundation, and the correct basis should be the theory of evaluation which is a branch of axiology. He also discusses the relations between the principles of evaluation theory and the criteria of translation criticism, claiming that the criteria of translation criticism are formed into a huge system, which consists of numerous concrete criteria, and if a universal criterion is really needed, it should be one telling the lowest requirement for a qualified translation, rather than a highest and ideal one. These articles help us reflect more on our study of translation criticism and indicate that the study of translation criticism should be guided by the evaluation theory in axiology and a discipline of translation criticism in light of evaluation theory is necessary.

The above review is only a much general one to the study of translation criticism in China. The following sections will offer some more detailed information, concerning the practice and the theoretical discussion of translation criticism.

2.4.1 Translation criticism in China at the practical level

At the practical level various translation criticisms have been done differing in their emphases on different elements of their evaluation — in the object of their criticism, in text types, in theories adopted and in criteria established and even in personal styles of the critics etc. As far as the object is concerned, there are criticisms on the translated texts and on the translators mainly. As far as the text type is concerned, there are criticisms on literary works and non-literary works. So far as the phases of translation are concerned, there are criticisms on the process, product and impact of translation. And translation criticisms bear different characteristics regarding the elements of evaluation emphasized: some are quantitative, others qualitative; some are analytic, others impressionistic; some stress the accuracy of information expressed, others fluency for a better reading.

Translation criticism in China has a long history and has been a constant company of translation practice. Luo Xinzhang's *Fan Yi Lun Ji* or *A Collection of Essays on Translation*，Ma Zuyi's *Zhong Guo Fan Yi Jian Shi* or *A Brief History of Translation in China* and Chen Fukang's *Zhong Guo Yi Xue Li Lun Shi Gao* or *A History of Translation Theory in China* — these books offer us many examples. Wen Jun (2006) has one chapter to the development of the practice and theory of translation criticism in China in his *Introduction to Scientific Translation Criticism*. Wen's discussion is fairly comprehensive except that he has missed Gu Zhengkun's influential theory of plurality and complementarities of translation criteria. To avoid much repetition, the authors of the this book will hence mention only a few.

In ancient China, one of the examples is the criticism made by Kumara jiva (344-

413) on the style of the translated text: "The Indian value much the elegance in their writing but such a feature is often lost when the Buddhist scripture is translated into Chinese and consequently, though the main ideas of the original are transferred, the style has been distorted, making the reading similar to the eating of food having been chewed by others—a really disgusting thing" (Chen Fukang 1992: 26). Another example is Dao'xuan (596-667), who once gave a review of the translation of the Buddhist scriptures before the Song Dynasty and pointed out there were many mistranslations and there were also good translations by Kumara jiva and Xuanzang (602-664) which not only captured the spirit of the original, but also offered a smooth reading (Chen Fukang 1992: 47).

In modern times, one of the famous examples is Wen Yiduo (1899-1946) making comments on Guo Moruo's translation of *Rubaiyat of Omar Khayyam*, pointing out mistranslations and at the same time the merits, and saying that some of the mistranslations are more poetic than the original. The other is Lu Xun's criticism or satire on Zhao Jingshen's translation of the "Milky Way" into "*niu nai lu*" (牛奶路).

In contemporary times, the well-known example is Qian Zhongshu's comments on Lin Shu's translations saying that he prefers Lin Shu's translation to the original text as the style of the translated is light and smooth, much better than the original which is heavy and rigid (Chen Fukang 1992: 425). And one can hardly forget the survey of reader's response to different Chinese versions of *The Red and the Black* in the 1990s which caused a hot debate on the criteria of translation among translators and critics.

Lv Jun and Hou Xiangqun (2001) list several models of translation criticism at present in China: source-text-oriented scientific criticism, target-text-oriented impressionistic criticism and theory or hypothesis testing criticism. The first model, which has been very popular for quite a long time, takes "faithfulness" and "equivalence" as the criteria. It can be qualitative and quantitative. One example of quantitative criticism is the analyses of equivalent transfer at different levels in the book *On Equivalent Translation* by Wu Xinxiang and Li Hong'an (1990). In the analysis of the equivalent degree of the two versions of a sentence, they describe the similarities and differences between the ST and the two TTs in the surface structures, the deep structures and the information structure at the phrasal level, the sentential level and the rhetorical level. After an extremely complicated comparison and analyses, they come to the conclusion about the equivalent degree of the two versions and this is showed in a table:

Table 2.1

Equivalent degree distribution	Referent (semantic level) (50%)	Interpretant (pragmatic level) (30%)	Sign (syntactic level) (20%)	Equivalent degree
Version 1	0.4	0.2	0.2	0.8
version 2	0.5	0.3	0.2	1

(Wu Xinxiang and Li Hong'an 1990)

There are also different approaches of translation criticism. Some are based on a linguistic theory, others on a literary or cultural theory, or simply one's own taste. One of the examples is criticism of the English version of Lu Xun's *Kong Yiji*, translated by Yang Xianyi and Gladys Yang made by Chen Hongwei (2002) based on fictional aesthetics, making a comparative study of the artistic accomplishments in those essential elements of fictional aesthetics such as character, time, space, plot, narration and language, showing how the translators have achieved affinity between the two artistic worlds conceived respectively in the source text and the target text by faithfully reproducing the aesthetic elements of the source text.

According to Wen Jun (2006: 161), since the introduction of different Western theories to China there have been more and more translation criticisms based on a certain theory: polysystem theory, information theory, functionalist theory, hermeneutics, stylistics, discourse analysis, pragmatics, textlinguistics, relevance theory and theory of communicative action etc., making translation criticism more scientific. Such ways of criticism should be encouraged as they can increase not only our awareness of theory and methodology, but also perspectives of our criticism. However, some criticisms of this model, as Cheng Aihua (2002) pointed out, just prematurely transplant a theory mechanically to draw a forced analogy and apply it to translation criticism, with the shortcoming of "methodology for methodology's sake".

Contrary to the bustling of translation criticism in journals applying all kinds of theories, there has been much less criticism on the current translation market. Xu Jun (2005) talks about it and calls our attention to the participation of criticisms on the quality of contemporary translations, on the choice of books to be translated and those phenomena harmful to the readers and to the society.

In fact, compared with the huge amount of documents translated into and out of Chinese, translation criticism is obviously far legged behind. On the one hand, the quality of many of the translations is dissatisfying. And on the other hand, as a famous translator Tu An once remarked that there has been little criticism in literary translation in today's China (Fu Xiaoping 2005). Another famous late scholar Yang Zijian (2006) also called our attention to the importance and weakness of translation criticism, especially criticism of literary translation in China.

2.4.2 Translation criticism in China at the theoretical level

Lv Jun and Hou Xiangqun (2001: 332) distinguish translation criticism and the study of translation criticism, saying that the former is a practice of appreciation, comparison and evaluation of a specific translated text based on translation theories or theories from other related fields, while the latter is the study of such a practice aiming at the theoretical discussion of the nature, the function, the criteria, the principle, the methods and other aspects of translation criticism. Lv Jun (2006) made a further distinction between the two, pointing that translation criticism is practical-oriented and it takes translated texts and the specific translation phenomenon as its object, while the study of translation criticism is the theoretical study of the general laws of the activities of translation and translation criticism, aiming to offer principles for the practice of translation criticism and to evaluate the worth of translation for human existence and for social development.

The study of translation criticism in China has a long history, but as is pointed out by Dong Qiusi, most of them are unsystematic and featured by translators' summary of their experiences as to what is and how to get to a good translation (Luo Xinzhang 1984: 540). Many people have written something concerning translation criteria and how to measure a translation in China, and it would be time-consuming to discuss their ideas one by one. Sun Zhili's article "Translation Criticism in the New Period" (1999), his book *Introduction to Translation of British and American Literature: 1949-1966* (1996), Wang Enmian's "On Translation Criticism in China" (1999), Huang Qiongying's "Translation Criticism in the Past Ten Years" (2002), Wen Jun and Liu Ping's "Translation Criticism in the Past 50 Years: Retrospective and Perspective" (2006), and some other articles and books all offer us good reviews of study on translation criticism in China. As translation criteria has been one of the key issues concerning translation criticism, the authors of this book intend to make a systematic study of all those versions of criteria based on a description and critical comments in light of Kuhn's theory of paradigm shift.

2.4.2.1 Concept of paradigm, paradigm shift and paradigmatic system

A. Paradigm and paradigm shift

The word "paradigm" is used as a technical term by Thomas S. Kuhn, the philosopher and historian of science. The concept of paradigm is developed in Kuhn's *The Structure of Scientific Revolutions* in 1962. Kuhn did not give an accurate definition to the term "paradigm". In the second edition of this book in 1970, Kuhn adds a "postscript—1969" and says that "a paradigm is what members of a scientific community share", including beliefs, values, techniques and models of behaviors (Kuhn 1970: 175-176). Paradigm, therefore, has a gestaltic feature encompassing the entire worldview of a community and all of the implications coming with it.

In Kuhn's view, "…the successive transition from one paradigm to another via revolution is the usual developmental pattern of mature science" (ibid: 12). This process of transition is called a "scientific revolution" or termed as "paradigm shift", denoting the progress of any science from the state of normal to abnormal and to normal again, only that the newly-formed normal state usually shows a radical change from the former one. A famous example is the transition from a Ptolemaic cosmology to a Copernican one.

Kuhn restricted the use of the term "paradigm shift" to natural sciences and held that in the humanities one may have constantly before him a number of competing and incommensurable solutions to a problem and thus paradigms do not exist in humanities or social sciences. Nevertheless, as has been said in the above paragraph, the term has been adopted and adapted in humanities and social sciences since the 1960s.

B. Paradigmatic shifts in humanities and social sciences

In humanities and social sciences, the term paradigm has been used to describe the set of experiences, beliefs and values that affect the way an individual (or a community) perceives reality and responds to that perception. In this sense, paradigm mainly refers to the world-view. The term "paradigm shift" is used to denote a change in how a given society goes about organizing and understanding reality. An example of paradigm shifts in social sciences is the cognitive revolution, away from behaviourist approaches to psychological study and the acceptance of cognition as central to studying human behaviour. Paradigm shifts also exist in linguistics. In an article "The Paradigm Shift: From structuralism to transformationalism", Dr. Anwar AL-thwary talked about the two senses of the term "paradigm": "[o]n one hand, it stands for the entire constellation of beliefs, values, techniques, etc. shared by the members of a given community. On the other, it denotes one sort of element in that constellation, the concrete puzzle-solutions which, employed as models or examples, can replace explicit rules as a basis for solution of the remaining puzzles of normal science" and the paradigm shifts from historical or comparative linguistics to structural linguistics, from structural linguistics to transformationalism (http://www.yementimes.com/article.shtml?i=1226&p=education&a=5). Wang Yichuan et al. (2009) also talked about the two senses of "paradigm" by Kuhn: one is primary referring to the constellation of the shared things of a scientific community; the other is secondary referring to the particular important rules drawn out. In literary studies, paradigms are those concrete schools such as Russian formalism, New Criticism and structuralism etc.

C. Paradigmatic system

When talking about the methodology of translation studies, Lv Jun and Hou Xiangqun (2001) point out that one of the effective ways is system approach in light of the system theory. System theory was proposed by the biologist Ludwig von Bertalanffy (1901-1972). A system is a complex of elements in interaction. Bertalanffy defines system as "a set of elements standing in interrelation among themselves and with environment". Some basic concepts of the general system theory are wholeness, open system in flux equilibrium, hierarchy and hierarchisation, primary activity, and "conservation" of the integrity. The system view is based on several fundamental ideas and among which the most fundamental one is that all phenomena can be viewed as a web of relationships among elements, or a system. Thus, paradigms can also form a system consisting of different competing paradigms, with some of them in the dominant position and others marginal. A "dominant paradigm" refers to the values, or system of thought, in a society that are most normative and widely held at a given time. Dominant paradigms are shaped both by the community's cultural background and by the context of the historical moment. The following factors are decisive for a paradigm to be accepted as a dominant one: 1), professional organizations that give legitimacy to the paradigm; 2), dynamic leaders who introduce and purport the paradigm; 3), journals and editors that disseminate the information essential to the paradigm, giving the paradigm legitimacy; 4), government agencies who give credence to the paradigm; 5), educators who propagate the paradigm's ideas; 6), conferences conducted that are devoted to discussing ideas central to the paradigm; 7), media coverage; 8), lay persons that embrace the beliefs central to the paradigm; 9), sources of funding to further research on the paradigm (http://en. Wikipedia.org/wiki/Paradigm).

Actually, in Kuhn's paradigm theory, the concept of a paradigmatic system has been implied. He says that a current paradigm may be challenged and thrown into a state of crisis. During this crisis, new ideas, perhaps those previously discarded, are tried till a new paradigm is eventually formed. Kuhn admits that "[e]ach of the schools whose competition characterizes the earlier period is guided by something much like a paradigm; there are circumstances, though I think them rare, under which two paradigms can coexist peacefully in the later period" (Kuhn 1970: ix). In applying Kuhn's paradigmatic approach to sociology, John Scott and Gordon Marshall found "a persisting lack of consensus around a single paradigm in sociology" and that we should "see sociology as a 'multiple paradigm' science" (Scott & Marshall 2005). Robert Brain Crotty (1980) combined system theory with Kuhn's paradigm theory to investigate the religious knowledge and came to the term of paradigmatic system of religious knowledge in his study of different research traditions and models in his doctorial dissertation (Crotty 1980).

To sum up, system theory helps us get a broader vision as it sees things as wholeness. Paradigm theory can help us see better the development of scientific research in a certain field. The core of a paradigm is the beliefs and values shared by a community. If there is the change of beliefs and values, there will normally be the change of paradigms. As far as translation criticism is concerned, we know that a real "revolution" can take place only when our belief about translation has changed. Translation criterion is something concerning our belief and value about translation, therefore a paradigmatic approach to it, with the guidance of system theory, should be helpful and reasonable for us to have a systematic overview of it.

2.4.2.2 Paradigmatic approach to study of translation criterion in China

A.The source-text-oriented paradigm

Translation principles and criteria have been regarded as the core of translation theories as well as translation criticism, therefore, we choose to focus on them for our discussion of translation criticism at the theoretical level.

Zhi Qian (223-253), a Buddhist monk and translator living in the period of the Three Kingdoms, in his Preface to Fa Ju Jing (法句经序) holds that a good translation of Buddhist scripture should be intelligible and faithful in meaning to the original (Chen Fukang 1992: 14).

Dao'an (314-385), who was in charge of the work of translating Buddhist scriptures in the Eastern Jin Dynasty, wrote many prefaces to the translated Sanskrit scriptures and his criteria of translation were often expressed in them. He is famous for his advocating a literal translation in order to be faithful to the original.

What needs to be mentioned here is the famous debate which took place in the year 224 on "*wen*" and "*zhi*" —whether the translated Buddhist scriptures should have a gaudy style (*wen*) or a plain style (*zhi*). And by the way, the authors of this book want to point out a mistake made by Andre Lefevere when he says that "the first translations of the Buddhist scriptures into Chinese were done in what was referred to as a 'simple' style, or *wen*" and "[a]fter Zhi Qian, translations were done in the elegant style, or *zhi*, suitable for literary translation" (Bassnett & Lefevere 2001: 21). Lefevere has mistaken *wen* for *zhi*. But anyway, Lefevere is excusable as in his article "Chinese and Western Thinking on Translation" he said that Yan Yang, his former graduate student's doctoral dissertation on Chinese thinking about translation has provided him with new insights (ibid: 24). In fact, the distinction between the Chinese character "*wen*" and "*zhi*" originated in Confucius' *The Analect*s to describe what a noble man should be like. According to Qian Mu (1895-1990), a famous historian, "*zhi*" means "plain" and "*wen*" means "gaudy". According to Lai Qinfang (2006), Confucius' view of the "harmony of *wen* and *zhi*" has been the highest standard for a good person and a good writing. "*Zhi*" refers to one's inner quality while "*wen*" one's outer appearance. It is Yang Xiong, a scholar in the period of the Three Kingdoms, who first discussed the issue of *wen* and *zhi* in literary studies. Later, another scholar named Wang Chong began to take the integrity of *wen* and *zhi* as the standard for excellent writings. However, "*wen*" and "*zhi*" can both refer to the formal style of a composition. Liu Xie, a famous scholar in literary studies in China, proposed in his *Shi Xu* (时序) that there have been changes of writing styles between *wen* and *zhi* from generation to generation and the ballads in the period of Tao Tang value the plain style while poetry in the period of Yu values more the elegant style. The "*wen*" and "*zhi*" discussed in Zhi Qian's Preface to Fa Ju Jing are just terms concerning the style of translation judging from the specific context. To cut it short, this debate on "*wen*" and "*zhi*", has the same nature as the debate on "beautiful" and "faithful" and has lasted more than a thousand years actually.

Xuanzang (602-664), the learned Buddhist monk and translator in the Tang Dynasty advocates faithfulness and intelligibility.

Ma Jianzhong (1845-1900), holds that good translation should be accurate and make the target reader response the same way as the reader of the original text (ibid:

102).

Yan Fu (1854-1921), in the preface to his Chinese translation of T.H. Huxley's *Evolution, Ethics and Other Essays*, says that there are three spheres of difficulties in doing translation, namely, *xin, da* and *ya* (translated differently as "faithfulness, expressiveness and elegance" or "fidelity, fluency and elegance" or as "loyalty, comprehensibility and embellishment" etc.). The three characters have been regarded as principles of translation and criteria for measuring the quality of translation by many translators and critics in China for more than a hundred years. Yan Fu thinks that the three requirements form an integrated whole and all for a better expression of the ideas of the original. To be faithful to the original is for the purpose of expressiveness and to be elegant (by means of using syntax of the pre-Han dynasty) is also in the interest of expressiveness. Though he is quite free with the way of expression of the original in his practice and has been criticized by many people for his "unfaithfulness", it seems that Yan Fu himself believes he is simply sacrificing the formal equivalence for the faithful expression of the meaning of the original and it seems also he is quite aware that he is doing translation sometimes in an abnormal way as he says that adding comments and notes where the translator thinks necessary "is not the right way to do translation" (Chen Fukang 1992: 128). Leo Tak-hung Chan (1997: 59) once commented,

> [T]o cut short the ongoing debate on whether Yan Fu regarded fidelity or fluency as the more central criterion, we need to note that, in principle (as against even his own actual practice), he stood on the side of fidelity to the original. In so doing, Yan Fu falls squarely within the tradition of the majority of Bible translator-theorists in the West, for whom faithfulness, or respect for the source text, was to be defended as a virtue.

Lin Yutang (1895-1976), as a translator and writer, holds that translation is an art, his criteria are similar to but somewhat different from Yan Fu's: fidelity is the foremost concern, then smoothness, and the then again, beauty. Beauty is the outcome of the translator's full play of his subjectivity to reproduce the style and spirit of the original (Chen Fukang 1992: 329-333).Yet, according to Yunte Huang (2002: 24), Lin Yutang, in doing translation from Chinese into English, "advocates Pidgin English, a hybrid of Chinese and English, as a more expressive language than standard English. He is critical of the tendency to standardize English by purging the so-called linguistic pollutants—that is, the kind of English spoken by immigrants and foreigners who, in Henry James's words, have played with the English language, 'dump[ing] their mountain of promiscuous material into the foundations of the

American'".

Chen Xiying (1896-1970) holds that translators should be faithful to the original text in every aspect and try to make the translated text resemble to the original in its form, sense and spirit. If one is translating a non-literary text, one has to strive to be faithful and expressive, and Yan Fu's "elegance" is unnecessary. Even if one is translating a literary text, if the original is not elegant, one should not make his translation elegant (Chen Fukang 1992: 323-327).

Lu Xun (1881-1936), a great translator and writer, and a translation theorist as well, thinks that translation should meet the requirements of faithfulness and intelligibility. As he insists that the main purpose of translation is to introduce the foreign cultures to the Chinese readers, he values much faithfulness to the original and believes that we can sacrifice smoothness for the sake of faithfulness if the two can not be achieved at the same time. To achieve faithfulness, he advocates literal translation in vernacular Chinese and an exotic atmosphere in the translated works and holds that literal translation can be an important means to enrich the mother tongue. Lu Xun argues that "all translations must have both intelligibility and the style of the original text" (ibid: 301). To achieve a set goal, Lu Xun suggests that we classify people into three types: those well educated, common readers having received a little education and the illiterate. The last type is not our target reader. For the other two, we should choose different books and adopt different methods (ibid: 314).

Zhu Shenghao (1912-1944) in his preface to his translation of Shakespeare, says that his foremost concern is to do all that he possibly could to preserve the spirit of the original (ibid: 334).

Fu Lei (1908-1966), just like Lin Yutang and Zhu Shenghao, also values "similarity in spirit". He thinks that in respect of the effect, translation is much like the drawing—what is more important is the likeness of spirit if the translator can not make his translation both similar to the original in spirit and in form or appearance (ibid: 394).

Qian Zhongshu (1910-1998), in his comments on Lin Shu's translation, says that a perfect translation or an ideal translation should be a "transmigration" in which the soul, the spirit of the original text is carried over to the target text and with the naturalness of the original in language (ibid: 421).

The year 1950 witnessed two important articles on translation criticism in China. One is entitled "The Criteria and Focuses of Translation Criticism" by Dong Qiusi, the other is "On Translation Criticism" by Jiao Juyin. The former suggests that we should set up a contemporary or realistic criterion for translation and the latter calls for our attention to the establishment of different criteria for different types of texts.

Liu Zhongde (1914-2008) holds that the principle for translation should be *xin*, *da* and *qie*, that is, faithfulness, expressiveness and closeness. "Closeness" means being as close to the original style as possible (Liu Zhongde 1991: 24).

Xu Yuanzhong (2000) regards literary translation as rivalry between two languages and even between two cultures which vie to express the original idea better. Translation should be faithful to the original at least, and beautiful at best. A literary translator should exploit the advantage of the target language, that is to say, make the fullest possible use of the best expressions of the target language in order to make the reader understand, enjoy and delight in the translated text. Based on his understanding of literary translation, Xu (2002) argues that the criteria of translation should be *xin*, *da* and *you*, that is, "faithfulness, expressiveness and the best words in the best order". In another article he explains the meaning of the word "*you*" as "the best way of expression" (Xu Yuanzhong 2003).

Yang Zijian and Liu Xueyun (1994) proposed that translation criterion can be expressed in a formula TC=F+E+X. "F" refers to "Faithfulness"; "E", "Expressiveness" and "X", the specific features of translation of a specific text-type. Later, in 2003, he modified his criteria offering a more practical system of criteria which consist of the external and internal parameters with "propriety" as the ultimate standard and takes faithfulness to the content or ideas of the original as the "ground-level requirement" (Li Xiaomin and Yang Zijian 2003).

Jin Di, co-authored with Nida the book *On Translation* (1984) holds that a good translation should achieve the effect of "dynamic equivalence" emphasizing the receivers' response to the translated works, requiring the translation to ensure the target reader to get the same feelings and thoughts as the reader of the original after their reading and hence the criterion of "equivalent effect" based on mainly the communication theory. The criterion of "equivalent effect" is further discussed in Jin's book *A Study on Translation of Equivalent Effect* in which he makes it clear that "effect" means "the feelings and thoughts" of the receptors, not the "response" by Nida. In fact, the criterion put forward by Jin Di and Nida is not something totally new. Some scholars both in China and in the West have already talked about it long ago. For example, in China, as has been mentioned, Qu Qiubai once said in 1931 that a translation should be faithful to the original meaning and enable the target language readers to have the same concept from the translated text as the source language readers get from the original text. Ma Jianzhong and Zeng Xubai also said something of the same nature as "equivalent effect". In the West, Tytler in his famous *Essay on the Principles of Translation* also said that "in a good translation, the merits of the original has been transferred totally to another language, enabling people of the target language to get a clear understanding and a strong response, equivalent to people of the original language" (Jin Di 1998: 13-14).

Sun Zhili (1997) holds a dialectical view on the criteria of translation. He believes that translators should seek the integrity of scientificity and artisticity, the unification of faithfulness and smoothness and the harmony of faithfulness with elegance.

Gu Zhengkun (1989) put forward his theory of plurality and complementarities of translation criteria arguing that there does not exist an absolute good-for-all and good-at-anytime criterion for translations, translators and readers, including critics. He developed a system of translation criterion which consists of the absolute standard, the highest standard and the concrete standards. The absolute standard is the original text itself, the highest standard is the maximal approximation which refers to the idealest approximation of the translated to the original in its imitation of the original's content and form (deep structure and surface structure). According to Gu, "the maximal approximation" is to be used to replace "faithfulness" or "equivalence" as it is more objective and realistic. As to the concrete standards, they are also called classified standards, which can be established in terms of different functions of translation, different levels of readers and translators, diverse aesthetic tastes of our human beings and so on. These various concrete standards are what term "plurality of translation criterion" refers to. Gu (2003) speaks of how to use concrete criteria to measure the maximal approximation, saying that it depends on the evaluator's needs to decide how many criteria should be used in his measurement. So far as the establishment of the maximal approximation, it is also flexible depending on the specific context. When talking about the "complementarities of translation criterion" Gu says that the merits of one concrete standard may just be the shortcomings of another and therefore different concrete standards can complement each other. This, as the authors of this book see it, is illogical. Supposing that we have come to the agreement that for poetry translation, it is essential to reproduce the poetic or aesthetic appeal of the original and for translations of technical texts, it is essential to reproduce the semantic information of the original, then can we say the excluding of poetic appeal is the shortcoming of the criterion set for technical translation? Certainly not. The reason is that we have classified poetry translation and technical translation into different types according to their dominant functions and have set up different criterion or criteria for each. As the criterion or criteria for each type is supposed to be suitable only for its own type, its own purpose and its own readers, it is even hard to say one has a merit compared with another. If we are going to know the merits and shortcomings of one criterion, we have to compare different criteria set up for one and the same type of translation. Otherwise, it would be almost meaningless. Even if we are criticizing a translation of one and the same type, say a poem, different criteria sometimes may be quite contradictory, instead of complementary, for the measurement. For example, the criterion of syntactic similarity may contradict with that of semantic and phonetic similarities.

Though Gu's theory of plurality and complementarities of translation criteria is quite valuable, after our careful reading of Gu's articles and books on the theory, the authors think that this theory has been, to a certain extent, over-estimated. First, the term "maximal approximation" as Gu says, is not initiated by him and some other scholars like Zhu Guangqian have used it before. Secondly, it does not have much difference from the traditional ideas of translation criterion as it still considers the source text as the ultimate yardstick for measuring the quality of a translation. And thirdly, there are parts that are not so strict in logic. Its main contribution is that it has brought us some epistemological thinking on the issue of translation criteria and is a significant effort to establish a system of translation criteria combining abstract criteria with concrete ones and it has illuminated that criteria are changeable in specific contexts and positions of a criterion in the system of criteria is also changeable. In his book *China and West: Comparative Poetics and Translatology* Gu Zhengkun (2003) illustrates the inevitability of the existence of plural translation criteria, arguing that in reality the multi-functions of translations, the diversity of people's aesthetic tastes and the multi-levels of the reader will lead to the diversity of the value of the translation and to the plurality of concrete translation criteria. All in all, we should say the theory of plurality and complementarities of translation criteria has taken a further step toward a systematic study of translation criteria in China.

The criterion of "harmony" was proposed by Zheng Hailing in 1999. Zheng claims that different from other abstract criteria, the criterion of "harmony" is concrete. The translator has to get a thorough understanding of the original, the whole and the parts, and then take every possible measure to make his translation to conform to the aesthetic standard of "harmony". The authors of this book can hardly agree on Zheng's claim. Actually, "harmony" is a term that is as abstract as "faithfulness" or "transmigration". The criterion of "harmony" actually can be said the contemporary version of Qian Zhongshu's "transmigration" or "sublime adaptation". Liu Miqing (2005) once talked about the literary and aesthetic origin of "*xin, da* and *ya*", "similarity in spirit" and "transmigration", saying that they are all strongly influenced by the traditional Chinese aesthetics and the aesthetic value of translation is fulfilled by imitating the beauty of the original work. Here, we want to add that such aesthetic-oriented translation criteria are all built on the belief that translation is an art.

Besides, there have been various translation criteria based upon various linguistic theories. One example is Ke Ping (1993; 1999) who, based on semiotics, thinks a good translation should guarantee the transfer of the most important meaning in a specific context and strive for the maximum equivalence between the ST and the TT. Ke Ping (1999) in light of the sociosemiotic theory of meaning, classifies meaning into three categories: referential meaning, pragmatic meaning and intralingual meaning. Another example is Si Xianzhu (2006) who proposed a model for translation quality assessment based on the systemic functional linguistics, saying that a qualified translation should achieve the functional equivalent including the language function and the text function. In another article Si (2008) re-explained his model saying that to measure a translation, according to systemic functional linguistics which sees translation as preserving the meaning, we have to see whether a translation is equivalent to the original concerning its ideational, interpersonal and textual functions.

One more linguistic criterion we should mention is the statistic approach adopted by Wu Xinxiang and Li Hong'an (1990) in their measurement of a translation at different levels: the higher the degree of equivalence, the better the translation.

There are some other scholars making efforts to establish quantitative translation criteria based on different theories. Fan Shouyi（1994）, for instance, borrows ideas from fuzzy mathematics and tries to quantify the fidelity and fluency of translation by the designed subjection values.

To sum up, all the above-mentioned criteria believe that the translator should and can be faithful to the original, either the intention of the author of the original or the meaning of the original text, and they value the faithful reproduction of the intention, or meaning or form or spirit of the original. What the criteria of equivalent response or equivalent effect stress is also the similarity of the feelings and thoughts of the target reader with those of the original. Therefore, there is little difference beneath the surface of these versions of criteria and in a sense we can say that they belong to the same paradigm, i.e. source-text-oriented paradigm.

B. The target-text-oriented paradigm

Quite different from the above-mentioned criteria is Zhou Zhaoxiang's criterion. Zhou (1998) holds that with the development of society, translation has changed into another thing, different in its essence and scope, and the translator has changed from a "slave" to a "gatekeeper". In one of his articles Zhou argues that the old criterion of *xin, da* and *ya* is out of date. He lists 12 parties involved in the process of translation and distinguishes "a good translating job" from "a good translation". He says that the former is what we need today and the criterion for measuring it is the intended function of the target text. In other words, the better the fulfillment of the commissioner, the more successful the translating job. From the terms used by Zhou, we can see that his criterion is greatly influenced by the skopos theory of the German functionalists, especially by that of Holz-Manttari.

Zhou's criterion can be regarded as a "revolution" in translation criticism in China or a new paradigm compared with the above-mentioned criteria. It views translation differently and values not the faithfulness or fidelity of the "translated text" to the original but rather, only the fulfillment of the purpose(s) of the "translated". Therefore, Zhou's criterion clearly falls into the target-text-oriented paradigm.

C. The balance-oriented paradigm

Besides the above-mentioned criteria, there are criteria that stand the middle of the two extremes, trying to take the original author, the original text and the purpose of the user all into consideration. This can be called a specific-situation-oriented or balance-oriented paradigm.

Li Yunxing (2001), from a systemic perspective and focusing on "text in communication" and "the translation situation", put forward a systemic criterion: "[t]ranslation quality should be judged by the degree of balance the translator has attained in handling the source text system and the target text system with the translation situation system as the fulcrum". And a comprehensive model for translation evaluation should comprise the three multi-faceted systems, namely the source text, the target text and the translation situation. To evaluate a translation, "the critic should first collect data and samples of all facets in each system and then describe them. This data collection and description process will certainly provide critics with panoramic views of what happened in the translation event" and then the critic can make his assessment by following the above-mentioned systemic criterion.

Yang Xiaorong (2001) comments on Gu Zhengkun's theory of plurality and complementarities of translation criteria saying that there seems to be "a missing link" and thinks that this missing link is "conditions". By "conditions", Yang means the decisive factors which are constraining elements in the establishment of translation criteria in a specific context including the nature of the original, translation purpose, target reader, translator and his views on translation, time and place of the translation activity etc. It is conditions that can determine translation criteria. No conditions, no criteria. The clarity of criteria conforms to the clarity of conditions. The function of conditions can be explained as the monitoring of context, both linguistic and extra-linguistic, over the whole process of translation. Theoretically, conditions bring determinacy to indeterminacy, or set limitation to it; practically, only if conditions are taken into consideration does it make sense to discuss about translation criteria. Actually, Gu (2003) does discuss those decisive factors and how they have made translation criteria plural in his above-mentioned book which has been seldom mentioned by translation scholars. Anyway, Yang's discussion is meaningful in that it lists more decisive factors for establishing translation criteria in specific contexts and gives these factors a generalized name "conditions". Yang (2005) gives a detailed review of study on translation criteria in China and in the West and distinguishes translation criterion from the criterion of translation criticism. She thinks that the former is consciously or unconsciously observed by the translator while the latter is by the critic. As there exist the differences in time and space and the subject, there will be the difference of the criteria. The differences also can be seen in the implementation, the units of examination and the degree of criterion awareness. But there are also many overlaps between the two as the critic should look at a translation from the perspective of the translator. Yang holds that the core of our discussion on translation criteria is how we can balance those constraining factors or "conditions" to make the translated text get to a well-modulated, well-balanced and harmonious state. This state can be called "the third state" and can be regarded as the criterion of translation. This criterion, as Yang says, implies a "middle way" philosophy.

D. The deconstructivist paradigm

There are other criteria based more clearly on philosophical approach. One is the deconstructionist view of translation that deconstructs translation and at the same time, the criterion of translation.

Wang Dongfeng (2004:3-9) holds that,

[T]he notion of "fidelity" is theoretically untenable. It embodies an all-or-nothing ethical judgment and hence can hardly function as a criterion for evaluating translations. The source text having lost its assumed determinant meaning under the dual impact from the New Critics' exposure of the "intentional fallacy" and Derrida's deployment of his famous non-concept differance, exactly what the target text is faithful to is called into serious question... Once "fidelity" is debunked, the time-honored myth of translation as cross-linguistic and cross-cultural transference of meaning will also collapse.

Wang also points out that in our traditional criteria for translation, there exist contradictions between faithfulness and other requirements. In reality, especially in today's translation market, translators are often forced to betray the author of the original as he or she is hired by the publisher. What is more, according to Derrida, nothing is translatable and nothing is untranslatable. What is translated can only be the translator's interpreting of the text (ibid).

E. The constructivist paradigm

The other philosophical approach is more constructive than deconstructive.

Lv Jun and Hou Xiangqun (2006) argue that traditional translation criteria come from people's belief that the meaning of a text or the author of the text is fixed and can be traced back through their intuition or linguistic analysis, therefore the criterion of "faithfulness" or "equivalence" to the original is popular and even a consensus for translators and critics. But deconstructionism with its theory of indeterminacy of meaning declares the total impossibility of faithfulness and even partial faithfulness, hence translation is only the "afterlife" of the original and the requirement of equivalence is meaningless. Consequently, there is no criterion for the translators and the critics to follow. The problem with deconstructionists is that they have over-exaggerated the subjectivity of the individuals and have neglected much of the objectivity of knowledge and the socialization of the individuals. Lv and Hou put forward a three-aspect criterion: 1), a translation should be able to stand the test of the objectivity of knowledge; 2), a translation should be plausible in its understanding of the original and valid in its interpretation of the original; and 3), a translation should go along with the intentionality of the original. Lv and Hou point out that "faithfulness" and "loyalty" can only be regarded as an attitude adopted by the translator. What is more, it is not suitable to seek and set up the highest standard as people of different cultures have different value systems. Therefore, a criterion telling the lowest requirement for a qualified translation is needed and the criterion proposed here can meet this demand. Such a criterion is preferable as it indicates the inevitability and possible validity of the existence of different interpretations to one and the same text. Another merit of this criterion is that it seeks the objective of criticism and at the same time does not deny the validity of subjective judgment in criticism. Compared with the above-mentioned criteria, one can find that this is more realistic and more tolerant—taking the original author, the source text, the translator and the target reader all into its consideration.

To sum up, there exists a paradigmatic system in the study of translation criteria in China. Some criteria are source-text oriented, others are target-text or client oriented; some are balance-oriented or middle-way oriented and others translator oriented. The translator-oriented paradigm has modern hermeneutics and deconstructionism as its philosophical background and views translation as something both impossible and possible and thus offers no criterion, leaving everything to the translator himself or herself, especially when the activity of understanding and expressing in translation is concerned. The balance-oriented or the middle-way-oriented paradigm is more influential in the field of literary translation and the source-text-oriented paradigm was once and for a long time the sole dominant paradigm, believing and requiring that the meaning or intention or function of the source text be reproduced in a translation by means of either the intuition or the linguistic analyses of the translator. We can even say that it still occupies the dominant position as fidelity to the original is still the basic requirement by the current professional standard. Yang Xiaorong (2001) also says that "faithfulness" and "smoothness" can be regarded as the dominant general translation criteria in contemporary China. According to Liu Miqing (2005), the criterion of the unity of "fidelity and intelligibility" ever since Xuanzang in the Tang Dynasty has been the dominant one in China and "faithfulness" to the original has been the foremost concern of translators just as Yan Fu says "to be expressive is for faithfulness to the original".

2.4.3 Professional and legislative criteria in China

Translation companies or agencies in China have set up their own professional standards for translation. Take the Nanjing Sunyu Translation Company for example. The "Standards of Translation Quality" of this company says that the concrete criteria are based on Yan Fu's *xin*, *da* and *ya*, especially xin and da. Errors are classified into three types: minor, major and significant. Minor errors include the improper use of punctuation marks, misspelling, inconsistency of terms, mistranslation of non-key words, not conformable to the idiomatic expression and errors of typing; major errors include misunderstanding, grammatical mistakes, improper terms, figure mistakes and mistranslation of key words; and the significant ones include mistranslation of important data and figures, loss of a whole sentence or a paragraph, loss of key words, mistranslation of key sentences, wrong terms. Errors of the first type should be controlled within the rate of 1/2000, for the second type, within 1/3000 and the third, 1/10000.

To regulate translation standards in China, "Specification for Translation Service—Part 1: Translation" was issued in 2003 which requires translations should be complete and content and terms be accurate. In 2005, "Target Text Quality Requirements for Translation Services" was issued by the Chinese government. The basic requirement for a translation is still "*xin, da* and *ya*" and faithfulness to the original, consistency of terms and smoothness are highly valued. The more concrete requirements concerning the norm of translating figures, proper nouns, units of measurements, symbols, abbreviations, neologies, poetry and advertisements and so on are all made clear. This national standard also offers principles and methods about how to measure the quality of a translation, saying that the measurement should be based upon the purposes of the translation and, at the same time, take both the errors of all kinds and the degree of difficulty of the original into consideration. In 2006, "Specification for Translation Service—Part 2: Interpretation" was issued and the criteria set for oral interpretation is accuracy and clarity. All these standards, as can be seen, require an accurate and faithful expression of the original. That is why we say criteria of source-text-oriented paradigm still hold a dominant position in China.

2.5 Translation Criticism in the West: An Overview

The practice of translation criticism in the West has a history almost as long as the activity of translation, but the history of study on translation criticism is much shorter and consequently there are not so many monographs on it. Hatim and Mason (1997: 197) once stated that:

> The assessment of translator performance is an activity which, despite being widespread, is under-researched and under-discussed. Universities, specialized university schools of translation and interpreting, selectors of translators and interpreters for government service and international institutions, all set tests or competitions in which performance is measured in some way. Yet, in comparison with the proliferation of publications on the teaching of translating—and an emergent literature on interpreter training—little is published on the ubiquitous activity of testing and evaluation.

Translation criticism in the West can also be classified into that in the broad sense and that in the narrow sense. In its broad sense, translation criticism, as has been said before, includes the criticism of translation theories. In respect of criticism of translation theories, some works are quite influential: *Translation Studies* by Susan Bassnett, *Contemporary Translation Theories* by Edwin Gentzler, *Translation Studies: An Integrated Approach* and *The Turns of Translation Studies: New Paradigms or Shifting Viewpoints?* by Snell-Hornby, *Introducing Translation Studies: Theories and Applications* by Geremy Munday—to name only a few. These books offer us historical and critical assessment of the development of translation studies with its various theories.

Studies and books on translation criticism in its narrow sense are underdeveloped compared with the amount of translations done and studies of other aspects of translation. In *Dictionary of Translation Studies* compiled by Shuttleworth and Cowie in 1997, we cannot find an item dealing with translation criticism, in *Routledge Encyclopaedia of Translation Studies* (1998/2004), one can only find the items of "translation quality" and "reviewing and criticism", and it was not until 2004 that in *An International Encyclopedia of Translation Studies* published in Berlin that one finds a group of articles (4 in fact) under the title of "on translation analysis, translation comparison and translation criticism in linguistic translation studies" (Hartmann 2006).

Monographs on translation criticism that can be mentioned are Katharina Reiss' *Translation Criticism:The Potentials and Limitations*, Juliane House's *A Model for Translation Quality Assessment* (1ˢᵗ edition in 1977 by John Benjamins Pub Co.; 2nd edition in 1981, Tubingen: Gunter Narr Verlag), *Translation Quality Assessment: A Model Revisited* (1997), Malcolm Williams' *Translation Quality Assessment: An Argumentation-Centered Approach* (2004).

Besides monographs, there are a collection of essays on translation quality assessment edited by Christina Schaffner named *Translation and Quality* in 1998 and a special issue of the journal *The Translator* focusing on Evaluation and Translation edited by Carol Maier in 2000.

What is more, many books have chapter or chapters on translation criticism, translation quality assessment or translation testing. Among which, Nida and Taber's *The Theory and Practice of Translation*, Peter Newmark's *A Textbook of Translation*, Wolfram Wilss' *The Science of Translation*, Christiane Nord's *Translating as a Purposeful Activity*—to name only a few—are very impressive. And there are some important articles found in some collections on translation studies such as *The Translation Studies Reader* and *The Translator's Handbook* etc.

2.5.1 Translation criticism at the practical level

Peter France, who is the chief editor of *The Oxford Guide to Literature in English Translation*, contributes to the above-mentioned volume an article entitled "Translation Studies and Translation Criticism" which offers us a picture of translation criticism in English. France (2000) begins with a translation criticism taking place in an imaginary "translation workshop" where Rudyard Kipling let his two characters talk about the comments of the different versions of the Bible in his story "Proofs of Holy Writ", France says that:

> Like many evaluations of translation, the judgments here are personal, metaphorical, and hard to argue with. Occasionally there is a reference to the source text (and even then not the 'real' source, the Hebrew, but to the Latin Vulgate), but above all the criteria concern the beauty of power of the target text. ... There is a kind of universalizing, absolute notion of good writing at work here, and one that remains powerful in spite of all one's awareness of the relative nature of taste judgments. A text works or it doesn't. If you feel its power, so much the better for you; if you don't, so much the worse. (France 2000: 3)

When talking about translation criticism and its criteria, France (ibid: 7) says that "[o]utside the specialized fields of Translation Studies, translator training, and the like, there are two widespread types of criticism, usually practised without a great deal of theoretical awareness: that of the language teacher (who may also be a teacher of foreign literature) and that of the journalist-critic". He then gives a detailed description of the situation:

> Almost all foreign language learning involves some element of translation, even if this is less prominent now than it once was. The teacher will propose a foreign text (often literary in nature) for translation, frequently offering a model version against which to judge the efforts of students. Judgments are in large part negative and local, noting errors in comprehension or failures to find adequate equivalents for particular expressions in the target language. The basic criterion here is one of adequacy to the source text.
>
> Against this, the journalist-critic, faced with a literary translation, will in many cases not comment on the translation at all, acting as if it gave unmediated access to the original. If the translation is noticed, the critic may compare it favourably or unfavourably with the original, but the dominant tendency is to judge it on its naturalness, fluency, elegance, and so on—is it well written? Venuti gives some characteristic examples, such as: 'the

style is elegant, the prose lovely, and the translation excellent' (Venuti 1995a: 2). Here the translation is judged according to the norms currently operating within the target culture—which may favour copiousness or brevity, plainness or decoration, and so on....The criterion here is one of acceptability to the target culture. (France 2000: 7-8)

In *Routledge Encyclopedia of Translation Studies* Edited by Mona Baker, there is an entry "Quality of translation" by Juliane House. According to House (2004: 197), "Approaches to translation quality assessment fall into a number of distinct categories: anecdotal and subjective, including neo-hermeneutic approaches; response-oriented approaches; text-based approaches". House gives further explanation of these approaches:

Anecdotal and subjective treatises on translation quality have long been offered by practising translators, philosophers, philologists, writers and many others. A central problem in such treatments is the operationalization of concepts such as 'faithfulness to the original', or 'the natural flow of the translated text'. Such intuitive treatments of translation quality are a theoretical in nature, and the possibility of establishing general principles for translation quality is generally rejected...An equally subjective and intuitive treatment of translation quality has more recently been proposed within the 'neo-hermeneutic' approach (e.g. Stolze 1992)...In Stolze's view, a 'good' translation can only come about when the translator identifies him/herself fully with the text to be translated. Whether such identification enables or in fact guarantees a translation of quality, and how this quality might be assessed, remains unclear. (House 2004: 197)

For response-oriented criticism, House says that:

Response-oriented approaches to evaluating translations are communicatively oriented and focus on determining the dynamic equivalence (Nida 1964) between source and translation, i.e. the manner in which receptors of the translated text respond to it must be equivalent to the manner in which the receptors of the source text respond to the source text. Nida postulated three criteria for an optimal translation: general efficiency of the communicative process, comprehension of intent, and equivalence of response. Upon closer scrutiny, these criteria prove to be as vague and non-verifiable as those used by proponents of the intuitive-anecdotal approach. Nida and Taber (1969: 173) propose another set of criteria: the correctness with which the message of the original is understood through the translation, the ease of comprehension and the involvement a person experiences as a result of the adequacy of the form of the translation. But the tests suggested for implementing such criteria, such as cloze tests or elicitation of a receptor's reactions to different translations, are not rigorous enough to be considered theoretically valid or reliable. (ibid: 197-198)

House (ibid: 198) then explains the psycholinguistic approaches: "[i]n the 1960s, psycholinguistists such as Carroll (1966) suggested the use of broad criteria like 'intelligibility' and 'informativeness' for assessing translation quality, together with a number of testing methods such as asking the opinion of competent readers, etc." She then says that the weakness of the two said approaches lies in their not taking the "black box", the human mind, into consideration and that in the test or evaluation of a translation, expert judges "simply take certain criteria for granted that are not developed or made explicit in the first place". What is more, "a norm against which the results of any behavioural test is to be judged" is missing.

For the text-based approaches, House thinks that it can be further divided into three models, i.e. linguistics, comparative literature or functional models. She then illustrates how each of them is implemented. For the linguistic model, she lists Reiss, Wilss and Koller:

> In linguistically-based approaches, pairs of source and target texts are compared with a view to discovering syntactic, semantic, stylistic and pragmatic regularities of transfer. An early and influential text-based approach to translation quality assessment is Reiss (1971/1978). Reiss suggested that the most important invariant in translation is the text type to which the source text belongs, as it determines all other choices a translator has to make. She proposed three basic text types on the basis of Buhler's (1934) three language functions: content-oriented, form-oriented, and conative. However, exactly how language functions and source text types can be determined, and at what level of delicacy, is left unexplained. Nor is the exact procedure for source text analysis given in two other influential publications. The first, Wilss (1982), stresses the importance in textual analysis of 'norms of usage' in the two language communities and suggests that deviations from these norms be taken as indicators of translation deficiencies. The second, Koller (1979/1922), suggests that the evaluation of a translation should proceed in three stages: (a) source text criticism, with a view to transferability into the target language, (b) translation comparison, taking account of the methods used in the production of a given translation, and (c) translation evaluation on the basis of native speaker metalinguistic judgments, based on the text-specific features established in stage (a). However insightful, this proposal remains programmatic in nature. (House 2004: 198-199)

And for the model of comparative literature described below, House points out that the main problem with this model is the lack or the fuzziness of the critic's standard for the measurement of a translation.

In approaches which draw on comparative literature, the quality of a translation is assessed according to the function of the translation in the system of the target language literature…first the translated text is criticized without reference to the source text, then specific solutions of translation problems are analyzed by means of the 'mediating functional-relational notion of translation equivalence'….it is not clear how one is to determine when a text is a translation and what criteria one is to use for evaluating a translation. (ibid 2004: 198-199)

While we admit what House said is true, we must say that House's criticism is somewhat unfair as such a model is usually not for the purpose of evaluating the quality of a translation and translation criticism.

For the functional model, House also expresses her dissatisfaction after her introduction:

In their functional theory of translation, Reiss and Vermeer (1984) claim that it is the skopos, i.e. the purpose of a translation, which is all important. The way the translated text is adapted to target language and culture norms is then taken as the yardstick for evaluating a translation….Of more relevance here is the failure of the authors to spell out exactly how one is to determine whether a translation is either adequate or equivalent, let alone how to assess its skopos. (ibid 2004: 198-199)

House then proposes her own functional-pragmatic model for translation quality assessment and says that:

The operation of the model involves initially an analysis of the original according to a set of situational dimensions, for which linguistic correlates are established. The resulting textual profile of the original characterizes its function, which is then taken as the norm against which the translation is measured; the degree to which the textual profile and function of the translation (as derived from an analogous analysis) match the profile and function of the original is the degree to which the translation is adequate in quality. (House 2004: 199)

What House says here has little difference from what she says in her *A model for translation quality assessment* (2nd edition) which also lists several practical approaches to translation quality assessment in a greater detail and then puts forward her own model. Here, we can see that the practice of translation criticism or translation quality assessment or evaluation is closely connected with translation theories and the theoretical study of translation criticism.

Juliane House's review is brief but considerably all-rounded. The authors of this book only want to add something more about Nida and Nord to offer a clearer picture of translation practice in the West.

In Nida and Taber's *The Theory and Practice of Translation*, there is one chapter talking about the testing of a translation. They discuss the problem of overall length of a translation, types of readers and illustrate some concrete procedures and methods for the tests, and in particular, the "Cloze Technique" for testing the ease of comprehension based on the principle of transitional probabilities which has the hypothesis that the easier it is for the reader to guess the next word, the easier the text is to be comprehended and hence a higher degree of intelligibility. In such a test, every fifth word is deleted and a blank is left in its place for readers to fill in those words that seem to fit the context best. And in an oral Cloze test, blanks are left for every tenth word. In both cases, the higher "degree of predictability", the easier a text or a translation is for comprehension; the fewer the number of incorrect guesses for the blanks, the easier the text is to read. And Nida and Taber say that "there is no absolute standard in the Cloze Technique" and "one should always test two different types of material on the same individuals" (Nida & Taber 2004: 169) .

More practical tests suggested by Nida and Taber (2004: 171-172) are: 1), reactions to alternatives, which requires one "read a sentence in two or more ways, often repeating such alternatives slowly (and, of course, in context), and then ask such questions as: 'Which way sounds the sweetest?' 'Which is plainer?' 'What words will be easiest for the people back in the villages to understand?'" 2), explaining the contents, which requires "someone read a passage to someone else and then to get this individual to explain the contents to other persons, who did not hear the reading"; and 3), reading the text aloud, which is regarded as "one of the best tests of a translation" requires that "several different people to read a text aloud. Such reading should take place before other persons, so that the reader will presumably be trying to communicate the message of the text" and "[a]s the text is read, the translator should note carefully those places at which the reader stumbles, hesitates, makes some substitution of another grammatical form, puts in another word, or in any way has difficulty in reading the text fluently in reading the text fluently"; 4), publication of sample material, which "can provide the kind of test necessary to judge the acceptability of a translation" while realizing that "the analysis of reactions to a published text is not a simple matter" and the popularity of a book may be affected by factors such as price, illustrations, attractive format, special distribution programs, and even quality of paper and therefore, "the ultimate judgment of a translation must be calculated in terms of reader hours per copy, not extent of distribution".

The German functionalist Christiane Nord, in her *Text Analysis in Transaliton Theory, Methodology, and Didactic Application of a Model for Translaiton-oriented Text Analysis*, talks about her "functionality plus loyalty" principle and gives us some description of the forms of translation criticism as well:

> Book reviewers rarely comment on the quality of a translation because normally a translated book is reviewed as if it were an original. If there is any reference to the book being a translation, the assessment is usually based entirely on a rather superficial analysis of the translation in relation to the target-cultural norms of language and literature. In other words, what is being reviewed is the product of the translation process. Therefore, this form of translation criticism (or rather, target-text assessment, because there is no way of judging the ST/TT relationship from only looking at the target text) is more relevant to the didactics of linguistics or literary studies than to translation teaching. For our purpose it could only be used as an indirect means of sensitizing the students to any contraventions of lexical or syntactical norms or of cultivating linguistic "intuition" (cf. Reiss 1971: 7), especially regarding the native language. Since most translations have to prove their functionality independent of the source text in a target-cultural situation, both Reiss (1971) and Koller (1979) suggest that this form of target-text assessment could be a first step in translation criticism. (Nord 1991: 163)

What is worth mentioning is that Nord pays much attention to translation criticism in teaching:

> For the translation teacher, translation criticism mainly means identifying, classifying and evaluating translation errors in order to develop methods of error prevention and error therapy. He may also want to find criteria for the marking of particularly "successful" solution—how are they to be accounted for in the evaluation of a translation? (ibid: 164)

This section serves only as a very brief survey. To describe in great detail of the practice of translation criticism we need more than one book and it is obviously beyond the objective of this book. We will, therefore, turn to discussions on translation criticism at the theoretical level where practice of translation criticism will also be touched upon.

2.5.2 Translation criticism at the theoretical level

As translation criticism in its broad sense is almost equal to translation studies, we will confine our review to that in the narrow sense. And as too many of the scholars have touched upon the subject of translation criticism, and some of them such as Nida, Newmark, Vermeer etc. are well-known to us, in this section we will only choose some of those less-known but at the same time representative researchers and make our review about the theoretical study of translation criticism in the West.

2.5.2.1 Reiss' study on translation criticism

Speaking of translation criticism, one can not but think of Katharina Reiss and her *Translation Criticism: The Potentials and Limitations* with a subtitle: *Categories and Criteria for Translation Quality Assessment*. Here, from the title of her book, one can see that Reiss, like other scholars in the West, makes no distinction between "translation criticism" and "translation quality assessment". The book was first published in 1971 in German and was not duly valued by scholars of translation studies outside of the German-speaking area as it was not written in English. Juan C. Sager has an article entitled "Katharina Reiβ : Translation Criticism: The Potentials and Limitations" in a special issue of *The Translator* focusing on Evaluation and Translation saying that:

> It is a sad fact, evidenced by the limited linguistic range of their bibliographical references, that most authors of English books on translation studies have insufficient knowledge of such important languages as French, German, Italian and Spanish—let alone Russian or any oriental languages—and are, hence, unfamiliar with the basic texts on the subject of translation written in these languages. (Sager 2000: 347)

Sager considers Reiss' book "truly seminal", "sound and sensible" and "will remain a classic" (ibid: 348). The translator of this book Erroll F. Rhodes (2000: vii) also speaks highly of it regarding it as a "pioneering presentation of the challenging possibilities and limitations of translation criticism" and the world-famous scholar Mary Snell-Hornby (2000: viv) in her Foreword of the English version of the said book speaks of Reiss' influence in the German-speaking area inferring that Reiss' approach must have been applied to hundreds of diploma theses as the classical model of translation criticism, provoking heated debates in scholarly journals right into the 1990s. Snell-Hornby comments that "[w]hile many observations must be seen against the background of the late 1960s, the model of translation critique and the thoughts that inspired it still make stimulating reading for anyone interested in translation".

Indeed, Reiss' *Translation Criticism: The Potentials and Limitations* deserves all these praises. It is the first effort to try to make the study of translation criticism systematic and many of Reiss' arguments are quite enlightening even at the present time.

In the Author's Foreword of the said book, Reiss first describes the unsatisfying situation of translation and especially that of translation criticism, saying that "[t]he standards most often observed by critics are generally arbitrary, so that their pronouncements do not reflect a solid appreciation of the translation process" (Reiss 2004: xi). She makes it clear that the purpose of her book is "to formulate appropriate categories and objective criteria for the evaluation of all kinds of translations" as this will help reduce the number of poor translations published and will pedagogically be a way of "honing an awareness of language and of expanding the critic's linguistic and extralinguistic horizons" (ibid).

Reiss insists that different kinds of texts call for different kinds of standards and therefore the first step toward a scientific evaluation is the establishment of a typology of texts to be translated as the distinguishing of text types will provide the critics the points of reference and the corresponding standards for evaluation. Based mainly on Bühler's theory of language function, she classifies the existing texts into four types, namely, content-focused, form-focused, appeal-focused and the audio-media type. She then relates text types with translation methods and the criteria for evaluation of each category. For a content-focused text, the yardstick might be fidelity or a faithful representation at the level of content; for a form-focused text, similarity of textual structure, style and the aesthetic value in form is required; for an appeal-focused text, similarity in reader's response should be a must; and for an audio-media one, the same effect on the hearer must be preserved and priority should be given to the conditioning factors of the non-linguistic media (Reiss 2004: 46-47).

To probe into the potentials and limitations of translation criticism, Reiss raises many questions that actually form a map of study on translation criticism. For example: What is translation criticism in the strict sense? What makes a qualified critic? In what way people are doing criticism? For criticism in translation teaching and learning, we may ask "whether the correctors give sufficient attention to the range of possibilities offered, expected, or even desired. What criteria are employed beyond the obvious ones of vocabulary blunders and misunderstood grammatical constructions? To what extent does the corrector simply rely on his own feelings?" (Reiss 2004: 3). Other essential questions are: do any objective points of reference or guidelines for evaluating a work of translation exist? What is meant by objective translation criticism? As every translation project is a balancing process achieved by constructing a target text under the constant restraint of a source text, "the specific individual translation, the result of this process, should be evaluated by objective and relevant criteria" (ibid: 4). But what are the "objective and relevant criteria"? Reiss gives a critical review of the previous approaches and finds no satisfactory answers.

According to Reiss, "objectivity means to be verifiable as in contrast to arbitrary and inadequate". To be objective means that,

> [E]very criticism of a translation, whether positive or negative, must be defined explicitly and be verified by examples. The critic should also always make allowance for other subjective options. In a negative criticism the critic should try to ascertain what led the translator to make the (alleged) error. (Reiss 2004: 4)

Reiss thinks that one of the causes for the inadequacies of translation criticism is due to "the wide variety of views as to what a translation can or should achieve, or even the doubt as to whether translation is in fact at all possible", and "the criteria and categories for critical evaluation cannot be formulated without a systematic account of the requirements, the presuppositions and the goals, of every translation process" (Reiss 2004: 7).

Reiss discusses different ways of translation criticism and holds that it is indispensable to compare the target texts with the source texts in translation criticism, especially for a constructive criticism and it is the comparison with the original that offers the critic an opportunity of choosing between different equivalents. Reiss gives us an explanation of the term "equivalence" in her annotation

> For the science of translating the term equivalence is a core concept. Equivalence may obtain both between the totality of the original text and its version in the atrget language, and between the individual elements in the text and its translation. Equivalence is not simply correspondence, nor is it reproduction of the original language unit Equivalence is, as its etymology suggests, "equal value." i.e., corresponding target language expressions may be considered optimally equivalent if they represent the linguistic and circumstantial context, the usage and level of style, and the intention of the author in the target language which carry the same value as the expressions in the source language. (ibid: 3-4)

What's more, Reiss emphasizes the importance of the critic's constructive translation criticism by offering counterproposals for rejected translations. She says that "[o]ur first principle, that translation criticism should be constructive, would rule out judging a translation solely on the basis of its faults ... it goes without saying that constructive translation criticism must also offer satisfactory alternative translations, substantiated with convincing evidence" (ibid: 15).

What is noticeable is Reiss' concept of translation, the product of the activity of translating: the version of a source text in a target language where the primary efforts has been to reproduce in the target language a text corresponding to the original as to its textual type, its linguistic elements, and the non-linguistic determinants affecting it (ibid: 90). For Reiss, "translation" is distinguished from "adaptation" in which the translated text "has achieved the special purpose for which it was intended" (Reiss 2004: 91). "Adaptation" falls into the category of translation in the broader sense and calls for a criticism different from that of a "translation".

In the concluding part, Reiss summarizes her ideas about translation criticism, saying that:

1. Translation criticism is proper if a translation (in the strict sense of the term) demanding a text-oriented translation method (accommodated to its text type) is examined by standards which are proper to its text type, ...

2. Translation criticism is proper if a translation (in the broader sense) demanding a goal-oriented translation method (directed to a special function or readership) is examined by criteria which are also derived from the functional category of translation criticism, adjusted to the standards of the special function or readership which the translation is intended to serve.

3. Both text-oriented and goal-oriented kinds of translation are affected by subjective influences: the subjective conditions of the hermeneutical process and of the translator's personality...

4. A proper translation criticism (whether text-oriented or goal-oriented) is accordingly objective only to the extent that it takes these subjective conditions into consideration. (ibid: 114)

To sum up, Reiss has set up a text-type-based framework for translation criticism. She classifies texts into four types and distinguishes translation from adaptation or translation in the strict sense from that in the broader sense. For translation in the strict sense, the criterion is basically source-text-oriented and for the latter, target-text-oriented. Reiss' discussion on translation criticism tells us that objectivity of evaluation can be achieved but subjectivity is hard to avoid. What we can do is only to try to reduce it to the minimum.

2.5.2.2 Wilss' study on translation criticism

Wolfram Wilss (2001) has a chapter on translation criticism in his *The Science of Translation: Problems and Methods*. Wilss develops a tentative framework for a "translation-critically motivated comparison" or translation criticism which requires the critic to compare the ST with the TT in three aspects, namely syntax, semantics and pragmatics, to see whether a translation is "wrong", "inappropriate", "undecidable" or "correct" and "appropriate". For Wilss, "[t]ranslating is an interplay of dynamic, text-related creative and non-creative formulation processes which permit at least to some—probably expandable—extent the application of intersubjective translation-critical criteria" (Wilss 2001: 226). And hence,

> [T]ranslation-critical insights rarely, maybe never, reach the level of natural science rigor, because translating is a case of language usage limiting the range of applicability of translation-critical results. It is therefore pointless to try to make TC (translation criticism, the authors of this book) more scientific than is sensible in view of its complex subject-matter and available methods. (Wilss 2001: 226)

Though Wilss thinks that some proposed frameworks could only be idealized to make translation criticism objective, he does hold that the linguistic approach can be helpful, "enabling the translation critic to differentiate, systematize and evaluate the linguistic and situational factors and rules operative in the process of translation" (ibid: 227).

2.5.2.3 House's study on translation criticism

According to Juliane House (1977/1981: 2), the problems existing in the translation quality assessment include the impressionistic, vague and general treatment of the subject from aesthetic, philosophical or stylistic viewpoints and "no explicit practical guidelines for a coherent analysis and evaluation of a translation". Pre-linguistic studies on translation quality assessment is featured by an anecdotal and largely subjective manner. As the criteria are often source-text-oriented emphasizing faithfulness to the original, "the retention of the original's specific flavour, local colour or spirit as opposed to a natural flow of the translation, and the pleasure and delight of the reader were discussed at great length" (House 1977/1981: 6).

House makes some comments on the response-based and the psycholinguistic studies as has been mentioned in the above section. She says that Nida's communicatively response-oriented studies and his three criteria namely, general efficiency of the communication process, comprehension of intent and equivalence of response, seem to be programmatic, general, and is not something totally new. Nida's ideas of equivalent effect have been mentioned by Leonard and Zilahy. According to the former, a good translation is "one which fulfill the same purpose in the new language as the original did" (Leonard 1958: 6), and according to the latter, "a translation is considered good when it arouses in us the same effect as did the original" (Zilahy 1963: 285).

Nida's principle of "Dynamic Equivalence" in 1964, changed to "Functional Equivalence" later, requires the manner in which receptors of the translated text respond to the translated text be equivalent to the manner in which the receptors of the source text respond to the source text. To measure whether equivalent effect is achieved, Nida and Taber (2004:163-173) offer some suggestions for testing the translation as stated in the above section. But many people have doubts about this test and therefore the theory of Functional Equivalence. Peter Newmark regards it illusive and House argues that the degree to which the equivalent effect is met can hardly be empirically tested. "If it cannot be tested, it seems fruitless to postulate the requirement, and the appeal to 'equivalence of response' is really of no more value than the philologists' criterion of 'capturing the spirit of the original'" (House, 1981: 9). House further points out that for the Cloze Technique suggested by Nida, as has been stated in the above section, it is "extremely difficult to analyze the results", and is hard "to find out exactly why incorrect guesses were being made". What is more, "for a detailed qualitative judgment of a translation's benefits and deficiencies, the Cloze technique seems to be too rough an instrument: it only attempts to measure intelligibility or ease of comprehension—criteria which cannot necessarily be equated with, overall quality of translation" (ibid: 10-11).

According to House, Nida's Cloze test is problematic also for its "total lack of reference to the source text". As "the source text itself may have a relatively low predictability rate", "the assumption that higher predictability rate and relative ease of comprehension equals higher quality in a translation is not necessarily valid" (ibid: 12). House, in addition, criticizes Nida's suggested elicitation of respondents' reactions to several translation alternatives, for "such a test merely compares several translations, but fails to undertake the more basic task of judging a translation against its source text" (ibid: 12-13). For the suggested "read out" test, i.e. reading out a translation to someone and asking him or her to explain the contents to several other individuals who were not present at the first reading of the translation, House regards it problematic for its relying "entirely on the individual, who is asked to report on the translation text, rather than on the translation". And for the method of reading aloud of a translation by several individuals before an audience to see where there is influency, House's comment is that "[a] major limitation of this test seems to be the fact that too many variables other than the mentioned 'problems of translation' may also be responsible for failure in the public presentation of the translation text" (House,

1981: 14).

Besides all theses criticism, we find that though Nida's criterion for measuring a translation values much of the reader's response, it is nevertheless, still source-text-oriented, as at the end of the chapter concerning the testing of a translation in the above-mentioned book by Nida and Taber we can read:

> The ultimate test of a translation must be based upon three major factors: (1) the correctness with which the receptors understand the message of the original (that is to say, its "faithfulness to the original" as determined by extent to which people really comprehend the meaning), (2) the ease of comprehension, and (3) the involvement a person experiences as the result of the adequacy of the form of the translation. (Nida & Taber 2004: 173)

Taking all the criticism on Nida's ways for testing a translation and the Bible's being not self-explanatory, we cannot help thinking that Nida's theory of Formal Equivalence and Functional Equivalence has been somewhat over-rated.

As she is not satisfied with the previous ways and criteria for translation criticism, House develops her own model for translation quality assessment in 1981. She first gives a definition to translation and says that:

> Before attempting to develop a model for translation quality assessment, we first have to be more precise about what we mean by translation. The essence of translation lies in the preservation of "meaning" across two different languages. There are three basic aspects to this "meaning": a semantic aspect, a pragmatic aspect, and a textual aspect of meaning. (House 1981: 25)

House's model (1981) is set up on the basis of pragmatics and the systemic functional linguistics. It requires the critic to make a detailed analysis of the SL text carefully to establish a textual profile and a careful study of the degree of match and mismatch between the ST and the TT on the distinction between ideational and interpersonal language functions developed by Halliday. House seems quite satisfied with her model and in 1997 when she published her *Translation Quality Assessment: A Model Revisited*, there is not much revision of her original model. In the concluding chapter, she says that:

> ...Central concepts of the original model have been retained, but made more accessible and more relevant to actual concerns in translational theory and practice. The book has therefore both introduced new concepts—specifically in terms of the analytic apparatus suggested for categorial linguistic analysis, and at the same time retained the central notion of source and target text comparison as the basis for translation quality assessment,

even when this text-based approach has for many specialists in the translational field been overtaken by a more target-audience-oriented notion of translational appropriateness. I believe this recent shift of focus in translational studies to be fundamentally misguided. (House 1997: 159)

House's comment on her revised model is that it "opens up the possibility of research into culturally-conditioned translational norms, which are likely to differ for different GENRES. More research with large corpora of texts belonging to different GENRES would thus give greater explanatory value to any individual translation analysis" and its "second major theoretical thrust" concerns "cultural filtering and the overt-covert distinction" (ibid: 161).

The authors of this book think that House has good reasons for her pride of and confidence in her own model and theory. Commenting on the contemporary studies, House says that many of them:

...appear to confuse a concern with translation as a phenomenon in its own right, i.e., as a liguistic-textual operation, with issues such as what translation is for, or what it should, might, or indeed must be for. A one-sided concern with the covert end of the cline not only reduces the importance of the source text in translation, but also blurs the borders between translations and other multiligual textual procedures. It is one of the purposes of the model developed in this book to provide means of conceptually separating a translation from a version, through positing functional equivalence between source and translation text as a sine qua non in translation. (House 1997: 166)

The objectivity and subjectivity and the relation between the two existing in translation quality assessment have been a puzzle to many researchers of translation criticism and this is expounded by House:

A distinction is to be maintained between the descriptive-explanatory, scientific moments in translation evaluation, as opposed to socio-psychologically based value judgments, which may well surface in any critical account. This does not mean that the attempt to develop a model of translation quality assessment is pointless. On the contrary. A detailed analysis of the "hows" and the "whys" of translated texts versus their originals has to be the descriptive foundation for an argued assessment of whether and to what degree a given translation may be seen to be adequate or not. Acknowledging the inevitably subjective element in any value judgment does not, then, invalidate the objective part of translation evaluation, it merely reinforces its necessity. Like language itself, translation quality assessment has two functional components, the ideational and the interpersonal. In other words, two steps may be distinguished: the first relates to analysis, description and explanation based on knowledge (of linguistic conventions), and empirical research, while the second relates to judgments of values, to social and moral questions of relevance and appropriateness and, of course, to personal preference or taste. Both components are implicit in translation quality assessments. The second is pointless without the first. To judge is easy: to understand is less so. If we can make explicit the grounds of our judgments, on the basis of an argued set of procedures such as those developed in this book, then, in the case of disagreement, we can talk and discuss: if we do not, we can merely disagree. (House 1997: 166-167)

Indeed, House's model has its theoretical and practical significance and in a sense we might say that her main contribution is in the theoretical aspect as her model is somewhat complicated and hard to implement. Her notion of the "cultural filtering" and her distinction between covert and overt translation are quite insightful and enlightening for our understanding of translation and important for the assessment of a translation:

A further theoretical issue here is the question of reciprocity of skew. In other words, if it is deemed appropriate and normative to filter when translating (in a certain way, namely covertly) from linguaculture A to linguaculture B, then we might logically suggest that it is equally warranted and indeed necessary to filter in the opposite way when translating from B into A. Is this logical conclusion justified? Firstly, how far such bi-directional skewing takes place is of course an empirical issue, but I know of no studies that explicitly address it. My own work—especially with children's literature—suggests for the translation pair English and German that skewing is in this case often but not necessarily always reciprocal, in that German children's literature translated into English is not consistently filtered towards the norm for children's literature written in English to the extent that children's books translated into German are also so filtered. I hypothesise that this is not an isolated case, and that there is such a thing as preferred direction of skew.... (House 1997: 162)

The notion of "cultural filtering" and the term "linguaculture" indicate House's idea about translation as a lingua-cultural activity. Consequently, translation and the measure of a translation have to take both the linguistic factors and the cultural factors into our consideration and to a great extent, the two kinds of factors are actually inseparable as House says:

Questions of cultural filtering are of course directly relevant to the question as to which type of translation is being attempted. The central distinction is between overt and covert translation. These translational types are seen, however, as endpoints along a continuum, such that unclear cases will in practice arise. An overt translation aims at what I called second-level-functional equivalence. At this secondary level the target text should attempt to match GENRE, REGISTER and LINGUISTIC STRATEGIES of the source text.... An overt translation allows members of the target cultures access to the function of the original... (House 1997: 162-163)

Overt translation and covert translation are two important terms given by House indicating two different kinds of translation. House's explanation to overt and covert translation is as follows:

In overt work, then, the translator is explicitly a mediator. Her role is important: the resultant text is clearly her work. This transparent role derives, however, not from the change to the original text caused by the translator's hand, but by virtue of the fact that the reader is thereby given access to a text in a new language (the most obvious case is the translation of literary works).

The paradox is then that in the overt case, the translator has the least leeway to alter the fabric and content of the text, but has a clearly recognisable role and function for the reader. In covert translation, on the other hand, it is the task of the translator to be invisible, but at the same time to transmute the original such that the function it has in its original situational cultural environment is re-created in the target linguaculture. To this end, various "filtering" devices, and translational compromises may well be necessary. At the levels of LANGUAGE/TEXT and REGISTER, the translation does not need, then, to be equivalent with its original. An equivalent function is to be aimed at, although it is differently framed, and operates in the target culture and discourse world...In covert translation, the translator's work is hidden. It is , essentially, the translator's task to cheat, i.e. to achieve in translation a second original, hiding its source. (ibid: 163)

House is aware that in making translation criticism there is the difference between the evaluation of the translation product and that of the translation process and that people may have different orients in their evaluation. In an article entitled "Translation quality assessment" in *Readings in Translation Theory* edited by Andrew Chesterman in 1989, House says that:

Evaluation the product means judging it in terms of two sets of standards: those based on the source text and culture, and those related to the target language culture. The first sets of standard is thus retrospective, concerning "faithfulness" to the original—the original content, style, function or intention, and in some cases also the form. The second set is prospective, concerning the degree to which the translation conforms to the norms of the target language and culture, and how well it achieves the goals assigned to it as a certain sort of text with a certain sort of function in that culture. (Chesterman 1989: 157)

House regards her model as one of the few full-length studies of the subject of translation criticism and refers to her own approach to translation criticism as "focuses on a retrospective comparison of ST (source text) and TT (target text), in particular on the degree of stylistic and functional equivalence between the two texts" (House 1997: 158). Indeed, House's paradigm, so far as the criteria for measuring the quality of a translation are concerned, is also source-text-oriented. This is made clear when she says that,

> ...it is important to clearly demarcate the lines between what is still a translation and what is "a new text for a new event in a new culture". In the terms provided in my model, a covert translation despite changes (brought about for example via cultural filtering) on the LINGUISTIC and REGISTER levels must be functionally equivalent to the original. (House 1997: 164)

To sum up, House's study on translation criticism is a step further toward making the subject of translation criticism more systematic, however, it is certainly not perfect, the complexity of model's procedures often make people shrink back and that is at least one of the important reasons why this model is seldom employed in reality. Besides, though House views translation as a lingua-cultural activity and her model has some advantages over the previous ones, yet, no reliable analytic instrument is offered to help the critic recognize and analyse the ideational and interpersonal functions of a text. This further weakens the application of House's model.

2.5.2.4 Nord's study on translation criticism

Christiane Nord, a representative of the German functionalists of the second generation, just like Reiss, shows much concern about criticism for translation and especially for translation teaching. In her book *Text Analysis in Translation Theory, Methodology, and Didactic Application of a Model for Translation-oriented Text Analysis*, she says that,

> If translation criticism is to be relevant to translation teaching, it has to integrate both methods: the analysis and assessment of the translation process and its determinants (including translation skopos and translating instructions) and the evaluation of the target text and its functionality for a given purpose.
>
> Such translation criticism is important for both teachers and learners...This is why Reiss (1974: 36; 1977: 540) suggests that translation comparison and translation criticism should have their place in an introductory phrase of translator training. (Nord 1991: 164)

As "effect" is a key word in translation criticism, Nord explains her idea about it in detail:

> Effect, as I understand it, has to be regarded as a recipient-oriented category. The recipient receives the content and form of the text against the background of his expectations deriving from his analysis of the situational factors and from his background knowledge. He compares the intratextual features of the text with the expectations built up externally, and the impression he gets from this, whether conscious or unconscious or subconscious, can be referred to as "effect"….The category of effect refers to the relationship between the text and its "users", and, therefore, the analysis of effect belongs to the area of interpretation and not to that of linguistic text "description". (Nord 1991: 130)

Nord further explains the category of effect and divides effect into "long-term effect" and "short-term effect". The long-term consequences may be "more difficult to anticipate than the immediate effect" and it does not include the "historical" effect, which is the history of the reception of a translation. Effect is affected by many factors, the medium, for instance, can play an important role and in fact, "[a]ll intra and extratextual factors can play a part in producing text effect" (ibid: 131).

Nord thinks that three relationships are the most important for the effect of a text. They are the relationships between intention and text, between recipient and text-world, and between recipient and "style". After a detailed analysis of these relations and types of effect, Nord concludes that,

> The types of effect based on these three fundamental relationships can be found in any text. This shows again that "equivalence" (in the sense of "equal effects of ST and TT") is not a very practicable criterion for a translation. The translator needs to know exactly which "type of effect" is required to remain unchanged, since the preservation of cultural distance (recipient/text relationship) often precludes the preservation of the interpretation (intention/text relationship). Moreover, the effect of the target text depends largely on whether the translation skopos requires a documentary, or an instrumental, translation. (ibid: 140)

To "objectivity", another key word in translation criticism, Nord gives her explanations, saying that a comparative analysis of both the source and the target text can be helpful as this can provide information about the similarities and differences between SL and TL structures and "the individual process of translation and the strategies and methods used", showing "whether the target text is appropriate for the required translation skopos" or not (ibid: 163). From this explanation we can see that Nord's values much description and analysis in order to be objective in translation criticism.

Nord also talks about the criteria for measuring the quality of a translation and regards it essential to have "a set of criteria" which may be established in several ways. The criteria can come from the translator's skopos or the critic's view of the translation skopos (Nord 1991: 165). And in any cases, the critic should observe "the overriding criterion of translation skopos" (ibid: 169).

While talking about translation errors and problems, Nord (2001: 74) says in her book *Translating As a Purposeful Activity: Functionalist Approaches Explained* that "[t]he basis for the evaluation of a translation is the adequacy or inadequacy of the solutions found for the translation problems". One thing we should pay attention to and Nord has actually called our attention to in her book is the different meaning of the word "adequacy" used by functionalists such as Reiss and Vermeer from that by Even-Zohar and Toury. For the former, "adequacy" means being proper, referring to "the qualities of a target text with regard to the translation brief: the translation should be 'adequate to' the requirements of the brief" and for the latter, it is "a translation which realizes in the target language the textual relationships of a source text with no breach of its own [basic] linguistic system" (Nord 2001: 35).

To sum up, we can say that Nord takes translation skopos as the criterion for translation assessment and the term "adequacy" used by Nord and Reiss in judging the quality of a translation is quite dynamic. Sometimes, there should be fidelity to the original or "a maximally faithful imitation to the source text", and sometimes there is no intertextual coherence. It all depends on the various specific purposes of the target text. Though both Nord and Reiss value the comparison between the ST and the TT, there is slight difference between the two. Reiss gives more weight to the source text because she distinguishes translation from adaptation; while Nord's comparison is all for the better fulfillment of requirements of the target text. The criteria of the skopos theory, especially those of Vermeer and Nord fall right into the target-text-oriented paradigm.

2.5.2.5 Williams' study on translation criticism

In 2004, Malcolm Williams published his *Translation Quality Assessment: An Argumentation-Centred Approach* which offers us a more comprehensive review of the study on translation criticism in the West. An overview of theories and models on translation quality assessment, including those literary and non-literary, helps the reader get a whole picture of the specific field and some of the models have been mentioned in the above paragraphs. Williams explores a discourse-based model, the potential of transferring reasoning and argument as the prime criterion of translation quality assessment. He argues that a judgment of translation quality should be based primarily on the degree to which the translator has adequately rendered the reasoning or argument structure of the ST.

Williams is more concerned about non-literary or pragmatic or instrumental translation. His goal is to propose solutions to the problems of sampling, quantification and borderline cases, type of error, and the level of seriousness of error. According to Williams, the main problems with the previous models for translation quality assessment (TQA), especially those have been applied to translation industry are microtextual:

> [T]hey tend to focus on discrete lexical and morphosyntactic units at the subsentence level and to be applied to short passages of texts. While this does not prevent the evaluator from detecting shortcomings and strong points in that text, microtextual models are not designed to assess each passage as an integral part of a whole, to take account of the fact that the translation of the short passage is, in principle at least, determined in part by, and in its turn influences, the text as a whole, or to evaluate the logic and coherence existing even within the sample passage itself. (Williams 2004: xvii)

Williams' purpose is to apply one particular aspect of discourse analysis—argumentation theory—to TQA and develops an assessment framework to complement existing microtextual schemes with specific reference to instrumental translation in a production context. Williams' model is text-based and flexible enough to incorporate microtextual TQA for specific purposes such as target-language quality assessment. He establishes a minimum level of acceptable overall quality for instrumental translations by proposing a new definition of translation error providing a coherent, defensible concept for error analysis and assessment and by the distinction of critical, major and minor errors believing that the higher in the macrostructure the error occurs, the more serious it is. Williams cites an authoritative U.S. manual to define the three kinds of errors:

> CRITICAL DEFECT. A critical defect is a defect that judgment and experience indicate is likely to result in hazardous or unsafe conditions for individuals using, maintaining, or depending on the product; or a defect that judgment and experience indicate is likely to prevent performance of the tactical function of a major item such as a ship, aircraft, tank, missile or space vehicle.
>
> MAJOR DEFECT. A major defect is a defect, other than critical, that is likely to result in failure, or reduce materially the usability of the unit of product for its intended purpose.

MINOR DEFECT. A minor defect is a defect that is not likely to reduce materially the usability of the unit of product for its intended purpose, or is a departure from established standards having little bearing on the effective use or operation of the unit. (Hayes and Romig, 1982:146). (Williams 2004: 67)

Williams (2004: 70) holds that "identification and appropriate rendering of the argument (reasoning) schema is the key to meeting the translation quality standard". His analytic process consists mainly of four stages. The first is to establish the ST argument schema, arrangement, and organizational relations to recognize what part or parts of the document contain "essential messages". The second is to examine the TT without reference to the original to assess the overall coherence and identify any potential problems concerning the essential passages. The third is to assess the TT against the ST in relation to the argumentation parameters: argument schema, arrangement/organizatioanl relations; prepositional functions and conjunctives/ other inference indicators; types of arguments; figures of speech (tropes); and narrative strategy. The last stage is an overall argumentation-centred TQA based on the evidence accumulated, together with a comparison with the results of some quantitative-microtextual TQA.

According to Williams, his model is both standard-referenced (fixed quality standards to be met) and criterion-referenced (varying quality criteria to be met depending on field or end use). It is based on theory rather than convention, experience, or arbitrary quantification of quality ratings and provides a minimum level of acceptable quality and performance:

> If the translation deviates from the argument schema, it does not meet the minimum quality standard. This serves to counter the criticism of excessive subjectivity often levelled against evaluators and TQA systems and provides evaluators with a theory-based solution to the thorny problem of borderline cases. (Williams 2004: 150)

To sum up, we can say that comparatively speaking, Williams' model has greater reliability, validity, comprehensiveness and criticality. Yet, as Williams himself says it seems "intensive and time-consuming" (Williams 2004: 74).

2.5.2.6 Other studies on translation criticism

Besides monographs and chapters in books on translation criticism, many articles about TQA appear in *Translation and Quality* edited by Christina Schaffner in 1998 and in a special issue of the journal *The Translator* focusing on evaluation and translation edited by Carol Maier in 2000 and in many other places.

Translation and Quality is centered around Hans G. Honig's paper "Position, Power and Practice: Functionalist Approaches and Translation Quality Assessment". Honig distinguishes functionalist and non-functionalist approaches in translation studies, saying that the former is target-text-oriented and the latter, source-text-oriented. He addresses the question of "supposed reader's response", pointing out that "[e]ven if assessment is based on functionalist translation (as, in my opinion, it should be) the speculative element will remain—at least as long as there are no hard and fast empirical data which serve to prove what a 'typical' reader's responses are like" (Honig 1998: 32). Honig also classifies all practical translation evaluation into therapeutic and diagnostic and offers a diagram of TQA in different situations. He concludes that there are no common TQA criteria; the most common criterion is that of meeting the text production standards in the target text and 50% of the evaluation is carried out without making it clear whether it is based on source text orientation or target text orientation, a mixture of therapeutic and diagnostic criteria.

Schaffner makes some comments on some critic's criticism that "in a functionalist approach the ST is dethroned, the role of the client is exaggerated, and that there is no clear delimitation between translation and adaptation or other textual operations". According to Schaffner,

> [S]ome of this criticism is due to misinterpretation and overgeneralization, and therefore unjustified, but it is also partly due to a confusing use of the keyword 'function' within functionalist literature. It is sometimes used in the sense of the function that the TT fulfils in the communicative setting of the target culture (in this sense, 'function' is synonymous with 'purpose'). But it is also used for the text function, e.g. informative or persuasive function (in this sense, it is linked to the speech acts and Buhler's function of language). Another use of the term concerns the function of a word or phrase within the whole text (i.e., the relationship of micro- and macro-structures). (Schaffner 1998: 3)

Articles in the special issue of the journal *The Translator*, focusing on "Evaluation and Translation", cover a wide range of TQA or translation criticism. They discuss not only TQA of written translation but also oral interpretation and corpus-based approach to student translations, showing that studies on TQA are becoming multi-perspective.

Translation, according to Ernst-August Gutt, is an instance of interpretative use of language, constrained and governed by the principle of relevance; it "should be expressed in such a manner that it yields the intended interpretation without putting the audience to unnecessary processing effort" (Anderman 2007: 58).

2.5.3 Professional criteria in the West

To ensure the quality of translation, some professional standards have been set up in many places of the world by different institutions.

The criteria set by Unesco's *Guidelines for Translators* makes "accuracy" "the very first requirement". The aim of translation is described as that "after reaching an understanding of what the ST writer 'was trying to say', the translator should put this meaning into (in this case) English 'which will, so far as possible, produce the same impression on the English-language reader as the original would have done on the appropriate foreign-language reader'" (Munday 2001: 31).

The Unesco's criteria also makes "allowance for the TT readers, who are sometimes non-native speakers of the TL" and translations can vary according to text types: "the style of articles translated for periodicals should be 'readable', while politically sensitive speeches require a 'very close translation' to avoid being misinterpreted" (ibid).

According to Munday, the Institute of Linguists' (IoL) Diploma in Translation in the UK gives criteria for assessing the translations in its *Notes for Candidates* as follows:

1, accuracy: the correct transfer of information and evidence of complete comprehension;

2, the appropriate choice of vocabulary, idiom, terminology and register;

3, cohesion, coherence and organization;

4, accuracy in technical aspects of punctuation, etc.

The question of 'accuracy' appears twice (criteria 1 and 4). 'Accuracy' is in some ways the modern linguistic equivalent of 'faithfulness', 'spirit' and 'truth'; … (Munday 2001:30)

Besides, we have other international standards such as ISO 9002 and many other national ones.

The International Association of Conference Translators requires the interpretation to be clear and accurate.

The Canadian government's Translation Bureau developed and adopted a model both as an examination tool and to help the Bureau assess the quality of the 300 million words of instrumental translation produced yearly. It makes distinction between two kinds of errors: 1), translation (transfer) and language errors and 2), major and minor errors. Translations are rated according to the number of major and minor errors in a 400-word passage: A—superior (0 major errors/maximum of

6 minor); B—fully acceptable (0/12); C—revisable (1/18); and D—unacceptable. A major translation error is defined as: complete failure to render the meaning of a word or passage that contains an essential element of the message; also, mistranslation resulting in a contradiction of or significant departure from the meaning of an essential element of the message. A major language error is: incomprehensible, grossly incorrect language or rudimentary error in an essential element of the message. As to what is "essential", it is up to the quality controller or evaluator.

The Ontario Government Translation Services (GTS) assesses the usability of the translation. Judgment of usability is based on a "guideline" for errors of transfer: a short text containing a 400-word sample with more than 5 minor errors or 1 major error could be considered unusable without revision. A major translation error is defined as one that seriously impedes the main message. As to what is of "seriously impede" or "main message", there is no definition.

The J2450 Translation Quality Metric was developed in 2000 by the U.S. Engineering Society for Advanced Mobility in Land, Sea, Air and Space. It distinguishes between the two categories: if an error clearly leads to serious consequences for a technician or affects the meaning of the translation, it must be considered major. Otherwise, it must be considered minor.

The American Translators Association (ATA) requires that a translation be as faithful and accurate as possible, conformable to the requirements of the clients.

To sum up, professionally, "accuracy" is almost unanimously required in translation. Some differences exist priorizing a certain aspect in accordance with the specific field. This is true both in China and in other countries.

Chapter 3
Studies on Criticism of Literary Translation:
Status Quo and Problems

We have given an overall review studies on translation criticism at the practical and theoretical levels both in China and in the West in Chapter 2. In this chapter, to know better the situation and problems of the field of criticism of literary translation, we will confine our discussion to the study of criticism of literary translation. As our discussion about translation criticism in general contains not only non-literary translation, but also criticism of literary translation, there will inevitably be some repetition in our discussion in this chapter, and we will try to keep it to the minimum.

3.1 Studies on Criticism of Literary Translation in China

To get a clearer picture of studies on criticism of literary translation in China, we divide it into three stages.

3.1.1 Studies before the 1980s

The study on criticism of literary translation in China underwent a long period centering upon the principles and criteria and most of the discussions do not distinguish principles from criteria.

Studies on criticism of literary translation in China before the 1980s, featured as a whole by fragmentariness, generally speaking, fall into the "philologist" paradigm. This paradigm believes that the intention or intentions or meanings of "the author" can be traced and obtained through intuition. That is to say, we can get to the essence of an object by means of intuitional experience. Faithfulness to the original author is not only necessary, but also possible and can even be guaranteed. Ever since Yan Fu put forward the tripartite "*xin, da* and *ya*", it has been adopted by most of the translators, especially literary translators, as the guideline and the yardstick for translation. Even if there are some scholars who are not for it, they never doubt that faithfulness (or *xin* in Chinese, and a problematic term) to the original should and can be achieved. However, it is not that all are for it. Some people, for example, Qu Qiubai, points out that Yan Fu's "*ya*" or "elegance" demolishes the other two parameters. What Qu Qiubai insists is the total fidelity to the original and by introducing some foreign ways of expression, the translators can enrich the target language and make it more delicate (Chen Fukang 1992: 312-313). Lu Xun holds almost the same view as Qu Qiubai, saying that fidelity to the original should be in the first place and foreignizing is a necessity and a right way to do translation as it is the task of the translator to retain the foreignness in his or her translation. Lu Xun's articles about translation touch upon many aspects of the activity, such as the ideology in translation, the issue of retranslation and so on. His classification of types of readers and his idea that translations for different readers should be different are also quite pioneering in China and in the world (ibid: 288-309). Therefore, Lu Xun's theory of translation can be regarded as a great step toward a systematic study of translation and translation criticism.

As we have already talked much about the studies of translation criticism in China in the above chapter, here we will only choose some of those that lead us to compare Western ideas with Chinese ones, concerning translation criticism in its broad and narrow senses.

Zheng Zhenduo (1898-1958) in an article "Three Problems in Translating Literaturary Works" in 1921 first introduced Alexander Fraser Tytler (1747-1814) to China and had a comparison between Tytler and Yan Fu, thinking that the former is in greater detail and the latter too concise. He, just like Qu Qiubai, also holds that Yan Fu's "*ya*" or "elegance" is unnecessary, and attention should be paid to avoid going to extremes, i.e. either too literal or too free (ibid: 220-238).

"Faithfulness to spirit" or "similarity to spirit" is a criterion that is proposed by Chinese scholars such as Chen Xiying, Zhu Shenghao, Guo Moruo, Mao Dun and Fu Lei etc. It is also the requirement of some Western scholars. But, one thing we should notice is that the word "spirit" in China is quite different from that in the West especially for the translator of the Bible. In China, it refers to the innate quality of a text that gives a text life and its most prominent characteristic. It is the opposite of "*xing*" or "form", associated with the "soul" of a literary work, hard to capture actually. In the West, it can refer to the "content" by some scholars and to "Holy spirit" or "the energy of words" by others (Munday 2001: 24). The terms such as

"Faithfulness to spirit" or "similarity to spirit" or "transmigration" and the philologist approach as a whole, as Lv Jun (2007d: 145) has pointed out, "inevitably will lead to mysticism" in translation criticism. Even if there are scholars, Dong Qiusi, for example, having realized we are rich in experiential statements about translation but short of systematic study and seeking to establish the science of translation for the establishment of a set of objective criteria for translation criticism, and even if there are scholars writing much about literary translation, their approaches unexceptionally fall into the philologist mode.

3.1.2 Studies in the 1980s

In the 1980s, influenced by linguistic approach and other approaches in translation studies in the West, some scholars in China began to study criticism of literary translation based on some linguistic theories or communication (information) theory. In such studies, the authorative position of "the author" first gives way to "the text" and "language". "Language" is taken as an instrument for accurate analysis. Linguistic analyses, such as syntactic analysis, semantic analysis, textual analysis, contrastive analysis, and the function of the original text are highly valued to guarantee and to measure equivalence in translation.

Since the term "equivalence" was introduced to China, some scholars think that it refers to equivalence in meaning, in style and in reader's response (Han Mingdai 1985), others confine it to equivalence in meaning (Xu Weiyuan 1987) and still others think that it includes structural equivalence, semantic equivalence and pragmatic equivalence.

Wu Xinxiang and Li Hong'an (1984) divide language into 15 crisscross planes in terms of "static ranks (word, expression, sentence, group of sentences and discourse) and dynamic levels (deep structure, rhetoric level, and surface structure)" and think that the measurement of a translation is to see to what degree the equal value transformations between the original and its version have achieved, seeking to establish a quantitative criterion of TQA to replace the traditional qualitative "*xin, da* and *ya*".

Jin Di (1986) argues that "resemblance in spirit" has "a tendency to ignore accuracy which is necessary for totality of effect" and that "equivalence of effects" means that "the impact of the TL text on its receptor should be as close as possible to that of the SL text on its own receptor". "Effect" means "impact" instead of "response" by Nida.

Tan Zaixi and Nida (1987) talk about the levels of translation criteria. They hold that there can be equivalence at eight aspects: 1) content; 2) form; 3) total equivalence; 4) partial equivalence; 5) functional equivalence; 6) text (discourse) type; 7) style; 8) pragmatic purpose.

Wang Tianming (1989) holds that equivalence in literary translation should strive to achieve equivalent effect, making the translation produce the same effect as the original in sound, form, style, rhetorical device, content, image and even association. Since total equivalence is impossible, the translator should first gurantte the equivalence in the central information contained in a word, a sentence or a text in a given situation.

Though there is the change of the authoritative position of "the author" to the "text" and the shift from the "text" to the "receptor of the target text", and the key term used has changed from "faithfulness" to "equivalence", the feature of source-text-orientation remains the same. The success of a translation is still to be judged using the source text as the yardstick, either its meaning or its function.

3.1.3 Studies since the 1990s

The 1990s witnessed a flourish in translation criticism, especially in criticism of literary translation. In 1991, a national symposium on criticism of literary translation was held and in 1992, there came the first monograph by Prof. Xu Jun on criticism of literary translation. In 1995, criticism of different versions of *The Red and the Black* and two versions of *Ulysses* was launched and a large number of people were involved. Ever since the middle of the 1990s, with the influence of the "cultural turn" in translation studies in the West, some Chinese scholars began to study literary translation from the perspectives of social factors and many MA theses began to study the mutual influence between the socio-cultural aspects and the translated literary works. The subjectivity of the translators also became a hot topic. Various cultural theories based on deconstructionism and modern hermeneutics began to be applied to criticism of literary translation.

At the end of the 20th century and at the beginning of the 21th century, criticism of literary translation became more multi-dimensioned. While there still existed some traditional approaches like fault-finding and intuitional comments (seeZhou Yi & Luo Ping 1999; Ma Hongjun 2000), there appeared some other approaches besides linguistic and cultural approaches. Lv Jun (2000) took a philosophical approach holding that translation criticism is a dialogue between the critic and the translator via the text. Based on the theory of communicative action put forth by Jurgen Habermas, Lv Jun (2002) pointed out that literary translation is a special kind of communicative action and requires a special standard for measurement. Jiang Qiuxia (2002) took an aesthetic approach in light of the Gestaut theory. Moreover, there appeared more quantitative statistic approaches and some of them were corpus-based making criticism of literary translation more objective. For instance, Xia Zhaohui and Cao Hejian (2003) made quantitative assessment concerning the stylistic equivalent. Hai Fang (2003) made statistic analysis of translating strategies used by different translators.

Efforts have been made to move criticism of literary translation toward systematization too. Xu Jun (1992) holds that literary translation is a recreation aiming at reproducing the original's formal value, cultural value, literary images and its semantic information. In his *Studies on Criticism of Literary Translation* he gives a detailed study of the principles and methods of criticism on literary translation. The four principles listed are: 1), the combination of judgment on the correctness or fault of the translation product and the analysis of the translation process; 2), a breakthrough of the intuitional impressionism comments based on the critic's own taste; 3), the integrity of the macro- and micro analysis and 4), criticism should be constructive and beneficial for the translator. He then suggests six basic ways of doing criticism of literary translation: 1), the logical-empirical method; 2), qualitative and quantitative analyses; 3), semantic analysis; 4), analysis of the sample; 5), comparison of different versions and 6), appreciation of good translation. And the last part of Xu's book is given to the discussion or criticism of literary translation in practice. The good combination of theory and practice makes this book quite enlightening.

Among books about criticism of literary translation, Wang Hongyin's *On the Criticism of Literary Translation* is characterised by its rich content, its profound thinking and its readability. Wang (2006: 49-50) regards criticism of literary translation as an advanced aesthetic research and proposes the combination of appreciation and academic research. He gives detailed analyses to many aspects of criticism on literary translation in light of literary criticism and translation studies. He talks about three functions of criticism of literary translation, namely the function of reading guidance, the function of quality evaluation and that of ideological guidance. He lists the qualities an ideal critic should possess: 1), knowing both languages with cultures; 2), knowing translation skills and appreciation; 3), with literary tastes; 4), knowing the original and translated texts; 5), empathy and understanding; 6), philosophical-minded; 7), with good manners. While this surely serves as a good summary of those prerequisites for a qualified critic, we must be aware that this list is actually far from complete. Some other qualities, for instance, the ability to offer a better version, might also be necessary for a more convincing comment.

According to Aristotle, the task of the critic is to evaluate genuinely a writer and his works (Wang Hongyin 2006: 103). Wang points out that though not all the criticism can be said to be evaluation and evaluation is not the end or the sole end of criticisms, it is inevitable that all criticisms including that of literary translation involve evaluation (ibid:104)

And in order to come to a satisfactory evaluation, one has to pay great attention to the methodology to be used. In this respect, Wang not only discusses carefully the methods that can be employed by critics, but makes some comments on the difference concerning methodologies between natural science and social science which is quite enlightening. Based on his criticism of the shortcomings of the pure scientism, he suggests that as the cardinal principles of criticism of literary translation, we should seek the combination of interpretation with empirical study, the combination of particularity with universality and the combination of personal aesthetic taste with social norms and values etc. (Wang Hongyin 2006: 92-93).

Wang's book is a great step taken toward systematic study of criticism of literary translation in China nowadays. It tries to be comprehensive in its discussion of every aspect of criticism of literary translation. This can be seen from its expounding of the five principles of doing translation criticism and the working definition of criteria for criticism of literary translation. The five principles—objectivity, wholeness, accuracy, economy, consistency—serve as a general guideline. "Objectivity" comes first as it is the fundamental principle of all scientific activities and hence the principle of criticism of literary translation. According to Wang, it requires us to adopt scientific methods to come to the reliable conclusions. It also means that we should try our utmost to avoid personal emotions and to reduce the subjective factors of the critics to the minimum in value judgment (ibid: 120). The principle of "wholeness" requires us to try to get rid of one-sidedness by looking at the object from different angles and in every possible ways. "Accuracy" is related to the accurate use of the categories, terms and the descriptive language. The critic should employ as less as possible those terms and expressions not recognized and established by the scientific community. "Economy" mainly refers to the brevity of language use and "consistency" is the requirement of clarity of our statements and for the sake of avoidance of self-contradiction in our discussion. The book is rigorous in that it does not forget to mention that there exists certain flexibility in practice which makes criticism artistic (ibid: 120-122).

Wang's book not only offers us the principles for criticism of literary translation, but also some operational guidance. The practicality of the book can be found in many aspects. For instance, readers are given detailed explanation to some concrete and practical methods such as close reading, sampling, quantitative method, evaluation etc. The expounding of criticism procedure also contributes to the practicality of the book. According to the book, six steps are involved in the activity of criticism of literary translation. They are: 1), reading of the original; 2), reading of the translation; 3), comparative study; 4), effect evaluation; 5), value judgment; 6), (choosing) the angle of commentary. Readers can find discussion of issues involved and things the critic should pay attention to in each of these steps (Wang Hongyin 2006: 93-115).

One of the features of Wang's book is its discussion of criticism of literary translation with reference to literary creation and literary criticism.

In talking about the criteria and grading of literary translations, Wang first discusses the criteria and yardstick for literary creation and then turns to the grading of literary translation accordingly. Wang classifies literary works into two kinds: reproductive and representative, each has different requirements in the three dimensions of "*xin, da* and *ya*". "*Xin*" is the requirement of facts and logic, "*da*" of language, and "*ya*" the overall aesthetic appeal. For translations that fall into the category of the "reproductive", they are expected to be objective, complete and well-knitted to meet the factual and logical demand; they are expected to be accurate, fluent and distinct to meet the linguistic demand; and they are expected to be concise, well-balanced and consistent to meet the aesthetic demand. For translations that fall into the category of "representative", our expectation is that they should be true to life, detailed and adequate in respect of the criterion of "*xin*", that they should be appropriate, vivid and novel in respect of the criterion of "*da*", and that they should possess the beauty of sound, image and form in respect of the criterion of "*ya*". Translations that conform to the criterion of "*xin*" can be said to have fulfilled its social function of exchange, translations that conform to the criterion of "*da*" is supposed to have fulfilled its social function of influence, and translations that conform to the criterion of "*ya*" can be regarded as having fulfilled the function of affecting the reader. The grading of the evaluation is based on the fulfillment of the three dimensions of "*xin, da* and *ya*". Fulfillment of "*xin*" is the basic requirement of an acceptable translation and is therefore graded as "plain" translation (here the term "plain" does not mean "bad", but rather, according to Wang, "plain", referring to the version's lack of aesthetic appeal and social influence); fulfillment of "*da*" is taken to be "good" translation and that of "*ya*" "excellent" translation (Wang Hongyin 2006: 122-132).

Wang's book holds that the three dimensions form an inseparable integrity and become a fairly stable evaluation system. However, this system is but the "primary norm" as there is another complementary evaluation system which can be regarded as the "secondary norm", a higher standard. This "secondary norm" system consists of three dimensions too: 1) innovation of translation methods; 2) novelty of language use and 3) enlightening for the development of translation theories (ibid: 133).

The "secondary norm" system put forward by Wang is quite refreshing. Factors such as "enlightening for the development of translation theories" are seldom considered by ordinary readers, critics and professional evaluators, and most possibly, it is some of the translation studies scholars who will give prominence to them.

Though no one can deny Wang's book is a great contribution to studies on criticism of literary translation, it is nevertheless not an all-solving scheme.

When discussing methods for criticism, Wang talks about the method of "evaluation". While saying that it is a method that is found in all criticism, he urges us to distinguish the value of the original work from that of the translation, the criterion of fidelity from similarity and objective factors from subjective factors (ibid: 93-105). This is, of course, very helpful for the practice of translation criticism, but a more detailed discussion is certainly needed if we consider the complexity of evaluation.

What's more, according to Wang, "*xin*" as a criterion only refers to the faithful transfer of facts and logical relationship contained in the original works. Here, we find again the different understandings and interpretings of the often-used term.

All in all, criticism of literary translation has been making progress in many ways. The scope has been enlarged from specific translated texts to translation phenomena and translational events; attention has been paid not only to the linguistic aspects but also to the cultural aspects of translation, and to the translator's subjectivity. Consequently, approaches to criticism of literary translation have become diverse—many perspectives, such as text-linguistics or discourse analysis, polysystem, functionalism, feminism, psychology, hermeneutics, pragmatics, relevance theory and communicative action etc. are adopted to make the criticism of literary translation more and more plural.

With the pluralization of criticisms on literary translation, there also comes the critical reflection of these criticisms and many people were puzzled by different criteria put forward by different approaches, some of the approaches are actually making the term "criterion" meaningless with their devouring of any "Center" (Lv Jun & Hou Xiangqun 2006). Scholars such as Xu Jun, Lv Jun and Hou Xiangqun, Liu Yunhong etc. have written articles and books to call for the establishment of the discipline of translation criticism.

3.2 Studies on Criticism of Literary Translation in the West

Criticism of literary translation in the West has something in common with that in China, i.e. concentrating mainly on the principles, the criteria and the methods of criticism, interwoven with the principles, the criteria and the methods of literary translation. It also underwent a process from impressionism to scientific analysis, as the discipline of Translation Studies over the world was in its infancy stage before the development of modern linguistics and it has followed the course in its development from random and unsystematic studies to systematic researches (Tan Zaixi 1998; qtd. in Zhu Chunshen 2008: 9).

Wilss (1982/2001: 216) when talking about the "absence of a systematic, methodologically stringent frame of reference" in translation criticism says that "TC (translation criticism, the authors of this book) was until recently largely anecdotal and spontaneous rather than systematically reflected, relying to a large extent on presumptions which may vary appreciably from one translation critic to another".

Though the above statement is basically true to the fact, we can not deny that there have been efforts to make translation criticism, including criticism of literary translation scientific and systematic. However, we must immediately add we can not either deny that there are few monographs on criticism of literary translation in the West.

3.2.1 Berman's study on criticism of literary translation

Antoine Berman is one of the few who pays special attention to criticism of literary criticism and who has not been given due attention in Translation Studies.

Berman is considered as the first to raise the issue of translation ethics in the modern time. His *The Experience of the Foreign: Culture and Translation in Romantic Germany* was first published in 1984 in German and was translated into

English in 1992. In this book, Berman says that the ethics of translation concerns about how "translation" and "fidelity" are defined. Translation cannot be defined solely in terms of communication, of the transmission of messages, or of extended rewording. Nor is translation a purely literary/esthetical activity, even when it is intimately connected with the literary practice of a given cultural realm. To be sure, translation is writing and transmitting. But this writing and this transmission get their true sense only from the ethical aim by which they are governed. "In this sense, translation is closer to science than to art—at least to those who maintain that art is ethically irresponsible" (Berman 1992: 5).

According to Berman, a bad translation "generally under the guise of transmissibility, carries out a systematic negation of the strangeness of the foreign work" and

> Cultural resistance produces a systematics of deformations that operates on the linguistic and literary levels, and that conditions the translator, whether he wants it or not, whether he knows it or not. The reversible dialectic of fidelity and treason is present in the translator, even in his position as a writer: The pure translator is the one who needs to write starting from a foreign work, a foreign language, and a foreign author—a notable detour. On the psychic level, the translator is ambivalent, wanting to force two things: to force his own language to adorn itself with strangeness, and to force the other language to transport itself into his mother tongue. (Berman 1992: 5)

In his *Translation and the Trials of the Foreign*, Berman proposes to examine the system of textual deformation that appears in every translation, preventing the translation from being a "trial of the foreign". He says that

> I shall call this examination the analytic of translation. Analytic in two senses of the term: a detailed analysis of the deforming system, and therefore an analysis in the Cartesian sense, but also in the psychoanalytic sense, insofar as the system is largely unconscious, present as a series of tendencies or forces that cause translation to deviate from its essential aim. (qtd. in Venuti 2000: 286)

Berman explains that his analytic framework is provisional, based mainly on his experience as a translator (primarily of Latin American literature into French) and to make it more systematic, the input of translators from other domains (other languages and works), the input of linguists, "poeticians" and psychoanalysts etc. are all needed.

Berman also says that "[t]his analytic sets out to locate several deforming tendencies. They form a systematic whole" (ibid: 288). Twelve tendencies are mentioned by Berman. They are: 1), rationalization; 2), clarification; 3), expansion;

4), ennoblement and popularization; 5), qualitative impoverishment; 6), quantitative impoverishment; 7), the destruction of rhythms; 8), the destruction of underlying networks of signification; 9), the destruction of linguistic patternings; 10), the destruction of vernacular networks or their exoticization; 11), the destruction of expressions and idioms; 12), the effacement of the superimposition of language.

These twelve deforming tendencies can be found in all translations, according to Berman, "at least in the western tradition".

"Rationalization recomposes sentences and the sequence of sentences, rearranging them according to a certain idea of discursive order" (ibid). It may make "the original pass from concrete to abstract, not only by reordering the sentence structure, but— for example— by translating verbs into substantives, by choosing the more general of two substantives, etc." (qtd. in Venuti 2000: 289). And all in all, it "deforms the original by reversing its basic tendency" (ibid).

Clarification "is a corollary of rationalization which particularly concerns the level of 'clarity' perceptible in words and their meanings. Where the original has no problem moving in the indefinite, our literary language tends to impose the definite" (ibid).

Expansion refers to the fact that "[e] very translation tends to be longer than the original" and is also called "overtranslation" (ibid: 290).

Ennoblement in poetry is "poetization" and in prose, a "rhetorization".

Rhetorization consists in producing "elegant" sentences, while utilizing the source text, so to speak, as raw material. Thus the ennoblement is only a rewriting, a "stylistic exercise" based on — and at the expense of— the original. This procedure is active in the literary field, but also in the human sciences, where it produces texts that are "readable," "brilliant," rid of their original clumsiness and complexity so as to enhance the "meaning."(qtd. in Venuti 2000: 290-291)

Qualitative impoverishment "refers to the replacement of terms, expressions and figures in the original with terms, expressions and figures that lack their sonorous richness or, correspondingly, their signifying or 'iconic' richness" (ibid: 291).

Quantitative impoverishment "refers to a lexical loss", neglecting the "certain proliferation of signifiers and signifying chains" in the original (ibid).

The destruction of rhythms is more often found in poetry and theater translation as poetry and theater are much more fragile than novel. One way to destroy the rhythmic movement of the original is "an arbitrary revision of the punctuation" (ibid: 292).

The destruction of underlying networks of signification refers to the deforming of the "hidden dimension" existing in literary works "where certain signifiers correspond and link up, forming all sorts of networks beneath the 'surface' of the text itself — the manifest text, presented for reading". The underlying chains "constitute one aspect of the rhythm and signifying process of the text" and if these chains are not retained and the networks are not transmitted, the "signifying process in the text is destroyed" (ibid: 292-293).

The destruction of linguistic patternings refers to the deforming of the original "beyond the level of signifiers, metaphors, etc." and extending to "the type of sentences, the sentence constructions employed" (qtd. in Venuti 2000: 293).

The destruction of vernacular networks or their exoticization refers to the deforming of the vernacular language in prose which "is by its very nature more physical, more iconic than 'cultivated' language" and is regarded as a virtue of the prose in the twentieth century. "The effacement of vernaculars is thus a very serious injury to the textuality of prose works" (ibid: 294).

The destruction of expressions and idioms refers to the distortion of the original proverbs and idioms by adopting the seemingly "equivalent" proverbs or idioms. And "it is evident that even if the meaning is identical, replacing an idiom by its 'equivalent' is an ethnocentrism" (ibid: 295).

The effacement of the superimposition of languages is the destruction of diversity of languages and a heterophony or diversity of voices in a novel. It "involves the relation between dialect and a common language, a koine, or the coexistence, in the heart of a text, of two or more koine" (qtd. in Venuti 2000: 295).

In the end of the essay, Berman calls our attention to the difference between his analytic of translation from "the study of 'norms' — literary, social, cultural, etc. — which partly govern the translating act in every society". He says that

> These "norms," which vary historically, never specifically concern translation; they apply, in fact, to any writing practice whatsoever. The analytic, in contrast, focuses on the universals of deformation inherent in translating as such. It is obvious that in specific periods and cultures these universals overlap with the system of norms that govern writing: think only of the neoclassical period and its "belles infideles." (unfaithful beauty, author of the dissertation) Yet this coincidence is fleeting. In the twentieth century, we no longer submit to neoclassical norms, but the universals of deformation are not any less in force. They even enter into conflict with the new norms governing writing and translation. (ibid: 296)

Berman then talks about the western tradition of "embellishing restitution of meaning, based on the typically Platonic separation between spirit and letter, sense and word, content and form, the sensible and the non-sensible" (ibid) and its influence on today's translation. He says that "[a]ll the tendencies noted in the analytic lead to the same result: the production of a text that is more 'clear,' more 'elegant,' more 'fluent,' more 'pure' than the original" (ibid: 297). Berman comments that "[t]ranslation stimulated the fashioning and refashioning of the great western languages only because it labored on the letter and profoundly modified the translating language. As simple restitution of meaning, translation could never have played this formative role" (ibid: 297). Therefore, Berman concludes that "the essential aim of the analytic of translation is to highlight this other essence of translating, which, although never recognized, endowed it with historical effectiveness in every domain where it was practiced" (ibid). This conclusion serves as an echo of what he has said about his analytic:

> This negative analytic should be extended by a positive counterpart, an analysis of operations which have always limited the deformation, although in an intuitive and unsystematic way. These operations constitute a sort of counter-system destined to neutralize, or attenuate, the negative tendencies. The negative and positive analytics will in turn enable a critique of translations that is neither simply descriptive nor simply normative. (qtd. in Venuti 2000: 286)

To sum up, Berman's negative analytic is "primarily concerned with ethnocentric, annexationist translations and hypertextual translations (pastiche, imitation, adaptation, free rewriting), where the play of deforming forces is freely exercised". Berman holds that no translator can escape this play of deforming forces. They are "unconscious" and "form part of the translator's being, determining the desire to translate". Therefore, it is "illusory to think that the translator can be freed merely by becoming aware of them", and only "by yielding to the 'controls' (in the psychoanalytic sense)" can translators hope to "free themselves from the system of deformation that burdens their practice" as "[t]his system is the internalized expression of a two-millenium-old tradition, as well as the ethnocentric structure of every culture, every language" (ibid).

For the methods of assessing a translation, Berman proposes to select some significant passages in the translation and compare them with the original, not only seeking to find out the shortcomings of a translation but also trying to analyze the qualities and originality of a translation as a work of art. Berman does not state clearly his assessment criteria. Yet, as the purpose of Berman is to try to prevent deforming or domesticating or ethnocentric translations, his criteria are clearly source-text-oriented. In this section, we quoted a lot from Berman as we think it better for readers to know what exactly has been said by Berman, to avoid "deforming" in a sense.

3.2.2 Other scholars' studies on criticism of literary translation

Besides Berman, we can find some other discussions about criticism of literary translation in the works of other scholars.

Most of the German functionalist scholars are supporters of the skopos theory, who believe that "translation brief" made by the "initiator" of the translation project is the most important yardstick to measure the quality of a translation, including literary translation. Accordingly, the starting point for the critic is the TT skopos or functions and the first step in the evaluation is to read the TT as a whole. And according to Nord (1991: 166), "...it is the text as a whole whose function(s) and effect(s) must be regarded as the crucial criteria for translation criticism".

Some scholars hold that functionalism does not work in literary translation because there is no way to know exactly who are the target audience or readers and what their needs or expectations will be. What is more, it is hard to know the purpose of a literary work; if a translation is purpose-oriented, it tends to limit the possibilities of grasping the entire meaning potential of the original from the start; and with the assumed audience in mind, it will limit the originality and transformative power of translated literature and infringe on the authoritative status of the source text. Against such ideas Nord (2001:122) argues that "[t]o make the originality of the source show through in the target text is, of course, a possible translation purpose. The problem is whether this can be done by simply reproducing what is in the text, since what is original in one culture may be less so in another, and vice versa". Nord further adds that "[t]he concept of function-plus-loyalty could perhaps make the functionalist approach even more directly applicable in literary translation".

Though also taking a functional approach, House is strongly against skopos theorists' "the end justifies the means". She holds that no judgment can be made without the comparison between the TT and the ST. Equivalence should be gained and measured based on the distinction between overt and covert translations. Generally speaking, overt translation is source-text-oriented and covert, target-text-oriented. Though House aims to dismiss the idea that TQA is by nature subjective, she has to admit that "[i]t is difficult to pass a 'final judgment' on the quality of a translation that fulfils the demands of objectivity" (House 1997: 119).

House meant to offer a general model for TQA, and therefore, no special attention is given to literary translation. Yet, her concept of "cultural filtering" is extremely useful for literary translation and the criticism of literary translation as this is closely connected with the cultural and political norm or standard of the translated works. House says that,

> A further theoretical issue here is the question of reciprocity of skew. In other words, if it is deemed appropriate and normative to filter when translating (in a certain way, namely covertly) from linguaculture A to linguaculture B, then we might logically suggest that it is equally warranted and indeed necessary to filter in the opposite way when translating from B into A. Is this logical conclusion justified?...but I know of no studies that explicitly address it. My own work—especially with children's literature— suggests for the translation pair English and German that skewing is in this case often but not necessarily always reciprocal, in that German children's literature translated into English is not consistently filtered towards the norm for children's literature written in English to the extent that children's books translated into German are also so filtered. I hypothesise that this is not an isolated case, and that there is such a thing as preferred direction of skew. (House 1997: 162)

Based on Even-Zohar's polysystem theory, Toury holds that TT is not introduced into but rather imposed upon the target literary polysystem, and the imposition may have positive or negative affects on the target linguistic and literary system. As to what kind of affects a translation will produce on the target literature and culture, it is governed and measured by norms. Usually, the initial norm determines whether the translator will have an adequate or an acceptable translation. Subordinate to the initial norm are preliminary norms and operational norms which in respective determine the translation policy (selection for texts for translation), directness of translation (through an intermediate language or not), completeness of the TT and the selection of TT linguistic material. In short, translation is a norm-governed activity and all the strategies used by translators are determined by the norms in action. Toury talked about the multiplicity of norms and the unstable, changing features of norms, and the active part the translator can play in the forming or retaining of a norm as well, admitting that "*non-normative behaviour* is always a possibility" (Toury 1995/2001: 64). All these translational norms in Toury's descriptive study are "only traceable", to be found by "examining the results of the often subconscious behaviour" of the translators (Munday 2001: 117). This certainly has given Toury's approach a tinge of unreliability. Even if Toury's concept of norm is useful to explain some translational phenomena, for the evaluation of the translational behaviour, it is not quite helpful, as is said by Toury, after all, norms observed by critics may be the same as those observed by translators and there may also be great difference between the two.

What we should also mention is Toury's distinction between the two senses of literary translation: one is that "the translation of texts which are regarded as literary in the *source culture*" and the other is that "the translation of a text (in principle, at least, any text, of any type whatever) in such a way that the product be acceptable as literary to the *recipient culture*" (Toury 1995/2001: 168). Such a distinction is significant as it helps us better realize the complexity of literary translation.

In connection with translation criticism, Andrew Chesterman's norm approach is, to some extent, more helpful than Toury. Chesterman (1997: 68) argues that all norms "exert a prescriptive pressure" and proposes another set of norms: 1), product or expectancy norms and 2) professional or process norms. The first norms are "established by the expectations of readers of a translation (of a given type) concerning what a translation (of this type) should be like" (ibid: 64). The expectations of the target readership concern the quality of the target text and the judgment of quality of the target text is then influenced by the prevalent translation tradition in the target culture, the norms of the same or similar text type and some social and economic factors. These norms may come from the common readers and they can also come from the "norm-authorities" such as teachers, literary critics and publisher's readers. Norms coming from the latter may be more influential and sometimes there may be contradiction between the authorities and the ordinary readers. But, anyway, the expectancy norms can be used to evaluate a translation.

Professional or process norms on the other hand are subordinate to the expectancy norms. They come from the behaviour of the best translators and "regulate the translation process itself" (ibid: 67). Professional or process norms can be further classified into three kinds: 1) the accountability norm, bearing some resemblance with Nord's principle of loyalty to all parties concerned in a translation act, concerning the translator's responsibility for the original writer, the commissioner and the target reader; 2) the communication norm, referring to the optimization of communication between the parties, a requirement for the translator as an expert in communication to accomplish; and 3) the relation norm, dealing with the relation between the TT and the ST, requiring the translation to maintain an appropriate relation with the ST. According to Chesterman, such a relation is to be judged by the translator "according to text-type, the wishes of the commissioner, the intentions of the original writer, and the assumed needs of the prospective readers" (Chesterman 1997: 69). It again reminds us of Nord's principle of "function plus loyalty". But Chesterman's study on norms offers us more insight into the norm-governed activity of translation than Toury and what is worth mentioning is that Chesterman further points out that "[v]alue concepts can be seen as prior to normative concepts, in that norms are governed by values" (Chesterman 1997: 172). He argues that "the four fundamental translational values are clarity, truth, trust and understanding" and descriptively rather than prescriptively, these values "appear to be the values held explicitly or implicitly by most translators" (ibid: 175). This is significant for us to look at translation criticism from the perspective of axiology.

Theo Hermans in his *Translation in System* has a more detailed study of norms. According to Hermans (1999/2004: 81), "[n]orms can be understood as stronger, prescriptive versions of social conventions. Like conventions, norms derive their legitimacy from shared knowledge, mutual expectation and acceptance, and the fact that, on the individual level, they are largely internalized". This means that many norms are actually observed unconsciously, but be they conscious or unconscious, norms can

> ...tell members of a community not just everyone else expects them to behave in a given situation, but how they *ought* to behave. They imply that there is, among the array of possible options, a particular course of action which is more or less strongly preferred because the community has agreed to accept it as 'proper' or 'correct' or 'appropriate'. The intersubjective sense of what is 'proper' or 'correct' or 'appropriate' constitutes the *content* of a norm. (ibid: 81-82)

Norms are not always observed by everyone. They "can and will be breached". As to "[w]hich norms are broken by whom will depend on the occasion, on the nature and strength of the norm and on the individual's position and motivation" (ibid: 82). There are strong norms and weak ones. Some norms may become stronger and stronger and consequently turn into "codified rules in the form of explicit obligations and prohibitions" (ibid). What is more, norms are constantly changing. They change to be readjusted to meet the changing conditions. "Different groups may judge particular norms more or less relevant or appropriate in certain circumstances" (Hermans 1999/2004: 84). Academic readers may have different expectations of a translation from those of non-professional readers. Norms of one text-type, in one society and in a given time may different from the other. "The internal history of translation could be written as an unfolding series of norm conflicts" (Hermans 1999/2004: 84). That is to say, there exist a multiplicity of different and competing norms in the world.

For Hermans, correct translation is a relative notion:

> There may be more ways than one of producing a correct translation. And what one section or community or historical period calls correct may be quite different from what others, or some of us today, may call correct. Correctness in translation is relative— linguistically, socially, politically, ideologically. (ibid: 85)

Hermans is right in pointing out the relativity of correctness in translation, he is also right in saying that "[i]n themselves, norms are neither true or false", but he is not so right in his pursue of the so-called descriptive study of norms not to pass any judgment on the correctness of a norm. It is true that norms are neither true nor false, but it is clear that some norms are considered more correct or more proper than others. After all, as Chesterman (1997: 68) points out, all norms "exert a prescriptive pressure". And we should realize that value judgment, including that of the norms, is inescapable in our life and it is one of the reasons for the changing of norms. It is with our value judgment of the norms that we get to know which norm can be used as the criterion of our translation criticism.

3.3 Different Forms of Criticism of Literary Translation

In practice, there exist different forms of criticism of literary translation. These forms can be roughly divided into several types: 1), criticism on translation theories, which belongs, according to our definition of translation criticism, to translation criticism in its broad sense; 2), criticism on translation events; and 3), criticism on translated texts; 4) criticism on the translator. And among the three, the third is what we traditionally have been focusing on and can be further divided into several subtypes: criticism of translated poetry, drama, novels, essays etc. What needs to be mentioned is that types of criticism can be classified from different angles and there are often overlaps between different types.

3.3.1 Criticism on theories of literary translation

According to Holmes, translation theory can be divided into general theory and theories of restricted areas. In the area of literary translation, there have been many controversial principles and criteria and one thing we should notice is that theories of literary translation are often closely connected and often expanded to translation theory in general.

Sachin Ketkar, as a writer and translator, makes some comments on the theoretical thinking about literary translation in his article "Literary Translation: Recent Theoretical Developments" (http://www. translationdirectory.com/article301. htm). He views traditional approach to literature and "literariness" as "essentialist" which sees the author as the sacred and unique creator and the translation as a mere copy of the original, greatly influenced by the dichotomy of "original" versus "copy" in the Western thought. In the traditional approach to literary translation, people are concerned about the finding of equivalents of lexis, syntax, concepts, styles etc. As the original is unique and by definition uncopyable, there has been hot debate on whether the translator should adopt free or literal translations, whether the verse should be translated into verse and can a translation be faithful and beautiful etc. The answers to these questions "range from one extreme to another and usually end in some sort of a compromise". "Even the approaches based on the 'objective' and 'scientific' foundations of linguistics are not entirely neutral in their preferences and implicit value judgments" as translation problems are not merely at the verbal or linguistic level. Different from the traditional approaches, Even-Zohar, Toury, Lefevere and Hermans etc. view literary translation as part of the cultural and literary system of the target culture and hold that the study of literary translation should begin with a study of the translated text within the system of the target culture. Toury talks about "pseudo-translation", which has no position in traditional approach, trying to discover and describe what is meant by equivalence within the target culture. Lefevere pays more attention to constrains over translators working within the target system—dominant poetics, patronage, ideology, etc. and thinking that translation is one of the typical forms of rewriting or refraction which includes criticism, translation, anthologization, the writing of literary history and the editing of texts. Ketkar points out these descriptive theories "have a limited use for the translator as well as translation criticism" and that the terms "rewriting" and "refraction" presupposes that "a text can be written *for the first time* and that it exists in a pre-non-refracted state" and hence Lefevere is facing the danger of belonging to the very system of thought he is criticizing. What is more, Lefevere "fails to point out the exact features and qualities of literary text which solicit refractions".

According to Ketkar, Raymond Van den Broeck's "Second Thought on Translation Criticism: A Model of its Analytic Function" in 1985 goes beyond Lefevere and Toury. Broeck, while stressing the importance of examining the norms involved in the production and reception of a translation, saying that it is the foremost task of translation criticism to create greater awareness of these norms, gives room for the critic's personal value judgments. The critic is entitled to doubt the effectiveness of the strategies chosen by the translator and can be "a trustworthy guide in telling the reader where target textemes balance source textemes and where in the critic's view, they do not" so long as the critic is familiar with the functional features of the source text and does not confuse his own initial norms with those of the translator.

Ketkar sees Venuti's advocating of "foreignizing" strategy as prescriptive, opposed to the above-mentioned descriptive approach. He argues that other approaches seemingly to be gaining ground "lay greater emphasis on the political dimension of literary translation" and are more influenced by New Historicism which "treats literary texts as a space where power relations are made visible". Tejaswini Niranjana finds that the relationship between the two languages and two cultures involved in translation is hardly on equal terms, and translations employing different strategies can either reinforce or reduce the hegemony of the colonizer, the stronger culture. Mahasweta Sengupta, for example, in her reading of Rabindranath Tagore's autotranslation of *Gitanjali*, finds that the translator "modified, omitted, and rewrote his poems in the manner of the Orientalists to cater to his Western audience", to "suit the English sensibility". Bassnett and Trivedi (1999) in their edited *Postcolonial Translation: Theory and Practice* believe that there exists the hierarchical opposition between the European colonizer culture and the colonized culture in translation. They hold that cannibalism is one of the ways former colonies trying to assert their own culture and reject the feeling of being derivative and at the same time not rejecting things that are of value from the colonizer. Spivak considers translation as a strategy to pursue the feminist agenda of achieving women's solidarity. Feminist approaches openly advocate manipulating the original text in translation to strive for the equal status between the woman (the translated text) and the husband (the original). All these political approaches throw light on the activity of translation but at the same time overlook the fact that "a literary text is far more complex artifact and the relationship it bears towards what is called 'cultural' and 'political' field is extremely intricate". They overlook the aesthetic aspect of a text which makes it a work of art. What is more, words like "culture", "politics" and "history" themselves are "polyvalent and open to various and often conflicting postures and interpretations". Ketkar's comments are to the point and similar criticisms on theories of literary translation can be found in Jeremy Munday (2001) and other critics such as

Newmark, House, Gentzler, Snell-Hornby etc.

Munday has a section to discuss and comment on the theories introduced in each chapter of his book *Introducing Translation Studies: Theories and Applications*. For example, after his introduction to systems theories, Munday (2001: 117) cites Gentzler's positive and negative comments on DTS and polysystem theory, pointing out that in Toury's study "there is still a wish to generalize (or even overgeneralize) from case studies, since the 'laws' Toury tentatively proposes are in some ways simply reformulations of generally-held (thought not necessarily proven) beliefs about translation" and "[i]t is debatable to what extent a semi-scientific norm/law approach can be applied to a marginal area such as translation, since the norms described are, after all, abstract and only traceable in Toury's method by examining the results of the often subconscious behaviour that is supposedly governed by them". He further points out that his own descriptive studies suggest that *"the law of interference"* proposed by Toury "needs to be modified, or even a new law proposed, that of *reduced control over linguistic realization in translation*" (Munday 2001: 118).

Munday contributes one chapter to the cultural approaches and gives it a title "Varieties of Cultural Studies". In the ending part of this chapter, he comments that

> To be sure, these new cultural approaches have widened the horizons of translation studies with a wealth of new insights, but there is also a strong element of conflict and competition between them. For example, Simon (1996: 95), writing from a gender-studies perspective, describes the distortion of the representation in translation of the French feminist Helene Cixous, since many critics only have access to that portion of her work that is available in English. However, Rosemary Arroyo (1999), writing from a postcolonial angle, claims that Cixous's own appropriation of the Brazilian author Clarice Lispector 'is in fact an exemplary illustration of an aggressively "masculine" approach to difference' (Arroyo 1999: 160). (ibid: 139)

In fact, criticism on theories of literary translation reveals the paradigmatic shifts in Translation Studies worldwide. The birth of a new paradigm is often accompanied by criticisms on the previous paradigm, previous theories. And even within the same paradigm, there often exist divergent voices and hence criticisms on each other, leading to different sub-paradigms in the whole system of paradigm or the modification of the same paradigm. The emergence of cultural approaches is accompanied by criticism of linguistic approaches. The best-known example is Susan Bassnett's dismissal of linguistic theories of translation in her *Translation Studies* published in 1980. Armed with deconstructionism, scholars like Bassenett accept Jaques Derrida's idea of translation, believing that translation ensures the survival of a text and becomes the after-life of a text, discarding the concept of "the original". Criticisms within the same paradigm are well shown in the case of functionalist approaches in Germany where differences can be found between Reiss and Vermeer, and between Holz-Manttari and Nord. Nord (1991), for example, once commented on Holz-Manttari's theory of translational action. Though she agrees that functionality is the most important criterion for the measurement of a translation, she is not satisfied with the latter's disregarding of the ST and thinks that we should not allow the translator absolute license in the decision-making in translation. As a result of such criticisms, we have actually, different versions of skopos theories in Translation Studies.

There is also criticism on theories of literary translation in China. Scholars like Chang Nam Fung (2004), Liu Miqing (2005), Lv Jun and Hou Xiangqun (2006) etc. have offered us some insightful criticisms on Chinese and foreign theories of literary translation. As translation criticism in its broad sense is not our focus in this dissertation, we will only briefly touch upon it and move on to criticism on translation events and translated texts.

3.3.2 Criticism on translation events

Criticism on translation events refer to comments on a specific translation activity, including translation policy, the choice of text to be translated by translators and publishers, the translator, the strategies and methods used by the translator and the reception and impact of the translated text, including the criticism of translators and the counter-criticism. The following are some examples of this kind of criticism in and out of China.

During the New Culture Movement at the early period of the first half of last century, there appeared many literary societies in China. One of such societies called "The Creation" founded in 1921 consists of famous writers and translators such as Guo Moruo, Yu Dafu, Cheng Fangwu, Zhang Ziping, Tian Han, Zheng Boqi etc. Another society called "Literary Studies Association" also founded in 1921 consists of famous writers and translators such as Zhou Zuoren, Zheng Zhenduo, Shen Yanbing or better known as Mao Dun, Zhu Ziqing, Liu Bannong, Xu Zhimo, Lao She etc. There was a heated debate between the two societies about literature and literary translation in the 1920s and some other scholars, writers and translators were also involved in it. First, in choosing texts to be translated, members of "The Creation" held that texts representing the spirit of the time marked by the liberation of personality and those with greater aesthetic value, loved, appreciated by and conformable to the taste of the translator should be translated rather than those literary works from the weaker and therefore impressed nations for the practical purpose of enlightening the target reader and making them realize the current social problems and the danger of the nation; secondly, different from the advocating of Lu Xun and members of "Literary Studies Association", scholars of "The Creation" held that retranslation and indirect translation of literary works, which was very popular among translators and publishers at that time, should be avoided. In respect of translation methods to be adopted, members of the "Literary Studies Association" advocated literal translation while members of "The Creation" value much translations that can preserve the spirit of the original. However, both of the societies criticized many of the irresponsible poor translations which are full of mistakes in understanding and expression. So far as the translator is concerned, Guo Morui thought that the translator should first have the sense of responsibility, and should then in a way "become" the author, "marry" the author of the original, integrate himself/herself into the author, getting a complete understanding of the author. Yu Dafu held that the translator first should be a scholar, an expert of the author to be translated, then spend time in thinking about how he/she can best transfer the ideas of the original author, and make sure that he/she has captured the spirit of the original work before setting hand in translation. Hu Shi thought that only those commonly accepted masterpieces should be translated and the translated language should be in the current vernacular language even if the original is in the form of rhymed verse or drama. He criticized Lin Shu for his translating Shakespeare into narrative old Chinese prose and considers Lin as having committed a big crime with his translating Shakespeare. As Lin was a good writer of the old Chinese, his translations were very popular at his time and won a lot of praises from critics. However, Lin was also criticized by some critics. Liu Bannong, for example, pointed out that Lin was not careful in choosing texts to translate and had translated both the excellent and the valueless. He also criticized Lin for his too many wrong translations and too many adaptations. What is more, Liu thought that the greatest mistake made by Lin was his not faithful to the original spirit and style by his domesticating strategy. After Lin Shu's death in 1924, Zheng Zhenduo wrote an article which gave Lin a fairly objective comment: Lin (together with his cooperator) has translated more than 150 literary works and among them more than 40 were excellent translation but more than two third belonged to the less valuable second or third class works in their original, yet it was through Lin's translations that many Chinese were able to know something about the Western literature and Lin's translation had greatly promoted the status of novel, which had been in a marginal position and was traditionally regarded as something "trivial" in the system of literature in China. Zheng further pointed out that Lin was not right to adapt a play into a novel and often with many additions and deletions, yet Lin should not be the only person to be blamed as he himself understood no foreign languages and his cooperator was also responsible for such faults. Cheng Fangwu wrote a long article criticizing Hu Shi for his criticism of Yu Dafu, saying that Hu Shi's attitude was not that of a scholar and was not discussing questions with the translator criticized. (Chen Fukang 1992; Zhou Jingshan 2003).

Sun Zhili (1999) once gave a detailed study on the literary translation after 1949 when the New China was founded. He says that there have been two periods of flourish of literary translation ever since 1949. One is in the 1950s; the other is the period from the end of 1970s to the present time (when Sun wrote the article). With the flourish of literary translation in the 1950s, there was also the flourish of criticism of literary translation. As the activity of literary translation was well planned and well organized by the government, there came many excellent translations of world classics. However, there were inevitably some poor translations at that time and these led to some hard-hitting comments from some hard-headed critics. For example, one of such articles criticized harshly on the translator Wei Congwu for his irresponsible money-making attitude in translation. Wei translated 12 books within two years. He spent only a month in translating a book of 422 pages and consequently made many ridiculous mistakes. Later, Wei made an open apology for his money-grubbing attitude and his careless working style. The monitoring institution and the publisher also apologized, promising that they will reinforce quality control and no books of poor quality will be published. With the policy of reform and opening to the outside world came the second climax of translation of all text-types including literary translation. But this time, to the disappointment of the readers, though there were many poor translations and many plagiarists in the retranslations of literary classics, there were not as many articles to criticize them. Even if there was an article criticizing the translators and the publishers, it was difficult to get published as journals were afraid of getting into troubles. As a result, poor translations could be seen everywhere in the market and almost all the articles in journals and newspapers were singing praises for some good translations. It is no wonder that serious scholars and critics have been calling for excellent translations.

Though we are not satisfied with the situation of criticism on literary translation in the past years, it was not that we have achieved nothing. In 1995, as has been mentioned in the foregoing chapters, there was a hot debate on different versions of Stendhal's masterpiece *The Red and the Black*, which involved many translators, translation theorists, critics and ordinary readers. People made various comments on topics like faithfulness and recreation, foreignization and domestication, author's style and the translator's style and so on, greatly promoting the development of criticism on literary translation in China.

Out of China, there are also many criticisms of translation events. Lawrence Venuti, for example, criticizes the dominant domesticating strategy in the Anglo-American tradition, especially in America since World War Two. In the diplomatic and business fields, "[t]ranslating and interpreting have served American political and economic interests over the past several decades, enabling the United States to achieve and maintain its pre-eminence in world affairs". In the publishing industry, "American publishers sell translation rights for more and more English-language books, including the global bestsellers, but spend disproportionately less on the rights to publish English-language translations of foreign books", exercising not only the political and economic hegemony, but also cultural hegemony over foreign countries, and choosing only those that can meet American expectations to translate. "In the decades after World War Two, American publishers emphasized a few modern Japanese novelists,…created a well-defined stereotype of Japanese culture (elusive, inconclusive, melancholic) which expressed a nostalgia for a less belligerent and more traditional Japan" (qtd. in Baker 1998/2004: 310-311). Venuti quotes Fowler (1992: 6) to make clear that the novels selected by American publishers "provided exactly the right image of Japan at a time when the country was being transformed, almost overnight in historical terms, from a mortal enemy during the Pacific War to an indispensible ally during the Cold War era". Consequently, Venuti points out that "[a] canon of Japanese fiction was established in English, one that was not simply unrepresentative, excluding comic and proletarian novels among other kinds of writing, but also enormously influential, determining readers' tastes for roughly 40 years" (qtd. in Baker 1998/2004: 310-311).

According to Venuti, besides political motivations, American publishers published translations out of their consideration of commercial profit. Most of the translated books were from European countries and "have had little or no impact on American culture" (ibid). "After British composer Andrew Lloyd Aebber successfully adapted The Phantom of the Opera to the musical theatre, American publishers scrambled to bring out translations of the original (1910) Gaston Leroux novel. When the show opened in New York during 1988 season, as many as four English versions were available in cheap paperback editions" (ibid: 312). Nevertheless, there were exceptions. The 1960s and 1970s saw the boom of Latin American literature marked by its experimentalism. Some Argentine and Columbian writers were translated into English, forming a new canon of foreign literature. The translation of Columbian Garcia Marquez's novel *One Handred Years of Solitude* in 1970 stayed on The New York Bestseller List for several weeks, "alerting the canon of contemporary American literature" (ibid).

Owing to the economic consideration, the strategy of fluent domestication has been dominant since the 1940s in America. This has not only "limited the recognition of translation as a significant cultural practice" but also "led to the marginalization of experimental translations that seek to broaden the translator's discursive repertoire beyond the most familiar forms of English" (ibid: 312). However, there has been "signs that the dominance of fluency is weakening, at least in the case of certain languages and literatures whose peculiarities resist it" in the 1990s (ibid). Venuti remarks that "[t]he questioning of fluent translation may well betoken a greater respect for cultural difference, a new American openness towards foreign languages and literatures that will give translation more authority and improve the status of the translator" (qtd. in Baker 1998/2004: 312). But Venuti further adds that the dominant current in America is still xenophobic.

Another example is Kundera's correction of translations of his own novels by irresponsible translators, editors and publishers. He complained about the misinterpreting, mistranslating of his novels and spent more time in correcting the translations than in writing the originals. He forced the publishers to produce a complete version of his novel *The Joke* in 1970 and asked a new translation, which came out thirteen years later. Snell-Hornby (2006: 107) thinks that this raises questions not only about cultural transfer but also "translation ethics, and the responsibility of translator, editor and publishers towards both the author and readers".

3.3.3 Criticism on translated texts

Criticism on translated texts is the majority of all criticisms. In China, it can be said that most of the existing criticisms belong to this kind. Criticism on translated texts takes different forms, varying in the genre and in the methods adopted by the critics. Most of such criticism focuses on the strategies and methods used by the translator(s), but other aspects such as the purpose(s) of the translator, the impacts of the translated text are also discussed. It can be criticism on a single translation or different versions of one and the same book. It usually involves the systematic or unsystematic comparison between the ST and the TT, but it can also be done without such comparison. If there is more than one version, there is normally the comparison between different versions. Sometimes the whole text is criticized, sometimes only part of it. Critics make comments on the translated from their personal impression or based on different analyses. There have been various linguistic approaches, literary and cultural approaches or hermeneutic approach to the text criticized. Theories of almost all kinds, in fact, can be found to be applied to criticisms on the translated literary texts—semiotics, systemic functional grammar, text linguistics, fuzzy linguistics, narratology, stylistics, reader response, reception aesthetics, psychology of visual art, relevance theory, rewriting, feminism, post colonialism and so on and so forth. As critics come to a translation with different theories and different criteria and again, different foreunderstanding, they often come to different conclusion as to whether the translation is well done or not. Famous examples are the dispute around different versions of Homer's epics and Xu Yuanchong's translation of one of Mao Zedong's poems etc. What should be mentioned is that recent years there have been some corpus-based criticisms on translated texts in China and some other countries which add more objectivity to the evaluative practice.

3.3.4 Criticism on the translator

Criticism on the translator involves comments on the translator's qualifications, his/her working attitude, motivations and purposes, his/ her own style, subjectivity, methods adopted, orientation of language and culture, ideology etc. Criticism on translators separately, as has been pointed out by Yang Xiaorong (2005), is not the dominance of our traditional criticism. There are criticisms on different translators of one and the same literary work, a single translator who has translated different works of one author or different authors, or several translators forming a group and cooperatively translating one book. What we should notice is that criticism on the translator has been often mixed with the other three kinds of criticisms.

3.4 Current Situation and Problems

The above historical review shows that our theoretical studies and practice of criticism of literary translation both in China and in the West have been carried out under the guide of or influenced by different theories. Efforts have been made to make criticism of literary translation systematic and some models have been established. Criteria for criticism of literary translation are becoming more and more plural.

Maier comments that "The co-existence of such numerous and diverse evaluative criteria and approaches offer a challenge to contemporary critics, readers and translators" (qtd. in Baker 1998/2004: 209). Critics have to decide on which criterion to use and "readers and translators must formulate evaluative criteria that will enable them to assess divergent, even contradictory critical evaluations" (ibid). Sir William Jones's translations of Indian literature into English were highly influential in the late eighteenth century. His translations have been studied by different critics recently. Some praised him for his promoting Europeans "to have a new respect for Indian literature", others found that there are many mistakes and his translation can lead to "misrepresentations of the Indian work", and still others, for example, Niranjana and Sengupta, criticized Jones for his "participation, principally through the 'outwork' of his translation, in the construction of the English-language Hindu character, psyche, and way of life", for his "oversimplification of Kalidasa's work that occurred as Jones shaped an 'image' for it that Europeans would find acceptable" (qtd. in Baker 1998/2004: 209). According to Maier, the above is the current situation of criticism on literary translation. Maier's judgment about the current situation of criticism on literary translation is true in China too as can be seen from our review and translation studies and translation criticism in China are greatly influenced by those abroad and many people like following the fashion, especially that of the Westerners.

Lv Jun (2007d) holds that the multi-theories and multi-criteria of translation and translation criticism have brought translation criticism a kind of "crisis": people doubt that whether there exist an objective criticism and if "anything goes", is it necessary for us to have translation criticism? Lv further points out that the "crisis" tells that we need to have a critical rethinking of the approaches we have taken to find the causes of the problems with criticism of literary translation and translation criticism as a whole.

What is more, our review also shows that some of the key terms such as "faithfulness", "equivalenct", "adequacy", "norm" and "*xin*" etc. are being used in different senses, adding on the one hand, confusion to public readers of translation and translation studies scholars, and on the other hand, obstacles to the establishment of the subject of translation criticism of its own right.

3.5 Causes of the Problems

According to Lv Jun (2007d), the problems with criticism of literary translation have something to do with the paradigmatic shifts in translation studies. With the philologist paradigm, both translators and critics believe that the author's intention should be and can be found and transferred faithfully if we know more about the author and try to integrate ourselves into the author. With structuralist paradigm based on structuralism linguistics and analytic philosophy, people believe that the meaning of the original is "out there" in the text and we can safely get to know the meaning of the original and safely transfer it to the target language by means of analyzing and comparing the structure, the semantic meaning of the ST and the TT, and the laws of language transfer. Having got rid of the interference of the author and with the belief that language is a reliable instrument for analysis, translation critics of the structuralist paradigm are making more objective criticisms. But with deconstructionist paradigm based on hermeneutic philosophy, meaning becomes something unstable and the meaning of the text to be translated is also indeterminate without exception. Translators and critics thus have nothing fixed to rely on. There is no "original", no "faithfulness" and no "equivalence" but rather "différance". And consequently, critics turn to factors out of text to seek interpretation of the process of translating and the translated works. Nevertheless, Lv Jun argues that we cannot thus totally negate the deconstructionist paradigm and in fact, it is this paradigm that leads us to a more comprehensive thinking of translation criticism—to take the socio-cultural factors into our consideration. If on the basis of our linguistic analysis and comparison we judge Yan Fu's translation as poor translation, it is unfair to him as his translation had its specific purpose to enlighten the target reader and played a fairly positive role on the reform and advancement of the then society. The problem with our translation criticism actually comes from our understanding of the nature of translation criticism. Criticism in fact should consider both the linguistic and socio-cultural factors and is a kind of value judgment. The critic is to judge the overall values of a translated text, including its artistic value, cultural value, moral value and intellectual value. Consequently, the study of translation criticism should be guided by evaluation theories instead of the linguistic or cultural theories or any translation theory.

The authors of this book think that the challenge the contemporary critics, readers and translators are facing is raised partly by the prevailing thoughts of post-modernism and post-structuralism which are anti-essentialism. It is also partly raised by the lack of systematic study of our criticism of literary translation. What is more, our understanding of criticism of literary translation needs to be deepened. In other words, our perplexity originates from our epistemological problem as well. We are not quite sure and can not come to an agreement about the nature of literature and that of criticism of literary translation owing to the unusual complexity of translation, especially literary translation. Ever since the beginning of translation practice and translation criticism, there have been different ideas of what translation should be. Theodore Savory (1957) once summarized those different opinions as follows:

1. A translation must give the words of the original.

2. A translation must give the ideas of the original.

3. A translation should read like an original work.

4. A translation should read like a translation.

5. A translation should reflect the style of the original.

6. A translation should possess the style of the translator.

7. A translation should read as a contemporary of the original.

8. A translation should read as a contemporary of the translator.

9. A translation may add to or omit from the original.

10. A translation may never add to or omit from the original.

11. A translation of verse should be in prose.

12. A translation of verse should be in verse. (Savory 1957; qtd. in Shen Yuping 2002: 258)

Literary translation is a fairly creative activity by nature. When it comes to judgment of literary translation, people first have again different ideas about literariness and then, polysemy, one of the prominent features of literary texts, together with people's cognitive and interpretive divergence, has made our criticism of literary translation a field of competing comments.

As we have discussed the essence of translation criticism and regard it as evaluation in the foregoing chapters, in the following chapters we will follow Lv Jun's advice and turn to evaluation theories and axiology in general to get a better understanding of criticism of literary translation.

Chapter 4
Axiology and Evaluation: Theoretical Foundation

As has been said at the end of the above chapter, the nature of criticism including criticism on literary translation is evaluation and the study of criticism on literary translation calls for the guide of an evaluation theory. We need here to make clear that the evaluation theory in this context has little to do with the appraisal theory in discourse analysis. Evaluation theories belong to the science of values or axiology. Such as it is, we will come to a general introduction and discussion of axiology, our theoretical foundation.

4.1 The Subject of Axiology

Values have been the objectives of various activities of our human beings. As values are so closely connected with our life, there has been interest in and efforts to understand the nature of them. According to Archie J. Bahm (1993), author of *Axiology: The Science of Values*, axiology is one of the three most general philosophical sciences (metaphysics, epistemology and axiology). Since there are different values, axiology, as the science inquiring into values, actually consists of different value sciences—aesthetics: the science of beauty, ugliness and fine art; ethics: the science of oughtness, duty, rightness and wrongness; religiology: the science inquiring into the ultimate values of life as a whole; and economics: the science of wealth relative to the production, distribution, and consumption of goods etc. Different as they are, they nevertheless share something in common, that is, the judgment of goodness and badness, of success and failure. Therefore, the study of what is value, how we understand value and value judgment have become the main concerns of axiology.

Though values have long been an inseparable part of our human life, and philosophers have touched upon it ever since Plato, according to Risieri Frondizi, there did not exist a value theory a century ago. "While metaphysics and ethics nourished in Ancient Greece, and theory of knowledge started in the 17th century, value theory, also called axiology, was not formulated until the end of the 19th century" (Frondizi 1971: 3).

In China, axiology for a long time was regarded as a branch either of ethics or of epistemology. It was not until the implementation of the policy of reform and opening-up that axiology was given its due position as an independent subject in philosophical study. Li Lianke (2003) says that there was no such a subject before the 1980s. In his book *New Axiology*, Li Deshun (2004) describes the basic structure of philosophy and holds that axiology, just like ontology, epistemology and methodology, is one of the fundamental branches of philosophy.

Bahm (1993) holds that Jeremy Bentham (1748—1832) and John Stuart Mill (1806—1873) are forerunners of modern axiology. The former's contribution is his idea of "calculus of pleasures" and the latter's, the extension of hedonistic pleasures to include mental pleasures with superior quality. Franz Brentano (1838—1917), the founder of intentionalism, also did great contribution to the value theory in the late nineteenth century, emphasizing presentational immediacy as the foundation for value judgments. According to Fang Yongquan (2007), German philosopher Eduard von Hartmann (1842—1906) was the first to use the word "axiology" in the fifth part entitled "Syllabus of Axiology" of his book *System of Philosophy in Outline*. According to Guy Axtell (2009), axiology "has been thought to have its official origin in Austrian/German value theory or Werttheorie as introduced by the economist von Neumann" and by philosophers including Meinong (1853—1920) and Ehrenfels (1859—1932). As a term in English, it "was introduced in Urban's book *Valuation: Its Nature and Laws* after his return from years of graduate study at two German universities identified at the time with the thought of Brentano, Rickert, and Windelband" in 1909. The Greek "axios" means "worth", "logos" means "science", and hence the English word "axiology" means the "science or study of value". In the 20th century, philosophy took an axiological turn with more and more people coming to think that a general theory of value is an absolute necessity, helping us comprehend systematically and scientifically all types of values and the world we live in.

At the end of the 19th century and at the beginning of the 20th century, while epistemology was advancing, axiology began to take shape and grew steadily with the development of phenomenology, made prominent by Edmund Husserl (1859—1938), and with the decline of logical positivism after its heyday in the midcentury.

According to Guy Axtell (2009), early in 1909 W. M. Urban (1873—1952) began to advocate an axiological standpoint on epistemology, trying to establish a value-driven epistemology or an epistemological axiology. Feng Ping and Chen Lichun (2003) hold that Urban's *Valuation: Its Nature and Laws* tried to establish an axiology that is scientific and objective. For Urban, if there is no objectivity, it is hard to establish a general theory of value. Therefore, discussions about the objectivity of value judgments became the critical issue for axiology. Urban holds that though the perception of value and that of knowledge both belong to epistemology, but epistemology can not cover the whole of value judgments and hence the term "axiology" is used and has almost the same meaning as "valuation" or "evaluation" in his book. He believes that the greatest obstacle blocking the study of value is the dichotomy of the so-called empiricism and rationalism, facts and values, appreciation and description. Value judgments actually are both subjective and objective as all values involve the feelings and desires of the subject which are again constrained by various factors in the process which the evaluation takes place in.

Axtell (2009) holds that the gains of analytic epistemology in the latter half of the twentieth century need not be abandoned, but rather set within a new philosophic context— the "value-driven" epistemology. This is actually an effort toward an epistemology in its wider sense which no longer sees the subject as "value-free" and takes both the object and the subject as the research object. And in this sense, we can say that axiology is not exclusive of epistemology and according to Feng Qi, there is an intrinsic unity among ontology, epistemology and axiology (Yang Guorong 2006). Nevertheless, axiology, focusing more on the knowing of value, is a philosophical discourse which is supposed to differentiate from epistemology in its narrow sense that separates subject from object and focuses on "being" rather than "value".

Greatly influenced by modern hermeneutics which emphasizes the qualitatively different understandings involved in intersubjective communication and different interpretations of meaning (compared with the objective understanding we have of the material world) and some schools of postmodern theories which seek a deconstruction of logocentrism, modern axiology shows a tendency of prevailence of relativisim over absolutism. Axiological relativism differs from axiological absolutism in that it accepts the thesis about the ontic dependence of all value on the valuers, considers intrinsic value to be epistemologically dependent on valuers and asserts the "nomological explainability and predictability of differences in valuations between valuers and of changes in valuations by the same valuer" (Norkus 1994: 102).

Here we need a few words about relativism. Relativism rejects absolute or universal standards. There exist relativism in different research fields and thus we have ethical relativism, epistemological relativism and axiological relativism. Epistemological relativism, for instance, views that there are no universal criteria of knowledge or truth. What counts as true is only relative to local cultures, historical periods, or socio-political interests. Ethical or moral relativism holds that there are no objective moral standards. Relativism was advocated as an alternative against positivism.

> Though often welcomed by sociologists in a spirit of tolerance and respect for cross-cultural difference, it is often forgotten that these views have strong historical links with political irrationalism, and (in particular) with European Nazism. It should be remembered that, from the standpoint of a thoroughgoing moral relativism, the values of respect and tolerance themselves have no general validity, but are mere peculiarities of particular, localized moral traditions (for example liberalism). (Scott & Marshall 2005)

The above quotation tells us that though relativism has many merits it is not proper to make relativity absolute. Thoroughgoing relativism can be especially harmful. Paul Feyerabend as a thoroughgoing relativist in his *Against Method* (1975) shows that "for each proclaimed methodological principle of science, an at least equally good case could be made for adopting its opposite" using historical studies of scientific changes as shown in Thomas Kuhn's "paradigm shift" and in this way gives his support to the principle of "anything goes" (Scott & Marshall 2005). However, if anything goes, there may be disaster caused by the misuse of our interests and will, and "the abandonment of reason has been historically no less destructive" (ibid).

One of the modern schools (paradigms) of axiology can be termed "constructive axiology" which differs from the classical axiology in that it prefers the idea of "the values of general significance" to that of "universal values" favoured by classical axiology. Values of general significance are thought to be values accepted by a particular community as necessary for the basic social and cultural functions of this community, amenable to expansion beyond the community to the nation or humanity as a whole, harmless to the other values, principles, sacred things and symbolism of varying cultures and social groups. Ethic values in the framework of each community may be considered as "supreme", "universal", or "central" but they are not obligatory for other communities to regard them as such (Rozov 1998).

The view of constructive axiology on the ethic values obviously accepts ethical relativism. In fact, Confucius's doctrine of the "golden mean" may be helpful in solving the problem of the long-term dispute between the two extremes. A more sound way is to accept relativism without going to any extreme. We should take a dialectical attitude to relativism, recognizing that there is absolutism in relativism in dealing with issues concerning values and evaluations and in our study of axiology.

4.2 Branches of axiology

The above section serves as a general introduction to the development of the subject of axiology. As there have been plural approaches to it, the subject has grown into one with several branches, two of which will be introduced and discussed below.

4.2.1 Ethics

Ethics is also known as moral philosophy and is called the first social science. "When we do moral philosophy, we reflect on how we ought to live. We ask what principles we ought to live by — and why we should follow these principles instead of others. We study various views and try to sort through them rationally" (Gensler, 1998). Ethics is therefore concerned with moral principles and values, with the ideas of "good" and "bad" as they apply to human affairs. According to Bahm (1993: 97), ethics is "a value science because oughtness and rightness are defined in terms of values". Here, the word "science" is used in its broad sense as Scott and Marshall (2005) point out that it is impossible to discover absolute foundations for moral judgements and contemporary ethical thought tends to adopt the view that ethics is contrasted with science.

"Ethics as value theory concerns itself with the evaluation of human conduct, with how human beings ought fundamentally to behave, particularly in relation to one another" (Levinson 2005). Almost all the ancient and modern philosophers show their concern implicitly or explicitly, directly or indirectly, for moral values in their ethics:

Socrates (469—399 BC) is known for his believing that virtue is knowledge and self-knowledge is necessary for success and inherently an essential "good" as anyone who knows what is truly right will automatically do it. Hence, knowledge and self-knowledge are the most valuable things in the universe.

Plato (427—347BC) is an objective idealist. He argues that the Idea of the Good is the eternal source of all existing goodness and all other beings, that the realm of ideas is absolute reality, forming part of The Soul. He believes that the Rational Soul or Thinking or Reason is the basis of the highest virtue of Wisdom; the Spirited Soul or Willing is the basis of the virtue of Courage and the Appetitive Soul or Feeling or Emotion, that of Moderation. Justice as a virtue itself, is the integrity of the above three and is more essential, and hence, more valuable.

Aristotle (384—322 BC) thinks that the value of one's life is to live with conduct governed by moderate virtue, in accordance with his nature and to realize his full potential. That is to say, "self-actualizationism" in doing the right thing, to the right person, at the right time, to the proper extent, in the correct fashion, for the right reason should be highly valued.

Epicurus (341—270BC) holds that the greatest good is prudence, exercised through moderation and caution. To him, excessive indulgence is destructive to pleasure. If one eats one food too often, it will cause him to lose taste for it and eating too much food at once will lead to discomfort and even illness.

Though modern philosophers in the West took an epistemological turn in the 17th century, yet the topic of ethic value was touched upon now and then in their thinking and writing.

Descartes (1596—1650) is regarded as the founder of modern philosophy. He thinks that the difference between good and evil is just like that between truth and fallacy. Thus, good is truth and truth is good.

Spinoza (1646—1716) holds that tolerance is a virtue as value is relative: good and evil is subject to individuals. Yet the freedom of Will must be governed by reason. Therefore, value is both relative and absolute.

David Hume (1711—1776) is the one who first put forward the difference between knowledge of "fact" and that of "value". The fact-value distinction is the distinction between what is (something that can be discovered by science, philosophy or reason) and what ought to be (a judgment which can be agreed upon by consensus). Hume argues that human beings are unable to derive "ought" from "is". As a subjectivist, Hume thought that value doesn't exist separate from us, but rather, it is based on our feelings.

Immanuel Kant (1724—1804) has been regarded as the last influential philosopher of modern Europe in the classic sequence of the theory of knowledge during the Enlightenment movement. Kant's works on epistemology attempt to make a compromise between the empiricists and the rationalists. The empiricists believe that knowledge is acquired through experience alone, but the rationalists maintain that such knowledge is open to doubt and that reason alone provides us with knowledge. Kant argues that reason should always be applied to experience. And in this way, the realm of what "is" and that of what "ought to be" are combined, with the primacy of the "ought", and thus the deep separation between fact and value established by Hume can be bridged (Kolak 2002; Li Lianke 2003).

Throughout the history of ethical philosophy, two main strands (paradigms) can always be found: ethical absolutism and ethical relativism. Ethical absolutism tends to exaggerate the universality and absoluteness of moral value, while ethical relativism holds that there is no common and absolute morality or the generally and absolutely correct morality universal to all societies. Relativists consider value to be epistemologically dependent on valuers. Ethical relativism includes cultural ethical relativism and normative ethical relativism (often shortened to cultural relativism and normative relativism). A dialectic view is that there is special and relative morality because of its specialty and relativity applicable to a certain society, and there is also universal and absolute morality becauseof its universality and absoluteness in application to a certain society (Wang Haiming 2004).

Jürgen Habermas (1929–), the leading contemporary representative of the Frankfurt school, distinguishes three cognitive interests common to human beings: the technical interest in knowing and controlling the world around us, the interest in being able to understand each other and join in common activity, and the interest in removing distortions in our understanding of ourselves, the last of which gives rise to the critical sciences. He is also famous for trying to develop a foundation for ethics in the notion of an ideal speech situation, a "discourse" oriented communicative ethics (Blackburn 1996). The contemporary Kantian ethical conceptions of Habermas form the basis for constructive axiology and in respect of ethical values, it suggests a breadth and tolerance for cultural, moral and religious diversity and requires a valid defense of those values which, having been accepted by communities or individuals, provide security and possibilities for the realization of any value system for themselves and their surroundings (Rozov 1998).

4.2.2 Aesthetics

Aesthetics is a branch of philosophy dealing with the nature of beauty, art, taste and the creation and appreciation of beauty. The Oxford Dictionary of Philosophy defines it as "[t]he study of the feelings, concepts, and judgements arising from our appreciation of the arts or of the wider class of objects considered moving, or beautiful, or sublime" (Blackburn 1996).

Aesthetic theory concerns itself with questions such as: what is a work of art? What makes a work of art successful? Can art be a vehicle of truth? Does art work by expressing the feelings of the artist, communicating feeling, arousing feeling, purging or symbolizing feeling? What is the difference between understanding a work of art, and failing to do so? How is it that we take aesthetic pleasure in surprising things: tragedies, or terrifying natural scenes? Why can things of very different categories equally seem beautiful? Does the perception of beauty have connections with moral virtue, and with seeing something universal or essential, and is the importance of aesthetic education and practice associated with this? What is the role of the imagination in the production or appreciation of art? Are aesthetic judgements capable of improvement and training, and hence of some kind of objectivity? (ibid)

The discussion of beauty and taste can be traced back to ancient Greek philosophers, but the term "aesthetics" was offered by A. Baumgarten (1714—1763), "father of aesthetics" in 1735. "Aesthetics" originates in the Greek word "aisthesis" which means experiencing an object through the senses apart from the intellectual act of interpretation. However, as can be seen from the above quotation, aesthetics is far more than what its Greek origin means. It also involves the analyses of the role of the artist's intention and imagination, of the nature of certain techniques like metaphor or symbolism, of the nature of beauty, sublimity in the form of music, painting or writing, the whole range of critical discourse, and in fact of all the appreciative experiences that may or have prompted the birth of a piece of art (Cooper 2007).

People have had different approaches to aesthetics. Some think that the essence of it is imitation or displaying of aspects of reality, seeking faithfulness to how things are. Others think that art is the expression of feelings and therefore there can be no necessary and sufficient conditions for the formally satisfying or the aesthetically correctness that can be settled once and for all. Some hold that the work of the artist is the creation of the new and creativity should be the central concept of the theory of art and aesthetics, others, like Kant, hold that aesthetic activity is a kind of play and judgements of taste occur in a "free play" of imagination and understanding, an occupation agreeable on its own account. It involves not merely the result of cognitive judgements on the object, but also the ability of the subject to see the aesthetic relationship between the object and the subject. There are also people who argue that works of art are to be appreciated as "object in their own right" and people who think that we cannot appreciate works of art without taking their moral or political or socio-cultural quality into our consideration (ibid).

In the course of the development of aesthetics, there are also turns from ontology to epistemology and then to axiology. In philosophical aesthetics it has proved hard to define features such as integrity, harmony, purity, or fittingness of works "in usefully specific, objective, terms; they are in any event qualities whose apprehension pleases and satisfies us" (Blackburn, 1996). Aesthetics in axiology can then be termed "axiological aesthetics". Axiologically, "beauty" does not purely derive from the object, it is, rather, a relationship, an axiological relationship between the property of the object and the aesthetic needs of the subject (Li Lianke 2003). Axiological aesthetics shows more concern about the subject in practice and views aesthetic experience as a value-production activity, hence, what we human beings get from the aesthetic experience is not simply knowledge of aesthetic properties of an object isolated from the subject (Huang Kaifeng 2001).

Axiological aesthetics has greatly influenced the field of literary studies. Bahm (1993: 96) says that "[s] ince fine art is not only made but also judged, a field of artistic criticism has developed. This field includes many varieties of literary criticism, musical criticism, dramatic criticism,…" The influence of axiological aesthetics on literary criticism comes mainly from the fact that the intuition or the immediate apprehension of the subject's aesthetic experience, reader's participation and response are given special value (Huang Kaifeng 2001). The activity of literary writing is a value-creation activity. It involves inevitably the fact judgments and value judgments of the author. The author's value judgments determine the content and the way of expression of his or her writing. And the realization of the value of a literary text relies on not only the author, but also the reader's participation (Min Ze & Dang Shengyuan 1999).

According to Chen Ming (2005), the historical starting point of axiological aesthetics can be traced back to Arthur Schopenhauer (1788—1860), a pioneer of the so-called voluntarist aesthetics based on the belief of irrationality of human nature. Voluntarist aesthetics comes from Schopenhauer's doctrine of the primacy of the Will as the ground of life and all beings and from his judgment that the Will is evil. For Schopenhauer the Will is an aimless desire and the source of all the sorrow in the world; each satisfied desire leaves us with either boredom or some new desire to take its place. Schopenhauer was among the first 19th philosophers to think that the universe is not a rational place, emphasizing that in the face of a world filled with endless strife and sorrow, we ought to minimize our natural desires to achieve a more tranquil frame of mind and a disposition towards universal beneficence. Schopenhauer believed that aesthetic experiences differ from other experiences in that the contemplation of the object of aesthetic appreciation temporarily allows the author and the reader a respite from desires and sorrows, and to enter a realm of purely mental enjoyment.

Friedrich Nietzsche (1844—1900) was greatly influenced by Schopenhauer. He thinks that beauty is the direct representation of the "Power to Will" (Wang Shunning 2002) and that the development of modern science and the increasing secularization in the world, especially in Europe, has killed the Christian God that has been the basis for meaning and value in the West. One of his famous remarks is "God is dead" and he is often quoted as appealing for the re-evaluation of all values since what should be valued is value in life itself. According to Nietzsche, all values come from the vital impulse of life. In his book *The Birth of Tragedy*, he talks of Apollo and Dionysus in Greek myth: the former standing for reason, logic and order; the latter, fertility, intuition, passion, rebellion and chaos. Nietzsche's idea has been interpreted as an expression of fragmented consciousness or existential instability by a variety of modern and post-modern writers.

Judgment of aesthetic value is made further complicated as it is often closely connected with ethics:

> [M]ost accounts of aesthetic evaluation, and more particularly, the evaluation of art, allow that ethical considerations play a genuine role in such evaluation, one more or less central according to the sort of artwork involved. Thus the ethical perspective embodied in, or conveyed by, a novel or film can be held to be ineliminably relevant to its evaluation as art, because appreciation of the work requires sharing or entering into that perspective to some extent, and yet such engagement might not be merited or justified. (Levinson 2005)

To sum up, axiological aesthetics is quite a complex issue. Besides the coexistence of subjectivity and objectivity of aesthetic judgments, there is also the issue of ethic value involved and in many cases ethic considerarions even play a vital role. And what needs to be mentioned is that the recognition of the aesthetic value and ethic value of an artwork, and the question whether a piece of work can be regardeded as an artwork, all concern with the problem of our capacity and ways of knowing an object and the axiological relationship between the object and the subject. That will inevitably make aesthetic judgment also an epistemological matter, a matter we will have to tend to in our discussion of value judgment as a whole.

To go into every detail about values and axiology is certainly not the objective of this research, nor is it possible for the authors. Therefore, we will not touch upon other branches of axiology such as religiology and economics. For our purpose of taking axiology and evaluation theory as something that can throw light on the study of criticism or evaluation of literary translation, in the following part of this chapter we will concentrate on the introduction of issues such as 1) what value is; 2) the classification of values; 3) evaluation and its nature; 4) types of evaluation; 5) principle of evaluation; 6) criteria for evaluation; 7) methodology of evaluation; 8) features of evaluation and criteria for evaluation and 9) criteria for evaluating an evaluation etc.

4.3 Value and Its Nature

What value is is the most essential question that axiology has to answer. Cambridge of International Dictionary of English defines it as "the importance or worth of something for someone". Historically, people have different ideas about what value is and where value is.

Wilhelm Windelband (1848—1915) was the leader of the German school of neo-Kantianism. He held that there could be no value without the subject's will and feeling.

Franz Brentano (1838—1917) argued that values are rooted in human emotions, in the contrast between favorable and unfavorable, between love and hate. Values are our attitudes toward objects and events (George 2003). His student Alexius Meinong (1853—1920) further elaborated his idea of value holding that "a value emotion is neither independent of publicly verifiable (scientific) fact, as Lotze claims, nor reducible to fact: It is a subjective feeling that can be judged to be reasonable or not by reference to the relevant facts" (ibid).

Li Lianke (2003) holds that value comes from practice. It is the relationship between the object and the subject. Value is the objectization of the subject and the subjectization of the object.

Li Deshun (2004) once summarized the existing views on value. The objective idealists hold that value is value itself, it exists independent of anything, beyond our human being and our life and beyond everything in the world. It is the ultimate objective, the final ideal and the absolute criterion of our human beings. This view of value has the obvious tinge of religious mysticism. Some people think that value is the object that possesses value, while others hold that value is the innate properties of an object that can meet the demands of our human beings and bring us pleasure, thus value is not the object itself but the properties attached to the object. Beauty, for example, does not exist by itself, but rather, embodied in some physical object.

Opposite to the view of value "entity", some people hold that value is something totally subjective, only existing in the interest, desire or emotion of the subjects. That is to say, value exists in evaluation. This view of value has the tendency to ignore the objective foundation of value and is liable to make value undefinable. Different from the above views, Li Deshun, similar to Li Lianke, holds that value refers to the process, result and extent of the subjectization of the object and is the unity of the subject and the object with the subject functioning as the yardstick. They both believe that value is objective but is not any dependent entity, nor the innate properties of the entity. Value exists in the interactive relationship between the object and the subject. Therefore, it is not simply the interest or needs of the subject either, but the product of the combination of the two, that is to say, value, in essence, is both objective and subjective (Li Deshun 2004). In brief, value, as the Cambridge of International Dictionary of English defines, is the importance or worth of something for somebody, hence, it involves an object and a subject and is the relationship between the two.

4.4 Classification of Values

Since value is a relationship between the object and the subject, it is hard to decide whether we should classify it from the perspective of the object or that of the subject. And in reality, people make different classifications for the sake of systematic study.

Bahm (1993) distinguishes twelve kinds of values in six pairs: 1) good and bad; 2) ends and means; 3) subjective and objective values; 4) apparent and real values; 5) actual and potential values; 6) pure and mixed values. Good and bad are non-contradictory opposites, but rather of relative, relative to other being and relative to its earlier or later being. This is seen from the words like "good", "better", "best" and "bad", "worse" and "worst" in our language. Good and bad are conceived as varying by degrees. Ends and means is the most important distinction necessary for understanding values. "Ends, that is, ends-in-themselves, are called intrinsic values because their value is contained within themselves. Means, that is, means to ends-in-themselves, are called instrumental values because their values derive from their usefulness in bringing about or maintaining intrinsic values" (Bahm 1993: 40). But to distinct the two this way, one may find that "some, possibly all, things that have intrinsic value also have instrumental value, and some things that have instrumental value also have intrinsic value" (ibid). We can distinguish objective values from subjective ones, but we need first to know what is meant by "subjective" and "objective". "To be objective is to be an object of attention. Analyses of experience normally distinguish a subject as that which attends and an object as that which is attended to" (Bahm 1993: 62). Thus, some intrinsic values are both subjective and objective at the same time. As when you exercise your body, you observe what you are doing and to identify your doing it with yourself as a subject, intrinsic goods and evils are experienced as both subjective and objective. Likewise, some instrumental values are both subjective and objective at the same time, but most instrumental values are neither subjective nor objective because they exist beyond experience. According to Bahm (ibid: 64-65), "[a]xiology as a science of values remains inadequate as long as the epistemology, the science of knowledge, used by the axiologist remains inadequate. An adequate theory of values involves an adequate theory about apparently real values and about real values" and difficulties in keeping clear distinctions between apparent and real values are sources of popular and professional confusion about values. What is more, most intrinsic values are experienced as mixed and blended in many different ways and the primary task of the axiologist is to understand values in general, especially intrinsic and instrumental values.

Here we need to say a few more words about intrinsic and instrumental values. Intrinsic value is an ethical value that an object has "in itself" or "for its own sake", while instrumental value (or extrinsic value) is the value which can generate intrinsic value. Something is of intrinsic value if it is good or desirable in itself; and it is of instrumental value if it can be a means to some other end or purpose. For example, music is regarded as worth having in itself and for itself while a radio is of instrumental value as it is worth having in order to enjoy music. Intrinsic and instrumental values are not mutually exclusive. For example, "receiving education" may be both worthwhile in itself and as a means of achieving other values.

Some axiologists also distinguish relative intrinsic value and absolute intrinsic value, regarding the former as subjective, varying from individual to individual and from culture to culture and the latter, independent of individual and cultural views.

However, there has been an ongoing debate as to whether there exists an absolute intrinsic value or not. John Dewey's empirical approach does not accept intrinsic value as an inherent or enduring property of things, but rather as an illusory product of our continuous ethic valuing activity. That is to say, goods are only intrinsic relative to a situation and there is only relative intrinsic value.

What is more, value can be classified according to specific research fields. There can be ethical value, sociological value, aesthetic value and economic value etc. Ethics tends to be focused more on moral goods than natural goods and often regards moral value as a unique and universally identifiable property, an absolute value rather than a conditional relative value. Sociologically, there are personal values popularly held by an individual or a community, subject to changes under particular conditions. Different groups of people may hold or prioritize different kinds of values that influence their social behavior. Economic value exists necessarily, according to Karl Marx, as our human beings are social and moral beings that must cooperatively produce and economize their means of life to survive, and in so doing subject to a certain relation of production.

The above discussion of the classification of values may make readers who have not much knowledge of axiology a little perplexed. Yet, it is significant for people to get a comprehensive understanding of values. Li Lianke (2003) once offered us a more clear-cut classification. He distinguishes material value from spiritual value. The former is further classified into natural value and economic value depending on whether it is naturally shaped or man-made. The latter is further divided into intellectual value, moral value and aesthetic value.

4.5 Name of Evaluation

Evaluation is actually one of the important elements of axiology. But as it is extremely essential for our concern about criticism of literary translation, we prefer to give it a position parallel to that of axiology as a whole. Another reason for such an arrangement is that evaluation in reality is often taken as a profession and consequently, it is both an axiological issue and a professional issue.

To evaluate, as Cambridge International Dictionary of English (2004) defines, is "to judge or calculate the quality, importance, amount or value of (something)". The term "evaluation" can refer to an outcome of the activity of an assessment. It can also refer to the process of the activity of assessment and as stated in the above paragraph, it can be used to refer to a profession as well.

According to Li Deshun (2004: 214), evaluation is assessment and judgment. It is the comparison of values and the main intellectual form of measuring values by human beings.

According to Li Lianke (2003: 104), evaluation is the reflection of value which is the relationship between the object and the needs of the subject.

Feng Ping in her book *On Evaluation* points out that "human cognition has two different orientations: one is to reveal what the world is, the other is to reveal the meaning and the value of the world....The former can be called knowledge, and the latter, evaluation". Feng argues that evaluation can be defined among various human activities "a cognitive activity with a purpose of reforming the world (a step further than knowing the world)" (Lv Jun 2007d: 262-263)

Chen Xinhan (2000) argues that evaluation falls into the category of epistemology. Logically, the activity of cognition comes before that of evaluation but from the perspective of epistemological genetics, evaluation comes first. However, in practice, it is hard to know exactly which is in the first place.

Most of the Chinese scholars think that evaluation is the reflection of value (relationship) and a special form of cognition aiming mainly to form value judgments (Chen Xinhan 2000; Xiao Xinfa 2004).

Su Fuzhong (2001) holds that evaluation is a purposeful cognition under the premise of the cognition of the object to be evaluated and with a certain criterion for measurement. And evaluation does not confine to value judgment.

C. I. Lewis (1883—1964), seeking to make value theory scientific, argues that "evaluations are a form of empirical knowledge. Their truth or falsity, is determined in exactly the same way as the truth or falsity of any other kind of empirical knowledge is justified" (George 2003). Lewis is obviously referring to the outcome of an assessment.

Bahm (1993: 69) thinks that evaluation is making evaluative judgments and "[e]valuative judgments express beliefs about comparisons of values that exist".

Matarasso (1996: 3) defines evaluation as "the process of calculating worth" and "a process which we carry out continuously" with its difficulty arising from the essentially relative nature of worth.

Some people essentially "equate evaluation with other concepts such as research or testing", others state that "evaluation involves comparing objectives and outcomes", and still others "call for a much broader conceptualization involving combined study of performance and values" (Stufflebeam & Shinkfield, 1985: 3).

Davidson (2005: 20) holds that "[e]valuation is something that prudent individuals, groups, organizations, and countries make a point of doing as part of good quality management". She says also that

> Evaluation, however, is much more than "applied social science research". Evaluation, as the term implies, involves not only collecting descriptive information about a program, product, or other entity but also using something called "values" to (a) determine what

information should be collected and (b) draw explicitly evaluative inferences from the data, that is, inferences that say something about the quality, value, or importance of something. Put another way, research can tell us "what's so", but only evaluation can tell us "so what". (Davidson 2005: xi)

Professionally, the definition by the Joint Committee on Standards for Educational Evaluation is: "Evaluation is the systematic assessment of the worth or merit of some object" (Stufflebeam & Shinkfield 1985: 3), whereas American Evaluation Association defines evaluation as "assessing the strengths and weaknesses of programs, policies, personnel, products, and organizations to improve their effectiveness". (http://www. evaluationwiki.org/index.php/Evaluation_Definition:_What_is_Evaluation%3F).

All professional evaluations are supposed to use data collected in a systematic manner. These data may be quantitative or qualitative. Successful evaluations often involve both kinds (Stufflebeam & Shinkfield 1985: 3).

As a brief summary, we can say that evaluation can be viewed both as a process and an outcome of an assessing program. It can also be viewed as profession. Broadly speaking, evaluation can be knowledge and judgments of everything and in its narrow sense, it only refers to the knowing (or knowledge) and the judging (or judgments) of the value(s) (or value relationship). That is to say, evaluation in its narrow sense means making value judgments. In this dissertation, evaluation is normally used in its narrow sense except stated otherwise.

A judgment usually takes the form of a sentence or a statement. Logical positivists embrace the principle of verification concerning the linguistic meaning of a sentence. This principle says that a sentence is strictly meaningful only if it expresses something that can be confirmed or disconfirmed by empirical observation. By the principle of verification logical positivists drive the problems of value out of the realm of philosophy as in the eyes of logical positivists, an axiological statement is only the expression of one's feelings and emotions which can not be verified as truth or falsity. However, there are exceptions. John Dewey (1859—1952), for example, accepts the principle of verification but disapproves logical positivism's anti-value theory and argues for the verifiability of value judgment, defending the validity of philosophical study on problems of value (Feng Ping 2006). The throughgoing logical positicism seems problematic especially when value judgment is concerned. Supposing all axiological judgments are meaningless, what are people doing when they say kindness is good and cruelty is bad? In a broad sense, "[e] very human action, implicitly or explicitly, is an expression of value or an assertion of preference" as "[w] ithout sets of values, all human actions are equally significant or equally meaningless" (Meehan, 1969: 25). A tentative definition of value judgment offered by Meehan (ibid: 28) is "an expression of preference or a choice among real options".

To get a better understanding of evaluation, and to seek a methodologically reliable approach to the evaluation of literary translation, we will cover the axiological and professional discussion, the theoretical-oriented and practical-oriented researches on evaluation in this book.

4.6 Nature of Evaluation

Most of the above definitions of evaluation say something about the nature of evaluation, but to get a clearer picture, we need a more detailed analysis. Davidson (2005: 1) says that "[i]n terms of the evolution of the human race, evaluation is possibly the most important activity that has allowed us to evolve, develop, improve things, and survive in an ever-changing environment". For some people, evaluation essentially is a form of empirical knowledge, whereras for others it is a special form of knowledge. However, we should realize that, as Davidson has put it,

[T]he special thing about evaluation—the part that makes it different from (and harder than) descriptive research—is that it involves more than simply collecting data and presenting results in "value-neutral" (i.e., purely descriptive) terms. Evaluation involves applying values to descriptive data so as to say something explicit about the quality or value of the evaluand in a particular context. (Davidson 2005: 85)

In other words, as can be seen from the definitions given by many Chinese scholars, evaluation is essentially an epistemological activity that is closer to human practice aiming at reforming the world or creating values. It is an advanced form of epistemic activity based on our cognition of the world and goes beyond it. The implication is, as Matarasso (1996: 9) puts it, that "evaluation is itself a part of the creative, artistic process" which is carried out continuously. To put it another way, evaluation bears some common traits with epistemic activity, but it has also its own peculiarities. To make clear the distinction and connection between the two, we may have a look at epistemology, the study of knowledge.

Epistemology as a branch of philosophy concerns mainly how we know what we know and how can we distinguish true knowledge from false knowledge. Epistemology is generally characterized by a division between two competing schools of thought: rationalism and empiricism. Disputes between rationalists and empiricists centre especially on the possibility of innate knowledge, of knowledge acquired a priori, independent of experience. Empiricism or positivist epistemology denies such a priori, holding that human mind is a blank sheet until marked by the impressions of sensory experience and truth is our objective understanding we have of the material world which can be verified or proved to be correspondent to the object. The anti-positivists argue that some conceptual or theoretical framework must be presupposed in any empirical research or factual judgement, and that there may be several competing conceptual frameworks or models, and no neutral standpoint can be found from which to adjudicate between them. Such an argument leads to epistemological reletivism. Another similar argument emphasizes the qualitatively different form of fore-understanding and understanding involved in intersubjective communication and the interpretation of meaning as in phonomenology and hermeneutics. According to such arguments, truth can only be a certain consensus arrived at by means of dialogues between the reader and the text, between the subject and the object. With the linguistic turn of philosophy and epistemology, while logical positivists insist that all knowable truths are either analytic or empirical and there is no room for the synthetic a priori, some deconstructionists, however, believe that we have no direct access to the realities about which our theories claim to provide knowledge. Some form of conceptual or linguistic ordering is necessary for even the most basic reports of our experiences or observations. We cannot step outside of language or discourse to check whether our discourse correspond to reality. Such a conclusion leads to radical or absolute relativism and makes the correspondence theory of knowledge totally unacceptable. Nevertheless, to avoid the state of chaos with epistemology, social constructivism sees consensus between different subjects as the ultimate criterion to judge knowledge. "Truth" will be given only to those constructions on which most people of a social group agree. Consensus theory of truth hence denies the possibility of criteria for truth claims outside the process of intersubjective communication (Hamlyn 2005; Scott & Marshall 2005).

Yu Zhenhua (2007) thinks that since the mid 20th century, there has been an important line of thought in Western philosophy which argues that inadequacy of traditional epistemology lies in the fact that it focuses only on "knowing-that" which pays more attention to the product of our cognition and is blind to "knowing-how" which sees cognition as a process in human practice. Influenced by the later Wittgenstein (1889—1951) there was a pragmatic turn in epistemology, a practice oriented approach to the theory of knowledge. John Dewey holds that "[v]aluation takes place whenever a problematic situation exists, whenever an expected enjoyment is blocked" (George 2003). That speaks well for his pragmatic standpoint: evaluation is to solve problems in practice.

Epistemology, like any research field, and as can be seen from the above introduction, is developing in the West and in China as well. Feng Qi holds that epistemology has its broad sense and its narrow sense. In its narrow sense epistemology is featured by different forms of positivism. In its broad sense, epistemology is the integrity of ontology, epistemology, methodology and axiology, including not only the perception of object in the outside world but also the subject itself (Chen Xiaolong 2005; Yu Zhenhua 2007).

Ren Ping (2000) argues that with the pragmatic turn there came a communicative and intersubjective turn in epistemology and in philosophy as a whole. An ideal approach is to set up an epistemology in its wider sense, taking a communicative and pragmatic turn in our philosophical study. Ren Ping in two of his books *Principle of Epistemology in Its Broad Sense* and *Communicative Practice and Intersubjectiveness* argues that traditional subject-object dichotomy, together with the subject-subject model of the postmodernists, should be replaced by a subject-object-subject framework to establish a new rationalism which can overcome the shortcomings of the other two (Fang Wentao 1999).

Lv Jun (2007d: 200-201) from the perspective of translation studies also analyzes the shortcomings of the above-mentioned subject-object dichotomy and the subject-subject model, emphasizing that only epistemology in its wider sense can be used as the foundation of a constructive Translation Studies, for such an epistemology, unlike epistemology in its narrow sense, put the individual subject in the structure of the social activity and views it as a subject in the communicative relationship with the subject of social groups as a whole. In the framework of epistemology in its wider sense there naturally exist the cognition of the object, the dialogue among different subjects and necessarily, the constrains of social institutions and social norms.

To sum up, we can say that evaluation does not fall into the category of traditional epistemology or epistemology in its narrow sense. It goes to the broader field of axiology which does not deny epistemology in its wider sense (a new paradigm) that embraces the consensus theory of knowledge, capturing the essence of the subjectivity of our cognition in evaluation, without giving up the objectivity of knowledge. As a category of axiology, evaluation is a creative social constructive activity or process concerning both our knowledge about something in general, value in particular, and our judgment of various values. From the perspective of system theory, axiology is not, and can not be totally isolated from other branches of philosophy such as ontology, epistemology and methodology, but rather, it is closely connected with them. As Lv Jun (2007c) points out that in axiology, epistemology is still very important, for if we can not explore and find the essence and laws of the object, we can not change it to meet the needs of the subject. Axiologically, what we want to know is mainly the value-relationship between the subject and the object for the purpose of acquiring greater value. Evaluation as comment on and judgments of values is both subjective and objective.

4.7 Types of Evaluation

For Meehan (1969: 28), a clear distinction should be made between a reasoned choice or judgment and a direct reaction or purely emotional response. Though emotional response is an important part of human life, and plays a part in value judgment, it cannot alone provide an adequate basis for evaluation as it involves no intervening calculations and has no cognitive dimension. "A judgment, on the other hand, implies a reasoned selection, a calculation of costs, a weighing of alternatives in terms of some sort of standard or ideal".

Similar to Meehan, Bahm (1993) argues that we should distinguish two common kinds of value judgments: valuative and evaluative. Valuative judgments express beliefs about the existence of values. Examples are: "this picture is beautiful" or "this chair is comfortable". Evaluative judgments express beliefs about comparisons of values that exist. Examples are: "this picture is more beautiful than that one" or "this chair is much more comfortable than that one". Bahm at the same time admits that "[k]eeping such a distinction in mind is difficult because, in practical experience, the enjoying of values, and both valuative and evaluative judgments, intermingle and flow together in lively occasions" (Bahm 1993: 69-70). Actually, the authors of this book think that all value judgments involve a certain comparison; some of them are implicit and others explicit. Here, in Bahm's valuative judgment, for instance, the comparison is implicit.

Michael Scriven (1991: 169; 340) distinguishes formative evaluation from summative evaluation. The former "is typically conducted *during* the development or improvement of a program or product (or person, and so on) and it is conducted, often more than once, *for* the in-house staff of the program *with the intent to improve*", the latter "is conducted *after* completion of the program ... and *for* the benefit of some *external* audience or decision maker". The terms formative and summative evaluation were originally put forward when talking about curriculum evaluation, but they have been widely adopted both inside and outside the educational community and may mean differently by different people in different contexts.

House and Howe (1999: 6) stress the difference between professional and non-professional evaluation. In their book *Values in Evaluation and Social Research* they first define what they mean by the term "value"—"the worth of a thing" and then, adopt the definition of evaluation from Scriven: "the determination of the worth, merit, or 'value' of something, particularly in the professional evaluation of products, programs, policies, and performance (Scriven, 1991)". They admit that there are different concepts of "value" and therefore, in their book, when they use the term "value", sometimes they refer to "value conclusions rationally determined" and sometimes, "preferences, beliefs, interests, and so on that are not subject to strong evidential support". According to House and Howe, "professional evaluation requires deliberation and is not based on unreflective cherishing or desiring".

What is also notable is that House and Howe (1999: 7) regard that "fact and value statements merge together on a continuum". The fact-value dichotomy from Hume holds that facts and values are separate different things and that values cannot be derived from facts. However, according to House and Howe, all our statements can be value-laden and facts and values are often mingled with each other, forming a continuum. "Whether a claim counts as a brute fact or bare value or something in between depends partly on context". And "[p]rofessional evaluative statements fall toward the center of the fact-value continuum for the most part". They say again that "[t]he context often determines whether statements are evaluative, and statements can be descriptive and evaluative at the same time" (ibid: 8).

Evaluation is normally thought to take three forms: process, outcome, and impact evaluation. Process evaluation describes and assesses program materials and activities. Examination of materials is likely to occur while programs are being developed. Outcome evaluation "assesses program achievements and effects". It studies "the immediate or direct effects of the program on participants". Impact evaluation looks "beyond the immediate results of policies, instruction, or services to identify longer-term as well as unintended program effects" (http://www. evaluationwiki.org/index.php/Evaluation_Definition:_What_is_Evaluation%3F). There are other scholars who tend to add a meta-evaluation which is the evaluation of a given evaluation.

According to Ma Junfeng (1999), evaluation can be divided into many kinds:

economic, moral, aesthetic, intellectual, individual, social, pre-activity, post-activity, comprehensive and specific etc. Each of them has its own particularity (criterion) and there are also generalities shared by all of them.

Ma Junfeng (1994) holds that social evaluation is the evaluation with the society as the subject, but Chen Xinhan (1997) argues that we should take certain social groups as the subject. The authors of this book think that their difference lies only in the scope and no essential discrepancy exists between them. Feng Ping (1995) thinks that social evaluation has three basic forms: institutional assessment, public opinion and the opinion of the media. All these discussions, have, no doubt, helped us get a better understanding of evaluation.

4.8 Objevtives of Evaluation

According to Davidson (2005), generally speaking, evaluations are conducted for one or two main reasons: to find areas for improvement and/or to generate an assessment of overall quality or value.

Davidson (ibid: 1) says that "[i]n terms of the evolution of the human race, evaluation is possibly the most important activity that has allowed us to evolve, develop, improve things, and survive in an ever-changing environment". This speaks well for the importance and function of evaluation.

Stufflebeam and Shinkfield (1985: 3) hold that while evaluation may employ procedures to obtain dependable and unbiased information, it is not value-free. "On the contrary, its essential goal is to determine the value of whatever is being assessed. … if a study does not report how good or bad something is, it is not evaluation". From the above-said, we can infer that one of the most essential objectives of evaluation is to tell not only in what way and to what extent something is good but also in what way and to what extent something is bad.

Meehan (1969: vii) holds that the purpose of evaluation is not only to make value judgments, but also to improve human performance. He stresses the practical orientation of evaluation by quoting Marx that "heretofore the philosophers have only interpreted the world, the important thing is to change it".

Feng Ping (1995) holds that the objective of evaluation is to reveal the meaning and the value of the world and to change the world.

Xiao Xinfa (2004) argues that the purpose of our human evaluation is to seek not only the "truth", but also "goodness" and "beauty" and to create value, meeting the needs of human life and social development.

In brief, though in reality evaluation may have various purposes depending on the specific situation, generally speaking, the objective of it is to reveal the meaning of the world and the value or value relationship existing. It is to tell good from bad, to solve problems, to better our practice, and to create greater value.

4.9 Principles of Evaluation

To make evaluation scientific, we surly need a sound principle as our guideline. In this respect, principles proposed by many scholars are very insightful. However, the discussions by Meehan, Matarasso, House and Howe in the West, and Lv Jun in China are especially inspiring.

Meehan (1969: 6) says that,

Value judgments, like explanations, are created to fulfill human purposes. They depend absolutely on empirical evidence and rational calculation.... While the content of the postulates needed for value judgment is different from the content of the postulates used in explanation, the forms and processes are the same and the role of empirical evidence and rational calculation is prime.

Meehan (1969: 6) thinks that the gap between fact and value is misconstrued and that value and fact should be welded into "an integral unit that is broken only analytically". He holds that in doing value judgments, we should reject idealism as "the kind of absolute, universal rules that it demands are beyond man's capacity to establish" (ibid: 7). Emotivism should also be "rejected as the sole basis for ethics because the results of emotional response are not sufficiently stable to provide a useful standard of choice or action" (ibid). What is more, "[r]igid empiricism or 'scientism' will not do because it denies even the possibility of defending value judgments by reasoned argument and leads eventually to normative 'know-nothingism'" (ibid).

Matarasso (1996: 7-8) shows more concern for the ethical principle. He thinks that a set of principles developed in educational assessment in America can be adapted to the context of arts workers in social contexts. Those adapted principles are: 1) due process, which means that procedures and standards used in evaluation must be reasonable, known and applied consistently; 2) privacy, which says that the information about an individual should be confidential, used in ways known to the person, and should be limited to job-related aspects of his activities; 3) equality, which means decisions should not be made on irrelevant grounds (e.g. gender, ethnicity etc.); 4) public perspicuity, meaning that the evaluation processes should be open to the public; 5) humaneness, referring to the consideration of feelings of those involved in evaluation processes; 6) client benefit, i.e. the interests of the "client"; 7) artistic freedom; and 8) respect for autonomy, which means individuals are entitled to exercise reasonable professional judgement in regard to their work and if the values of different clients are irreconcilable, make it clear to avoid latent conflict.

The discussion of House and Howe (1999) is quite helpful for professional evaluation. In their book *Values in Evaluation and Social Research* House and Howe give a detailed review of different assumptions about value and evaluation and suggest that we adopt a deliberative democratic principle.

A list of conflicting ideas and advice for evaluation is as follows:

1.Evaluators should be value-neutral.

2.Evaluators should be advocates for certain groups.

3.Evaluators should treat all stakeholder views as equally worthy.

4.Evaluators should weigh and balance stakeholder views.

5.Evaluators should admit all stakeholder views as legitimate.

6.Evaluators should take the views of the sponsors of the study.

7.Evaluators should engage in dialogue with stakeholders.

8.Evaluators should remain aloof from stakeholders.

9.Evaluators should act only as facilitators.

10.Evaluators should draw conclusions in their studies.

11.Evaluators should not draw conclusions.

12.Evaluators should draw partial conclusions.

13.Values determine methodology.

14.Values have nothing to do with methodology.

15.Values are subjective.

16.Values are objective. (House & Howe 1999: xiii-xiv)

House and Howe point out that these different opinions stem from different conceptions and assumptions of value and evaluation. Logical-positivists make a distinction between facts and values. Their fact-value dichotomy view holds that evaluators can legitimately or objectively determine facts as facts have to do with the real world but can not do so with values as values have to do with worth humans place on factual situations and are subjectively chosen by the subject involved, hence can not be reached by rational determination. In this case, evaluators can only make evaluative statements based on client values and can not criticize those values or they can try to find evidence to make their claims correspond to values of the client. House and Howe do not think this logical-positivist view can work as a basis for professional evaluation.

Interpretivists share a "constructivist view" which regards knowledge as actively constructed through interaction and dialogue which is culturally and historically grounded and laden with moral and political values, often serving particular interests. While this view in general denies the fact-value dichotomy and is more acceptable, the individual or radical constructivist view should be rejected. Radical constructivists give privileged positions to insiders and exclude the outsider perspectives in evaluation, ignoring the fact "that insiders may well be wrong or biased in their interpretations" just as the outsiders might be (House & Howe 1999: xviii), holding that both facts and values are subjectively chosen by the individual to form a world of his own and therefore, everything is relative to the individual. Obviously, the radical constructivist view is not proper to function as the basis of professional evaluation.

Postmodernists, seeing public knowledge and professional expertise as oppressive in general and in their seeking to deconstruct the logo-centrism, undermine any value judgments, including their own. Consequently, there is no position for a scientific evaluation except radical relativism that claims "anything goes". Therefore, it can not serve as the proper basis for evaluation either (House & Howe 1999: xix).

For House and Howe, a preferable view is the deliberative democratic view which "is dialogical but, unlike radical constructivism, it does not assume that insiders are always correct". And "[u]nlike postmodernism, it employs public criteria to evaluate and contribute to public knowledge" (ibid).

According to House and Howe, facts and value statements are not dichotomous, but rather melded together, existing on a continuum and blending into one another, hardly to be fully distinguished from each other. "This is especially true of evaluative statements and the concepts from social research that evaluators often employ" (ibid: xvi). They argue that "Evaluative statements consist of fact and value claims intertwined" (House & Howe 1999: xv) and "evaluators can draw objective value conclusions by collecting and analyzing evidence and following the procedures of their professional discipline" (ibid). They believe that "[s]uch a view legitimates professional activities and opens the way to a stronger social role for evaluation" and "provides evaluation with more authority in public decision making, a much-needed service in contemporary society" (ibid).

House and Howe actually are talking about different paradigms in evaluation studies. The deliberative democratic view proposed by House and Howe is identical with the social constructivism which we think proper to adopt as the foundation of evaluation and of Translation Studies. It also echoes Habermas' theory of communicative action in a way, advocating the consensus theory of knowledge. Therefore, we will accept most of the principles of evaluation based on this deliberative democratic view.

Some general principles of evaluation based on the deliberative democratic view can be summed up as follows:

"Evaluations should meet three explicit requirements: inclusion, dialogue, and deliberation" (House & Howe 1999: xx). "Inclusion" means we should consider the interests and opinions of all major parties involved in the evaluation. "Dialogue" means that we should allow the authentic interests and opinions represented and interacted in the process of evaluation. "Deliberation" means that we should use sufficiently the expertise of evaluators. "When the evaluation meets such requirements, as well as those typically associated with proper data collection and analysis, we call the study democratic, impartial, and objective" (ibid).

Other principles are:

"Evaluators should not ignore imbalances of power or pretend that dialogue about evaluation is open when it is not". In other words, evaluators should strive to remedy the unequal power relationships between different parties among their dialogue for the adjudication of public value claims. At the same time, "[e]valuators should not assume that all group opinions are equally correct" (ibid: xix-xx).

"Evaluators do not have to consider all criteria or all potential audiences, only those relevant to a particular time and place in a particular context" (House & Howe 1999: xvi-xvii).

Lv Jun (2007a) from another perspective also put forward some principles of evaluation which we think quite insightful and significant for the practice of evaluation.

Through his detailed analysis of the relationship between subject and object in the cognitive activity, Lv Jun argues that evaluation activity is a complicated process which involves both subject-object relationship as that in traditional epistemology which gives priority to objective principle and minimizes the involvement of the subject and the subject-object relationship as that in epistemology in its wider sense which sees subject as part of the object and calls for a subjective principle. Lv Jun further points out that the two seemingly different cognitive forms cannot be clearly distincted and separated in evaluation in reality. Subject is always there in all our cognitive activities especially in human and social sciences. To get a valid and a comprehensive value statement, we must take both objective principle and the subjective principle into our consideration. In evaluation, the subjective principle does not deny the objective principle, rather, the former entails the latter. Therefore, we should put more weight on the subjective principle, guarding against, at the same time, going to the extreme of radical relativism as the deconstructionists do.

According to Lv Jun (2007a), one way to avoid going to any extreme, especially that of deconstructionism, is to combine the subjective principle with the normative principle. The subjective principle in evaluation is closely connected with the individual's needs and the needs of the individual may vary from person to person and have the character of diversity and fluxion. Such characteristics are the main factors leading to the negative view of the deconstructionists on evaluation and objective criteria of evaluation in particular. Nevertheless, deconstructionists have neglected a fact that any individual is an individual of a society which has great influence on his beliefs and ways of behaviour owing to the cultural tradition shared by all members of the society. And as a member of the society, the individual's needs, either material or spiritual, are inevitably influenced and to an extent determined by the society he lives in and by the human nature he shares with his race. That is to say, an individual's view on value is not totally decided by himself and is shaped in a certain degree by the community. What is more, any society has its laws and norms which require its members to observe. If an individual's needs are unlawful or irrational, and hence unacceptable by the society, his needs will surly be judged as unreasonable and be criticized and even expelled by the society. This means that the subjective principle must be modulated and constrained by the normative principle.

"In sociology a norm is a shared expectation of behaviour that connotes what is considered culturally desirable and appropriate. Norms are similar to rules or regulations in being prescriptive, although they lack the formal status of rules" (Scott & Marshall 2005). Chen Xinhan (1995:155) says that, "norms are the crystallization of the basic views on value of a society". Norms can be found in each society and in the individual's view on value, and therefore have the property of objectiveness. The combination of subjective principle with normative principle is bound to give evaluation the character of objectiveness.

In brief, evaluation, according to Lv Jun (2007a), should adhere to the integrity of the objective principle, the subjective principle and the normative principle.

The authors of this book hold that to fulfill the objectives of evaluation and to make our evaluation more scientific, we can adopt the principles proposed by Meehan, Matarasso, House and Howe and those by Lv Jun as our guideline.

4.10 Criteria for Evaluation

For the purpose of carrying out a scientific evaluation, besides sound principles, we need, among many things, the criteria for value judgments. Yet, there have been many different arguments about value and different criteria for value judgments since the ancient times. As the criteria of value judgments are closely connected with people's views on value, we have already touched upon the issue of criteria for value judgments in the section on "value and its nature". To avoid unnecessary repetition, in this part we will only talk of one or two of the criteria given by the ancient and modern philosophers and concentrate on criteria given by the contemporary.

Ancient philosopher Protagoras (490—420 BC or 481—411BC) is most famous for his saying that "Man is the measure of all things: of things which are, that they are, and of things which are not, that they are not" (Li Lianke 2003: 24). This idea has become an important foundation of those later subjectivists in axiology and in value judgments especially.

Modern philosopher John Duwey (1859—1952) is regarded as the most prominent figure of the pragmatists. He is famous for his instrumentalism holding that effectiveness should be the only yardstick for the testing and measuring of truth and value.

In China, the evaluative criteria put forward by ancient philosophers such as Confucius (551—479BC), Xun Kuang (298—238BC) and Wang Shouren (better known as Wang Yangming, 1472—1528) etc. all have far-reaching influence on the modern criteria for measuring human practice including the practice of translation.

Confucius's belief that "do unto others as you would be done by" has been regarded as the most basic ethical criterion of human behavior. Xun Kuang values "*Li*" or ethical norms, loyalty and faithfulness by essence, and regards it the ultimate criterion for measuring the quality of a person and his performance. As norms are always social, such a criterion requires the needs of the individual should give way to the needs of the society or a certain community if there are conflicts between the two (Li Lianke 2003). Wang Yangming's theory of mind advocates that the criterion for assessing everything in the world is human conscious, the sense of knowing right and wrong. He once explained the relationship between the flower in the wild and the person who comes to the flower, saying that it is the person and his capacity of appreciation of beauty that gives aesthetic value to the flower with pleasing color (Zhang Xianghao & Chen Yi 2009).

Contemporary Western and Chinese philosophers and axiologists have many remarks about the criteria for value judgments as well. When talking about the criteria for evaluation, some of them do not distinguish criteria or standard of value from criteria for value judgments or evaluation.

Meehan (1969: 39), for example, says that "[e]very use of a value judgment or an explanation can and must be treated as an experiment; no complete, final, or general value structure is possible.Value standards will vary among societies and within societies, over time and within a limited time span".

As is pointed out by Shi Fuwei (2006), many scholars in China do not always distinguish "criteria of value" from "criteria for value judgments" and often use the former to refer to the latter in their writing. And actually, many of them do not think it necessary or possible to make the distinction.

Actually, the issue of criteria for evaluation is the most debatable in axiology. Stufflebeam and Shinkfield (1985: 5) identify three crucial sources of difference in evaluative criteria: different expectations of clients, the merit or excellence of the evaluation in question and the extent of need for the evaluation. Other sources concern people's idea as to whether evaluations need to be comparative or not, the main uses of evaluation and the extent to which evaluators need special qualifications.

Bahm (1993: 70) talks about, descriptively, how a value judgment and the standard or criterion for the judgment are made:

A particular value judgment (valuative or evaluative) may spring forth on any occasion when a person is enjoying or suffering intrinsic value or observing causal relations. When a person has made a particular kind of value judgment several times, its recurrence may endow it with a standardized character. When several persons make similar value judgments many times, their common recurrence may endow them with a socially standardized character and develop into a cultural trait. In cold weather, people commonly prefer warm clothing, and in hot weather, people commonly prefer cool clothing. Once a judgment acquires social establishment, it functions as a prejudgment about values.

Bahm here has touched upon the problem of individual evaluation (the subject of the evaluation being an individual) and social evaluation (the subject of the evaluation being a group of people or a community), and that of subjectiveness and objectiveness of evaluation. In China, as traditionally we prefer the needs and interests of the collective to those of the individual, social evaluation has been given more weight. Li Deshun holds that the criteria for social evaluation are the objective needs of the society and the dominant ideology of the society. Chen Xinhan argues that the criteria for social evaluation should be the realized reasonable needs of a society. Zhang Lihai holds that the criteria for social evaluation are the social norms shaped on the basis of the fundamental interests and ideals of the society in a certain period (He Haibing & Qin Hongyi 2008). However, our emphasis on social evaluation does not mean that individual evaluation is unimportant or less important. Individual evaluation includes the evaluation of the evaluator himself or herself. Individual evaluation usually adopts the individual's own criteria, but sometimes, the individual may also employ the social criteria. What needs to be mentioned is that social evaluation sometimes may be made by an individual, usually an expert of a certain field (Li Lianke 2003).

Davidson (2005) gives a detailed account about five main factors influencing an evaluation: first, consumers, the actual or potential recipients or impactees of the program; second, values, basis on which you determine whether the evaluand is of high quality or valuable, and the criteria determining "how good is good"; thirdly, the evaluand's content and implementation; fourthly, the impacts (intended and unintended) on immediate recipients and other impactees of the program; and fifth, comparative cost-effectiveness (compared with alternative uses of the available resources that might feasibly have achieved outcomes of similar or greater value). Each of the five factors can be adopted as the dominant orientation of our evaluative criteria.

In the field of criterion studies, there also exist different paradigms. Davidson (2005) identifies two main orientations in choosing the criteria for evaluation. One is goal-oriented or target-oriented, the other is need-oriented.

According to Davidson (2005: 25), most evaluands have some overarching purpose that we might refer to as a "goal" that "can often take us part of the way toward working out how good (or how valuable, how effective, etc.) an evaluand is" . However, the "goal" alone cannot ensure a valid conclusion about how well the product, project, or program is doing. Davidson is greatly influenced by Scriven. She offers us a list of problems with goal achievement evaluation, which is an adaptation of Scriven's (1991) with some explanations:

Table 4.1   Problems with Using Preset Targets or Goals as the Only Criteria

Problem	Example
Overruns and shortfalls	Should we (a) call Program X a "failure" because it missed one of its targets, (b) say that it did very well because it exceeded one of its targets by much more than it missed on another, or (c) something in between?
Goal difficulty	What if the goal that Program X barely missed (Goal 2) was a particularly challenging one, whereas the goal it far exceeded (Goal 3) was easy?
Goal importance	What if the easy target was actually the more important one (i.e., it was more valuable to meet that goal than to meet the other one)? (How would we find out independently whether it was or was not?)
Side effects	What if Program X also had an excellent side effect that was not included in the list of goals? Should we disregard that? If not, how would we know whether it compensated for the target it missed?
Synthesizing mixed results	What if we need to rank (or choose between) two programs, one of which is Program X and the other of which exactly met each of the three targets without exceeding any? On what basis could we say that one is better than the other?
Reasonableness of target levels	Suppose you find out that Program X came in "on budget" (i.e., met its cost goal), but then you find out that it cost five times as much as any comparable project that achieved roughly the same thing. (A similar problem occurs if Program X goes just over a very lean budget.)
Ignoring process: Do the ends justify the means?	What if Program X came in on budget by forcing the project staff to work overtime every weekend for 3 months so that in the end the top three team members quit their jobs and went to work for a competitor?
Whose/Which goals to use?	

(Davidson 2005: 26-27)

Since the goal-based evaluative criterion is problematic, some people turn to the goal-free needs-based evaluation. "Goal-free" as a term in evaluation does not mean that we will not consider the goal of a program or the goal of the evaluand. It only indicates that we cannot take the goal-oriented criteria or the intended effect (ignoring the process and the unintended effect) as the sole standard.

Needs-based evaluation requires us to know what the true needs of consumers or impactees are. The needs that we identify will be the main criteria we use for the evaluation. What is more, the data collected during the needs assessment phase can often become part of the criteria.

Generally speaking, consumers or impactees refer to those for whom something changes (or should or might change) as a result of a particular product, service, program, or policy. According to Davidson (2005: 30),

> Consumers can be divided into two groups: (a) immediate users or recipients and (b) other downstream impactees. Immediate recipients are the people who actually bought a product, signed up for a program, or received services directly from the evaluand, whereas downstream impactees are those who were not direct recipients but who were affected nevertheless.

Consumers or impactees can be individuals or the organization where direct recipients work, and they can be the local community, or the whole society in general.

Actually, according to Davidson (ibid: 33), the needs-based criteria are also problematic. The first problem is we have to distinguish "needs" from "wants". The second is to distinguish between different kinds of needs. A true need "might not be something that someone desires or is conscious of needing. It might even be something that is definitely not wanted. A seriously dehydrated person wandering in the desert might strongly desire a beer on arrival at an oasis, but what he or she really needs is water".

Davidson defines a need as "something without which unsatisfactory functioning occurs" and a want as "a conscious desire without which dissatisfaction (but not necessarily unsatisfactory functioning) occurs" (Davidson 2005: 33).

In using needs-based criteria, we need to be aware that needs are highly context dependent, geographically, culturally and historically:

> Another important point here is that needs are highly context dependent, with context having many dimensions such as geographical, cultural, and historical. A century ago, we did not need to be able to get from one side of the Pacific Ocean to the other in less than a day, but in today's business environment, that is expected. A firm doing business overseas would fall way behind its competitors (a clear example of unsatisfactory functioning) if representatives traveled only by sea and took weeks to get to their overseas customers. The context has changed, and the need has changed with it. As another example, basic living condition needs are defined differently in different countries because "satisfactory functioning" is defined differently. (ibid: 34)

Needs are context dependent, but that does not mean they all are arbitrary and everything becomes totally relative. What the evaluator needs to do is "clearly define the context and justify why we classify certain things as needs" (ibid).

According to Davidson (ibid: 35), we can distinguish three different kinds of needs: 1) conscious needs versus unconscious needs; 2) met needs versus unmet needs and 3) performance needs versus instrumental needs. Davidson explains that

> The distinction between conscious needs and unconscious needs is a fairly straightforward one—the things we know we need versus the things we do not know we need. ... there are things that we think we do not need but that we actually do need. The term unconscious is not meant to imply that these needs are not known to anyone; rather, it just implies that the needs are not known to the person who has the needs.

Met needs are those needs of the evaluand that have already been met and if they were taken away, it would probably cause seriously unsatisfactory functioning. Unmet needs are those that have caused or will cause problems for the evaluand. A performance need is "the actual or potential problem, whereas the instrumental need is the proposed solution. In needs assessment, we are concerned with the performance needs and not the instrumental needs" (Davidson 2005: 36).

Davidson (ibid: 23) offers us a Key Evaluation Checklist (KEC) (an adaptation of Scriven's, and for detail, see the next section) and suggests that the evaluative criteria are most relevant in five of the checkpoints in the KEC:

> Consumers, where we identify who might be affected by the evaluand; Values, where we explain broadly how we define what is "good" (or what is "valuable"); Process Evaluation, where we evaluate content and implementation of an evaluand; Outcome Evaluation; and Comparative Cost-Effectiveness.

Davidson (ibid: 24) further explains the five points as follows:

> Consumers —who are the actual or potential recipients or impactees of the program; Values — on what basis will you determine whether the evaluand is of high quality, is valuable, and so forth? Where will you get the criteria, and how will you determine "how good is good"? Process Evaluation — how good, valuable or efficient is the evaluand's content and implementation? Outcome Evaluation —how good or valuable are the impacts (intended and unintended) on immediate recipients and other impactees? Comparative Cost-Effectiveness— how costly is this evaluand to consumers, funders, staff, and so forth, compared with alternative uses of the available resources that might feasibly have achieved outcomes of similar or greater value? Are the costs excessive, quite high, just acceptable, or very reasonable?

For Davidson (ibid: 28-29), if we want to set up a criterion list, the essential factors or tools also needed are: 1) a needs assessment; 2) a simple logic model that links the evaluand to the needs; 3) an assessment of other relevant values; 4) checklists for thinking of other relevant criteria under the headings of Process, Outcomes, Cost-

Effectiveness and 5) a strategy for organizing your criterion checklist.

Though Davidson suggests that we adopt the needs-based evaluative criteria, she does not offer us a hierarchy of needs. That is to say, concrete criteria are not given by her. This, in fact, is quite natural if we consider that needs are context dependent.

"A need is something that is deemed necessary, especially something that is considered necessary for the survival of the person, organization, or whatever" (Scott & Marshall, 2005). Needs are different from wants as has been pointed out by Davidson. The former refer to things necessary, the latter, to those desired.

American psychologist Abraham H. Maslow (1908—1970) is famous for his theory of self-actualization or the hierarchy of needs. According to Maslow, food, sleep, protection from extreme hazards of the environment is the need that must first be met. Then come the needs for safety and security: some kind of order, certainty, and structure in our lives. What follows is the need to belong and to love. After that, there will be the need for self-esteem, both self-respect and esteem from other people. Finally there comes the need for self-actualization, or the desire to become everything that one can become (Scott & Marshall, 2005). Maslow holds that the first three kinds of needs belong to needs that are felt and caused by the deficiency in reality, whereas the other two kinds belong to needs for development.

Li Lianke (2003) thinks that human needs can be divided into biological needs and social needs. They are subjective in the sense that they are the expression of human desires and objective in the sense that they are to a great extent socially and historically determined in a certain context and are represented in social practice.

Li Deshun (2004) argues that while Maslow's hierarchy of needs is inspring, we should take a more dynamic attitude toward the hierarchy of needs. Li himself tends to divide needs into two kinds: the material needs and the spiritual needs and each of them can again be classified into realistic needs and developmental needs. The material needs include the basic biological needs and needs for economic development which are connected with the most fundamental value and the material value. The spiritual needs are needs for knowledge of the world, the society and human life and needs for the satisfactory political and ethical life, and for aesthetical enjoyment etc. The ultimate needs are the developmental value featured by a harmonious combination of the development of material needs and spiritual needs, which finds expression in the unity of the realization of truth, good and beauty. Consequently, we can evaluate things in terms of quality and quantity of the realization of all kinds of material and spiritual values. The more values and the more important, the higher it will be in the hierarchy of value. Yet, we should be aware that importance is relative.

To sum up, criteria for evaluation is closely connected with our views on value and the latter is again closely linked with human needs. Logically, human needs have become the basis and sources of value and our criteria for evaluation. However, as human needs are highly context dependent, there can not be a list of criteria that can be used anytime and anywhere. In other words, there will always be, as there have been, from the ancient to the present, different criteria suitable for a specific context. But does that mean all the criteria are totally relative and we have to accept the idea of "anything goes"? Frondizi (1971: 18) once commented that

> How can chaos be avoided, unless there are standards of value, norms of behavior? If every one carries his own yardstick of valuation, by what standard shall we decide axiological conflicts? Esthetic and moral education would be impossible; moral life will be meaningless; repentance of sin would seem absurd.... If we make man the measure of esthetic value and moral law, it would appear that there would be, strictly speaking, neither "good taste" nor morality.

What Frondizi says tells us that the paradigm of absolute relativism in evaluation will ruin evaluation and the orderly life of our human beings. The wayout we suggest is as follows: first, we can identify some values that are widely accepted and have some general criteria concerning the highest and ultimate values and especially the lowest and fundamental values, the former kind can be standard put forward by Li Deshun—the unity of the realization of truth, good and beauty, and the latter kind can be standards that meet the lowest needs or requirements of a specific context; secondly, we should adhere to the principles for evaluation given in the above section and consider carefully the essential relevant contextual factors listed by Davidson to set up a comprehensive and workable list or a framework of evaluative criteria for a specific situation; and thirdly, we can accept the suggestion by Frondizi (ibid: 28) — to give priority to methods. Frondizi remarks

> John Dewey is one of the thinkers who believe that the main problem today is methodological. After having concerned himself with axiological questions for several decades, Dewey, at the age of 90, wrote: "In the present situation, as concerns the problem of values, the decisive question is of a methodological type".

4.11 Methods and Procedures of Evaluation

From our discussion about different ways of translation criticism and different principles of evaluation in the above chapters, we know that there are different paradigms in any field and people have different approaches to evaluation. Though evaluation concerns many factors, the most important one is criterion or the basis of a standard. Giving priority to methods does not solve all the problems of evaluation, as we soon will find that first, when methods are concerned, there exist again different paradigms, and secondly, the core of any paradigm is the basis of standards or criteria. Graham Low (2002) says that "[e]valuation requires in essence two things, firstly that a task is defined in such a way that criteria for 'success' can be derived and secondly that data can be produced which may be matched against the criteria". Though it seems that our discussion of methodology will bring us back to the discussion about criteria, yet it will certainly be helpful for us to discuss the merits and shortcomings of different methods and choose from them the one we think best. What is more, by adopting a well-established framework and by following certain steps that are logically arranged, the evaluators will no doubt come to more scientific (reasonable) and more acceptable evaluative conclusions that may bear greater value for the improvement of a program in practice.

As to how evaluation is or can be made, Meehan (1969) holds that value judgment involves description and explanation.

> A description organizes perceptions by grouping them into classes, by relating them according to a rule of inclusion or exclusion, and by linking those classes with appropriate relational concepts… Structurally, a description consists of a set of variables or concepts whose values have been determined by observation. Descriptions are always specific and particular; they relate to the past and never to the future; they contain no general terms such as "all" or "some." The set of concepts used to describe a situation depends on both the perceptions of the observer and the conceptual apparatus he employs. If an observer is not interested in daisies, he will not include them in his description of a field even if they are present; on the other hand, he cannot include them in the description if none are to be seen—though he might, of course, state in the description that there were none to be seen if that was important. (Meehan 1969: 19)

For Meehan, evaluation can be scientific as "[d]escriptions and explanations are the heart of the scientific enterprise, the foundation on which reasoned human action with reference to the environment is built" (ibid: 25). An explanation not only generates expectations about changes in the environment, but also suggests the way in which variables interact to produce those changes, and can provide an intervention strategy by which man might exert some measure or control over the situation. Though explanations can be problematic, they can be very reliable, so long as it has logical coherence and is compatible with other well-established explanations in the field, experimental evidence, and various other factors.

According to Meehan (1969: 40),

Value judgments are always made with reference to the future; retrospection, the examination of past choice and its consequences, is an important way of testing the adequacy of a value principle but affects present choice only indirectly. Normative questions appear in the general form: "What changes are needed in this situation?" or "What choice should be made in this situation?" They are answered by referring to the alternatives attainable in that situation and by making comparisons and calculations based on accepted standards and purposes.

Meehan (ibid: 31) actually adopts a consequence-based model of evaluation. He holds that the consequences of human choices can serve as a basis for evaluation. We can compare the consequences actually chosen with those that might have been chosen in the same situation by the same actor, in terms of impact, direct or indirect, on man.

Bahm talks of how things are known and the ways of knowing the value of things. For him, "[o] bjects are known in two ways: directly and indirectly. Thus, two basic kinds of knowledge exist: intuitive or direct knowing and inferential or indirect knowing" (Bahm 1993: 71). Intuition refers to the immediacy of apprehension of the object you are studying and trying to know, while inference is going from something given or known to something else. Inference can again be divided into, mainly, perceptual inference and conceptual inference. Perceptual inference involves sensation: from what you have seen or tasted or felt you can infer what you have not. Conceptual inference involves both sensation and conception, inductively and deductively. Inductively, you can infer from repeated enjoyments of reading translations by a certain translator that reading a translation by this translator always produces the same kind of intrinsic value. Deductively, you infer from the premise that reading the translation by this translator always brings you enjoyment that you will also enjoy or feel the value next time you come to the translation of this translator. Bahm (ibid: 86) says that "[v]alues are known in the same ways that other objects are known, that is, by intuition and inference".

For Bahm, besides the epistemological problem, value judgments may also have to do with the linguistic competence of the person who reports his or her value experiences. Experiment shows that in the distinguishing of different varieties of colors, people who can distinguish pink from scarlet and maroon have a better vocabulary for describing their color experiences and feelings associated with them than those who can not.

Matarasso (1996: 15) says that:

All evaluative studies rely on two types of information: quantitative evidence, expressing the size of various measures, and qualitative evidence, which expresses more obviously subjective judgements about worth. The increasing emphasis on evaluation in the public sector has relied heavily on quantitative evidence (albeit of increasing complexity) because it is easier to get, easier to use, and appears authoritative.

However, Matarasso thinks that quantitative information only pretends to be objective. "Its weakness lies both in the unspoken or unrecognized assumptions which underlie it and in its susceptibility to manipulation" and therefore, "efforts have been made to balance statistical information with other more subtle forms of qualitative measure" (ibid: 16). He also mentions that cost-effectiveness ratio has a relevance to arts programmes with social objectives, but in the field of arts, the subjective, personal response is central to the meaning (ibid: 17).

So far as the process and procedure of evaluation is concerned, House and Howe (1999: xvi) hold that "the logic of evaluation consists of finding criteria for the evaluation, setting performance standards for each criterion, collecting relevant data, and summing the data and criteria into overall judgments of success or failure of the policies, programs, products, or whatever is under review". They further explain that

The actual evaluative process is more complex and is dependent on many substantive and contextual considerations as well as the nature of the entity being evaluated. The context of the evaluation is critical in limiting the logical possibilities of evaluations and making solutions possible. Evaluators do not have to consider all criteria or all potential audiences, only those relevant to a particular time and place in a particular context. Although evaluators differ as to how agreement on criteria is obtained, who participates in the evaluation process, and how performance criteria and data are handled, they can nonetheless arrive at reasonable levels of agreement using the concepts and tools of their discipline. (ibid: xvi-xvii)

House and Howe, as has been mentioned before, think that fact and value are not dichotomous, but rather, form a continuum. Their idea about the continuum of fact and value is inspiring for value judgments, especially the professional evaluation which, according to House and Howe (1999), often contains both the epistemological statements and the evaluative statements. To pass on a value judgment, one has usually to identify the existing value(s). Yet, to know or to identify the value(s) of something is closely connected with epistemology, which studies how things are known and the nature of knowledge, all kinds of knowledge, including scientific knowledge, religious knowledge, literary and artistic knowledge, and knowledge of values as well. Besides, House and Howe's emphasis on the importance of contextual factors in evaluation is also insightful.

According to Davidson (2005: xi-xiii), "[n]o one has thought more deeply or critically about what evaluation really is, how it is different from other undertakings, and what very specific procedures are required to answer truly evaluative questions than has Scriven". Michael Scriven has made the greatest contributions to the development of a unique logic and methodology that is truly evaluation specific and has provided a solid theoretical foundation for evaluation practice. An evaluation-specific logic and methodology is "a set of principles (logic) and procedures (methodology) that guides the evaluation team in the task of blending descriptive data with relevant values to draw explicitly evaluative conclusions" and "[a]n explicitly evaluative conclusion is one that says how good, valuable, or important something is rather than just describing what it is like or what happened as a result of its implementation".

Greatly influenced by Scriven, Davidson (ibid: 26-27) advocates a goal-free needs-based approach to evaluation. A goal-free evaluation (GFE) requires "the evaluation team deliberately avoids learning what the goals are (or were) so as to avoid being overly focused on intended outcomes. The rationale behind this approach is that both intended and unintended effects are important to include in an evaluation" and it "is sometimes called needs-based evaluation because a needs assessment is one of the primary tools used to identify what effects (both positive and negative) should be investigated".

For Davidson (ibid: 37-39), needs assessment consists of two phases: the first is to identify and document what she terms as "performance needs", the unmet needs causing the actual or potential problem which have caught the attention of clients; the second is to investigate the underlying causes of performance needs. The first may be called the "severity documentation phase" whereas the second, "diagnostic phase". In the first phase, we document the extent of the performance needs "by gathering some hard evidence (usually quantitative data) about the magnitude of the problem" and "[i]n many cases, it is helpful to locate some comparative information (e.g., similar statistics from earlier years, data from similar communities in the city or state) to gain a comparative sense of the severity of the problem". In the second phase, we try to understand the underlying causes of those needs, and "[i] n many cases, there is more than one cause of a performance need (or the causes are different for different people), and a multifaceted solution (or different solutions for different people) is required".

Davidson calls us to pay attention to the difference between the two phases:

Note that the diagnostic phase of the needs assessment is an inherently open-ended inquiry. That is why qualitative methods are most prevalent here. In contrast, the earlier documentation of performance needs in the community usually focuses on the magnitude of needs that are thought to exist. That is why the methods used for the first phase of the needs assessment are typically more quantitative. (Davidson 2005: 47)

Davidson offers us a framework for evaluation which the author of this dissertation thinks fairly comprehensive. The following framework used for planning and conducting an evaluation and presenting its results is an adaptation of Scriven's Key Evaluation Checklist (KEC) by Davidson with a few modifications and simplifications:

Table 4.2   The Key Evaluation Checklist (modified from Scriven's 2003 version)

I.Executive Summary One- to two-page overview of the evaluand and findings	II. Preface Who asked for this evaluation and why? What are the main evaluation questions? Who are the main audiences?		III. Methodology What is the overall design of the evaluation (e.g., quasi-experimental, participatory, goal free) and (briefly) why?	
1.Background and Context Why did this program or product come into existence in the first place?	2.Descriptions and Definitions Describe the evaluand in enough detail so that virtually anyone can understand what it is and what it does.	3. Consumers Who are the actual or potential recipients or impactees of the program (e.g., demographics)?	4. Resources What resources are (or were) available to create, maintain, and help the program or policy succeed?	5.Values On what basis will you determine whether the evaluand is of high quality, valuable, and so forth? Where will you get the criteria, and how will you determine "how good is good"?
6.Process Evaluation How good, valuable, or efficient is the evaluand's content, (design) and implementation (delivery)?	7.Outcome Evaluation How good or valuable are the impacts (intended and unintended) on immediate recipients and other impactees?	8 & 9.Comparative Cost-Effectiveness How costly is this evaluand to consumers, funders, staff, and the like, compared with alternative uses of the available resources that might feasibly have achieved outcomes of similar or greater value? Are the costs excessive, quite high, just acceptable, or very reasonable?		10. Exportability What elements of the evaluand (e.g., innovative design or approach) might make it potentially valuable or a significant contribution or advance in another setting?

11. Overall Significance Draw on all of the information in Checkpoints 6 through 10 to answer the main evaluation questions (e.g., What are the main areas where the evaluation is doing well, and where is it lacking? Is this the most cost-effective use of the available resources to address the identified needs without excessive adverse impact?).	12. Recommendations and Explanations [optional] A more in-depth analysis of why/how things went right/wrong, perhaps including recommendations for improvement	13. Responsibilities [optional] A more in-depth analysis of exactly who or what was responsible for good or bad results (Note: This is very tricky and is usually not the kind of territory you want to get into unless you are highly skilled.)	14. Reporting and Follow-up Who will receive copies of the evaluation report and in what form (e.g., written, oral, detailed versions, executive summary)?

15. Meta-evaluation
A critical assessment of the strengths and weaknesses of the evaluation itself (e.g., How well were all of the Key Evaluation Checklist checkpoints covered?) and conclusions about its overall utility, accuracy or validity, feasibility, and propriety (see the Program Evaluation Standards for details)

(Davidson 2005: 6-7)

Davidson points out that the above framework is "a guiding framework for the evaluation team members (be they organizational members, external evaluators, or a mix) to make sure that all important ingredients that will allow valid evaluative conclusions to be drawn are included" and as "the KEC was designed primarily for application to program evaluation, some of the points might need reframing when the KEC is used for other evaluands or evaluees (the term used in personnel evaluation)" (Davidson 2005: 5). What is more, though not all checkpoints must always be included in all evaluations, the omission of certain elements should be carefully justified. "This is particularly important for Checkpoints 5 through 9 and 11, which form the core of the evaluation" (ibid: 7).

Despite of Davidson's advocating for a needs-based approach, she has made it clear that multiple perspectives should be adopted "depending on what primary need the evaluation is addressing (e.g., building organizational learning capacity, meeting accountability requirements) and on the time and resources available to get the evaluation done" (Davidson 2005: xiv). That is to say, the approach to evaluation should also be context dependent.

Davidson (ibid: 4) holds that steps involved in an evaluation are: 1) defining the main purposes of the evaluation; 2) identifying the evaluative criteria (using needs assessment and other techniques); 3) organizing the list of criteria and choosing sources of evidence (mixed method data); 4) dealing with the causation issue; 5) understanding which values should legitimately be applied in an evaluation and how to navigate the different kinds of "subjectivity"; 6) importance weighting: figuring out which criteria are the most important; 7) merit determination: figuring out how well your evaluand has done on the criteria (excellent? good? satisfactory? mediocre? unacceptable?); 8) meta-evaluation: how to figure out whether your (or someone else's) evaluation is any good.

To sum up, in this section we have discussed the methods and procedures to make a scientific or reasonable evaluation. The ideas of those scholars reviewed are all inspiring. We suggest that the evaluator take the ideas of the above-mentioned scholars into his or her consideration and strongly recommend the framework by Davidson which allows some modifications to meet the requirements of a specific evaluation in a specific context.

4.12 Main Features of Evaluation Based on Social Constructivism

Evaluation is a very complex activity. It involves axiology, ethics, politics, economy, epistemology, psychology, linguistics, aesthetics, methodology…in fact, almost every aspect of our human life. Because of its complexity, it is one of the most debatable areas of the humanity and social science and there exist many ideas and different paradigms concerning value and evaluation.

Among all those paradigms discussed by House and Howe (1999), we prefer the deliberative democratic view or the social constructivist view of evaluation. Consequently, either the principles or criteria for evaluation or the methodology of evaluation we recommend are of social constructivism, which is mainly featured by context dependence.

The feature of context dependence inevitably gives rise to relativism. As a matter of fact, the 20th century in the West has witnessed a flourish of relativism in the philosophical field. The contemporary axiological-inclined thinker Hilary Putnam uses "rational acceptability" as the criterion for truth. Habermas often uses "rationality" and "legality" to refer to "truthfulness" (Lv Jun 2007b).

Though social constructivism embraces relativism, it does not go to extreme as the individual or radical constructivism does. Evaluation based on social constructivism bear the following subfeatures: dynamic, dialogic and dialectic; integrity of relativism and absolutism; integrity of subjectivity with objectiveness, integrity of description and prescription and explanation, integrity of quantitative and qualitative studies and so on.

The distinction between relativism and absolutism are mainly concerned with our epistemological attitude toward and assumptions about value and evaluation. Social constructivism or the deliberative democratic view of evaluation put forward by House and Howe holds that anything, including truth, is both relative and absolute. Value is closely connected with human needs and human needs can vary from person to person, from culture to culture and from context to context. This will inevitably make value and evaluation relative. However, Within a specific context or society, as an individual is always an individual of a certain community, there exist some objective laws, rules or norms that are supposed to be observed by all the members of the society. In this sense, the criteria for value and evaluation are absolute.

Objectivity has been thought to be the touchstone of scientific authority. Matarasso (1996: 14) argues that though philosophers and social scientists have written extensively on the issue of objectivity in social research, it is easy to recognize that the day-to-day business of program evaluation is fundamentally subjective as "[s] ocial policy generally, and arts projects specifically, are value-driven". For Matarasso (1996: 24), "[o]ver-zealous pursuit of scientific objectivity, and the internal validity of evaluation processes, is inappropriate and unhelpful approaches to the evaluation of social programmes and especially arts projects".

So far as the objectivity of value judgment is concerned, House and Howe (1999: 9) hold that the positivist notion of objectivity should be rejected and instead, being objective means "working toward unbiased statements through the procedures of the discipline, observing the canons of proper argument and methodology, maintaining a healthy skepticism, and being vigilant to eradicate sources of bias".

Machael Scriven argues for the valid position of subjectivity in evaluation and thinks so long as an evaluation "is free of inappropriate personal or cultural biases" it can be an objective evaluation. He also talks of "the intersubjective experience of a community or group" and thinks that subjectivity has an objective ground as the intersubjective experience of a community or group cannot exist independently of people's shared perceptions and intersubjective sensemaking (Davidson 2005: 90-91).

In fact, the question of subjectivity and objectivity is closely connected with that of relativism and absolutism. Though human beings may have different goals or needs and hence different values, yet within a specific society of a given time, our goals and needs may have a universal character. And for the realization of the goals or needs, the society will have some laws or norms to govern the behavior and desire of all the members of the society. In this case, the objective social laws and norms function as constraining forces that to a great extent determine the individual's subjective needs. That is to say, in a given context, a need that seems totally subjective has actually an objective base.

4.13 Criteria for Evaluating an Evaluation

Evaluation, as has been discussed, can be classified into different types. One of them is meta-evaluation. Meta-evaluation is as important as evaluation itself because to make evaluation scientific and to promote the development of the science of axiology and evaluation, we need critical reflection on the evaluations done. In this respect, besides Davidson's checklist, Stufflebeam and Shinkfield (1985) offer us some advice and the criteria for evaluate an evaluation in their book *Systematic Evaluation: A Self-Instructional Guide to Theory and Practice*. The criteria for measure the quality of an evaluation, to a great extent, overlaps the principle and the criteria for evaluation, but there are surly some differences.

According to Stufflebeam and Shinkfield (1985: 10), the requirements for a valid (good) evaluation are as follows:

An evaluation should be useful. It should be addressed to those persons and groups who are involved in or responsible for implementing what ever is being evaluated. It should help them to identify and attend to strengths and weaknesses in the object. It should place heaviest emphasis on addressing the questions of most importance to them. It should issue clear reports in a timely manner. And, in general, it should provide not merely feedback about strengths and weaknesses but also direction for improvement.

Other requirements for a good evaluation are:

It should be feasible. It should employ evaluation procedures that can be implemented without major disruption. It should take into account and exert reasonable controls over political forces that might otherwise subvert the evaluation. And it should be conducted efficiently.

It should be ethical. It should be founded on explicit agreements that ensure that the necessary cooperation will be provided, that the rights of all concerned parties will be protected, and that the findings will not be compromised. Moreover, it should provide a balanced report that reveals both strengths and weaknesses. (ibid)

For Stufflebeam and Shinkfield (ibid: 11), we can have a check on the following factors to see whether an evaluation is good or not: 1) audience identification, the identification of the audiences involved in or affected by the evaluation for the purpose of addressing their needs; 2) evaluator credibility, maximum credibility and acceptance to be achieved by trustworthy and competent evaluators; 3) information scope and selection, information collected able to address pertinent questions about the object of the evaluation and responsive to the needs and interests of the specified audiences; 4) valuational interpretation, a clear and careful description of the perspectives, procedures, and rationale used to interpret the findings; 5) report clarity, a clear report of the findings of an evaluation concerning its context, motivations, purposes, procedures, conclusions and recommendations etc.; 6) report dissemination, evaluation findings to be disseminated to clients and other persons who have the rights to know for their assessment and use of the findings; 7) report timeliness, a timely release of the evaluation reports for the best use of the specified audiences; and 8) evaluation impact, the impact produced by the evaluation leading to better performance of the audience and better result.

In brief, meta-evaluation is significant for both the improvement of our evaluation practice and for our theoretical study of evaluation as well. It might be the end of an evaluation and it can also mark the beginning of another evaluation.

Chapter 5
Criticism of Literary Translation in Light of Evaluation Theories and Axiology in General

If the meaning of "value judgment" can be stipulated in terms that relate to human capacities and human needs, value judgment can be made amenable to reasoned criticism. That is, once a definition of the concept is agreed, the conditions that must be satisfied before value judgment is possible, the structures and processes involved in the act of judging, and the points in the process that are open to criticism can be identified. It should then be possible to suggest standards of criticism or at a minimum the conditions needed for reasoned criticism. (Meehan 1969: 2)

The above words by Eugene J. Meehan (1969) in his *Value Judgement and Social Science: Structure and Processes*, though written many years ago, remain insightful and are quite suitable to be used here as the opening remarks for the discussion of criticism of literary translation in light of the evaluation theory in axiology. If we want to make a reasoned translation criticism, especially criticism of literary translation, we need first come to an agreement of the concept of "criticism" and then, "the conditions" to satisfy to make our criticism, the structures and processes involved in the act of judging or criticizing, and then the "points" or factors open to criticism in the process and then again, the criteria for criticism. For criticism of translation, especially literary translation, as has been made clear in Chapter 2 and Chapter 3, is a kind of evaluation in essence. In Chapter 4 we have given a general introduction of axiology and the related evaluation theories in order to get a better understanding of evaluation. In this chapter, we will take a closer look at criticism of literary translation in light of the evaluation theories in axiology.

5.1 Evaluation of Literary Works

To discuss the evaluation of criticism of literary translation, it is better for us to inquire into the values and evaluation of literary works first as the evaluation of criticism of literary translation and the evaluation of literary works are closely connected.

5.1.1 Value of literary works

People may have different ideas in different times as to what is the value of a literary work. Yet, this does not mean the evaluation of a literary work is totally subjective and relative. In fact, we can always find some popular ideas about the value of literary works during a certain historical time in a specific context. Axiologically, all our human activities are value creation and literary writing is no exception. The value of a literary work is closely connected with its function in practice in a certain society. According to Min Ze and Dang Shengyuan (1999), in China, the value of poetry in its earliest stage lies mainly in serving various religious needs. As time goes on, in different periods, the value of literary works is viewed as meeting various needs: representing the pleasure of labour, relaxing people physically and mentally, singing praises for rulers and their government or criticizing their faults alternatively, health care, emotion expression, life recording, moral and intellectual education and enlightenment, aesthetic experience and even state governing concerning the reform or revolution of a society etc. Though a literary work certainly has its material value, from the above views we can see that what we value is mainly its spiritual value. In the West, there is not much difference concerning the ideas of value of literature, and art as a whole. People see it as meeting the needs of seeking pleasure, expressing truth and beauty, enlightenment by means of amusement, liberation of human nature, aesthetic education and social criticism etc.

Actually, people's ideas about the value of a literary work are changing mainly with their understanding about the nature of literature and their different needs for literary texts. It is also the case with evaluation of literary works.

5.1.2 Evaluation of literary works

What should first be made clear is that here we are using the word "evaluation" in the sense of "criticism" as evaluation is the essence of any criticisms.

There have been different approaches or paradigms concerning the evaluation of literary works. The criteria of evaluation vary in accordance with people's understanding of literariness, the supposed function of literary works and some other factors. However, axiologically, all the discrepancy over the issue of criteria originates from our different views on value.

In literary studies, some people think that value is the innate properties of a literary work that can meet the demands of our human beings and bring us pleasure, others think that value is something both objective and subjective, existing in the literary text itself and the interest, desire, emotion, interpretation of the subjects. And still others regard literature as an arena of conflicting cultures and political interests. Russian formalists and some scholars labeled as New Criticism value the aesthetic function of literature very much and try to find the literariness which they think the main origin of aesthetic values from the literary texts themselves while Marxist Criticism and the reception aesthetics believe that the aesthetic values exist in the interaction between the text and the reader.

Terry Eagleton once spoke of the evaluative nature of literary criticism and held that there does not exist a wholly disinterested statement:

> All of our descriptive statements move within an often invisible network of value-categories, and indeed without such categories we would have nothing to say to each other at all. It is not just as though we have something called factual knowledge which may then be distorted by particular interests and judgements, although this is certainly possible; it is also that without particular interests we would have no knowledge at all, because we would not see the point of bothering to get to know anything…. The claim that knowledge should be 'value-free' is itself a value-judgement. (Eagleton 1983: 14)

Eagleton makes some comments on I. A. Richards' experiment to seek to demonstrate how subjective literary value-judgments can be by giving his undergraduates some poems, withholding from them the titles and authors' names, and asking his undergraduates to evaluate them. The evaluations are known to be highly variable: time-honoured poets were marked down and obscure authors celebrated. Eagleton thinks that such a result is not surprising at all as there actually exist a consensus of unconscious valuations underlying these different judgments. The readers' assumptions and expectations of literary works, especially poems, in this experiment are quite similar. The participants were, "presumably, young, white, upper- or upper middle-class, privately educated English people of the 1920s, and how they respond to a poem depended on a good deal more than purely 'literary' factors. Their critical responses were deeply entwined with their broader prejudices and beliefs" (ibid: 15). Eagleton holds that all critical responses are so entwined, and literary critical judgements or interpretations are context-dependent and context-determined. What is implied here is that behind the seemingly "subjective" evaluation, there exists an objective foundation. He further explains that:

> In eighteenth-century England, the concept of literature was not confined as it sometimes
> is today to 'creative' or 'imaginative' writing. It meant the whole body of valued writing
> in society: philosophy, history, essays and letters as well as poems. What made a text
> 'literary' was not whether it was fictional—the eighteenth century was in grave doubt
> about whether the new upstart form of the novel was literature at all—but whether
> if conformed to certain standards of 'polite letters'. The criteria of what counted as
> literature, in other words, were frankly ideological: writing which embodied the values
> and 'tastes' of a particular social class qualified as literature, whereas a street ballad, a
> popular romance and perhaps even the drama did not. At these historical points, then,
> the 'value-ladenness' of the concept of literature was reasonably self-evident. (Eagleton
> 1983: 17)

Wolfgang Iser is known for his aesthetics of reception that holds that literary
reading is a process of the interaction between the text and the reader. Iser is greatly
influenced by Roman Ingarden when he proposes that the text has its response-
inviting structure (Ling Chenguang 2001). Ingarden (1985: 92) argues that the work
of art is the product of the intentional activity of the artist, but the completion of the
work and "the actualization of its moments of potentiality" depends on the reader and
therefore it is actually the common product of the artist and the observer (reader).
Readers may come to the text with different purposes, for aesthetic experience,
scientific research, or information about the life of characters depicted in the work
or some other extra-literary facts. What is more, there are different potential readers
and at different times, a fact that adds difference to evaluations of one and the
same literary text. Hence, the idea that the artistic value of a literary work is totally
subjective is quite popular. But, value judgments of the work of art are not merely
subjective.

> When an observer ceases to react emotionally to it or is no longer sensitive to it as a work
> of art, so far as it is treated as an instrument of enjoyment, it is not valued by him either
> positively or negatively but becomes an object of indifference. But the work of art itself
> undergoes no change in its property during these modifications of subjective mood and
> response. (ibid: 96)

Ingarden talks of the importance of the capacity of the reader too. According to
Ingarden, it is not that all readers have the ability to evaluate properly the artistic or
aesthetic value of a work of art. The reader must first interact with the text and then
possess the required apprehensive and appreciative capacity as otherwise neither

the properties nor the values of the text will reveal themselves to him. Readers may be in one way or another inefficient—lack of artistic culture or unequipped with the required background knowledge or unable to appreciate a particular work at a particular moment.

Ingarden (1985: 100) also talks of the virtues for a good text to have. "Lucidity, clarity of expression and precision of construction" are properties of linguistic components that are "value qualities characterizing the literary work itself". On the contrary, "unclarity, obscurity, unintelligibility" are regarded as defects that will bring negative value to a text.

In his conclusion, Ingarden (ibid: 106) says that:

...aesthetic value, made concrete on the basis of a given work of art, is nothing else but a particular quality determination marked by a selection of interacting aesthetically valuable qualities which manifest themselves on the basis of the neutral skeleton of a work of art reconstructed by a competent observer.

Of course, a literary work may contain not only aesthetic value, it may own many other values as has been said in section 5.1.1. The existence of multiple views on value of literary works has determined the existence of multiple criteria for evaluating literary works.

Literary criticism in the 20th century has undergone a process marked by the turn from text to reader and from reader to culture and politics. Feminist Criticism, New Historicism, Post-colonialism and Ecocriticism etc. have drawn our attention to things like power relation, social and historical context, cultural identity and environmental protection etc. and etc. Literariness and aesthetic value of literary texts were marginalized and the evaluation of artistic value of them gave way to the socio-cultural value. The evaluation of literary works has almost become the evaluation of various social ideologies. New Historicism, for example, is "characterized by (1) resituation of literary text in the historical context 'defined primarily in terms of hierarchies of power determined by gender, race, and class' and (2) redefinition of literary studies in terms of an activist agenda 'which is ideologically committed to the goal of the subversion of hierarchies of power'" (Zhu Gang 2001: 260). Post-Colonialism sees literary works as "discourse" which, according to Foucault, "is a set of 'rules' which determines the sorts of statements that can be made, 'a system that defines the possibilities of knowledge,' or the criteria for truth" (Zhu Gang 2001: 286). What is closely connected with "discourse" is "power". For "power" in Foucault's sense exists everywhere in our human life and is often found with "discourse" and "knowledge" which presuppose and constitute various power relations. Post-colonialists show great concern about the cultural relation between the First World and the Third World and find that literary works can be a tool to reinforce or to deconstruct Western cultural hegemony. And literary criticism itself is thus seen as a textual event which is more like a value-judgment process (ibid; Zhu Liyuan, 1997).

No matter how many different models of evaluation of literary works we have, according to Min Ze and Dang Shengyuan (1999), the most common model is featured by various normative requirements. And as has been said by Li Deshun (2004), the needs of the subject are the general yardstick which is used in our evaluation or criticism. Min Ze and Dang Shengyuan (ibid) hold that in evaluating literary works, it is the aesthetic needs and aesthetic ideal that mainly function as the yardstick. Evaluation based on mainly the aesthetic needs or ideals does not mean the criteria for the evaluation of literary works are purely and solely subjective; another criterion is the inherent properties and laws of literary works. What is more, the needs of the subject are not formed in vacuum, but rather in a specific context and are controlled by various objective and subjective contextual factors. There will be consensus concerning the criteria of literary works in a given society and in a given time. Consensus is something intersubjectively agreed upon and according to Popper, has the status of objective knowledge. To make it clear, Andre Lefevere (1978: 11) once quoted Popper's distinction of "three worlds": the world of physical objects or physical states; the world of states of consciousness, or mental states, or perhaps of behavioral dispositions to act; and the world of objective contents of thought, especially of scientific and poetic thoughts and works of art. According to Popper,

> What matters is world three, because that is where we find "knowledge in the objective sense... knowledge without a knower... knowledge without a knowing subject" (Popper 1972: 109). The objectivity of this kind of knowledge lies in the fact that "it can be intersubjectivity tested" (Popper 1961:44) ...Truth, at any given moment and inside any given discipline, lies not in the subjectivity of one man's mind, but in the evolving intersubjective consensus of the qualified practitioners of that discipline. (qtd. in Lefevere 1978: 11)

To sum up, from the above discussion we can say that the evaluation of literary works, especially their spiritual value, be it moral, intellectual, political and aesthetical, should seek the organic unity of subjectivity and objectivity. The criteria should be based on the needs and ideals of the subject for a certain value in a certain context. They also stem from the innate law or properties of literary creation itself. Criticism of literary works is always value-laden and axiologically, even the descriptive statements in it are never value-free. Literary works may have various positive or negative values depending on the criteria adopted by critics in a specific context. Compared with the spiritual value of literary works, the material value or the economic value seems much easier for us to measure and has been neglected for long. Yet, with critics' or evaluators' paying more attention to reader's participation, the economic value of literary works is in a sense connected with the spiritual value, as reception aesthetics holds that it is the reader's readering that actualizes the aesthetic value of a literary work.

5.2 Evaluation of Literary Translation

As has been stated when talking about the criticism of literary works, in this section and the following part of this dissertation in fact, we will also use the word "criticism" in the sense of "evaluation" as criticism is evaluation in essence. Therefore, the term "criticism" and the term "evaluation" are interchangeable in the following discussion.

5.2.1 Value of literary translation

Axiologically, we live in a world of value and the purpose of all the human activities is to create greater value. As has been said in the above section, literary texts have various values; the same can be said to translation of literary works. Actually, translation, no matter what kind of it, literary or non-literary, is never value-free, ethically, aesthetically or economically. Venuti in his *The Scandals of Translation* formulates an ethics enabling translations to be read and evaluated in their socio-cultural contexts "with greater respect for linguistic and cultural differences" (Venuti 1998: 6). In the introductory part of the above-mentioned book, Venuti draws our attention to the nonlinguistic aspect of translation by saying that "[t]ranslation is stigmatized as a form of writing, discouraged by copyright law, depreciated by the academy, exploited by publishes and corporations, governments and religious organizations" (ibid: 1). He goes further to criticize those linguistics-oriented approaches and saying that:

Translation research and translator training have been impeded by the prevalence of linguistics-oriented approaches that offer a truncated view of the empirical data they collect. Because such approaches promote scientific models for research, they remain reluctant to take into account the social values that enter into translating as well as the study of it. Research thus becomes scientific, claiming to be objective or value-free, ignoring the fact that translation, like any cultural practice, entails the creative reproduction of values. (Venuti 1998: 1)

Jose Lambert also calls our attention to the close relationship between translation principles and value principles:

No translation, no communication is possible without conventional principles which turn out to involve value principles as well. The interesting point is that in the situation of translation, at least from the point of view of the scholar, there are generally clear juxtapositions of value principles from various cultural backgrounds; hence value oppositions (conflicts) may become systematic, in lexical, syntactic, socio-cultural, generic matters, and so on…Instead of being a matter of mere technical communication (or of language systems only), translational activities are inevitably influenced by traditions and norms of all kinds. (Delabastita, D' hulst & Meylaerts 2006: 91)

Literary translation as the translation of literary texts, from the perspective of axiology, is a form of human practice to create values. Axiology tells us value can be divided into many kinds from different perspectives: ethic value, intellectual value, aesthetic value, actual value, potential value, intrinsic value, instrumental value, material value, spiritual value and economic value etc. As has been said in the part talking about the classification of values, we think that the general distinction between material value and spiritual value put forward by Li Lianke (2003) is suitable to be adopted in our discussion of value and evaluation of literary works. Li further divides material value into natural value and economic value depending on whether it is naturally shaped or man-made and spiritual value into intellectual value, moral value and aesthetic value. According to this classification, a literary text has both material value and spiritual value as it is man-made and is supposed to meet the needs of our mental enjoyment and social development both cultural and economic. A translation of a literary text, accordingly, is supposed to have its material value and spiritual value as well.

5.2.2 Criticism or evaluation of literary translation

In the above section we speak of briefly the value and classification of the value of translation of literary works. In this section, we will concentrate on the evaluation of literary translation. The main issues to be discussed will be 1) criticism of literary translation and its nature; 2) objectives of criticism of literary translation; 3) types of criticism of literary translation; 4) principle of criticism of literary translation; 5) criteria for criticism of literary translation; 6) methodology of criticism of literary translation; 7) features of evaluation and criteria for criticism of literary translation; and 8) criteria for criticizing a criticism or an evaluation etc.

5.2.2.1 Criticism of literary translation and its nature

When discussing the essence of criticism and the essence of translation criticism we reviewed many definitions of translation criticism to show that the most essential feature of criticism is evaluation. Literary translation is the translation of literary works. Criticism of literary works as has been showed in section 5.1.2, is highly evaluative. It belongs mainly to humanity and social science which have much difference from natural science. Criticism of translation of literary works is, likewise, highly evaluative.

In light of evaluation theories in axiology, criticism of literary translation can be viewed both as a process and an outcome of an assessing program of literary translation. It can be viewed as a profession as well. And it is more than applied social science, as Davidson (2005: xi) points out, in that it "involves not only collecting descriptive information about a program, product, or other entity but also using something called 'values' to (a) determine what information should be collected and (b) draw explicitly evaluative inferences from the data, that is, inferences that say something about the quality, value, or importance of something".

Criticism of literary translation, implicitly or explicitly, is comparative. It is the comparison of values of literary translations. Our judgment of the value of a literary translation comes from our comparing it with another translation. What is more, its comparative nature is also seen from the fact that the critic or the evaluator is constantly, consciously or unconsciously; compare a literary translation with a certain criterion in order to pass on the value judgment.

If we view evaluation as a process, as Matarasso (1996) does, then criticism of literary translation will also be a process, implying that we will carry it out continuously and will often come (back) to the criticism of one and the same translation (s) of a literary work again and again, owing to the relative nature of value. What is also implied is that criticism of literary translation as an outcome of an evaluation may just a value judgment for the evaluated work for the time being. That is to say, one criticism will be challenged or even replaced by another later coming criticism.

The idea that evaluation can be viewed as a profession reveals that there might be some criticisms that are not professional. Professionally, evaluation is the systematic assessment of the value of something. The word "systematic" shows that evaluation and criticism alike is an activity that requires the critic to follow a certain rule or principle in the discipline. All professional criticisms are supposed to use data, quantitative or qualitative, collected in a systematic manner. Though professional criticism thus described may sound more scientific, it does not mean non-professional criticism is redundant. And in fact, non-professional criticism may appear very important for a comprehensive criticism.

Wang Hongyin (2006) regards criticism of literary translation as an advanced aesthetic research. It differs from ordinary appreciation of a literary translation. From the perspective of evaluation, Wang is almost expressing the same idea, as there exist professional and non-professional criticisms. However, it does not seem so proper to confine criticism of literary translation to "aesthetic research" only as axiologically we know a literary translation may have various values.

As has been said when we discuss the nature of evaluation, though evaluation certainly has something to do with knowing the object, it does not fall into the category of traditional epistemology or epistemology in its narrow sense. Rather, it goes beyond it and to the broader field of axiology which embraces epistemology in its wider sense, believing in the consensus theory of knowledge. Criticism of literary translation therefore, should capture the essence of the subjectivity of our cognition and at the same time acknowledge the objectivity of knowledge. Criticism of literary translation is a creative social constructive activity or process concerning both our knowledge about a literary translation and our judgment of the various values of it. The axiological-oriented criticism of literary translation is not supposed to be totally separated from epistemology. What is rejected is epistemology in its narrow sense, typically represented by logical positivism. Just as Davidson (2005: 85) says that "the special thing about evaluation—the part that makes it different from (and harder than) descriptive research—is that it involves more than simply collecting data and presenting results in 'value-neutral' (i.e., purely descriptive) terms". A most significant implication we can get from evaluation theory and axiology in general is that the object of our criticism is not simply a substantial object that exist "out there", but rather, the value relationship between the subject and the object. That is to say, the object of our criticism includes both the subject and the object. In other words, the subject has become part of the object in criticism as evaluation.

To sum up, we can say criticism of literary translation has some common features with epistemic activity, but it also has its own distinct peculiarities. It is a practical-oriented and axiological-oriented process of evaluating the various negative and positive values of literary translations.

5.2.2.2 Objectives of criticism of literary translation

Knowing the objectives of criticism of literary translation is of great importance. In light of the evaluation theory, criticism is a purposeful activity and may have different objectives depending on the specific context. However, generally speaking, a criticism has to tell how (in what way and to what extent) good or how bad something is. It is to find the overall significance, the overall quality or value of something evaluated or to find areas for improvement.

Finding ways to improve the quality of literary translation should be the final goal as evaluation is always practical-oriented. Criticism should be for the purpose of solving problems and creating greater values to better meet the needs of our human beings. Just as Karl Marx points out that the interpretation of the world is necessary, but the more important thing is to change it (Meehan 1969), thus, though criticism of literary translation may involve description and interpretation of the evaluand, it should offer satisfactory alternatives to make the criticism constructive—as Reiss has proposed in her *Translation Criticism: The Potentials and Limitations*.

5.2.2.3 Types of criticism of literary translation

There have been different types of criticism of literary translation both home and abroad. Though as scholars such as Reiss, Wilss and Snell-Hornby etc. have pointed out, most of them are largely anecdotal, spontaneous and unsystematic, our review finds out that there have been much efforts to make criticism of literary translation more systematic. We talked about different models or criteria in Chapter 3. Here, in this part, we will not go into every detail and will mainly concentrate on the types of criticism of literary translation from the perspective of evaluation classification.

Different types of criticism exist and have been classified from different angles by different scholars. Lv Jun and Hou Xiangqun (2001) point out that there exist the source-text-oriented scientism criticism, the target-text-oriented impressionism criticism and the theory-based criticism. They also argue that translation criticism can be divided into extra-text and intra-text criticisms. The former includes socio-political, historical and moral criticism, while the latter aesthetic, linguistic and cultural. Yang Xiaorong (2005) distinguishes criticism of English-Chinese translation, criticism of Chinese-English translation and that of back translation in terms of the direction of translation. In terms of the genre, Yang distinguishes criticism of literary translation and non-literary translation, and she says that generally speaking literary translation refers to translations of novels, plays, poems and essays etc. Wang Hongyin (2006) distinguishes three types of criticism of literary translation in terms of the purposes of criticism: 1) criticism for theorization; 2) criticism for creation and 3) criticism for translation. The first kind of criticism is mainly carried out by theorists and professional critics based on a certain belief and follow a certain paradigm. The second mainly by writers and writers who are, at the same time, translators or critics. But the typical of this type of criticism is made by those who are writers only, paying more attention to the issues such as language, techniques, structures and styles. The third is mainly carried out by translators based mainly on their own experience, their own understanding about translation and criteria for translation. In this type of criticism, translators of literary works and those of non-literary works and translators of different literary genre may have different criteria for their evaluation of a translation.

In Chapter 3, we summed up different types or forms of criticism of literary translation at the practical level in terms of objects of criticism in China and in the West. They are: 1) criticism on translation theories which belongs, according to our definition of translation criticism, to translation criticism in its broad sense; 2) criticism on translation events; 3) criticism on translated texts; and 4) criticism on the translator. We reviewed also some approaches to criticism of literary translation, for instance, Berman's analytic of translation focusing on the ethic of translating, Umberto Eco's notion of the "model reader" and those norm-based approaches by Nord, Toury, Chesterman and Hermans etc. Though doubtlessly each of the above-mentioned scholars and some other scholars have tried to draw a clear picture of the types or models of criticism of literary translation, none of them investigated distinctly from the perspective of evaluation theory and axiology in general. Herein below, we will take a look at this issue from an evaluation perspective in the hope that some new insights can be gained.

In terms of the nature of evaluation, Meehan (1969) distinguishes reasoned judgment from a direct reaction or purely emotional response. Similar to Meehan, Bahm (1993) distinguishes evaluative judgments from valuative judgments. For them, reasoned judgments or evaluative judgments involve analytic comparison and have a cognitive dimension, resembling a scientific research, whereas direct reactions or valuative judgments only express the belief of the critic that there are some values in the object or a pure emotional response to the object—liking or disliking, satisfying or unsatisfied, valuable or unvaluable. But they two never deny that direct reactions or valuative judgments also play an important role in our human life and in value judgment, only that for an adequate evaluation, we need both reasoned judgment and a direct reaction, both evaluative judgments and valuative judgments. This reminds us of the distinction between ordinary appreciation of literary translation and scientific study of literary translation made by Wang Hongyin (2006) who holds that criticism of literary translation is the combination of aesthetic appreciation and aesthetic study.

Scriven (1991) distinguishes formative evaluation from summative evaluation. The former is typically conducted with the purpose for improvement during the development of a program or product and the latter is conducted after the completion of the program. This way of distinction is helpful for us to see that criticism of literary translation does not only exist when a literary translation is finished and published. There are criticisms of literary translation during the process of translating and after the completion of a literary translation.

Diachronically, evaluation can be roughly divided into process evaluation, outcome evaluation, impact evaluation and meta- evaluation. In the above paragraph we have touched upon actually the process evaluation, outcome evaluation and impact evaluation. Process evaluation describes and assesses a program process. It may occur while a program is being developed or after its completion. Outcome evaluation pays more attention to the immediate achievements and effects of a program, while impact evaluation assesses mainly the longer-term effects, including those unintended effects. In fact, impact evaluation can be included in the outcome evaluation. Meta- evaluation is the assessment of a made evaluation to check whether an evaluation is a reasoned judgment and has fulfilled its objectives. This classification of evaluation suggests that in criticism of literary translation we can also carry out our criticism during and/or after a translation program, describing and assessing its process or results and long-term impacts, both intended and unintended. And a criticism can be reasonable or simply emotional or impressional. It also calls for criticism and evaluation. In other words, we can have process criticism, outcome criticism and meta-criticism in the criticism of literary translation.

Synchronically, many types of evaluation can co-exist. Ma Junfeng (1999) classifies evaluation into economic, moral, aesthetic, intellectual, individual and social evaluation. Li Lianke (2003) distinguishes material value from spiritual value. The former is further divided into natural value and economic value, depending on whether it is naturally shaped or man-made while the latter intellectual value, moral value and aesthetic value. This shows that in the criticism of literary translation what we will evaluate is the material value and spiritual value of a translation and to be more exact, we will have to evaluate the economic value, the ethical or moral value, the intellectual value and the aesthetic value of a translation in order to know its overall significance. What is more, we can classify criticism in terms of the criticism subject. The subject of the criticism can be an individual or the society or a group of people and therefore, we can have individual criticism and social criticism as well.

House and Howe (1999: 6) distinguish professional from non-professional evaluation. The former refers to "value conclusions rationally determined" and the latter, "preferences, beliefs, interests, and so on that are not subject to strong evidential support". For House and Howe, "professional evaluation requires deliberation and is not based on unreflective cherishing or desiring". They hold that all our statements can be value-laden and facts and values are often mingled with each other, forming a continuum. And "[p]rofessional evaluative statements fall toward the center of the fact-value continuum for the most part" (ibid: 8). From House and Howe's distinction we can infer that criticism of literary translation can also be professional or non-professional and non-professional criticism is after all criticism except that it is not strongly evident-supported. That is to say, impressionism can still have its place in criticism.

5.2.2.4 Principle of criticism of literary translation

Principles are guidelines for our human practice, and for criticism of literary translation there is no exception. Since we view criticism essentially as evaluation, we will naturally take those principles for evaluation as the principles for criticism and for criticism of literary translation in particular in the current context.

In Chapter 4, when talking about the principles for evaluation, we discussed some principles proposed by several scholars and suggest that we adopt them as our guidelines in evaluation. We mentioned Matarasso who pays great attention to the ethical principle, Meehan who thinks that the gap between fact and value is misconstrued and should be welded into an integral unit, only analytically broken, House and Howe who hold that fact and value forms a continuum instead of a dichotomy, suggest that we adopt a deliberative democratic principle which in essence bear the same feature as social constructivism advocated by Lv Jun etc. Their principles can be summed up as some do's and don'ts as follows:

1.We should seek the proper combination of Idealism and Realism in setting up criteria for criticism.

2.Emotivism should be rejected as the sole basis for value judgment.

3.Rigid empiricism/logical-positivism or scientism should be rejected because it denies even the possibility of defending value judgments by reasoned argument. The fact-value dichotomy holds that evaluators can legitimately or objectively determine facts as facts have to do with the real world but can not do so with values as values have to do with worth subjectively chosen by the subject involved and can not be reached by rational determination.

4.Individual or radical constructivism should be rejected as it holds that everything, fact or value, is subjectively chosen by the individual to form a world of his own and therefore, everything is totally relative to the individual.

5.Postmodernism should be rejected as it sees public knowledge and professional expertise as oppressive in general and in seeking to deconstruct the logocentrism, it undermines any value judgments and our judgments about any value judgment.

6.Social constructivism or the deliberative democratic principle should be adopted as it echoes Habermas' theory of communicative action, embraces the idea of the consensus theory of knowledge and public criteria, advocates authentic dialogues intersubjectively and admits the objectivity in criticism.

7.Both objective principle and subjective principle should be taken into our consideration in our criticism. In criticism, as the subjective principle entails the objective principle, we should put more weight on the subjective principle, guarding against, at the same time, going to the extreme of radical relativism as the individual constructivists and deconstructionists do.

8.Subjective principle should work together with the normative principle to ensure a reasoned criticism as norms usually stand for the social needs and interests and have priority over the individual needs.

9.Critics should follow the procedures of a well-established framework of evaluation.

10.Critics do not have to consider all criteria or all potential audiences, only those relevant to a particular time and place in a particular context.

5.2.2.5 Criteria for criticism of literary translation

Criteria have been the core of any evaluation. The same can be said with criticism of literary translation. As has been noticed, there have been various criteria for the assessment of quality of a literary translation both home and abroad. While this is something annoying for some people, it is nonetheless quite natural since we know from our study of evaluation theories and axiology in general different people may have different views on value. In this section, we will center upon, in light of the evaluation theory and axiology in general, the following issues: 1) criteria for literary translation and criteria for criticism of literary translation; 2) the bases of the criteria for criticism of literary translation; 3) the subject of the criticism; 4) the highest criteria and the ground-level criteria; and 5) criteria for the judgment of different values etc.

A. Criteria for literary translation and criteria for criticism of literary translation

Speaking of criteria for criticism of literary translation, we have first to make it clear the difference between translation criteria and the criteria for measuring a translation. As has been said when discussing criteria for evaluation, some scholars tend not to distinguish value standard from standard for measuring value, others hold that there does exist the difference between the two and it is even impossible to make such a distinction. Wang Yuliang (2000; 2006) says that most of the scholars take the needs of the subject as value standard (criteria of value) and the extent to which the needs of the subject are satisfied as standard for evaluation (criteria for value judgments), while Shi Fuwei (2006) argues that many scholars do not always distinguish criteria of value from criteria for value judgments. Similar to it, in the field of Translation Studies, we find that many scholars do not distinguish translation criteria and criteria for evaluating a translation. Wang Hongyin (2006: 65) remarks that the criteria for translation criticism used by the critic are not necessarily identical with the criteria observed by the translator. However, Wang (ibid: 131) equates translation criteria with criteria for evaluating translations when he explains his parameters for grading a translation of literary work. Yang Xiaorong (2005: 102-103) says that we can distinguish translation criteria from criteria for evaluating translations as a translator's translation criteria may not be totally the same as those of a critic and there may also exist some other differences, but in many cases, the two criteria may be identical and it is unnecessary for us to make a distinction.

The authors of this book think we had better keep such a distinction, as it is helpful for a systematic research not to blend two different conceptions. Generally speaking, our evaluation is based on a certain criterion or a set of criteria as Julius Kovesi (1998: 36) talks of moral judgment saying that "[i]t is characteristic of evaluation that we evaluate according to criteria of goodness". "Criteria of goodness" is one thing, while the criteria for judging the goodness may be the same thing and it may also be quite another, depending on contextual factors such as who is the evaluator, for what purpose he is evaluating and what a model or procedure he is following etc. If the critic is the translator himself or herself, he or she may adopt the criteria for evaluation that are the same as the translation criteria. And even if the critic and the translator is the same person, it is not impossible that criteria for evaluation may not be the same as the translation criteria if he has changed his view on translation. After all, one's view on value may change and one's value standard will change accordingly.

B. The bases of the criteria for criticism of literary translation

The next question we have to address is where the criteria for value judgment come from or on what basis we establish a certain criterion. As has just been mentioned, it is the view of value that determines one's value standard and value standard is actually determined by the needs of the subject. Therefore, in evaluation and criticism alike, what we are going to evaluate is the extent to which the needs of the subject are satisfied. That is to say, we judge the value of a literary translation on the basis of a criterion that is determined by the extent to which the needs of the subject are met. In other words, our criteria for evaluation are needs-based. This seems a reasonable answer to the above-raised question. However, two more things need to be discussed. One is that as has been pointed out by some scholars such as Scriven, Davidson, Wang Yuliang and so on, needs-based criteria may not be quite scientific, as the needs of the subject are not all reasonable and the satisfaction of those unreasonable and unhealthy needs can only be harmful to the subject and hence bears negative "value". Thus, needs-based criteria call for the distinction between needs and wants or desires. We talked about their difference in Chapter 4. The former refer to something that is deemed necessary, especially for the survival of the person, organization, or whatever whereas the latter refer to a conscious desire without which dissatisfaction occurs. But here, we have to actually make another distinction between desire and ideal. Yet, such a distinction is obviously very subtle and difficult, especially for an individual. A possible solution is to put it in a specific context and take the social norms into our consideration. That is one of the reasons we recommend the combination of subjective principle and the normative principle as one of our guidelines for criticism. What is more, if we consider "needs" in its broad sense, "ideal" may also be regarded as a kind of need. That is why Min Ze and

Dang Shengyuan (1999) in their *Value of Literary Works* (*Wen Xue Jia Zhi Lun*) say that the aesthetic needs and aesthetic ideals of the subject should be the yardstick for measuring the quality of a literary work. To sum up, we can say that the criteria for criticism of literary translation are based on the reasonable needs (including the reasonable ideals sometimes) of the subject. But then, we have to answer another question immediately: who are the subject?

C. The subject of the criticism

Axiolohically, value is the relationship between the object and the subject. Therefore, value is always the value of the object for the subject. Bahm (1993: 70) once described how the criteria for value judgment are set up:

> When a person has made a particular kind of value judgment several times, its recurrence may endow it with a standardized character. When several persons make similar value judgments many times, their common recurrence may endow them with a socially standardized character and develop into a cultural trait…Once a judgment acquires social establishment, it functions as a prejudgment about values.

The above description shows that the subject of evaluation/criticism is generally divided into two kinds: individual and social. When the subject is an individual, it can be the translator himself or herself, it can be an editor, a teacher teaching translation, especially literary translation, a public reader who knows nothing about the source language and the source culture, a reader who knows a little about the original writer, a bilingual reader who knows something about the two languages and cultures involved, a bilingual reader who are quite familiar with the original work and its author, a friend of the translator, an enemy of the translator, the author of the original work, an expert in literary studies, an expert in translation studies, a writer in the target culture, another translator, another translator who has translated the same work, a professional critic, an authority in the profession… Each of these individual subjects may have their own criteria for their value judgment owing to the differences in their backgrounds, professions, social positions, purposes and many other factors. These differences will inevitably bring about the differences of their understanding of literature, literary translation, their needs and expectations of literary translation, views of values and their criteria for value judgment. Some critics may prefer the accurate expression of the meaning of the original, others the form and style of the original, and some may value more the likeness of the spirit of the translated to that of the original, others only the readability of the target text and the aesthetic appeal of the translated. Still others may prefer the long-term impact of the translated. All in all, this reminds us of all those different forms of criticism of literary translation in China and in the West we talked about in Chapters 2 and 3. What is more, the maximal criteria for literary translation set by the individual may be quite different just as the maximal criteria set for literary creation by different writers and critics. In the field of literary creation, the maximal criteria for literary writing can be found quite different. Du Fu in one of his poems expresses his criterion for poetry writing, saying that he will never feel satisfied with his poems if they can not have the effect of striking the reader. Zheng Banqiao, the great painter and poet in the Qing Dynasty, values much brevity, novelty and the lofty spirit and considers meeting requirements in these aspects as his criterion for judging the value of the art of work. The couplet in his study says that brevity is the soul of wit and novelty is the goal of writing. And by such criteria, it is said, Zheng Banqiao burnt out many of his poems which he evaluates as valueless. On the contrary, some critics point out that many of the contemporary Chinese writers prefer the economic value of their works to the ethic values and there is the tendency of vulgarity. For some writers and critics alike, "best-seller" has become their criterion for evaluating a literary work. Similarly, in the field of literary translation, some scholars and translators such as Qian Zhongshu, Fu Lei and Nida, make "sublime adaptation", "similarity in spirit" and "equivalent effect" as the maximal criterion, Guo Muoruo and Cheng Fangwu hold that the best situation is that the translator of a poem should be a competent poet himself and the translator should completely identify himself with the author of the original poem. Others, like Zeng Xubai, argue that different translators of Homer all claim they have captured the spirit of Homer, but this is absolutely impossible. However, the criterion for translation is only one, that is, to translate accurately the translator's understanding of the original (Chen Fukang 1992). Facing so many different criteria for criticism, it is not surprising that people generally hold that criticism is but something subjective.

However, if we think that criticism of literary translation is totally subjective, we are totally wrong. For we know that evaluation is both subjective and objective. It is objective because the seemingly subjective value judgments have their objective ground. Any individual is an individual of a certain society in a certain time. He or she is thereby constrained by the physical world and the spiritual world in which he or she lives. Their needs, their outlooks of value are all influenced and even governed to a certain extent by the environment of their living and by people around them. We talked about in the foregoing chapters the changing of values in different historical periods. According to scientists, the ancients needed only 18 elements in the Nature to survive the world, whereas we human beings today need at least 80 elements (Li Deshun 2004: 48). This shows that the individual's needs and outlooks of value are actually objectively constrained by space and time. It also shows that criteria of value judgment are an objective existence in a certain society and during a certain developmental period of the society.

Comparatively speaking, social subject—the subject of the criticism being a group of people or a community—is more objective, though it is also subjective. This is because the criteria for criticism are based on the needs and outlooks of value of the society instead of the individual. Li Deshun holds that the criteria for social evaluation are the objective needs of the society and the dominant ideology of the society (He Haibing & Qin Hongyi 2008). As the Chinese traditionally value the needs and interests of the collective much more than those of the individual, the criteria for criticism of the social subject tend to possess more power and more validity.

It is reasonable for people to put on more weight on social criteria. First, it is agreeable that the needs and interests of the society are more important than those of an individual. Secondly, social criteria are based on social norms that are often made and observed by most of the members of the community. Social norms can be classified into different kinds: technical norms which regulate mainly the conduct of the human being's knowing and reforming the physical world, legal norms which take the form of laws and political and ethical norms which govern and regulate mainly the conduct of the interpersonal communication. All these norms are the realized or conscious reasonable needs and values of a society and therefore have the property of consensus of truth. When we adopt them as the criteria for evaluating or criticizing any social activity including literary translation, there will be more reasonable value judgments. For example, most people adopt "fidelity" and "readability" as criteria for translation. That is because such criteria are widely accepted and reflected the needs and expectations of most of the readers and hence have become part of our social norms.

Though social subject and social criteria seem more important than individual subject and individual criteria, it does not mean we can do without individual criteria and individual criticism. Actually, as Chen Xinhan (1994) points out, social subject can be a group of people, a class of people or a nation, but it is the individual that functions as the realistic subject. Social evaluation means that an individual or an institution consisting of different individuals makes value judgments in accordance with the social criteria. This indicates that though individual evaluation usually adopts the individual's own criteria, an individual may also employ the social criteria. And in this case, the distinction between individual criticism and social criticism is no longer clear-cut.

D. The maximal criteria and the minimal criteria

We mentioned the maximal criteria given by different subjects in the above paragraphs. In the following paragraphs, we will center upon the issue of the maximal criteria and the minimal criteria. We know from axiology that the criteria for evaluation can be goal-based or needs-based and the latter is preferred by us. We also know that needs may be of different importance for the subject and therefore we have to set up the order of importance of various needs for the establishment of needs-based criteria. That naturally brings us to the question of the ranking of values. Frondizi (1971) once made some remarks on the polarity and hierarchy of values. Values often present themselves in a positive and negative aspect: good or bad, beautiful or ugly, positive value or disvalue/negative value. For value is the relation between the subject and the object, and polarity implies a break with indifference and the establishment of an evaluative relation.

> In the presence of objects of the physical world, we can be indifferent. On the other hand, the moment a value attaches itself to an object, such indifference is broken and we like it or dislike it, accept it or reject it, seek it or avoid it. We are not neutral when confronted with a work of art or a dishonest act. (Frondizi 1971: I)

If we think an object has positive values, we have also to rank these values especially in a professional criticism. And actually the ranking of values is significant for the development of the individual and the society as a whole. For the purpose of our human practice, including evaluation, is to create greater value, as has been said many times. Ranking values or listing the hierarchical order of values is often revealed in the subject's preference and choice. Yet, it is here that we need to make our best endeavors to reach a reasoned judgment. Our ranking should not be solely emotional; rather, a rational calculation supported by sufficient relevant data is badly needed. Of course, it is much easier to point out that we need a set of criteria that can tell us the hierarchical order of values than to state concretely what that order is. There have been axiologists who have proposed such a table of values, but were severely criticized and forgotten. The problem is that the importance of value, just like needs or values, is highly context dependent. It is hard to say whether a sweet song is more beautiful or valuable than a delicious meal without taking the specific context into our account. However, that does not mean criteria for value judgment are absolutely arbitrary, relative and can never be fixed. What is implied is that criteria can be set up in a specific context and be adopted to reach a valid judgment. What is more, efforts have been made to set up kind of minimal criteria that are accepted by the majority of a community or even agreed cross-culturally. Tang Yijie, a famous philosopher in Beijing University proposes that we adopt Confucius's belief "do unto others as you would be done by" (or "do not do to others what you do not want them to do to you" or "never impose on others what you would not choose for yourself") as the ground-level criterion (code) of conduct, which he considers acceptable to any culture and any country (Lv Jun 2002). Early in 1988 in the Nobel Prize Winners' Conference held in Paris focusing on the threats and promises of the 21st century, the Sweden physician Hannes Alfvén was reported to declare that in order to survive in the 21st century we human beings have to turn to Confucius for wisdom (Yang Yitang 2009). In 1993, The Parliament of the World's Religions proclaimed the Golden Rule as the common principle for many religions. The "Declaration Toward a Global Ethic" was signed by 143 leaders from different faith traditions and spiritual communities. It states "[w]e must treat others as we wish others to treat us. We make a commitment to respect life and dignity, individuality and diversity, so that every person is treated humanely, without exception" (http://www.religioustolerance.org/parliame.htm). According to Yi Zhongtian (2008), Confucius's belief "do unto others as you would be done by" has been inscribed on the wall of a hall in The United Nations Headquarters.

Confucius' teaching of "do unto others as you would be done by" as a ground-level criterion can throw some light on the issue of translation criteria. Facing various needs and desires or ideals of our human beings, it is difficult to come to an agreement as to what should be the highest value and the highest value standard. According to Li Deshun (2004), we should take a more dynamic attitude toward the hierarchy of needs and values. Li classifies needs into two kinds: the material and the spiritual. The material needs include the basic biological needs and needs for economic development, whereas the spiritual needs are needs for knowledge of the world, the society and human life and needs for the satisfactory political and ethical life, and for aesthetical enjoyment etc. The ultimate needs are the developmental value featured by a harmonious combination of the development of material needs and spiritual needs, which finds expression in the unity of the realization of truth, good and beauty. Thus, we can adopt the measurement of the quality and quantity of the realization of all kinds of material and spiritual values as the criteria for evaluation. The quality and quantity of values decide the hierarchy of value. Wang Hongyin (2006) once offered a set of highest criteria for criticizing literary translation. Wang classified literary works into two kinds: reproductive and representative. Each of the two kinds has its needs of "truthfulness", "goodness" and " beauty" to meet. When it comes to literary translation, "truthfulness" becomes "*xin*", "goodness", "*da*" and " beauty", "*ya*". The needs of the two kinds of literary translations are concreted into several demands and one dominant social effect (for details, see Chapter 3). The best translation is one that can meet the demands of all the three aspects, the organic unity of the realization of values of "*xin, da* and *ya*". What comes next is the translation that can meet the general requirement of "*xin*" and "*da*", translations that only meet the demand of "*xin*" will be ranked as the third.

While we admit that it is reasonable to rank the translation that can meet the needs of the realization of "*xin, da* and *ya*" the best as such a realization indicates the fulfillment of the intended value, the ranking criteria under discussion are problematic. For it is often difficult to make a clear distinction between the requirement for "*xin*" and "*da*" as Yan Fu said that "to be *da* is to be *xin*". Zheng Zhenduo also remarks "faithful translation means expressive translation. It is doubtful that a translation that is not expressive is faithful" (Chen Fukang 1992: 231). Indeed, it is hard to imagine a translation that is faithful is not expressive if the original is expressive and since either "*xin*" (faithfulness) or "*da*" (expressiveness) is to be realized by means of language, the two criteria can actually be expressed as one criterion: "faithful expression". In fact, "faithfulness" is a problematic term to be used as a criterion for translation, as it has two senses: one is "fidelity", the other is "loyalty". When it is used in the first sense, it can mean "true" or "follow the original exactly", when in the second sense, "honest" or "loyalty" (Cambridge International Dictionary of English). The first sense has mainly to do with the quality of a product in terms of the transfer of information, while the second, mainly with the quality of a person's conduct in terms of his attitude (needless to say, it also has something to do with the product as the product is always the product of an agent, a translator with a certain attitude). Similarly, the Chinese character "*xin*" that has long been taken as a criterion for translation is also problematic. For the system of traditional Chinese ethics keeps a distinction between "*zhong*" (忠), which refers to mainly the second sense of "faithfulness" in English as can be seen from the grapheme of the Chinese character "*zhong*" (忠) from "*xin*" (信), which originally is used mainly to mean "keeping one's words" as can be seen also from the grapheme of the Chinese character "*xin*" (信). But as time went on, the semantic meaning of the character "*xin*" (信) gradually expanded and has been used to refer to "loyalty", "fidelity" and to the concept of "faithful" and "creditable". That explains why the character "*xin*" (信) has been translated into English quite differently by different scholars nowadays as "faithfulness" or "fidelity" or "loyalty". And in our daily use and scholarly discussion of translation criteria alike, people often have different interpretations of it and use it to refer to different things. In discussions of literary translation especially, there has always been the question of "faithful to whom, to what and to what extent". Some scholars use it to mean that the translated should be totally the same as the original in every way, others refer it to the accurate transfer of meaning of the original, and still others the exact or similar effect or function of the original (Yang Xiaorong 2005). Wang Hongyin (2006) uses it in the sense of "fidelity" to refer to the requirement of the exact transfer of the facts and logical relationship of the original work, whereas Wang Dongfeng (2004) holds that "the notion of 'fidelity' is theoretically untenable. It embodies an all-or-nothing ethical judgment and hence can hardly function as a criterion for evaluating translations". Of course, for those deconstructionists, either "faithfulness" or "fidelity" is meaningless—an idea we are strongly against. Nevertheless, all these have made the English "faithfulness" and Chinese character "*xin*" two problematic terms. The authors of this book suggest that we use "fidelity" (accuracy) and "creditability" mainly in our discussion of the relation between the translation and the original texts for the measurement of the intellectual value of a translation and regard "loyalty" as a criterion in judging the politic and ethic values of a translation and a translational event. In the sense that nothing is perfect in the world, the maximal criteria for criticism is often thought to be impractical, but it is still valuable as a goal for the translators to achieve and as a direction of all human practice.

Comparatively speaking, it is more realistic, and in a sense more important, for us to come to a consensus concerning the minimal criterion for value and value judgment. This suggests that in setting up criteria for translation and translation criticism including criticism of literary translation, we should seek a minimal criterion for different needs: political and ethical needs, intellectual needs, aesthetic needs, economic needs and social developmental needs etc. And indirectly, this suggests we should set up criteria for texts of different types as people usually have different expectations and needs for different texts. In this respect, Lv Jun (2002) has made some fruitful attempts. A set of criteria offered by him requires first that a translation should be able to stand the test of the objectivity of knowledge, secondly that a translation should be plausible in its understanding of the original and valid in its interpretation of the original and thirdly, a translation should go along with the intentionality of the original. Such criteria are more acceptable especially for literary translation as different interpretations to one and the same text are allowed so long as they are reasonable. The feature of polysemy of literary texts is taken fully into consideration in such criteria. The merit of such a set of criteria lies also in its seeking the objectivity of criticism and at the same time does not deny the validity of subjective judgment. From the perspective of evaluation theory, we can say such a set of criteria is suitable for measuring the ethical value, intellectual value and part of the aesthetic value and cultural value of a literary translation. Though such a set of criteria is not perfect, nevertheless, it is a significant step taken toward the systematicity and scientificity of translation criticism, especially criticism of literary translation, in the context of plurality of criteria for criticism.

E. Criteria for the judgment of different values in literary translation

In the above paragraph we spoke of the minimal criteria for measuring different values of a literary translation. We mentioned ethical value, intellectual value and aesthetic value etc. In fact, a literary translation may have a lot more different values and to evaluate a literary translation we need to establish criteria for each of them. However, that is far beyond the ability of the authors and seems unnecessary, for practically we need only to know some of the main values to come to a reasonable value judgment. In what follows, we will mainly discuss those prominent factors concerning the establishment of criteria for judging the political and ethical value, intellectual value and aesthetic value.

a) Political and ethical value

When talking about branches of axiology in Chapter 4, we say axiology, as the science inquiring into values, actually consists of different value sciences—aesthetics: the science of beauty, ugliness and fine art; ethics: the science of oughtness, duty, rightness and wrongness; religiology: the science inquiring into the ultimate values of life as a whole; and economics: the science of wealth relative to the production, distribution, and consumption of goods etc.

Ethics as value theory concerns itself with the evaluation of human conduct. It is also called moral philosophy, a science about the principles we ought to live by. According to Rozov (1998), one of the modern schools (paradigms) of axiology that can be termed "constructive axiology" differs from the classical axiology in that it prefers the idea of "the values of general significance" to that of "universal values" which is favoured by classical axiology. Values of general significance are thought to be values accepted by a particular community as necessary for the basic social and cultural functions of this community, amenable to expansion beyond the community to the nation or humanity as a whole, harmless to the other values, principles, sacred things and symbolism of varying cultures and social groups. Such a school admits the relativity of ethic value and at the same time holds that there are some values that possess general significance. The relativity is evident as we can find that some ethic values in one community may be considered as "supreme" or "universal" may not be obligatory for another community.

The contemporary philosopher Jürgen Habermas tries to develop a "discourse" oriented communicative ethics which requires a valid defense of those values accepted by communities or individuals. Habermas' theory of communicative action has great influence on the re-establishment of rationality of human communication including ethics.

T. M. Scanlon is an influential contemporary moral philosopher who did great contribution to the re-establishment of rationality of human morality. Scanlon is a pluralist and contractualist about both moral and non-moral values. Contractualism, in a broad sense, indicates the view that morality is based on contract or agreement, and in a narrow sense, a particular view developed by Scanlon, especially in his book *What We Owe to Each Other*, that thinking about right and wrong is thinking about what we do in terms that can be justified to others and that others can not reasonably reject, and hence, moral standards come from "mutual recognition", wrongness consists in unjustifiability. Scanlon argues that contractualism allows for most of the variability in moral requirements that relativists have claimed, it also accounts for the full force of our judgments of right and wrong. The concept of contract is of social as moral conclusions such as fairness and responsibility can be understood through mutual justification and criticism. (http://www.hup.harvard.edu/catalog/SCAWHA. html)This contractualist view is obviously identical with social constructivism and the consensus theory of truth which we are for and provides us with a sound foundation for the judgment of ethic values. According to Scanlon, benign relativism acknowledges both moral relativism and moral objectivity. Values with general significance are usually justified and cannot be reasonably rejected by most cultures and hence are objective. Such contracted values form the core of the ethic norms and other values may vary from culture to culture and from community to community (Chen Zhen 2008).

Ethic relativism is also called cultural relativism. But here, cultural relativism in moral philosophy is different from cultural relativism in anthropology as the latter usually does not make value judgment as to which culture is superior (in the descriptive approach). Actually, ethic relativism can be said a result of cultural diversity. As people in different culture may have different ethic values, we should be cautious to make judgments of ethic value cross-culturally. Cross-cultural judgments of ethic value can only be made based on the criteria (values of general significance) that are cross-culturally accepted. Otherwise, if we adopt criteria that are only acceptable to a specific culture in a specific time to measure the ethic value of another culture, we will make the mistake of being ethno-centralism.

All value judgments involve subjectivity. The judgment of ethic values has no exception. But this by no means can stop us from making reasonable judgments of ethic values and other values. First, those values including ethic values once pursued by people in different historical periods have objective constrains over individual subject (Han Dan 2009). Secondly, the needs and outlooks of value including ethic value of an individual subject are objectively constrained or influenced by the social norms. That is to say, subjectivity will become intersubjectivity in a specific social context. And the intersubjective experience of a community or group exists dependently of people's shared perceptions and intersubjective sensemaking. Thirdly, as House and Howe (1999: 9) say that in value judgments we do not accept the positivist notion of objectivity. Being objective in value judgments means "working toward unbiased statements through the procedures of the discipline, observing the canons of proper argument and methodology, maintaining a healthy skepticism, and being vigilant to eradicate sources of bias". All in all, the attitude of benign relativism we take in evaluation and criticism does not deny the objectivity of the criteria for value judgment. Rather, as has been made clear in our discussion of principles of evaluation in Chapter 4, we insist on the integrity of subjectivity with objectivity and the integrity of relativity and universality.

The above discussion is helpful for the establishment of criteria for judging the politic and ethic values of literary translation as translation is an interlingual and intercultural activity. Here, the authors prefer to discuss ethic value together with politic value because these two kinds of values are closely linked. Politics, as is known, is closely connected with power as power with interests of individuals or collectivities or classes or nations. Politics is in a way defined by morals of different classes or nations: people's beliefs about right and wrong, good and bad, right ways of living, virtues to pursue, vices to fight, responsibilities and duties to shoulder, and the outlooks of value as a whole. All these have made politics an ethical matter. The only difference lies in the fact that politics seems to show more concerns with the ethical value of classes and nations than that of individual's whereas ethics concerns moral principles of individuals and collectivities both. Here, we can see why moral philosophy has been called the first social science, why many translation studies scholars and scholars in other fields of social researches nowadays appeal to go back to ethics, why some translation studies scholars are talking about the politics of translation, and why we prefer to discuss criteria for evaluating ethic values together with politic values.

Since we have made it clear our view of translation as a social activity, an interlingual and intercultural speech event and also as a profession (a fact often neglected by many theoretical studies), let us begin with the professional ethics of translation. Williams and Chesterman (2004: 19) state that:

> At a more practical level, many national professional associations of translators have an official code of good practice which states the ethical principles that professional translators are expected to abide by. These codes are attempts to translate abstract ideas and values into concrete form, and also to meet the needs of translation as a business activity, involving e.g. the requirement of professional secrecy....
>
> There are also internationally agreed documents concerning ethical translatorial behavior. One is the Translator's Charter, and another is the Nairobi Declaration.

The above-mentioned Translator's Charter is issued by FIT. It is mainly about the obligations, rights of translators and the issue of copyright etc. Among those obligations, one finds that "[e]very translation shall be faithful and render exactly the idea and form of the original— this fidelity constituting both a moral and legal obligation for the translator" and "[a] faithful translation, however, should not be confused with a literal translation, the fidelity of a translation not excluding an adaptation to make the form, the atmosphere and deeper meaning of the work felt in another language and country" (http://www.fit-ift.org/en/charter.php).

The FIT Regional Centre Europe (FIT Europe) has also issued its Code of Professional Practice, laying down the basic rights and obligations of translators and interpreters as a non-exhaustive guide for its member associations. The following is one of its requirements: "Translators and interpreters shall not knowingly mistranslate or misinterpret. Instructions received from the client cannot justify deviation from this Code" (http://www.fit-europe.org/vault/deont/CODE_PROF_PRACTICE.pdf).

In Chapter 2 we talked about some other requirements issued by other translator associations in the world, each concerning some ethical criteria. The common is that translators are to be faithful to the original. Thus, it seems that "faithfulness to the original" can be taken as a criterion. Yet, the term "faithfulness" as a criterion is problematic especially with literary translation as we will see in the following discussion.

Out of the professional circle, much of the discussions about the ethic values or ethic criteria for literary translation are more theoretical-oriented, especially with descriptive translation studies. However, as translation is a kind of social practice and translation criticism, as is shown by evaluation theory and axiology in general, is more practical-oriented, our discussion here will try to guide our theoretical research to the direction of problem-solving in practice.

When setting up criteria for measuring the politic and ethic values of a literary translation, Confucius's teaching of "do unto others as you would be done by" is especially enlightening as it mainly concerns the interpersonal relationship, the code of conduct of our human beings. Normally, a writer hopes his or her work to be translated as accurately as possible, with the maximum loyalty to him or her. For to be loyal is to show due respect to the author and another culture. In other words, "loyalty" to the author of the original and to a foreign culture is an ethical requirement for the translator. "Loyalty" as Nord has put it, is "an ethical concept governing translators' responsibility to their partners in the cooperative activity of translation, beyond 'fidelity' as a relation between texts" (Nord 2001). And in this sense, translators are required not only to respect the original but also the reader and the client. Being not loyal to the original means a cheating for the reader as this will lead to unfaithful translation. Normally, the reader hopes to read a translation that is translated without much distortion by the translator. By "normally", I mean that there will be exceptions. And it is the exception that proves the rule. We talked about Berman's criticism on various distortion of the original and Venuti's criticism on the Western cultural hegemony by means of domesticating the foreign and the publishers' connivance and support of the strategy of fluent translation for the sake of making greater profit, leading to the marginalization of experimental translations and depriving the readers of the rights of accessing those unfamiliar forms of literary works. Their criticisms actually indicate that we need to make "loyalty" an ethical criterion for translation.

Another example we gave in Chapter 3 when talking about the criticism of translation event is Kundera's correction of translations of his own novels by irresponsible translators, editors and publishers. Kundera complained about the misinterpreting, mistranslating of his novels and spent more time in correcting the translations than in writing the originals. Snell-Hornby (2006: 107) comments that this raises questions not only about cultural transfer but also "translation ethics, and the responsibility of translator, editor and publishers towards both the author and readers".

One more example is given by Lv Jun and Hou Xiangqun (2001: 76-77). They talk about Even King's translation of Lao She's novel *Luo Tuo Xiang Zi* to show the importance of respecting the original. The author was made quite angry by the translator's changing the tragedy ending into a comedy with large amount of distortion of the plots of the original novel. Lao She declared that what Even King has translated was not his novel. When the translator translated another novel named *Divorce* by Lao She, the author was forced again to make the same declaration and asked to confine the issue of the translation because the translator has again changed hugely the plots of the original. Lv Jun (2002) points out that the translator's "violence" against the original is actually manipulated by the power of ideology of American society when the novels were translated in the beginning of the 1940s. At that time the dominant ideology was to create a joyous atmosphere to reduce and cover up the mental sufferings of the public in the sacrifice of loyalty to the original.

The above example also shows that translation is not simply an interlingual and intercultural activity, it is a political event as well. Translation can reveal the conflicts of interests between different classes and nations and the unequal power relations between the two languages and cultures involved. In the history of Bible translation, Martin Luther's version was banned and William Tindale was even hanged as their translations threatened the interests of the Church and were judged as having negative value and harmful to the society by the dominant ideology. Here, there rises another issue that is often neglected: the respect to the translator, to the needs and interests of the translator and those with the same needs and interests as the translator. It is not that the translator is always wrong when there is contradiction and conflict between the translator and the society or the other parties involved in the translation event. On the contrary, it is often the translator that may stand for the long-term needs and interests of the society. Thus, when we make criticism of literary translation, we should also pay attention to the long-term value of the translated and to the unequal power relations that may exist between the critic and the translator and between the two cultures as well. "Loyalty" is not the sole yardstick by which we assess a translation. Respect and tolerance should also be taken into our consideration.

Everyone wants to be respected. This is what Maslow's theory of needs tells us and the Golden Rule proclaimed by the Parliament of the World's Religions in its "Declaration Toward a Global Ethic" signed by 143 leaders from different cultural backgrounds. To "respect life and dignity, individuality and diversity" should also be made a golden rule in translation for the translators, editors and publishers especially. The examples given in the above paragraphs have spoken well for it: since we do not want others to disdain us, we should not disdain others. This is especially significant in the current context of globalization marked by more and more cultural exchange. If we do not want our own writing translated at the translator's will, and if we do not want our own culture to be distorted through translation, we should try to avoid doing so to the writing and culture of others. To show due respect to the original author and his or her culture, to show due respect to the translator and the reader, and to show due respect to critics each other should be included in the ground-level ethical criteria for evaluating a literary translation. However, as there might be different needs and expectations or ideals among the parties involved in the translation event, there might be conflicts between these respects. Chesterman once pointed out readers will make evaluative judgments about a translation according to their expectations and "will approve of a translator who confirms to these expectations" (Munday 2001: 119). Meanwhile, a teacher, a literary critic and publisher's reader, acting as norm-authority, can confirm the prevalent norm by encouraging translations that conform to the norms they accept. According to Chesterman, this may be that a translation should meet TL criteria of readability and fluency or "[a]lternatively, a literary critic may criticize a translation that offends the norm, and this criticism may damage the reception of that book amongst ordinary readers" (ibid). And "there may sometimes be a clash between the norm 'authorities' and society in general". In this case, there will be different criticism on one and the same translation and translation event. If we think of the fact that there exist so many different needs and interests, the above-mentioned phenomenon is not surprising at all. A descriptive study will only tell us the fact, but an axiological study cannot stop at that. Facing such a phenomenon, we should, and indeed have to, pass on our judgments on it. We might acknowledge that each of the criticism may be right or partly right. We might also make our own judgment by specifying the context, the contextual objectives, the reasonable needs of the individual subject and the society etc. and by means of careful observation, data collection, analysis and comparison etc. That is to say, we should adjust our criteria to the specific context and follow strictly the models or frameworks of the criticism. Since we suggest a needs-based approach, the most important thing for the critic is to know the real and reasonable needs of the individual subject and the society as a whole. Usually, we will put the needs and interests of the society as a whole in the first place. In other words, the social norm will be normally regarded as superior to that of the individual and that of a certain authority. But what we should bear in mind is that norms form a system and in the norm system there are various norms struggling for the dominant position. Historically, norms that conform to the needs and interests of the majority of the members of the society, norms that indicate the brighter future of the society and the world a whole, norms that stand for the scientific progress of the society will finally win out. This indicates that the current social norms are not always right, and they are changeable. By adopting a norm that is different from the dominant social norm may not be always wrong. We acknowledge the plurality of values and plurality of criteria or norms for evaluating values, but we recommend more the authentic dialogue between different criteria and norms. In this sense, Habermas' communicative ethics can well serve as our guideline for discussing the criteria of politic and ethic values in literary translation. Our discussion here also indicates that, as Juan C. Sager (1983: 121) says "[t]here are no absolute standards of translation quality but only more or less appropriate translations for the purpose for which they are intended". Another implication of our discussion here is that, as the evaluation theory tells us, criticism is a continuous process toward a consensus (truth), it is part of our human practice to create greater values. In this way, we are actually suggesting a practical-oriented dialectical sociological approach to criticism of literary translation, especially when the evaluation of the political and ethical values of a literary translation is concerned. Though there exist many different values and criteria or norms, the specific context and our detailed analysis of the main contextual factors will suggest the proper criteria to be adopted (Zhang Zhiqiang 2008). In the context of globalization, we treasure more the criteria of loyalty and respect to the original author and his or her language and culture as first, this is beneficial for the equal exchange of different cultures. Secondly, it can improve our understanding and tolerance of other literary traditions, other politic and ethic values, and in a way, better our understanding of ourselves. Thirdly, it is beneficial too for the preservation of cultural diversity, good for the dehegemonizing the cultural hegemony, ethno-centralism and the increasing cultural conflicts, and good for avoiding imposing our values and beliefs on others. And all in all, it conforms to the needs and interests of our human beings to build a harmonious world to live in.

There have been some politic and ethic criticism of literary translation in Translation Studies. Scholars such as Lefevere, Bassnett, Trivedi, Chesterman, Nirajarna, Simon, Venuti, Spivak, Bhabha, Robinson, and Pym etc. all showed great concern for the politics of translation. However, as most of them are greatly influenced by poststructurism and take a deconstructivist approach to the cultural and political aspects of translation, and as they have different academic backgrounds, they view literary translation from different perspectives and come to different understanding about the politic and ethic values of literary translation. They either find in literary translation the manipulation of ideology of the target culture or the power imbalance between the two languages and cultures. Some of them relate translation with the question of gender and find a language of sexism in translation studies. For example, translation has been compared to a woman either beautiful but not faithful or faithful but ugly. They also see the male-orientation in Steiner's metaphorical explanation of the four stages of translating concerning his hermeneutic motion. These feminist translation theorists seek to promote the status of the translated texts and women as well, taking translation as a political activity to fight for women the equal power or rights with men or for the equal power of the language and culture of the less powerful nation with that of the powerful nations. Sherry Simon (1996: 2) sees translation as a committed project and holds that "fidelity is to be directed toward neither the author nor the reader, but toward the writing project—a project in which both writer and translator participate". G. C. Spivak as a postcolonialist and feminist theorist criticizes the "ideological consequences of the translation of 'Third Word' literature into English and the distortion this entails" (Munday 2001: 133). She speaks out "against Western feminists who expect feminist writing from outside Europe to be translated into the language of power, English" in "translatese"—a term used by Spivak to refer to the kind of domestication which "eliminates the identity of politically less powerful individuals and cultures" —that consequently leads to the fact that "the literature by a woman in Palestine begins to resemble, in the feel of its prose, something by a man in Taiwan" (ibid). Spivak also makes comments on some translations from Bengali to English. She thinks that these translations "too often fail to translate the difference of the Bengali view because the translator, albeit with good intentions, over-assimilates it to make it accessible to the Western readers" (ibid: 134). She says "[t]he status of a language in the world is what one must consider when teasing out the politics of translation. Translatese in Bengali can be derided and criticized by large groups of Anglophone and anglograph Bengalis" (Venuti 2000: 406-407). Such phenomena suggest that readers from powerful and less powerful nations may have different value judgments on the one and the same translation. Niranjana (1992) speaks of asymmetrical relations of power between the colonizer and the colonized and the fact that translation has been used by the colonial power as a tool to rewrite the image of the "East" and to reinforce the power of the colonizers. She calls for an "interventionist" approach from the translator not to be assimilated by the Western culture and make visible the difference between the two languages and cultures involved in a translation.

There are some other postcolonialists like Bhabha and Robinson, who value the equal cultural exchange, thinking that translations of literary works with the feature of hybridity may produce a better effect of reducing cultural hegemony and ethno-centrism. The term "hybridity" is, according to Gina Wisker (2007: 189), originated in horticulture, and refers to "the cross-breeding of two species by grafting or cross-pollination to form a third, 'hybrid' species". In postcolonial theory, "hybridity" is "both widely used and disputed, referring to the creation of new transcultural rather than multicultural (crossing and fertilizing rather than fragmented) forms within the space produced by colonization where people, indigenous, immigrated, settled, colonizing and colonized, live and move". The word "hybridization", therefore, "involves new mixes of linguistic, cultural, political and racial beliefs and forms" (Wisker 2007: 190). "Hybridity recognizes a polyphony of voices, narrative forms and viewpoints... aligns itself with a sense of a cultural equity despite difference, through these varieties of voices" (ibid). Wisker further explains that

> Hybridity as a concept and lived experience is rich with cultural meaning drawn from the varieties of culture which are affecting any individuals or groups. It is more than just a cross-cultural exchange since for those included there is a wealth of expected issues to do with the language, politics, values and identity. (ibid)

Homi K. Bhabha (1994) talks about the significance of hybridity in that it can impair the hegemony of powerful culture by means of impurifying the hegemonic language and the colonizer's culture. Schaffner and Adab (2001) (re)define hybrid text as follows: "Hybrid text, in addition to being products of text production in a specific cultural space, which is often in itself an intersection of different cultures, can also result from a translation process". They think that hybrid texts show features that somehow seem "out of place", "strange" or "unusual" for the target readers. Douglas

Robinson (1997) holds that hybridity is a process of linguistic, cultural, political and racial properties and is welcome by most postcolonialists as it can enrich the culture of our human beings as a whole. According to this hybridity view, the translator should show respect both to the original author and to the target reader. He or she should try to bridge the gap between the two languages and cultures to accomplish the task of cross-cultural communication. The criterion for judging a good translation hence is set up based on the task of translation serving for the equal exchange and better understanding between and of different literary traditions and different cultures.

The above discussion shows that deconstructivist cultural approaches to translation will bring some contradictory conclusions as to what the translator should pay their loyalty and respect to and by what means. Some theorists propose to give full play to the subjectivity of the translator regardless of the loyalty to the original, others may advocate strategies to make the features of the original prominent, paying adequate respect to the source language and culture, and still others suggest the respect of the translator to both the source and the target texts and cultures. Seen from the perspective of evaluation theory and axiology in general, this indicates different people have different ideas about ethic values and different ways of ranking the ethic values. Comparatively speaking, we prefer the hybridity view as it entails not only the requirement of loyalty and respect but also another very important political and ethical value, i.e. equality and fairness. In other words, besides loyalty and respect and tolerance, equality and fairness between the two languages and cultures should also be taken into our consideration when we try to set up criteria for literary translations.

What is more, studies have shown that criteria for criticizing the politic and ethic values of literary translations may also have to consider factors of text types and ways of our doing translation. Cay Dollerup (1997) holds that translation can be classified into translation as "imposition" and translation as 'requisition', 'Imposition' is normally driven by the source culture, often with little regard for the receptor culture, and pays much attention to the intention of the original text; whereas 'requisition' comes from the target culture and implies a more relaxed attitude towards the sender's intentionality. He argues that "[s]cientific and educational material is translated mostly as requisition but there is a difference in the fidelity towards the source text: scientific texts will tend to be loyal and literal, whereas educational ones allow for more latitude and adaptation" (Dollerup 1997: 47-48). According to Dollerup, "[a] daptation will apply, in particular, to literary translation where successful translation is characterized by an overall requisitioning attitude" (ibid: 48). Dollerup (ibid: 54) adds that "[a]s far as literature is concerned, ideologically-driven translation is unlikely to survive into the next century, for the simple reason that computer networks will bypass censorship". Dollerup seems to have been a little too optimistic, but there has been a tendency of showing more respect to the original in the 21st century.

The development of computer science and the science of artificial intelligence has brought about some revolutionary changes in our ways of translation, especially translation of scientific and technological materials and other non-literary texts. Anthony Pym (1992: 152) once thought that "The essential problem of translational ethics is not how to translate in any given situation, but who may decide how to translate". However, Pym (2003) seems to have changed his view of translational ethics in the contemporary time. He reviews some of the traditional translation ethics and comes to what he terms as the "translational ethics" of the present time, i.e. fidelity to memory. He talks of the overall tendency to give loyalty to the original text and author in the long history of translation and the exception "in medieval discourses on translation, where teamwork was the norm, authors were either collective or absent, and target-side acceptability mixed with source-side slavishness in accordance with the nature of each task". Traditionally, responsibility of being loyal to the original is put on the individual translators. The ethics of fidelity in action could make those who were seen as having breached the principle of loyalty severely punished. A famous example is Dolet, who insisted on the notion of fidelity himself and "was burned at the stake for adding three words to Plato". This reminds us of other victims of such an ethics, William Tindale and Martin Luther, for instance. And this also shows that people or the dominant ideologies usually have more requirement of fidelity concerning the translation of the classic and sacred texts.

Let us go along with Pym. Pym (2003) gives us a description of the current situation of some professional translation:

> Translation projects are increasingly done in teams, bringing together translators, terminologists, revisers, technology engineers, DTP (Desk Top Publishing, the author) experts, project managers, and even an author and client or two. In such situations, the individual translator is no longer responsible in any sovereign way.
>
> A growing amount of translation works from "authorless" texts, produced by teams in successive drafts and rewrites (we might think here of document-production processes in EU institutions). This means there is no longer any one author to whom the translator might be faithful. The impact of those changing conditions is most obvious in the fields

now freely called "localization" rather than "translation".

Consequently, Pym says "[i]n the adaptation of software, product documentation and websites, fidelity is no longer an adequate ethical frame". We have to consider other ethic norms such as "collective responsibility", "the primacy of purpose" as proposed by the Skopostheorie, "loyalty to people" as put forward by Nord and "human virtues" such as understanding, truth, loyalty, clarity, trustworthiness with understanding of (what the client wants, the source text, what the readers can be expected to understand and so on) as the primary task. This "human virtues" ethic norm is suggested by Andrew Chesterman. Pym (2003) also mentions the "ethic of resistance" by Venuti. He argues that these ethic norms are all problematic and inadequate. Foe example, Nord's principle of loyalty, like the general Skopostheorie, "is unable to judge or prioritize individual purposes. It thus cannot offer guidelines in situations where the translator has to choose between divided loyalties, perhaps to a client (who wants one kind of translation) and actual end user (who might need quite another kind, to the best of the translator's judgment)". And

> For all the above approaches, the translator has to make ethical decisions in view of quite a complex array of factors. One must be aware of not just the source text, but some kind of sending subjectivity, some kind of end purpose for the translation, some kind of paying client, ideally some kind of improvement to the target culture, and even more ideally some kind of improvement in the status of the translator's profession. Somehow, one has to see all of that, then decide. (Pym 2003)

Alternatively, Pym suggests a "fidelity as memory". He explains that

> Most of our contemporary ethics oblige translators to see a wide range of factors, increasingly an array of human and cultural factors. At the same time, our language technology is removing precisely the same range of factors, ostensibly to keep translators focused on language-replacement exercises. This technology (but there is a bit of the same everywhere) reduces virtue to nothing but consistency and efficiency, since the translator who uses the memory is encouraged to keep looking back at what has been translated in the past (such is the function of memory). All the other virtues, indeed the whole range of recent reflections on ethics, are no longer in the domain of the technological translator. (Pym 2003)

What Pym has said is not confined to non-literary translation. In the net-era, for the netizens cyberspace is supposed to be an open space of freedom, justness and equality and it is to a great extent more open and free than the traditional way of communication. The rapid development of the Internet has given rise to net literature and online translation of literary works or network-based literary translation. A group of articles appeared in *Journal of Comparative Literature* in China, in 2002 discussing the impact of online translation of literary works on the readers, translators and publishers, and criticism of literary translation in general. Zhang Xu (2002) holds that most of the online translators enjoy great freedom in choosing texts to translate and in choosing strategies of translating. Usually they value speed more than accuracy. They are often for their own amusement and show not much respect to the original, often adapting the original at will. Such translation has proved that translation is a "rewriting" in Lefevere's sense and has been a huge satire to traditional literary translation.

Xu Jun and Gao Fang (2006) argue that cyberspace has offered ordinary readers more discursive power of criticism of literary translation. They hold that criticism of literary translation online or "literary translation cyber-criticism", as they termed it, has the characteristics of spontaneity, extensiveness and acuteness. Some publishing houses, such as Shanghai Translation Press and Yilin Translation Press in Nanjing, have offered readers online forums for criticism of literary translation. The dialogue between readers and publishers has had positive impact on the improvement of the quality of literary translation and is significant for criticism of literary translation in Translation Studies. Criticisms on the translations of Milan Kundera, J. Tolkien's the *Lord of the Rings* and the series of *Harry Potter* have attracted a wide public. Some readers even offered their own translation of J.K. Rowling's *Harry Porter and the Order of the Phoenix*. Some of the criticisms are quite reasonable and acute, but others irrational and vulgar. But anyway, it is the extensive participation of the readers that on the one hand has enriched the value of the literary translation and on the other hand, has promoted the timely dialogue between readers and translators and publishers.

Zhang Yanqin (2007) speaks of the spread of HTML on the Internet and the revolution of reading mode of readers brought forth. It is much easier for readers nowadays to access the original and consequently many bilingual readers who are not satisfied with the translation set hands on translation. Competing versions or versions by a group of translators can be seen online and this has greatly promoted the intersubjective communication between readers, translators, authors and publishers, confirming Habermas' communicative ethics.

Though the network-based literary translation and criticism of literary translation have some positive value, proper ethic norms are badly needed. Translation without the permission of the author or the original publisher is certainly tortious. It may become a trespass of the interests of the author or the original publisher, the translator and the publishing house that has purchased the copyright. Therefore, even if these translations are not for money-making, we cannot encourage such a behavior.

When we discussed text types of literary works and types of literary translation in Chapter 1, we analyzed some of the prominent features between literary and non-literary works and offered a list of those literary genre: poems, novels, novella, short stories, science fiction, essay in its narrow sense (essays expressing the writer's experiences, feelings and thoughts), autobiographies, fairy tales, folklores etc. according to their content (subject-matter) and their formal structure. And accordingly, while there is criticism of literary translation in general, there should be criteria for criticism of novel translation, poetry translation, drama translation, essay translation and translation of other texts that are regarded as literary texts in different cultures. For example, in literary creation in general and in versification in particular, what is known as poetic license produces more unusual, unique and even ungrammatical expressions in literary works than we have in non-literary writing and poetry is, generally speaking, more symbolic and polysemous than essays and novels. Readers come to different literary works with different expectations. Virginia Woolf says in her essay "How Should One Read A Book" that "[m]ost commonly we come to books with blurred and divided minds, asking of fiction that it shall be true, of poetry that it shall be false, of biography that it shall be flattering, of history that it shall enforce our own prejudices". Similarly, readers come to translation of different literary works also with various expectations. Usually, readers can be tolerant more with the betrayal of the original in the translation of a free verse as they often pay much more attention to the emotion that is expressed in the poem than to what is said and how. Books for children are normally translated fairly freely, and "in such a way as to mask their foreignness: often enough the translator's identity or even the fact of translation goes undeclared (when I first read Jules Verne, I had no idea he was French)" (France, 2000: 9). Poetry translation "(particularly when the original is printed alongside the translation) often foregrounds the element of translation, and notions of acceptability here will be more elastic than for prose fiction" (ibid). Moreover, there exist the difference of degree of difficulty in translating different types of literary works. As most people acknowledge poetry translation is the most difficult and some even hold poetry is untranslatable, readers are supposed to be more tolerant of adaptation in poetry translation than that in an essay. Another reason for reader's development of a greater tolerance to the adaptation with poetry translation lies in the belief that poems are more open to interpretation as they normally possess more obviously the feature of multiplicity of meanings common with literary works. However, the author has to add immediately that there also exist different forms of poems that have different degree of translatability. Such a fact is not always realized by readers who have little knowledge about poetry.

The above discussion shows that the criteria for evaluation of the politic and ethic values mainly concern about translation events and the parties (subjects) involved in it. It also shows that types of literary works and ways of doing literary translation have something to do with it as well. However, these are not all the factors about the political and ethical evaluation of literary translation. To make a comprehensive political and ethical judgment, we have to evaluate the political and ethical values found in the translated literary works themselves.

Criticism of literary translation is a complex activity involving many aspects. It requires us not only to study many socio-cultural factors surrounding it, but also to scrutinize the original text and the translated text. For the politic and ethic values are to be found not only in various interpersonal and international relationships, but also in the (reading of) literary texts. Questions involved are: what are the morals or themes of the original, what are the morals or themes of the translated and what are the difference existing between the two. Here, translation criticism is almost the same as literary criticism. Readers should give detailed analysis to the plots of the literary work and its social background, trying to find out the politic and ethic attitude of the author and the translator. For example, in reading *Robinson Crusoe*, we can find the unequal relationship between the colonizer and colonized from the behavior of Crusoe and Friday. We can also find the sharp criticism of the capitalist's greed from the description of Domby's making his wife and children the instruments of making money, the criticism of dishonesty and the moral declination in a capitalist society from the description of the cunning scheme of Mr. Carker the Manager in Charles Dickens' novel *Dombey and Son*. Readers of the translations of the two novels, supposing they are equipped with the adequate background knowledge, will most possibly realize the political and ethic values of the translations if what they have read are translations that are faithful to the original. Similarly, if one reads an English translation of *Jin Ping Mei* which translates those plots of sexual behavior in Latin and other parts in English, one can judge it to have greater ethic value than another version which preserves all the description of sexual behavior and deletes most of the other plots, supposing he or she is a reader who believes frenzy sexual behavior immoral.

But after all, the value judgments are made by readers. Therefore, the politic and ethic value judgments of a literary translation depend largely on the politic standpoint and the ethic outlook of the readers. Readers may have different understandings, assumptions and beliefs about the above discussed factors concerning politic and ethic values such as loyalty, respect, tolerance, equality, fairness etc. Consequently, there have been different responses and criticisms on one and the same translated text. Lin Shu's translations were known to be often with much adaptation of the original, but they were once very popular among ordinary readers and even highly praised by the great bilingual scholar Qian Zhongshu. Ezra Pound's translation of the Chinese classical poems were very popular among the Western readers but were heavily lashed by many bilingual Chinese scholars for his irrespect of the original.

Difference in criticisms of the politic and ethic values of literary translation also has something to do with the intensity of awareness of the criteria for criticism, such as loyalty, respect, tolerance, equality, fairness etc. If the critic does not even possess these criteria when making the value judgment, then criticism can only be a kind of emotional response, and from the perspective of evaluation, it cannot be regarded as scientific, though we cannot say it is not a criticism. Besides, different conclusions of the politic and ethic value judgments of a literary translation have to do with the methodology involved in criticism. If the critic does not follow strictly the procedure of careful description, explanation, analysis and comparison, one could not expect a reasonable evaluative conclusion.

Up to now, our discussion seems to suggest that the most important factor in criticism of literary translation is the critic. It is the critic's standpoint, outlook, criteria and methods that play key roles in the process of criticism. With the development of philosophical hermeneutics, poststructurism and the spread of postmodernism in the 20th century, in the fighting against logocenteralism, in the field of literary studies and translation studies as well, as has been observed, there has been the tendency to give priority and authority to readers and translators as readers. Such a tendency has challenged the traditional criteria of loyalty and respect to the original and the long-standing notion of the translated as inferior to the original. Rosemary Arrojo (1997) speaks of the "death" of the author, a concept from Roland Barthes and the indeterminacy of meaning derived from Derrida's notion of "différance" and intertextuality. According to Derrida, the meaning of a sign comes from its relation with and distinction from other signs, with the author's absence and the reader's participation, and it is always endlessly deferred. Thus, there is no fixed meaning and no "original" text. Consequently, Arrojo holds that there should be a through revision of the traditional relationship between originals and translations, between authors and translators and between translators and their readers.

The deconstructivist approach to translation, as can be seen from the above analysis, has totally deconstructed the traditional criteria of loyalty to the source text and its author. While making Translation Studies plural, it has actually undermined as an independent discipline, especially translation criticism. For in the eyes of the deconstructionists, there can only be various "rewriting" of a text and the result is "anything goes". Consequently, one can adopt some feminist strategies in translation to make the sexism in texts visible and to fight for the equal rights for women, one can adopt some postcolonialist strategies to foreigninzing a text from the less powerful culture, one can domesticate a text from a powerful culture, one can also try to dehegemonize any cultural hegemony by means of hybridizing a translation. Despite of the fact that deconstructivist approach has broadened our vision of translation studies and has made explicit the complexity of the activity of translating and the plurality of the criteria for assessing the activity of translating, deconstructivist approach to translation seems to draw translation studies farther and farther away from the "internal knowledge" of translation, paying too much attentions to the external social factors, as Pym (1995) says, and is far from an ideal one for the practical-oriented subject of translation, especially when the issue of criteria for translation criticism which calls for an integrity of descriptive study and prescriptive study in order to make reasonable value judgments is concerned.

Carol Maier (2004: 208) points out that "[r]ecent work in literary criticism and theory, linguistics, anthropology, philosophy, and cultural studies has direct, albeit at times contradictory implications for the evaluation of literary translations". The authors of this book think that radical constructivism (deconstructionsm) which over-exaggerates the individual subjectivity and the individual "différance" or divergence contributes much to the "contradictory implications". Anthony Pym (1995) is right when he says that deconstructionist approach "turns translation into what could only be an inferior form of the kind of readings undertaken by deconstruction itself" and that "[i]n a world where everything is to be constructed, deconstructionist theory can and should raise passing doubts on the way to concrete action. But translation theory has a lot of other work to do, awaiting the philosophers' return from Derridean islands".

But do not think Pym is totally against deconstructionism. He is just more pragmatic than other cultural studies scholars and against the "away-from-practice" philosophical approach to translation and is speaking from mainly the professional perspective of translation. According to Pym (ibid),

> Deconstructors are correct to react against simplistic theory. But they should first locate their opposition with some precision. Meaning transfer is, to be sure, a common basis for twentieth-century linguistic theories of translation, especially those suited for mechanizing translators. The notion has further been assisted by the development of service ethics and a broad feminization of the translator's profession.... No translator or translation critic need believe that translation is the transfer of stable meaning.

In other words, we can say Pym holds that there is unstable source-text plurality of meaning, yet this does not prevent the translator from translating from one language into another. In the actual process of translating, the source-text plurality is either "reduced or conveyed or augmented". Translators "have to make choices between available alternatives, many of which involve potentially beneficial reductions of plurality. Such choices require ethical guidelines. And yet the question of ethics, which is where translation theory needs real help from philosophers, is precisely the point obscured by fixations on origins" (Pym, 1995). For Pym (2007), translation is a problem-solving activity, its correctness and validity depend on both the linguistic and social norms of the target culture.

As an interlingual and intercultural social activity, translation and our translation criticism naturally have to be constrained by various social norms. Yet, as Chesterman (1997: 172) has said, "[v]alue concepts can be seen as prior to normative concepts, in that norms are governed by values". He further points out that "the four fundamental translational values are clarity, truth, trust and understanding" and descriptively rather than prescriptively, these values "appear to be the values held explicitly or implicitly by most translators" (ibid: 175). If this is true, "clarity, truth, trust and understanding" are all factors we need to consider when establishing criteria for criticism of literary translation and translation in general as Chesterman is saying "translational values" in general.

From all our foregoing discussions, we know that the problem of criteria for evaluating the politic and ethic values of literary translation concerns so many factors that it is really difficult for us to set up criteria universally applicable. What is more, it is harder for us set up a hierarchy of the importance of these factors that are acceptable to all the people. The fundamental reason for this is that there exist different and conflicting social norms and outlooks of values.

One of the efforts to solve the problem is to turn to siociology for a breakthrough as translating, translation criticism as well, is essentially a social practice. In this respect, it is Daniel Simeoni's (1998) who first employed Bourdieu's notion of habitus to account for the translators' action. He points out "[t]he habitus of a translator is the elaborate result of a personalized social and cultural history". Translatorial habitus is caused by the translator's backgrounds, translation contexts and individual life experiences which may vary from person to person.

The application of Pierre Bourdieu's theory of sociology to translation has been considered as part of the reflection on the so-called descriptive approach to translation. The key concepts borrowed from Bourdieu's theory of sociology are field, capital and habitus.

According to Bourdieu (1983, 1984, 1992, 1993), a society as a space contains a number of fields, within which individuals and institutions struggle for power in accordance with the specific logic of each field. Fields are historically constructed, specialized and relatively autonomous social areas of material or symbolic production. Each field has its own institutions, laws, and its own value systems. The largest field in society is the field of power, defined strictly in terms of power relations:

> The field of power is a field of forces defined by the structure of the existing balance
> of forces between forms of power, or between different species of capital. It is also
> simultaneously a field of struggle for power among the holders of different forms of
> power. It is a space of play and competition in which the social agents and institutions [...]
> confront one another in strategies aimed at preserving or transforming this balance of
> forces. (Bourdieu and Wacquant 1992: 76, note 16; italics in original. qtd. in Raila 2009).

Bourdieu's concept of "field" itself implies the concept of system. As we can see that within a certain field, there are smaller sub-fields and each field is primarily positioned and defined through its relation to the field of power and to other fields, particularly in terms of economic and cultural capital. Thus, the field of literary production is located within the larger field of cultural production, which is eventually placed in the largest the field of power. The field of literary production can again be divided into smaller sub-fields: drama, novel, poetry etc. Each field follows its own specific logic, but there certainly exist some properties common to all fields. The field can also be understood as the sum of intersecting and combating subjectivities.

Thus, social norms can be regarded as the results of the conflicts and struggles.

The term "capital" is usually narrowly defined as economic category of monetary exchange for profit. However, Bourdieu's concept of "cultural capital" regards culture also as a form of capital. There are different capitals existing in a society: symbolic capital—the accumulation of prestige, and linguistic capital—linguistic competence or advantage etc. In general, "cultural capital" refers to acquired education, culture, technical skills, etc. "cultural capital" is often unequally distributed and maintained. The status an agent holds in a society or within a field is closely connected with the capital he acquires in a specific field.

Individuals, groups or institutions within a certain field are bestowed with a specific "habitus", a concept referring to a system of durable dispositions which normally guide unconsciously the ways of thinking and behavior of the individuals, groups or institutions. "Habitus" therefore, bears some resemblance with Jung's "collective unconscious". Thus, we can see that the concepts of field, capital and habitus are interrelated in Bourdieu's sociology and are more explicative for the translation activity than those existing norm theories.

Vasso Yannakopoulou (2008) argues that

When dealing with actual translations, norms seem to be insufficient to account for translation choices. They are indispensable if one is to understand the context in which a translation came into being, they can also describe the position a particular translation had in the target culture, but cannot account for the motivations behind the translator's choices. Therefore, in my view they should be supplemented with the notion of habitus in order to achieve a more thorough outlook of the work of a particular translator. In Simeoni's (1998:33) words, "norms without a habitus to instantiate them make no more sense than a habitus without norms. Incorporating conflict in one single construct attached to the person of the translator should also help us better understand the tension behind the individual choices during the decision process".

According to Yannakopoulou, "[t]he translator's awareness of the norms pertaining in a particular field is only one of the many considerations he tackles with while making his translation decisions". The translator's personal disposition should also be taken into our consideration. What is more, "norms cannot effectively account for cases of deviant translation practices". The translator "can at all times decide to translate counter to them". Though Yannakopoulou is too absolute here, she is right to call our attention to the subjectivity of the translator. She further quotes Gouanvic (2005:158) to support her opinion:

Norms do not explain the more or less subjective and random choices made by translators who are free to translate or not to translate, to follow or not to follow the original closely. If a translator imposes a rhythm upon the text, a lexicon or a syntax that does not originate in the source text and thus substitutes his or her voice for that of the author, this is essentially not a conscious strategic choice but an effect of his or her specific habitus, as acquired in the target literary field. (Yannakopoulou 2008)

Yet, Gouanvic is only partly right too. For in Bourdieu's sociology, "habitus" is both individual and social. From the perspective of social constructivism, "habitus" falls largely into the "collective unconscious". Any individual is an individual of a society, as has been said many times, therefore, the individual subject can not be totally free "at all time" and in any place. Generally speaking, the individual translator's freedom is limited. He or she is explicitly or implicitly constrained by social norms or laws. But, according to Jung, individuals also have "individual unconscious", the power that drives his action unconsciously. Here, we have to hasten to add that Bourdieu's "habitus" is not the same as Jung's psychoanalysis and we have to admit that in the history of translation, there did exist many translators who translated against the dominant ideologies and social conventions consciously and that we can often find translator of the same era have different ways of doing translation. That is why we say Bourdieu's sociological theory is more explicative. In fact, in the course of social progress, once a norm becomes dominant, it begins to show the tendency of conservativeness as it tries to maintain its dominant position. It is largely the translations by translators who translate against the dominant norm that have contributed a lot to the change of social norms and systems, and to the progress of the target cultures and even the whole race. Translators are not always passively constrained by the dominant norms and dominant norms are not always and forever "correct" in the course of the social development. On the contrary, as has been pointed out by Lv Jun and Hou Xiangqun (2010), "dominant ideologies are often conservative and deceptive, and a text against them may be progressive when revolutionary ideas are contained in it and it is good for social progress".

In light of Bourdieu's sociology, we can find that decisions and products made by the translator are the results of the struggles in a field or between fields. The individual's choice, decision or action is the internalization of the social field and the social field is the objectification of the intersecting individual's choice, decision or action. Everything is determined by the field which is, dialectically speaking, both stable and changing. The authors of this book hold that Bourdieu's concept of "field" can be replaced by a term most people are familiar with, i.e. context. Additionally, for the subject of criticism which is highly prescriptive, mere description and explanation is far from enough, we have to get to know whether the dominant norms are progressive or not and what are or might be the correct or proper criteria or norms that can be used as yardsticks in our criticism.

As we view translation as an interlingual and intercultural social activity, Bourdieu's sociology is certainly enlightening for translation and translation studies, including the politic and ethic aspects of translation criticism. Yet, as we see translation also as a speech event and communication (see our definition in Chapter 1), the communicative ethics of Habermas we mentioned before can also throw some light on the issue under discussion.

Facing the trend of irrationality of postmodernism in the 20th century, Habermas is one of the greatest thinkers who endeavor to re-establish the communicative rationality for the world we live in. He divides the world into 1) "the external world" as the totality of existing states of affairs, 2) "our social world" as the totality of all normatively regulated interpersonal relations that count as legitimate in a given society, and 3) "a particular inner world" (of the speaker) as the totality of his intentional experiences. As he thinks communicative rationality is to be acquired and formed in the process of linguistic communication, he tries to construct a theory of universal pragmatics, which is later changed into formal pragmatics as an extension of "formal semantics" aiming to identify and reconstruct universal conditions of possible understanding or general presuppositions of communication. For Habermas, the task of a communicative action is to reach understanding between acting subjects, and for the purpose of reaching an agreement at last:

> The goal of coming to an understanding [Verstandigung] is to bring about an agreement [Einverstandnis] that terminates in the intersubjective mutuality of reciprocal understanding, shared knowledge, mutual trust, and accord with one another. Agreement is based on recognition of the corresponding validity-claims of comprehensibility, truth, truthfulness, and rightness. (Outhwaite 1996: 119)

From the above quotation we can see that Habermas highly values understanding. His concept of understanding means 1) uttering something understandably; 2) giving [the hearer] something to understand; 3) making himself thereby understandable; and 4) coming to an understanding with another person (Outhwaite 1996: 129). Coming to an understanding is the process of bringing about an agreement on the presupposed basis of validity-claims. And validity-claims are proposed to offer a mutually recognized normative background.

Habermas' validity-claims are actually the socio-cultural norms for the purposeful-rational actions that have concrete significance only for acting subjects who meet one another on the level of intersubjectivity. Norms with validity on the level of intersubjectivity must be agreed upon in communication and the normative validity is different from power in that it is built on the belief that one can justify the norm and defend it against critique in a given case. Norms produced this way are dialogical, intersubjective, rational, pragmatic and practical consensus.

According to Ciaran Cronin (1993: xi), the translator of Habermas's *Justification and Application: Remarks on Discourse Ethics*, "Habermas is rowing against the prevailing tide of skepticism concerning the possibility of universally validity claims in ethics". For Habermas, an unrestricted relativism of values and ways of life whose logical consequence would be complete practical disorientation. Speakers may raise different kinds of claims to validity, yet, claims raised in moral judgments admit of rational criticism based on publicly intelligible reasons. The goal of Habermas' discourse ethics is thus to emphasize rationality in argumentative discourse. Though some people think that Habermas' consensual theory of ethics is too ideal, Cronin (1993: xv) comments that:

> Regardless of our assurance that a particular consensus is rational, it can always transpire that it involved ignoring or suppressing some relevant opinion or point of view, that it was influenced by asymmetries of power, that the language in which the issues were formulated was inappropriate, or simply that some evidence was unavailable to the participants….Yet the notion of consensus under ideal conditions of discourse is not an empty ideal without relation to real discursive practices. Habermas maintains that the ideal has concrete practical implications because, insofar as participants in real discourses understand themselves to be engaging in a cooperative search for truth or rightness solely on the basis of good reasons, they must, as a condition of the intelligibility of the activity they are engaged in, assume that the conditions of the ideal speech situation are satisfied to a sufficient degree. And it is this normative presupposition that Habermas exploits in developing his "quasi-transcendental" grounding of a basic moral principle.

Discourse ethics put forward by Habermas has offered us kind of a reasonable middle-ground criterion for judging the politic and ethic value of literary translation as a communicative action. For the consensual criteria are valid claims that are practical-oriented, pragmatic, rational and normative reached for the satisfaction of the needs and interests of all those potentially affected participants. Habermas

(1993) holds that ethical questions concern what "ought" to be. Those "oughts" are independent on subjective purposes and preferences and yet are not absolute. The consensual "oughts" mean that what you "should" or "must" do is "good" for you and for "me" to act in this way in the long run, all things considered, as there are common interests recognized and justified. And in this way,

> [I]t is ultimately my self-respect that is endangered when I act immorally. One who violates moral norms not only exposes himself to the contempt of others but also feels contempt for himself because he has internalized this sanction. A norm counts as "justified," therefore, only insofar as it is in the interest of each, viewed from his own perspective, that everyone should engage in a practice regulated by the exchange of signs of respect. (Habermas 1993: 44)

What should be noticed is that Habermas is using the term "respect" in the sense of the contemporary German moral philosopher Ernst Tugendhat, who holds that respect has some shade of difference from esteem in that the latter implies admiration. "By contrast, respect for a person as a person admits of no gradations; we respect a person as such not on account of some outstanding characteristic or other. We respect a person as such on account of his capacity to act autonomously, that is, to orient his actions to normative validity claims" (Habermas 1993: 45).

Ethical judgment therefore, should take respect to all the parties, no matter how strong or weak he or she is as there might exist asymmetries of power in reality. Habermas (ibid: 48-49) states that "[i]mpartiality of judgment, by contrast, is essentially dependent on whether the conflicting needs and interests of all participants are given their due and can be taken into consideration from the viewpoint of the participants themselves". He further points out that "[w]e cannot attain an impartial standpoint by turning our back on the context of linguistically mediated interaction and by abandoning the participant perspective completely, but only by extending the individual participant perspective in a universal fashion" (Habermas 1993: 49).

From the above discussion we can see that the Habermasian logic of the discourse ethics is that: communicative actions are purposeful, aiming at understanding and consensual ethic codes or norms which we should abide by to ensure the success of communication. In order to come to an agreement or consensus some presupposed validity-claims such as comprehensibility, truth, truthfulness, and rightness, are necessary. Consensus reached conformable to these validity-claims are "quasi-transcendental" and can be used as criteria for value judgment. Respect should be highly valued as it implies equality and impartiality.

To sum up, as literary translation is an extremely complicated cross-cultural social event, criticism of literary translation becomes also extremely complicated. There are too many factors involved in it and even if we can list some of the essential concepts and factors concerning the politic and ethic values of a literary translation such as loyalty, respect, tolerance, trust, understanding, clarity, fairness, equality, text types, readers and so on, it is not that easy for us to know the exact importance of these different factors. What is more, since all these factors concerning our views on value and criteria for assessing the values, as value theory has told us, are but context dependent, to set up criteria for the criticism of specific contextual factors concerning the politic and ethic values of a literary translation will also be context dependent. The author of this dissertation once remarked that any change of the contextual factors in the translatorial speech event may bring forth changes of the criteria for translation, ways of doing translation and criteria for criticizing a translation (Zhang Zhiqiang 2008).The existing various criteria as we talked about in Chapter 3 and in this chapter show that highest criteria aiming at meeting the demands of people's needs for "truth", "good" and "beauty" are idealist and abstract, but axiologically speaking, they are also significant as they indicate the direction of our human practice aiming at creating the greatest value. We talked also about setting up a ground-level criterion based on the bottom ethic requirements concerning the spiritual human needs and interests. Our discussion shows that though respect seems a consensual norm or criterion, it is yet not concrete enough as there exist different conflicting respects. Our analyses show that all these conflicts come from the competing norms and habitus indicating different needs, interests and habitus of the subjects involved, both individual and social. However, there is one fact that has often, if not always, been neglected especially by the descriptive study of translation, by the "semi-scientific norm/law approach" (Munday 2001: 117), that the found norms are actually only "traced" norms by scholars with different outlook of value. If we are satisfied with our criticism in adopting these descriptively found norms or criteria, there will always be contradicting and conflicting value judgments which will reinforce the existing norms that each group or class or school holds on, and criticism will lose large part of its value. For the purpose of improving the world we live in—and that is exactly the goal of our evaluation and criticism—we need to take a step further, to make critical reflexion on the existing norms or paradigms for revising or modifying them, and encourage the truthful dialogue between different classes, schools and paradigms to reach new consensus, or more practically, a compromise. Moreover, we should realize that we live in a changing word, in which facts and ideas are changing and that our description in humanities is always to a certain extent subjective and value-neutral is almost impossible. This subjectivity in humanities (in its broad sense, including social sciences) does not mean there is no objectivity in humanities. It only implies that objectivity in humanities is somewhat different from that in natural science (see "objectivity" defined in Chapter 4). In fact, subjectivity is the right starting point of our perceiving and transforming the world and "hermeneutics (the science of interpretation) has often been thought of as the basic research method of the humanistic disciplines" and "translation quality assessment…is overtly evaluative" (Williams & Chesterman 2004: 58; x). What we mean is that mere description and explanation, though necessary, is not enough for our axiological approach to criticism of literary translation. In order to make more constructive criticism aiming to better the world, to better our literary translation, we need not only to find the existing criteria, that is, the "individual" "Is", concerning what translation is, but also the "consensual Is" and the "consensual Ought" which are what the set of criteria should be based on. And it is here the "consensual Is" begins to merge into the "consensual Ought". Statements concerning what translation is and what translation should be are both value judgments (We see again there is no "pure" description). We need first a consensus about what translation is and then what good translation is and then again, the best. We admit that there is no easy solution to the long-standing issue of criteria for criticism of literary translation. Previous cultural and sociological studies have made the complexity of this issue more prominent, especially in the respect of the politic and ethic values of literary translation. As translation is a social practice and translation criticism we advocate is also practical-oriented, we should not neglect those existing professional ethics for translators in our theoretical reflexive discussion. Based on the social constructivism, Habermas' communicative ethics or discourse ethics, and in light of value theory, we believe that if all participants in the translatorial event can make rational reflexions and dialogue on the pre-existing norms and their expectations, especially their real needs and interests, especially their long-term needs and interests and of the human race in the era of globalization, they should be able to come to an agreement, a consensus, or to be more realistic, a compromise at least, which can then be used as the criteria. They should be able to realize that showing respect to others and the Other, and to be exact, the needs and interests of others, is actually to show respect to themselves and their own interests. Though the general conclusion we come to is that concrete and practical-oriented criteria for criticism of literary translation can only be set up when a specific context is given and when detailed analysis of the hierarchy of the importance of various values are made, so far as the politic and ethic values of literary translations are concerned, in the current context of globalization, respect to the OTHER should be our first and foremost concern in passing value judgments on a literary translation.

We have been lingering long over the criteria for judging the politic and ethic values of literary translations. One of the reasons for doing so is that in many societies, the concern for the politic and ethic values of literary translations prioritizes the other values, just as Lefevere (2004: 39) remarks that "on every level of the translation process, it can be shown that, if linguistic considerations enter into conflict with considerations of an ideological and / or poetological nature, the latter tend to win out". Another reason is that what we have discussed here is closely connected with what we will discuss in the following part and therefore seems more fundamental for the whole criticism of literary translation.

b) Intellectual value

Intellectual value refers mainly to the knowledge that adds to our understanding about the world and our human beings. In literary works, it is mainly revealed in the forms of literary works and the content describing human life, socio-cultural customs, and people's perceptions and feelings of the physical world and their partners in the social world. Usually, such descriptions are about the Other. By reading a translation we expect to know what things are like in other places. Therefore, it seems easier for us to set up criteria for measuring the intellectual value of a literary translation. However, things are not as easy as one might have thought. The first difficulty concerns the often unique features of literary works and the second the polysemous nature of literary works. Both of the two facts add to the difficulty in setting up criteria for the measurement of the intellectual value of literary translations. For we have to make judgments about the quality and quantity of the intellectual value of literary translations. In other words, our judgment shall tell how much and how well the translated literary texts have succeeded in transferring the intellectual values of the original. And also, we have to consider the possibility of translating, and to what extent, the intellectual values contained in the original. Moreover, different needs, expectations and responses of different readers should also be taken into our consideration. After all, values are the value to a certain subject. All these factors have made the measurement of the intellectual value of literary translations not only a matter of understanding and interpretation, but to a certain degree, an ethic and aesthetic matter as well. To make the complex matter simpler, our discussion will mainly concentrate on two aspects: form and content.

Speaking of intellectual value, we are almost talking about the value of knowledge. And speaking of knowledge, we have to consider the understanding, interpreting, transferring and receiving of knowledge. Based on our discussion about the politic and ethic values of literary translation, we can say the more information of the original text is transferred, the better quality of a translated text, and similarly, the more information received and understood by the reader, the better quality of the translated. For such translated texts could be said to possess not only adequate respect to the original and the target readers, but also the maximum information or knowledge.

Knowledge we expect to get from our reading of a literary translation is not confined to what is expressed (the content). Forms of literary works also have their formal meaning, a fact closely connected with the aesthetic value of a literary translation and will be discussed later.

From the reading of a literary work, we expect to know what is said and in what way it is said. For example, there exist quite a number of different forms of poetry. The following is part of a list of different types of poetry from a webpage (http://www.poemofquotes.com/articles/poetry_forms.php):

ABC: A poem that has five lines that creates a mood, picture, or feeling. Lines 1 through 4 are made up of words, phrases or clauses while the first word of each line is in alphabetical order. Line 5 is one sentence long and begins with any letter.

Acrostic: Poetry that certain letters, usually the first in each line form a word or message when read in a sequence.

Ballad: A poem that tells a story similar to a folk tail or legend which often has a repeated refrain.

Ballade: Poetry which has three stanzas of seven, eight or ten lines and a shorter final stanza of four or five. All stanzas end with the same one line refrain.

Blank verse: A poem written in unrhymed iambic pentameter and is often unobtrusive. The iambic pentameter form often resembles the rhythms of speech.

Burlesque: Poetry that treats a serious subject as humor.

Canzone: Medieval Italian lyric style poetry with five or six stanzas and a shorter ending stanza.

Cinquain: Poetry with five lines. Line 1 has one word (the title). Line 2 has two words that describe the title. Line 3 has three words that tell the action. Line 4 has four words that express the feeling, and line 5 has one word which recalls the title.

Couplet: A couplet has rhyming stanzas made up of two lines.

Epic: An extensive, serious poem that tells the story about a heroic figure.

Epigram: A very short, ironic and witty poem usually written as a brief couplet or quatrain. The term is derived from the Greek epigramma meaning inscription.

Epitaph: A commemorative inscription on a tomb or mortuary monument written to praise the deceased.

Free verse: Poetry written in either rhyme or unrhymed lines that have no set fixed metrical pattern.

Ghazal: A short lyrical poem that arose in Urdu. It is between 5 and 15 couplets long. Each couplet contains its own poetic thought but is linked in rhyme that is established in the first couplet and continued in the second line of each pair. The lines of each couplet are equal in length. Themes are usually connected to love and romance. The closing signature often includes the poet's name or allusion to it.

Haiku: A Japanese poem composed of three unrhymed lines of five, seven, and five morae, usually containing a season word.

Horatian ode: Short lyric poem written in two or four-line stanzas, each with its the same metrical pattern, often addressed to a friend and deal with friendship, love and the practice of poetry. It is named after its creator, Horace.

Iambic pentameter: One short syllabel followed by one long one five sets in a row.

Italian sonnet: A sonnet consisting of an octave with the rhyme pattern abbaabba followed by six lines with a rhyme pattern of cdecde or cdcdcd.

Limerick: A short sometimes vulgar, humorous poem consisting of five anapestic lines. Lines 1, 2, and 5 have seven to ten syllables, rhyme and have the same verbal rhythm. The 3rd and 4th lines have five to seven syllables, rhyme and have the same rhythm.

Name: Poetry that tells about the word. It uses the letters of the word for the first letter of each line.

Ode: A lengthy lyric poem typically of a serious or meditative nature and having an elevated style and formal stanza structure.

Petrarchan: A 14-line sonnet consisting of an octave rhyming abbaabba followed by a sestet of cddcee or cdecde.

Pindaric ode: A ceremonious poem consisting of a strophe (two or more lines repeated as a unit) followed by an antistrophe with the same metrical pattern and concluding with a summary line (an epode) in a different meter. Named after Pindar, a Greek professional lyrist of the 5th century B.C.

Quatrain: A stanza or poem consisting of four lines. Lines 2 and 4 must rhyme while having a similar number of syllables.

Rhyme: A rhyming poem has the repetition of the same or similar sounds of two or more words, often at the end of the line.

Rhyme royal: A type of poetry consisting of stanzas having seven lines in iambic pentameter.

Rondeau: A lyrical poem of French origin having 10 or 13 lines with two rhymes and with the opening phrase repeated twice as the refrain.

Senryu: A short Japanese style poem, similar to haiku in structure that treats human beings rather than nature: Often in a humorous or satiric way.

Sestina: A poem consisting of six six-line stanzas and a three-line envoy. The end words of the first stanza are repeated in varied order as end words in the other stanzas and also recur in the envoy.

Shakespearean sonnet: A 14-line sonnet consisting of three quatrains of abab cdcd efef followed by a couplet, gg. Shakespearean sonnets generally use iambic pentameter.

Sonnet: A lyric poem that consists of 14 lines which usually have one or more conventional rhyme schemes.

Tanka: A Japanese poem of five lines, the first and third composed of five syllables and the other seven.

Villanelle: A 19-line poem consisting of five tercets and a final quatrain on two rhymes. The first and third lines of the first tercet repeat alternately as a refrain closing the succeeding stanzas and joined as the final couplet of the quatrain.

Most of the above types of poetry have certain requirement on the form. They are part of the literary traditions from different cultures and contribute to the diversity of our human culture. In translating these poems, translators should do their utmost to transfer as much as possible their formal features in order to inform target readers of the fact that the ideas and feelings of the poet they are reading are expressed in a specific way. Of course, there have been voices of the untranslatabilty of poetry, for there evidently exist great differences in versification in different cultures, and the unique features of each language certainly bring forth great difficulty in preserving the form while the translator tries to transfer the meaning and emotions of the poem.

Bassnett (2004: 83) once pointed out "[w] ithin the field of literary translation, more time has been devoted to investigating the problems of translating poetry than any other literary mode". She mentioned Lefevere's discussion of the seven strategies employed by English translators of Catullus' poem: 1) Phonemic translation, aiming to reproduce the SL sound in the TL whlie at the same time producing an acceptable paraphrase of the sense; 2) Literal translation, in a word-for-word way distorting the sense and the syntax of the original; 3) Metrical translation, where the dominant criterion is the reproduction of the SL metre; 4) Poetry into prose, with distortion of the sense, communicative value and syntax of the SL text; 5) Rhymed translation, with double bondage of metre and rhyme; 6) Blank verse transaltion, with greater accuracy and higher degree of literalness and certain restricts on the structure; and 7) Interpretation, versions where the substance of the SL text is retained but the form is changed or imitaions where the translator produces a poem of his own which has "only title and point of departure, if those, in common with the source text" (Bassnett, 2004: 84). Though what Bassnett wanted to emphasize is that interlingual transaltion is bound to reflect the translator's own creative interpretation of the SL text, her discussion on the translation of spatial arrangement in free verse, showed well that form may also be quite meaningful in poetry and actually form and content are hardly separatable. She stated that if we arrange Chomsky's famous "meaningless" sentence: "Colourless green ideas sleep furiously" in the following way:

Colourless

green ideas

sleep

furiously

[T]he apparent lack of logical harmony between the elements of the sentence could become acceptable, since each 'line' would add an idea and the overall meaning would derive from the association of illogical elements in a seemingly logical regular structure. The meaning, therefore, would not be content bound, but would be sign bound, in that both the individual words and the association of the ideas would accumulate meaning as the poem is read. (Bassnett 2004: 103-104)

In *Constructing Culture: Essays on Literary Translation*, Bassnett (2001: 69) makes it further clear that "a poem is a text in which content and form are inseparable" and that it is not beneficial to argue which one, form or content, is more significant. She suggests that we follow James Holmes' suggestion that

[E]very translator establishes a hierarchy of constituent elements during the reading process and then re-encodes those elements in a different ranking in the target language.

If we compare translation and source, then the ranking of elements becomes visible. Holmes describing this process as a 'hierarchy of correspondences' (Holmes, 1978). (Bassnett & Lefevere 2001: 70)

However, Bassnett is against using the comparative method to "place the translation in some kind of league table, rating x higher than y" (ibid). She holds that this method can only be used to "understand what went on in the actual translation process" (ibid). But, for our purpose of making criticism that favours respect to the Other, we have to say that the translation that has transferred more information of the original culture is superior to the other.

Our discussion here indicates that though we aim at the maximum transfer of the information contained in the ST, when setting up criteria for assessing the intellectual value of literary works, we have to take the degree of difficulty of translating and the issue of untranslatability into our consideration. Our discussion here also reminds us of our foregoing discussion about the ethic criteria for judging the value of a translation. That is: the factor of text types is essential for our establishment of a set of criteria for literary translation. What is more, our discussion of axiologically criticism of literary translation seems often to bring us back to ethics. As Berman (1992: 3) remarks, "…in this domain, fidelity and treason are incessantly at issue. Translating, as Franz Rosenzweig wrote, 'is to serve two masters'; this is the ancillary metaphor. The work, the author, the foreign language (first master) have to be served, as well as the public and one's own language (second master)".

What Berman says and quotes is such a commonplace in translation practice that has been often neglected by some critics. Critics of literary translation should have sympathy with the translators who are not only often in a dilemma as to decide to whom they should give their loyalty and respect, but also what and how to translate the Other.

Zhang Zhiqiang (1998) once proposed to make "informational adequacy" as the yardstick for measure a translation based on the assumption that translation is to translate information from one lingua-culture to another. The degree of informational adequacy is decided by the comparison of the quantity of information contained in the translated with that of the original. Here, we should be aware that quantity is closely connected with quality and quality with accuracy. In other words, we should realize that adequacy is closely connected with accuracy in measuring the information transferred in a translation. This again indicates that we will give priority to the original author and text. But how can we know the exact meaning of the author and the original text and how can we know how much information is transferred and more importantly perceived by the target readers. These questions suggest that judging of the intellectual value of a literary translation is much more complex than one might has expected. It only involves ethic factors, but also the issue of epistemology. We have also to consider 1) the subjectivity and objectivity of knowledge; 2) understanding and interpreting of the meaning of the original; 3) the expression of the meaning in the target language; and 4) the understanding and interpreting of the meaning of the translated text. To make clear all these questions, we have to ask the theories of knowledge and hermeneutics for help.

To discuss the understanding and interpreting of the meaning first brings us to the issue of subjectivity and scientificity or objectivity of knowledge in literary studies. We know that literary works in general are not concerned with knowledge the same way as other non-literary texts, and literature with other disciplines in natural science.

There have been efforts, influenced by scientism, to make the understanding and interpreting of the meaning of a literary text scientific. In seeking a scientific basis to it, people once turned to linguistics and structuralism attempting to construct various models. They hold that meaning is "there" in the text, treating literary text as an object which can be observed and studies by an outside observer. In this paradigm, the writer of a text is the encoder and the reader is the decoder who can know the exact meaning of the author which is objectified in the text. The reader or the observer, can trace the signifier to know the signified as there exist an object which corresponds the signifier. "Anything that can be said in one language can be said in another, unless the form is an essential element of the message" (Nida & Taber 2004: 4).

However, the above idea is denied by poststructuralism which argues that meaning is inderterminate, is not "there" in the text, but rather is generated in the reading process varying from one reader to another and from one time to another. Consequently, there is no objectivity with the poststructuralist or deconstructionist paradigm.

Both the above approaches have gone to extremes. The first approach has made literary translation the same as non-literary translation, ignoring the specific polysemy of literary text. The second has made it impossible for critics to judge the "truthness" of a literary translation as all translations seem equally "correct" and equally "wrong" in terms of interpretation.

Questions of understanding and interpreting of the meaning of the original, the expression of the meaning in the target language and the understanding and interpreting of the meaning of the translated text are actually all connected with hermeneutics. Richard Palmer in his book *Hermeneutics: Interpretation Theory of Schleiermacher, Dilthey, Heidegger, and Gadamer* admits "the advantages of the 'separatist' position, that is, of regarding the text of a literary work purely as an 'aesthetic object,'" but questions "the concomitant assumption that a text should be 'analyzed in strict separation from any perceiving subject'" (Gerhart 1979: 91). Ricoeur sees Schleiermacher the first major figure of Romantics in the hermeneutical tradition which depends mainly on the marriage of reflection and intuition. Schleiermacher believes in the reconstruction of another's intuition and it is possible for a reader to understand an author better than the author can understand himself. "For Ricoeur, Schleiermacher's hermeneutics emphasizes subjectivity at the expense of objectivity" (Gerhart 1979: 100). Dilthey shifts his starting-point from nature to humankind, proposing that "the individual is better understood against a whole history of humankind rather than in terms of an isolated natural being" (ibid: 101) and thus offers understanding an object structure. Ricoeur tries to bridge the gap between subjectivtity and objectivity of interpretation, He suspends the relation of the word to the thing, thinking that only when a speaker actualizes the referential function of the language can that relation occur. In the reading of a text consisting of signs, linguistic signs are understood to refer only to other signs, without any reference to some thing in the world. For Ricoeur, "[a]ny word is potentially polysemic; it passes into actual meaning only in the event of a given sentence" (ibid: 115).

Ricoeur holds that it is misleading to say that the "reader is in dialogue with the author through his work". He does not think the nature of the relationship of the reader to the text is of the same kind as that to a dialogic situation which consists of questions and responses. For one cannot find such exchange between reader and author (ibid: 125). According to Ricoeur, text, "appears to be an occasion which allow the interpreter to be transposed to a new horizon of understanding" (ibid: 127-128).

Ricoeur shows great concern for translation. He believes that there is no absolute criterion for good translation because such a criterion requires us to be able to "compare the source and target texts with a third text which would bear the identical meaning that is supposed to be passed from the first to the second" (Ricoeur 2006: 22). For Ricoeur,

> …a good translation can aim only at a supposed equivalence that is not founded on a demonstrable identity of meaning. An equivalence without identity. This equivalence

can only be sought, worked at, supposed. And the only way of criticizing a translation— something we can always do—is to suggest another supposed, alleged, better or different one. …Indeed, it seems to me that translation sets us not only intellectual work, theoretical or practical, but also an ethical problem. Bringing the reader to the author, bringing the author to the reader, at the risk of serving and of betraying two masters: this is to practice what I like to call linguistic hospitality. (ibid)

In other part of his book *On Translation*, Ricoeur remarks "just as in the act of telling a story, we can translate differently, without hope of filling the gap between equivalence and total adequacy" (Ricoeur 2006: 10).

Richard Kearney (2006) in his "Introduction: Ricoeur's philosophy of translation" says that

Translation can be understood here in both a specific and a general sense. In the specific sense — the one in common contemporary usage — it signals the work of translating the meanings of one particular language into another. In the more generic sense, it indicates the everyday act of speaking as a way not only of translating oneself to oneself (inner to outer, private to public, unconscious to conscious, etc.) but also and more explicitly of translating oneself to others. (Kearney 2006: xiv-xv)

Ricoeur argues that good translations involve some element of openness to the other. All translations involve some aspect of dialogue between self and others. Ricoeur's "linguistic hospitality" means that the translator should be aware that "[t] he world is made up of a plurality of human beings, cultures, tongues. Humanity exists in the plural mode. Which means that any legitimate form of universality must always — if the hermeneutic model of translation is observed — find its equivalent plurality" (ibid: xx). If we follow Ricoeur's philosophy of translation, we can be fully aware of the plurality of meaning. Ricoeur's "equivalent plurality" admits "equivalent" and is inspiring. It gives us edification for the measurement of the intellectual value in that the critic should be tolerant to different reasonable interpretation and edifies that in making judgments about the aesthetic value of a literary translation, we should seek the "equivalent plurality", allowing the target reader to access the plurality of meaning.

In his *A Theory of Semiotics*, Umberto Eco (1975) asserts that the ideal reader or decoder is always respectful to the original text and its author. The respectful decoder only enjoys a limited inventive freedom of interpreting the text. Guided by the contextual relationships in a text, he can get to know the intended message of the author which is emitted in a certain historical environment.

Eco is obviously unsatisfied with those deconstructionists who give the reader "license" to a limitless and uncheckable flow of reading. He explores the nature of meaning and the possibilities and limits of interpretation. Eco holds that "the aim of the text must be to produce the Model Reader, that is to say, the reader who reads it as it is in some sense designed to be read, where that may include the possibility of being read so as to yield multiple interpretations" (Collini 1992: 10). Eco argues that

> [T]he properties of the text itself do set limits to the range of legitimate interpretation. He does not appear to maintain that there are any formal criteria by which these limits can be established in theoretical terms, but he invokes instead a kind of cultural Darwinism: certain readings prove themselves over time to the satisfaction of the relevant community. He also points to the way that all the discussants, whatever their explicit theoretical allegiance, in practice look for some kind of unity of belief and sensibility behind the various texts written by a single author, and in line with this he allows himself to speak with some authority on the meaning of those pieces of writing known as *The Name of the Rose* and *Foucauit's Pendulum* as well as those which will henceforth be known as his Tanner lectures on Interpretation and Overinterpretation. (Collini 1992: 16)

Eco's idea has been supported by some present novelist-critics such as Malcolm Bradbury and David Lodge, who "evidently sympathized with Eco's desire to limit the range of acceptable interpretation, suggesting that the working practice of the writer clearly presupposed some such limits, some reason for the work being written this way and not that" (ibid: 15-16).

Facing the challenge of those deconstructionsits, Eco defends his theory quite convincingly by saying that

> But by what criterion do we decide that a given textual interpretation is an instance of overinterpretation? One can object that in order to define a bad interpretation one needs the criteria for defining a good interpretation.
>
> I think, on the contrary, that we can accept a sort of Popperian principle according to which if there are no rules that help to ascertain which interpretations are the 'best' ones, there is at least a rule for ascertaining which ones are 'bad'. We cannot say if the Keplerian hypotheses are definitely the best ones but we can say that the Ptolemaic explanation of the solar system was wrong because the notions of epicycle and deferent violated certain criteria of economy or simplicity, and could not coexist with other hypotheses that proved to be reliable in order to explain phenomena that Ptolemy did not explain. (Eco 1992: 52)

The basic essence of Eco's criteria for limiting interpretation reads as follows:

Any interpretation given of a certain portion of a text can be accepted if it is confirmed by, and must be rejected if it is challenged by, another portion of the same text. In this sense the internal textual coherence controls the otherwise uncontrollable drives of the reader. (ibid: 65)

Eco also gives us vivid examples to illustrate his idea about the limited and valid interpretation and overinterpretation:

I remember that in 1985, during a debate at Northwestern University I said to Hartman (refer to Geoffrey Hartman, me) that he was a 'moderate' deconstructionist because he refrained from reading the line

'A poet could not but be gay'

as a contemporary reader would do if the line were found in Playboy. In other words, a sensitive and responsible reader is not obliged to speculate about what happened in the head of Wordsworth when writing that verse, but has the duty to take into account the state of the lexical system at the time of Wordsworth. At that time 'gay' had no sexual connotation, and to acknowledge this point means to interact with a cultural and social treasury.

In my The Role of the Reader I stressed the difference between interpreting and using a text. I can certainly use Wordsworth's text for parody, for showing how a text can be read in relation to different cultural frameworks, or for strictly personal ends (I can read a text to get inspiration for my own musing); but if I want to interpret Wordsworth's text I must respect his cultural and linguistic background. (Eco 1992: 68-69)

While insisting on the limit of valid interpretation, Eco is fully aware of the plurality of meaning of literary works. He states that

During my lecture, speaking both of interpreters and of other authors and of interpreters of my own novels, I have stressed that it is difficult to say whether an interpretation is a good one, or not. I have however decided that it is possible to establish some limits beyond which it is possible to say that a given interpretation is a bad and far-fetched one. As a criterion, my quasi-Popperian stricture is perhaps too weak, but it is sufficient in order to recognize that it is not true that everything goes. (ibid: 144)

Forgive our long quotation here as we see it necessary for readers to know the inherent logic of Eco. By limiting the validity of interpretation, Eco does not deny that people can read a text differently for different use, but to interpret a text, readers have to show due respect to the author and his culture. This is especially important in the current context of globalization as has been shown in our above discussion of the politic and ethic value of a literary translation. Moreover, we should be aware that people could have different purposes of reading and using a text in reality. There have been many purposeful misreading of what is said or written by others. This is obviously against the communicative ethics proposed by Habermas.

The analytic philosopher Donald Davidson (2001: 177) in his *Epistemology and Truth* says that "[m]any philosophers in recent decades have held that truth is an epistemic concept; even when they have not explicitly held this thesis, their often implied it".

We talked about epistemology in Chapter 4 and we know that there have been different approaches to knowledge. There exist objectivism and relativism (radical or weaker). There are "correspondence theory of knowledge" and "consensus theory of knowledge". For our discussion here about the judging of intellectual value of literary translation, we find that besides Eco, Popper's theory of knowledge and Habermas's ideas are quite enlightening as well.

Karl Popper (1972: 106) in his *Objective Knowledge: An Evolutionary Approach* identifies three worlds: "first, the world of physical objects or physical states; secondly, the world of states of consciousness, or mental states, or perhaps of behavioral dispositions to act; and thirdly, the world of objective contents of thought, especially of scientific and poetic thoughts and works of art". Popper's three-world distinction is significant for our understanding of the subjectivity and objectivity of knowledge and text interpreting. His first world, "world 1", is the physical universe, mainly of material objects, consisting of the actual truth and reality that we try to represent but do not always perceive it and represent it correctly. "World 2" is the world of our subjective personal perceptions, experiences, and cognition, consisting mainly of personal knowledge. "World 3" is the total of the objective abstract products of the human mind, consisting of such artifacts as books, tools, theories, models, libraries, computers, and networks etc. While "world 3" mainly describes and predicts "world 1", some of the objects also belong to "world 1". According to Popper, "world 3" is where we find "objective contents of thought" and knowledge there is intersubjectively tested and can be criticized or potentially falsified. In one of his lectures Popper remarks

> I assert that we can, and that indeed we must, distinguish sharply between knowledge in the subjective sense and knowledge in the objective sense. Knowledge in the subjective sense consists of concrete mental dispositions especially of expectations; it consists of concrete world 2 thought processes, with their correlated world 1 brain processes. It may be described as our subjective world of expectations. Knowledge in the objective sense

consists not of thought processes but of thought contents. It consists of the content of our linguistically formulated theories; of that content which can be, at least approximately, translated from one language into another. The objective thought content is that which remains invariant in a reasonably good translation. Or more realistically put: the objective thought content is what the translator tries to keep invariant, even though he may at times find this task impossibly difficult. (Popper 1978)

Thus, for Popper, "[t]ruth, at any given moment and inside any given discipline, lies not in the subjectivity of one man's mind, but in the evolving intersubjective consensus of the qualified practitioners of that discipline" (Lefevere 1978: 11).

Obviously, "truth" in Popper's sense, is objective in that it is intersubjectively consensual and can be falsified. In this respect, we can say Habermas' classification of the world has something common with Popper's distinction between the three "worlds" of physical objects, mental states, and cultural products, and is in a way also enlightening for translators and translation critics as it speaks from the perspective of language and communication. Habermas also distinguishes three worlds and views that they are interrelated by language as the medium of communication:

Table 5.1   **(Habermas' three worlds)**

Domains of reality	Models of communication: basic attitudes	Validity-claims	General functions of speech
"The" world of external nature	Congnitive: objectivating attitude	Truth	Representation of facts
"Our" world of society	Interactive: performative attitude	Rightness	Establishment of legitimate interpersonal relations
"My" world of internal nature	Expressive: expressive attitude	Truthfulness	Discourse of speaker's subjectivity
language		Comprehensibility	

(Outhwaite 1996: 131)

In Habermas' framework "Our" world, the society, is where people exchange their perceptions and where consensus and consensual norms are shaped. "My" world's, the individual's, understanding of the first world, the external nature, has to be intersubjectively accepted in the "our" world to be "truth" and "rightness", and then can be used as objective and legitimate yardstick for criticism.

Besides the questions concerning the understanding and interpreting of the meaning of literary texts, in our evaluation of the intellectual value of a literary translation, we have also to consider the contextual needs of the subject (the translator and the reader) in plural form. It might not be, sometimes, the more information transferred the better. The information should be able to meet the real needs of the target society and be beneficial for the socio-cultural progress of the target culture.

To sum up, our discussion here tells us that translation of a literary text should convey as much as information or meaning contained in the ST. The meaning of a text is both subjective and objective. We do not deny the plurality of meaning of literary texts, but as a text is always a text in a certain time of our human society and reader, translators as well, are always subjects in a given society, if they pay due respect to the original work and its author, there can be a consensus about what intellectual value (information about human practice in various forms, social life in a certain place and time, customs, historical events, moral codes, attitude toward and feeling about certain behavior etc.). Moreover, our discussion once again shows the importance of context. Consensus that can be used as criteria for judging the intellectual value of a literary translation can only come from a specific context and detailed analysis of the contextual factors involved. We will hereto end this section by Hermans' quotation of Luhmann:

> Luhmann maintains, because contexts are always historically unique, meaning is prevented from sliding into a Derridean labyrinth of "difference" and deferral. When we look at texts in this way, through their "temporalized semantics", we may be able to glimpse the speaker's agenda: how likely was this communication in these particular circumstances, why was this theme, and this mode of transmission, selected at this moment, how does it alter the existing state of affairs? (Hermans 1997: 12)

c) Aesthetic value

Aesthetic value has been said to be the most prominent feature that distinguishes literary texts from non-literary texts. However, the judging of the aesthetic value of a literary work and that of a literary translation is also the most debatable in literary studies and translation studies. The reason, as the authors of this book see, is that judgment of the aesthetic value of a literary translation involves too many factors. It is not simply the judgment of aesthetic value, but that of ethic and intellectual values as well. Such being the case, the issue of criticism of the aesthetic value of a literary translation will definitely be more complex. The authors of this book could only hope to contribute a little to it from the perspective of evaluation theory and axiology in general.

Aesthetics, as has been discussed in Chapter 4, deals with the nature of beauty, art, taste and the creation and appreciation of beauty. It concerns not only what we have just talked about—the understanding and interpreting of a work of art—but also how beauty is conceived and enjoyed, whether the perception of beauty has connections with moral virtue or the receiver's outlook of moral value, and can aesthetic judgements be objective and so on.

Judgment of the aesthetic value is, as axiology and axiological aesthetics tell us, mainly dependent on the critic's outlook of beauty. If one holds that "truth is beauty", s/he will judge what s/he sees as "true" as beautiful. In literary criticism, those who think that the essence of beauty is imitation or displaying of aspects of reality will seek faithfulness to how things are in literary works. Accordingly, in judging the aesthetic value of a literary translation, they will take fidelity to the original as the most important criterion. Those who believe that literature is one of the forms of art and is the expression of feelings would argue there is no aesthetically "correctness" or "wrong" that can be settled once and for all. That is to say, there does not exist an absolute criterion for judging aesthetic value. Accordingly, they hold that for literary translation no absolute criterion exists for the judgment of aesthetic value. Those who value the novelty think that a literary work should offer them something new or strange tend to grade high the literary text showing great creativity and dissimilarity. In the similar way, they will grade high such a literary translation. Those taking aesthetic value as a matter of taste will deny any objectivity in the aesthetic activity, and accordingly, they will also deny the existence of any criterion for the judgment of aesthetic value in literature and in literary translation alike. What is more, there is often, if not always, ethic judgment involved in aesthetic judgment which will turn some translation with great aesthetic value in the eyes of some people a disgusting and ugly work. All these seem to indicate that, as axiology shows, the aesthetic value is the value realized by the subject. As subjects may have different understanding about beauty and possess different expectations and needs for a literary work and its translation, their aesthetic judgments to one and the same translation may be quite different. That is why we said aesthetic judgment is also connected with that of intellectual value and hermeneutics we talked about in last section.

As the aesthetic value is realized by readers, there has been a shift from the author and text to readers' interpreting and response. Martin Heidegger (1889—1976) who is greatly influenced by Nietzsche and whose ontological hermeneutics shifted the focus from interpretation to existential understanding—a more direct and more authentic way of being in the world than a way of knowing, from the methodological level to the ontological level, holding that understanding itself is the existing mode of being. Hans-Georg Gadmer (1900—2002) in his book *Truth and Method* developed Heidegger's ontological hermeneutics and emphasized that a reader or an interpreter inevitably has his or her prejudices and prejudices are rooted in one's concrete tradition which may be alien to a particular tradition of the author of a text the reader is reading. Prejudices are not the blockades to our understanding; they form a condition of understanding and contribute to the interpreter's specific horizon. "Hans-Georg Gadmer describes the process of interpreting a text as the fusion of one's own *horizon* with the *horizon of the text*". "Horizon" is defined by Gadmer as "[t]he totality of all that can be realized or thought about by a person at a given time in history and in a particular culture" (http://en.wikipedia.org/wiki/Hermeneutics; http://www.newworldencyclopedia.org/entry/Hans-Georg_Gadamer). "[T]he horizon of the present is being continually formed, in what we have continually to test all our prejudices. An important part of this testing is the encounter with the past and the understanding of the tradition from which we come" (Gadamer 1999: 273). Hence, the concept of "fusion of horizons" which can generate a third horizon or our understanding of a text. What is more, as no one can step outside the history of his or her understanding and all human understanding involves interpretation which is itself historically conditioned by particular cultures and languages, there comes the concept of "historicity of understanding". And "[t]here is thus room for constant reinterpretation and re-evaluation, as different meanings are projected upon the work concerned" (Blackburn 1996). Gadamer's philosophical hermeneutics has greatly influenced Hans Robert Jauss (1921-) and Wolfgang Iser (1926-) — two best known figures of German Reception Aesthetics that sees "[h]istory of literature is a process of aesthetic reception and production that takes place in the realization of literary texts on the part of the receptive reader, the reflective critic, and the author in his continuing productivity" (Zhu Gang 2001: 186). For Jauss, textual interpretation is largely "a question of reconstructing the reader's 'horizon of expectation'" (ibid: 183) and "the quality and rank of a literary work result neither from the biographical or historical conditions of its origin [Entstehung], nor from its place in the sequence of the development of a genre alone, but rather from the criteria of influence, reception, and posthumous fame, criteria that are more difficult to grasp" (ibid: 185). That is to say, criteria for judging the aesthetic value of a literary work has become more and more diversified because of the existence of many different horizon of expectations.

Despite the prevailing subjectivity in the judgment of aesthetic value, there has always been the idea of objectivity of aesthetic judgment. And some people have come to accept that judgment of aesthetic value is both subjective and objective.

> [T]here is public discourse about aesthetic standards, and aesthetic judgments are usually put forward as true, not merely as reports of one person's subjective response. The central problem concerning aesthetic value is that it is not merely in the eye of the beholder, while yet it seems to require the eye of the beholder in order to exist. (Janaway 2005)

In the field of translation studies, in respect of judging the aesthetic value of a literary translation, things are more complicated than literary studies, though in many ways closely connected with it, by the involvement of two languages, two cultures, politic power, ethics, literary tradition and translation tradition of literary works, reader's concept of literature, the difference of literary genre, reader's aesthetic tastes and expectations, critic's understanding of translation and literary translation, his cognitive competence, his aesthetic capacity, his imagination, his way of doing criticism, his ability of presenting his opinion and so on and so forth. For those who expect fidelity or equivalence, there is equivalence of different kinds. The following citations will give us a glimpse of people's different ideas about literary translation from different corners of the world. "[t]here is greater freedom and subjectivity in interpretation in the case of the translation of a literary text...a literary translation, aesthetic in nature, is an independent text because it tolerates and encourages deviations, additions and omissions" (Singh 1996: 67). Raymond Van den Broeck (1978: 31) once remarked

> [T]he criterion for the functional correspondence between a literary text and its translation cannot simply derive from the linguistic system in its ordinary sense, but must be determined by the aesthetic function of the literary text. The translator of a literary text does not aim primarily at establishing equivalences on the level of natural language, for his proper aim is to exhibit equivalence of artistic procedures.

Michelle Yeh (1995: 275) says that "[w]hat is poetic in one language may not be so in another, and the associations of imagery are dependent on cultural context".

Yunte Huang (2002: 165) says that "literary translation involves rendering aesthetic or cognitive concepts specific to one linguistic culture into their approximations specific to another culture".

What the above scholars said indicate that aesthetic judgment of literary translation is not merely a question of aesthetics, but rather, a series of factors involving epistemology and moral philosophy etc.

In *Children's Literature in Translation: Challenges and Strategies*, Anette Oster comments on the translation of children's literature to show the tradition of great adaptation in English translations of Hans Christian Andersen. The "irony, latent sexuality and dynamic or disturbing use of language" in Andersen's writings and the beginning of the tales were often changed into the conventional "Once upon a time", "a phrase which Andersen himself very rarely used" (Adams 2006: 93). "And while Andersen's approach to storytelling was complex and hybrid, refusing to distinguish between adult and child in his peculiar development of the oral folk tale into an evolving literary genre, the tendency was to translate him back into the conventional mould of the Brothers" (ibid).

For many people, imagery is more important than meaning, and therefore, the translator is required to pay more attention to the transfer or representation of the imagery of the original or to offer some inventive imagery of the translator as Pound has done. The Chinese tend to talk about the beauty of *Yijing* (or artistic conception), which is difficult to translate into English accurately (as there simply exist no corresponding concept in English, roughly, the artistic and poetic or romantic appeal or atmosphere). Another term we are familiar with that is also often used by the Chinese and the Westerner, also hard to pin down, is "spirit" which has caused many debates among translators and critics.

Style is also an important element for the judging of the aesthetic quality of a literary work and its translation. Berman (1992: 15) once commented, "A. W. Schlegel's translation of Shakespeare has been overestimated. Schlegel was too soft and too much immersed in Romance and Goethean verse to capture the majestic barbariousness of Shakespearean verse; his verses are more Italian verses than English verses".

And then the factor of the receptor. The trial of the foreign is actually given by the target reader. A comment on Minford's translation of *The Deer and the Cauldron* (*Lu Ding Ji*) by Louis Cha (better known as Jin Yong in Chinese) reads:

> [W]hen I read an "action" Kungfu novel, I am eager to throw off my academic gown along with other parts of my disposable culture, and allow the text to wash over me, carrying me forward, imparting subtly (if I am lucky) aspects of the "foreign" culture I do not know but which I wish to learn. In Minford's translation there are too many words— and a strong whiff of academe which drag me away from direct experience. To be frank, at the end of chapter 2, I asked myself whether I would bother to read on if the remaining

chapters were available and I was far from certain I would. But this is not because a western reader is ill-equipped or unwilling to approach Kungfu fiction with an open mind. It is also not because Chinese culture is so alien as to be inaccessible. It is because the quality of the English text is flawed. Whether a flawed version of The Deer and the Cauldron is better than no version remains as open question. (Liu ching-chih et al. 1997: 161-162)

The aesthetic judgment of a literary translation is indeed a complex event. It is not a task one can finish without being criticized by others. Yet, as axiological aesthetics shows, it is not an issue that is totally subjective. Liu Miqing (2005: 168-197) in his *Introduction to Translation Aesthetics* says that aesthetic subject and aesthetic object are dialectically inseparatable concepts. One of the essential features of the aesthetic subject is that it is constrained by the aesthetic object. In translation practice, the subject is the translator and the object the original text. Translation is different from writing because of this objective conditioning. The constrain of the aesthetic object lies first in the beauty of form of the original, secondly in the non-formal spiritual beauty which is fuzzy but can be felt "there". It also lies in the cultural difference and the difference of aesthetic experience from the difference of time and space. The other essential features of the aesthetic subject are the translator's subjectivity or "subjective dynamics" as Liu puts it. The translator's subjectivity lies in first his aesthetic feeling, aesthetic perception or sense of beauty, and secondly his capacity of knowing and then his capability of linguistic analysis, aesthetic analysis and aesthetic expression. It also lies in the tenacity or will to finish the artistic representation with his translation. Liu (ibid) offers his aesthetic criteria for literary translation asking essay translation to be plain, simple and elegant, novel translation to be fluent and intelligible and poetry to be elegant both in form and content with appealing images and *Yijing*. We can see that Liu is mainly talking about the aesthetic criteria from the perspective of style, a comprehensive set of criteria for judging the aesthetic value of a literary translation could actually much more complicated than it. Nevertheless, what Liu discussed in his book indicates that beauty is something both subjective and objective. In making aesthetic judgments we are not left totally relying on our emotions or individual response, but rather, aesthetic judgment can be made by means of reasonable analysis too. And as Janaway (2005) has said, there does exist "public discourse about aesthetic standards". Consensus about beauty can be arrived at in a given context otherwise we human beings will lose our direction of reforming the world. Reasonable criteria for judging the aesthetic value of literary translation can come from the integrity of the critic's subjectivity and the objective analysis of the above-mentioned list of factors involved in the concrete aesthetic activity.

To sum up, the establishment of sets of criteria for judging the politic and ethic values, the intellectual value and the aesthetic value of literary translation all interwoven and context dependent. Generally speaking, our criteria should be based on the detailed analysis of the contextual factors involved in the evaluation or criticism. Reasonable criteria come from our reasonable analysis of the object, the value-relationship between the subject and the object, and consensus or at least compromises can be reached which can tell us the real needs and the order of our needs, which can then be used as our criteria. There can be the highest criteria aiming at realizing the ultimate highest value of the integrity of truth, good and beauty, there can also be more realistic ground-level criteria that tell the bottom needs of an acceptable literary translation. In setting up reasonable criteria for criticism of literary translation, which should be practical-oriented and is also a form of reforming the world for achieving greater value, mere description and explanation is not enough, therefore, critical reflection on the pre-existing norms or consensus is always necessary. Dominant norms may not be always the "correct" and a historical and dialectical view on the values and criticism of the values of literary translation is of great importance. Moreover, finding proper ways of doing criticism is also of great significance and that is what we will talk about in the next section.

5.2.2.6 Methodology of criticism of literary translation

We talked about different existing ways and forms of doing criticism of literary translation in Chapter 3: 1), criticism on translation theories, which belongs, according to our definition of translation criticism, to translation criticism in its broad sense; 2), criticism on translation events; and 3), criticism on translated texts; 4) criticism on the translator. We should realize that if we view translation as an interlingual and intercultural communicative event, then criticism on translated texts and criticism on the translator are all entailed in criticism on translation events. And again, if we view translation criticism as an evaluation, then criticism of literary translation will be evaluating the various values of a literary translation as is our above discussion. Evaluation theory which we talked about in Chapter 4 tells us that to make an evaluation scientific, methodology and observing the methodology of the discipline is one of the key elements. Hence, it is essential for us to look at criticism of literary translation in light of methodology of evaluation.

Since we regard Davidson's needs-based evaluation framework reasonable, and we have been advocating establishing needs-based criteria and consensus-based criteria, and as we value more social evaluation than individual one, the authors of this book would like to offer a framework for criticism of literary translation by making some necessary adaptation to Davidson's framework of evaluation which is a modification of Scriven's Key Evaluation Checklist (see Chapter 4).

Table 5.2   The Key Checklist for Criticism of Literary Translation (modified and simplified from Davidson's 2005 version)

1. Background: Who asked for this evaluation and why? What are the main evaluation questions? Who are the main audiences? The overall design of this criticism	2.Descriptions and Explanations: Describe the evaluand in enough detail so that virtually anyone can understand what it is and what it does. Why did this program (event) or product of literary translation come into existence?	3. Consumers: Who are the actual or potential recipients or impactees of the program and its product	4. Resources: What resources are (or were) available to create, maintain, and help the program or policy succeed?	5. Values: On what basis will you determine whether the evaluand is of high quality, valuable, and so forth? Where will you get the criteria, and how will you determine "how good is good"?
6.Process Criticism: How good or efficient or in what way is the translation done?	7.Outcome Criticism: How good or valuable are the impacts (intended and unintended, short-term and long-term) on immediate recipients and other impactees?	8.Comparative Cost-Effectiveness: How costly is this evaluand to consumers, funders, staff, and the like, compared with alternative uses of the available resources that might feasibly have achieved outcomes of similar or greater value? Are the costs excessive, quite high, just acceptable, or very reasonable?		9. Exportability: What elements of the evaluand (e.g., innovative approach) might make it potentially valuable or a significant contribution or advance in another setting?

10. Overall Significance (Value Judgment): Draw on all of the information in Checkpoints 6 through 9 to answer the main evaluation questions (e.g., What are the main areas where the evaluand is doing well, and where is it lacking? Is this the most cost-effective use of the available resources to address the identified needs without excessive adverse impact?).	11. Recommendations and Explanations: A more in-depth analysis of why/how things went right/ wrong, including constructive recommendations for improvement	12. Responsibilities A more in-depth analysis of exactly who or what was responsible for good or bad results	13.Reporting and Follow-up: Who will receive copies of the criticism and in what form

14. Meta-criticism:
A critical assessment of the strengths and weaknesses of the evaluation itself (e.g., How well were all of the Key Criticism Checklist checkpoints covered?) and conclusions about its overall utility, accuracy or validity, feasibility, propriety and room for improvement

A few words about the framework or checklist. First, in this framework, needs include ideals but exclude and should be distinguished from desire. Secondly, recommendations and responsibilities are thought to be necessary instead of optional as we hold that criticism is practical-oriented and for problem-solving and improvement. Just as Reiss (2004: 15) says "it goes without saying that constructive translation criticism must also offer satisfactory alternative translations, substantiated with convincing evidence". Thirdly, though we make a distinction between process criticism and outcome criticism, they two are actually closely connected and therefore it is not a clear-cut distinction. Fourthly, criteria and the criticism are equally context dependent. Fifth, comparison between the ST and the TT should be involved in our analysis, though in reality there are some criticisms that do not consider the ST. Matarasso (1996: 2) points out that "[e]valuation without comparison is as meaningless as trying to measure a room without holding one end of the tape measure down". Reiss (2004: 15) also says that even judgment of consistency with "the overall spirit of the book" should be based on a comparison with the original, as the original serves as "objective criteria". Fifthly, an example of checkpoint 9 is Pound's translation of the classical Chinese poem which contributed a lot to the Imagist Movement, a revolution in versification and poetics as a whole. Gentzler (2004: 24) once commented that

> Pound, thus, successfully used translation to challenge and change the prevailing literary norms....Pound relentlessly attacked the prevailing Victorian/Edwardian literary tastes. As Pound used translations as a tool in his cultural struggle, so too have Euro-American translators of the sixties and seventies used translation to challenge prevailing tastes and cultural conceptions in Western (North American) society as well as to lend energy to the counter-culture movement.

Sixth, in our analysis of the resources available, we should grade the difficulty of translation tasks. Last but not least, according to the specific purpose of our criticism, we can pick up just one or two of the checkpoints in our criticism, bearing in mind its incomprehensiveness. We can center upon one or two of the values of a literary translation in our criticism, either politic and ethic or intellectual at one time.

Meehan (1969: 61-62) once pointed out "[i]t is impossible both in practice and in principle to examine every aspect of every situation or to seek to determine every possible consequence of every possible choice. There must be a selection of variables, an order of priorities". What Meehan says indicates two aspects of criticism of literary translation. First, as we have countless contextual factors to consider in our making criteria and making evaluative judgments, practically, we can choose some of the main factors. This is what exactly the author of this dissertation advocates. Inspired by the sociologist D. H. Hymes' framework of analyzing speech events, he has chosen factors such as "addressor and his / her cognitive status, addressee and his / her cognitive status (translator being both the addressee of the original author and the addressor of the target text), topic, setting, channel, code (what language or dialect or style of language is being used), message-form, event—the nature of the communicative event within which a genre may be embedded, key (tone and style), purpose, effect" as the main factors to be considered in translation and translation criticism and suggested that we can even choose from these main factors a few more contextually important ones (Zhang Zhiqiang 2008). Secondly, our criteria for criticism must include a hierarchy of value in the given context. Normally, the aesthetic value of literary translation priorizes the other values. But this is not always the case. Here again, context has the final say.

5.2.2.7 Features of criteria for criticism of literary translation

Criteria for criticism of literary translation, as has been discussed in the above paragraphs, are context dependent and pluralized. The main reason is the plurality of our outlook of values and the plurality of our human needs. Two prominent features of criteria for criticism of literary translation are subjectivity and relativity. It is nothing shameful to admit the subjectivity and relativity in criticism of literary translation as we accept that axiologically value is always the value to a certain subject and as social constructivism holds that anything, including truth, is both relative and absolute. Values, no matter what kind of, moral or intellectual or aesthetic, are both subjective and relative and at the same time objective (see our discussion in Chapter 4). Hence, another feature of criteria for criticism of literary translation is objectivity. Eco's discussion about the interpretation of literary text, Popper's three-world theory and Habermas' three-world theory, together with the consensus theory of truth, all show that subjectivity has an objective ground as the intersubjective experience of a community or group cannot exist independently of people's shared perceptions. Despite of the plurality of the needs and values of human beings, within a specific society of a given time, human needs are constrained and conditioned by the society people live in. The existing objective social laws and norms will to a great extent determine the individual's subjective needs. What is more, objectivity in humanities, especially in literature and literary translation, is not the same as that in the natural science and hence radical logical positivism is rejected. Instead, we accept what Scanlon termed "benign relativism", and consequently radical constructivism and radical relativism are also rejected. Thus, criteria for criticism of literary translation become plural, normative, consensual, dynamic, dialogic, critical, reflexive and dialectic. And dialectically, we can find the integrity of relativity and absoluteness, and the integrity of subjectivity and objectivity in the criteria for criticism of literary translation.

5.2.2.8 Criteria for criticizing a criticism

Evaluation can both be a product and a process. So can criticism of literary translation. One evaluation and one criticism always leads to another and hence the progress of our society. The later coming criticism always, directly or indirectly, entails some critical refelxion of the preceding one. Such criticism is called meta-criticism as meta-evaluation in axiology. In light of meta-evaluation, we know that the criteria for criticizing a criticism overlap to a great degree the principle and the criteria for criticism, but there are also some differences between them. The following are some requirements for a good criticism of literary translation to meet:

1. A criticism should fulfill its objectives.

2. A criticism should be useful and beneficial for those involved and especially those responsible for the program of translation and its product.

3. A criticism should be ethical. This requirement implies many other. A criticism should include reports revealing both strengths and weaknesses of the translation. It should be reasonable and well-grounded in its analysis and value judgments. The critic should give due respect to the evaluated, taking the difficulties of the task into the consideration. Try to be impartial, following strictly the procedure of the discipline. The data collected should be authentic and the feeling expressed should be truthful and friendly, allowing a counter criticism.

4. A criticism should be timely.

5. A criticism should be constructive, offering alternatives and pointing out the direction for improvement.

6. A criticism should try to be comprehensive, taking as much as the relevant contextual factors into consideration.

7. A criticism should be well-organized, opinions should expressed clearly and intelligible.

8. Criteria adopted should be consistent with those applied to the same genre.

All in all, meta-criticism is as important as criticism itself. It is in a sense more important in that it is more critical, potentially leading to better criticism by reflecting the shortcomings and merits of the preceding criticisms. It is also significant for the development of Translation Studies and for the establishment of a subject of translation criticism.

Chapter 6
Summary and Conclusion

Translation criticism has been an underdeveloped area in Translation Studies. Criticism of literary translation is even more underdeveloped despite of the fact that there have been numerous articles on it, especially compared with the extra large number of literary translations produced in the world. While we can say the insufficiency of study of criticism of literary translation owes partly to the relatively short history of Translation Studies as an independent discipline, and partly to the complexity of literary translation and criticism of it, our study in this book shows that it also owes to the lack of unanimity in the understanding and use of some of the key terms such as "faithfulness", "adequacy", "equivalent", "*xin*", "*ya*" and even "translation" and "literary translation" in our scholarly discussion. In this book, the authors gave detailed reviews and analyses of the previous studies translation criticism and criticism of literary translation trying to find where we are in the field of criticism of literary translation. They made some comments on the existing criteria and based on the assumption that criticism essentially is evaluation, they turned to evaluation theories and axiology in general. The axiological findings, including some value-driven epistemological findings, have been used to study the main aspects concerning criticism of literary translation. The main content of this research and some major findings and implications are summed up as follows.

6.1 Summary of the Research

In order to know the current situation of translation criticism and criticism of literary translation at the theoretical and practical levels, the authors first made a general review of the related studies at home and abroad. In their review, the authors adopted a paradigmatic approach for a clearer picture of the divergence and development of the related studies. Reviews and analyses of the previous studies show that people both in China and in the West have different understandings about translation, literariness, literary translation and criteria for criticizing a translation. There exist different paradigms in the system of Translation Studies and even within the same paradigm there are subparadigms indicating different assumptions and viewpoints of translation, literariness, literary translation and criticism of literary translation. There have been philological approach, linguistic approaches, cultural approaches and sociological approaches to translation and literary translation. In linguistic approaches, some scholars tend to find equivalence between the two texts by means of semantic analysis, others by pragmatic analysis, still others by cognitive and function analysis. In cultural approaches, there have been feminist view on translation and postcolonialist view on translation. Within functional approach, there exist difference between Nida and Newmark and those German functionalists. Even within a single theory, for instance, the skopos theory, one can find different beliefs about translation. All these different views on translation, on literariness give birth to different criteria for translation, for literary translation and different ways of translation criticism. There have been source-text oriented criteria, target-text oriented criteria, target-reader oriented criteria and translator oriented criteria. There exist various theory-based criteria and also some professional criteria. Some scholars adopt qualitative study, others quantitative. Some approaches are more descriptive, others more prescriptive. And some deconstructionist approaches are actually deconstructing the term "translation" by devouring any "Center" and making the term "criterion" meaningless. Our comparatively thorough review of criticism of literary translation at the theoretical level and the practical level both in China and in the West finds quite plural approaches which are controversial, inconsistent, incoherent or discrepant. Such a situation has made Peter France (2000: 10) claim that "in the day-to-day process of evaluating the thousands of translations that are published, critics will continue to negotiate between rival claims". Our analyses show that such a situation is caused seemingly by the fact that people are following different theories but actually by the plurality of people's outlook of value. Hence, value and evaluation theories can be applied to our study of translation criticism and criticism of literary translation.

Reviews of the previous studies also show that there have been efforts to make translation criticism and criticism of literary translation scientific and systematic both in China and some other countries. Some books and articles have given in-depth analyses of the subject of translation criticism and criticism of literary translation, formulating different models for translation quality assessment and adopting different approaches to translation criticism and criticism of literary translation: Reiss's model based on text types and goals, House's general model for TQA (strongly against skopos theorists' "the end justifies the means", holding that no judgment can be made without the comparison between the TT and the ST) and her concept of "cultural filtering", Berman's analytic of translation, Nord's prescriptive "norm of functionality", norm approaches by Toury, Chesterman and Hermans, and philosophical, aesthetical and literary approaches by Chinese scholars such as Xu Jun, Liu Miqing, Yang Xiaorong, Wang Hongyin, Lv Jun and Hou Xiangqun etc. All these studies help us to know better the nature of translation criticism and to make translation criticism including criticism of literary translation a subject of its own right. And among them, Lv Jun's approach to translation criticism is based on social constructivism and in light of evaluation theories and axiology in general and is therefore, especially enlightening. Inspired by the previous studies, especially that of axiological approach to translation criticism, the present research aims at a further endeavor toward a more systematic study of criticism of literary translation.

In this book, detailed reviews and discussions about concepts of criticism, literary text, literariness, literary criticism and literary translation were made as these concepts are closely connected with each other and are key terms for the present research. Our reviews and discussions about the essence of these concepts and terms helped not only make clearer our research object— criticism of literary translation and the nature of it: evaluation, but also know better the generality shared by criticism of literary translation and literary criticism and the particularity possessed by the activity of criticism of literary translation. Based on our discussion and analyses, translation criticism is defined, in a broad sense, as an evaluative practice involving quantitative and/or qualitative description, interpretation, comparison, discrimination and value-judgment concerning any translational event (including the motivations and purposes of translation, the choice of texts to be translated, translation policies, the implementation of translation, translators, strategies and methods adopted, translation contexts, the outcome of translating, translation theories etc.) in accordance with implicit or explicit criteria. In its narrow sense, translation criticism is defined as the evaluation of the process, outcome and impact of an interlingual and intercultural speech event in a specific context in accordance with implicit or explicit criteria, involving quantitative and/or qualitative description, interpretation, comparison, discrimination and value-judgment.

For the purpose of seeking a solid foundation and framework for criticism of literary translation, the authors introduced some related axiological theories concerning main branches of axiology, value and its criteria, evaluation and its objective, principles for evaluation, classification of evaluation, criteria for evaluation, methods of evaluation, features of evaluation and meta-evaluation etc.

In light of evaluation theories and axiology in general, the authors discussed first value and criticism (in the sense of evaluation) of literary works, value of translation of literary works and then criticism or evaluation of literary translation. They analyzed the nature of criticism of literary translation, the objectives of criticism of literary translation, types of criticism of literary translation, principles of criticism of literary translation, and criteria for criticism of literary translation. As criteria have been regarded as the core of criticism, they gave detailed analyses to topics such as criteria for literary translation and criteria for criticism of literary translation, the bases of the criteria for criticism of literary translation, the subject of the criticism, the highest criteria, the ground-level criteria and the hierarchy of values, criteria for the judgment of different values including the politic and ethic values, the intellectual value and the aesthetic value. Moreover, methodology of criticism of literary translation, features of criteria for criticism of literary translation, and criteria for criticizing a criticism were all discussed in detail.

6.2 Major Findings and Conclusions

Our axiological approach to criticism of literary translation finds that literary translation is a form of human practice to create values and values of a literary work and its translation are closely connected with its function of meeting different needs in practice in a certain society.

Criticism of literary translation is a purposeful activity and may have different objectives depending on the specific context. Generally speaking, a constructive criticism has to tell how (in what way and to what extent) good or how bad a literary translation is. It also has to find the overall quality or value of the translation and to find areas or alternatives for improvement. Finding ways or offering suggestions to improve the quality of literary translation should be the final goal of a practical-oriented criticism. Criticism of literary translation should aim to solve problems, to create greater values and to better meet the needs and interests of our human beings.

Diachronically, criticism of literary translation can be roughly divided into four kinds: 1) process criticism which takes place during the process of a translation program or after it passing judgments on various factors involved in the translational event; 2) outcome criticism which focuses more on the short-term effects of the translation; 3) impact criticism which pays more attention to the long-term effects of the translation; and 4) meta-criticism which is the assessment of a made criticism to check whether the made criticism has given a reasoned value judgment and whether it has fulfilled its objectives.

Synchronically, there can co-exist many types of criticism: criticism on the ethic value, politic value, intellectual value, aesthetic value, actual value, potential value, intrinsic value, instrumental value, material value, spiritual value and economic value etc. Theoretically speaking, there will be as many types of criticism as there will be different types of values viewed from different angles. If we want to draw the overall value of a literary translation, we will have to tend to all these kinds of values.

In terms of the criticism subject, there are individual and social criticisms. Individual criticism refers to the case when the critic is an individual: the translator himself or herself, an editor, a teacher teaching translation, especially literary translation, a public reader who knows nothing about the source language and the source culture, a reader who knows a little about the original writer, a bilingual reader who knows something about the two languages and cultures involved, a friend of the translator, an enemy of the translator, the author of the original work, an expert in literary studies, an expert in translation studies, a writer in the target culture, another translator, another translator who has translated the same work, an authority in the profession… Each of them may come with their own criteria for value judgments, making prominent the subjective feature of criticism of literary translation. However, it is not right to think that criticism of literary translation is totally subjective, because the seemingly subjective value judgments have their objective ground. Any individual is an individual of a certain society in a certain time. He or she is thereby constrained by the objective physical world and the spiritual world in which he or she lives. Their needs, their outlooks of value are all influenced and even governed to a certain extent by the environment of their living and by social norms. Social criticism on the other hand, refers to criticisms with a group of people or a community, an institution as the subject of criticism. Criteria for social criticism are normally the objective needs of the society or the normative intersubjective consensus often made and observed by most of the members of a community. Criteria adopted in individual criticism and in social criticism may sometimes overlap and it is the individual that functions as the realistic subject in both kinds of criticism. When an individual critic employs the social criteria in his criticism, the distinction between individual criticism and social criticism is blurred.

Criticism of literary translation can also be professional or non-professional. Here, we are not referring to professional critics or non-professional critics. We are only speaking of the property of two different criticisms. Non-professional criticism usually relies mainly on the critic's preferences, beliefs, interests, and so on that are not subject to strong evidential support and has the property of impressionism. Professional criticism on the other hand, as professional evaluation requires, should involve not only collecting descriptive information about a program of literary translation, the process or the product, but also using a certain set of criteria of value to determine what information should be collected and based on data analysis to make value judgments. What we need is, obviously more professional criticisms to make our criticism of literary translation more scientific and more reasonable. Actually, compared with the number of professional translators, there have been few professional critics of literary translation.

In criticism of literary translation, what is evaluated is the value relationship between the subject and the object. That is to say, the object of our criticism is not simply a substantial object existing "over there" separated from the subject. Subjectivity is therefore something inevitable in our criticism. Nevertheless, to pass on reasonable value judgment, we have to know the subject and the object and their relationship. In other words, criticism of literary translation cannot be separated from epistemology. But one should be aware that rigid logical positivism favored by epistemology in its narrow sense is rejected by our axiological-oriented criticism of literary translation. Thus, criticism of literary translation embraces subjectivity of cognition and at the same time acknowledges objectivity of knowledge. It bears some common features with epistemic activity, but it also has its own distinct peculiarities. Axiologically, there will always be subjectivity concerning error identification and merit appraisal in translation criticism and criticism of literary translation. The existence of subjectivity in criticism does not mean there is no objectivity in translation criticism and criticism of literary translation. Texts and contexts are always historically unique, and Eco's theory of text interpreting tells us the properties of the text itself do set limits to the range of legitimate interpretation beyond which it is possible to say that a given interpretation is a bad and far-fetched one. Popper's theory of knowledge, his three-world distinction and Habermas's three-world theory all indicate that there is objectivity existing in humanities, only that this objectivity is different from that in natural sciences which have been dominated by the "correspondence theory of knowledge" and logical positivism. What we believe in our study of criticism of literary translation is the social constructivism which embraces the "consensus theory of knowledge" and accepts the benign relativism of truth.

As criteria for criticism have been the core of criticism of literary translation, much of the discussion was given to questions concerning the establishment of a proper set of criteria. Discussions in this book show that we should keep a distinction between the concept of translation criteria and that of criteria for measuring a translation for a systematic study of the subject of translation criticism and criticism of literary translation as there can be similarities and great differences between them. It also shows that mere descriptive and explanatory study of criteria for translation criticism is not enough for criticism of literary translation. Description and explanation is necessary, but if we are satisfied with adopting some descriptively found norms as criteria, there will always be contradicting and conflicting criticisms which will in turn reinforce the existing norms. This will possibly make criticism lose its value, failing to fulfill its objectives of improving the world we live in, in case the existing dominant norms have become conservative. By the way, description here is different from descriptive study of translation which tries to be value-free and refuses to make value judgment. What is more, axiology tells us there could not be "pure description" in humanities. We need to make critical reflexion on the existing norms or paradigms and encourage the truthful dialogue between different classes, schools and paradigms to reach new consensus which is more progressive. Critical reflexion is the most prominent feature of criticism. In fact, in the course of social progress, once a norm becomes dominant, it begins to show the tendency of conservativeness as it tries to maintain its dominant position in the system. Our study indicates that translators are and should not always be passively constrained by the dominant norms and dominant norms are not always and forever "correct" in the course of the social development. The critics should therefore constantly making critical reflexion on the normative criteria or the dominant paradigm. What we need first is a consensus about what translation is and then what a good translation ought to be.

Axiological approach to criticism shows that one's view of value and value standards are determined by the needs of the subject. Therefore, consensus is actually need consensus and in evaluation and criticism alike, what we are going to evaluate is the extent to which the needs of the subject are satisfied. This means our criteria for criticism should be needs-based. However, we have to admit that there is no easy solution to the issue of criteria. Needs-based criteria may also be problematic, as we have to determine what are the real, reasonable and hence proper needs of the subject, which is absolutely no easy job. For we have to distinguish needs from wants and desires and ideals. But this also indicates that we can set up different criteria, the highest criteria and the ground-level criteria.

To set up criteria of various heights means to rank values or to list the hierarchical order of values. As value is always the value to a certain subject, in singular and in plural forms, we have to endeavor to know the needs and the hierarchical order of the needs of both of the two subjects. Usually, we put more weight on the latter. In other words, we value more social needs than individual needs as translation of literary works is viewed as a form of social practice to create social values. Yet, it is difficult even for us to set up proper social criteria since we know a literary translation may have various values and there exist different social groups and nations. The authors of this book offered some possible solutions to seek proper criteria for measuring the ethic and politic value, the intellectual value and the aesthetic value of literary translation. One of them is that through our theoretical discussion, we can set up certain general maximal idealized criteria like the actualization of the harmonious integrity of truth, good and beauty, and certain minimal criteria that is more realistic telling the minimal requirements for a qualified translation. The other is that we should pay due attention to the existing professional criteria in establishing the working criteria. Thirdly, we can specify the context and give detailed analysis to those contextual factors involved and then determine the criteria to be used. Criteria are thus fully context dependent, and any change of the contextual factors may bring forth the change of our criteria. In the current context of globalization, we recommend the respect for the "Other" (the original) as a basic criterion as it is beneficial for an equal exchange of cultures and is good to dehegemonize any cultural hegemony and ethno-centralism. We should realize that showing respect to others and the Other, and to be exact, the needs and interests of others, is actually to show respect to ourselves and to meet the needs and interests of ourselves in the long run. Normally and traditionally, the aesthetic value of a literary translation priorizes the other values in literary translation, but there will always be exceptions to this hierarchy and our axiological approach shows that the aesthetic value and the intellectual value and those of the ethic and politic are interwoven.

The main features of our axiological-oriented criticism of literary translation can be summed up as: purposeful, rational and reasonable, critical, reflexive, dialogical, intersubjective, normative, consensual, comparative (implicitly or explicitly), pragmatic, practical and constructive. It is also featured by the integrity of subjectivity and objectivity, the integrity of description, explanation and prescriptive evaluation, and by the dialectics of relativity and absoluteness.

For carrying out the axiological-oriented criticism of literary translation properly, we put forward some principles for the critic to follow. Our axiological-oriented criticism of literary translation is based on social constructivism which rejects rigid logical-positivism or scientism, embraces a benign relativism but is strongly against unrestricted radical relativism whose logical consequence, as Habermas holds, would be complete practical disorientation. "Everything (anything) goes" does not go.

To make our axiological-oriented criticism of literary translation reasonable, convincing and systematic, the authors of this book offered one general framework for carrying out criticism of literary translation and one comparatively concrete framework for contextual analysis. As there are many contextual factors to consider, they suggested that the critic should choose to take some of the main factors into his/ her consideration depending on the specific contextual objectives of the criticism.

In the last part of this book, the authors talked about meta-criticism, which is not only significant for the implementation of translation criticism and criticism of literary translation, but also important for the theoretical research of criticism of literary translation. Actually, what the authors have done in this book can be regarded as a metacriticism of our Translation studies concerning mainly translation criticism. It is hoped that this research can make due contribution to the establishment of a subject of criticism of literary translation and translation criticism as a whole in its own right.

6.3 Suggestions for Further Studies

As our reviews made in this book could have missed some important documents and points in the field of translation criticism, criticism of literary translation and axiology and as criticism of literary translation is a very complex activity, more comprehensive and more in-depth studies of different literary genre, the environment and the effect of criticism etc are called for. More case studies of criticism of literary translation can be carried out too. Other methods, for instance, corpus-driven analysis, can be explored to make our value judgment more convincing. It is also suggested that many other disciplines such as psychology, sociology and aesthetics etc. that are closely connected with criticism of literary translation be further studied to ensure a better understanding of criticism of literary translation and an establishment of a discipline of criticism of literary translation.

Bibliography

Alvstad, C. 2020. 'Literary translator ethics'[A]. in K. Koskinen & N. Pokorn (eds). *The Routledge Handbook of Translation and Ethics*[C]. London: Routledge.

Anderman, G. 2007. Linguistics and Translation[A]. in Kuhiwczak & Littau. (eds.). A Companion toTranslation Studies[C]. Clevedon / Buffalo / Toronto: Multilingual Matters Ltd.

Angelelli, C. (ed.). 2014. *The Sociological Turn in Translation and Interpreting Studies*[C]. Amsterdam and Philadelphia, PA: John Benjamins.

Arrojo, R. 1997. The Death of the Author and the Limits of the Translator's Visibility[A]. in Snell-Hornby, Jettmarová & Kaindl. (eds). *Translation as Intercultural Communication: Selected papers from the EST Congress, Prague 1995*[C]. Amsterdam: John Benjamins.

Axtell, G. 2009. *General Theory of Value 1909-2009: Reflections on the First Centennial of American Axiology*[OL]. http://janusblog.squarespace.com/janusbloglibraryofpapersd/General%20Theory%20of%20Value%201909.doc.

Bahm, A. J. 1993. *Axiology: The Science of Values*[M]. Amsterdam / Atlanta, GA : Rodopi.

Baker, M. (ed.). 2004. *Routledge Encyclopedia of Translation Studies*[Z]. Shanghai: Shanghai Foreign Language Education Press.

Baker, M. 2006. *Translation and Conflict: A Narrative Account*[M]. New York: Routledge.

Bassnett, S. (ed.). 2021. *Translation and World Literature*[C]. London and New York: Routledge.

Bassnett & Lefevere, 2001. Constructing Culture: Essays on Literary Translation[C]. Shanghai: Shanghai Foreign Language Education Press.

Bassnett & Trivedi. (eds). 1999. *Postcolonial Translation: Theory and Practice*[C]. London and New York: Pinter.

Bassnett, S. 2004. *Transaltion Studies*[M]. Shanghai: Shanghai Foreign Language Education Press.

Bell, R. T. 2001. *Translation and Translating: Theory and Practice*[M]. Beijing: Foreign language Teaching and Research Press.

Berman, A. 1992. *The Experience of the Foreign: Culture and Translation in Romantic Germany*[M]. Heyvaert, S. (trans.). New York: State University of New York Press.

Berman, A. 2000. Translation and the Trials of the Foreign[A]. in Venuti, L. (ed. & trans.). *The Translation Studies Reader* (2nd ed.) [C]. London and New York: Routledge.

Bhabha, H. K. 1994. *The Location of Culture*[M]. London and New York: Routledge.

Blackburn, S. (ed.). 1996. *The Oxford Dictionary of Philosophy*[Z] [OL]. Oxford University Press. *Oxford Reference Online*. Oxford University Press. Manchester University. 25 July 2007 <http://www.oxfordreference.com/views/ENTRY.html?subview=Main&entry=t98.e991>.

Bourdieu & Wacquant. 1992. *An Invitation to Reflexive Sociology*[M]. Cambridge: Polity Press.

Bourdieu, P. 1983. *Language and Symbolic Power*[M]. Raymond and Adamson (trans.). Massachusetts: Harvard University Press.

Bourdieu, P. 1984. *Distinction: A Social Critique of the Judgement of Taste*[M]. Nice, R. (trans.). Massachusetts: Harvard University Press.

Bourdieu, P. 1993. *The Field of Cultural Production: Essays on Art and Literature*[C]. Johnson, R. (ed.). Cambridge: Polity Press.

Brown & Yule. 1983/2000. *Discourse Analysis*[M]. Beijing: Foreign Language Teaching and Research Press

Brunette, L. 2000. Towards a Terminology for Translation Quality Assessment[J]. *The Translator*, Vol. 6, No 2, 169-182.

Carbaugh, D. 2007. Ethnography of Communication[OL]. in Wolfgang, D. (ed). *The Blackwell International Encyclopedia of Communication*[Z]. Blackwell Publishing. Blackwell Reference Online. 30 October 2007 http://www.blachwellreference.com/

Catford, J. C. 1965. *A Linguistic Theory of Translation*[M]. Oxford: Oxford University Press.

Chan, L. T. 1997. The impressionistic approach to translation theorizing; or: Twentieth-century Chinese ideas of translation through the Western looking-glass[A]. in Snell-Hornby, Jettmarova & Kaindl (eds). *Translation as*

Intercultural Communication: Selected papers from the EST Congress - Prague 1995[C]. Amsterdam / Philadelphia: John Benjamins Publishing Co.

Chang Nam Fung. 2004. *A Critical Study of Chinese and Western Translation Theories* [M]. Beijing: Tsinghua University Press.

Chesterman & Wagner. 2002. *Can Theory Help Translators? A Dialogue Between the Ivory Tower and the Wordface*[M]. Manchester: St. Jerome Publishing.

Chesterman, A. (ed.). 1989. *Readings in Translation Theory*[C]. Oy Finn lectura Ab: Oy.

Chesterman, A. 1997. *Memes of translation: the spread of ideas in translation theory*[M]. Amsterdam & Philadelphia: John Benjamins Publishing Co.

Cheung, M. P. Y. 2005. "To translate" means "to exchange"? A new interpretation of the earliest Chinese attempts to define translation ('fanyi') [J]. *Target*, Vol.17, No.1, 27–48.

Classe, O. (ed.). 2000. *Encyclopedia of Literary Translation into English*[Z]. London and Chicago: Fitzroy Dearborn.

Collini, S. (ed.). 1992. *Interpretation and over-interpretation*[C]. Cambridge: Cambridge University Press.

Cooper, D. E. *A.* 2007. *Companion to Aesthetics*[OL]. Blackwell Publishing. Blackwell Reference Online. 07 July 2007 <http://www.blackwellreference.com/ subscriber/book?id=g9780631196594_9780631196594>

Cronin, C. 1993. Translator's Note. in Cronin, C. (trans.). *Justification and Application: Remarks on Discourse Ethics*[M]. Cambridge: Polity Press.

Crotty, R. B. 1980. *A Study of Paradigmatic System of Religious Knowledge and Associated Religious Social Groups with Special Reference to Thelogical Education in the Roman Catholic Church*[D]. University of Adelaide. Doctoral dissertation.

Davidson, D. 2001. *Epistemology and Truth*[M]. Oxford: OUP.

Davidson, E. J. 2005. *Evaluation Methodology Basics: The nuts and bolts of sound evaluation*[M]. London/ California/ New Delhi: Sage Publications, Inc.

Davis, K. 2004. *Deconstruction and Translation*[M]. Shanghai: Shanghai Foreign Language and Education Press.

Delabastita, D' hulst & Meylaerts. (eds). 2006. *Functional Approaches to Culture and Translation: Selected papers by Jose Lambert*[C]. Amsterdam & Philadelphia: John Benjamins Publishing Co.

Delisle, Lee-Jahnke & Cormier. 2004. *Translation Terminology*[Z]. Kong Yifeng &

Zhong Weihe (trans.), Beijing: Foreign language Teaching and Research Press.

Dollerup, C. 1997. *Translation as Imposition vs. Translation as Requisition*[A]. In Snell-Hornby, Jettmarova & Laindl. (eds). *Translation as Intercultural Communication*[C]. Amsterdam/Philadelphia: John Benjamins Publishing Co.

Eagleton, T. 1983. *Literary Theory: An Introduction*[M]. Oxford: Blackwell.

Eco, U. 1975. *A Theory of Semiotics*[M]. Bloomington: Indiana University Press.

Eco, U. 1992. Between author and text[A]. In Collini, S. (ed.). *Interpretation and over-interpretation*[C]. Cambridge: Cambridge University Press.

Eco, U. 1992. Overinterpreting texts[A]. In Collini, S. (ed.). *Interpretation and over-interpretation*[C]. Cambridge: Cambridge University Press.

Eco, U. 1992. Reply by Eco[A]. In Collini, S. (ed.). *Interpretation and over-interpretation*[C]. Cambridge: Cambridge University Press.

France, P. (ed.). 2000. *Oxford Guide to Literature in English Translation*[Z]. Oxford & New York: Oxford University Press.

Frondizi, R. 1971. *What Is Value?——An Introduction to Axiology* (2nd ed.) [M]. Illinois: Open Court Publishing Company.

Gensler, H. J. 1998. *ETHICS: A Contemporary Introduction*[M]. London and New York: Routledge.

Gentzler, E. 2004. *Contemporary Translation Theory* (2nd edition) [M]. Shanghai: Shanghai Foreign Language Education Press.

George, A. 2003. "Value, Value Theory". *Encyclopedia of Science and Religion*[Z] [OL]. The Gale Group Inc. Retrieved December 27, 2009 from Encyclopedia. com: http://www.encyclopedia.com/doc/1G2-3404200530.html

Gerhart, M. 1979. *The Question of Belief in Literary Criticism: An Introduction to the Hermeneutical Theory of Paul Ricoeur*[M]. Stuttgart: Akademischer Verlag Stuttgart.

Gouanvic, J. 2005. "A Bourdieusian Theory of Translation, or the Coincidence of Practical Instances: Field, 'Habitus', Capital and 'Illusio'" [J]. *The Translator*, 11(2), 147-166.

Habermas, J. 1993. *Discourse Ethics*[M]. Cronin, C. (trans.). Cambridge: Polity Press.

Habermas, J. 1993. *Justification and Application: Remarks on Discourse Ethics*[M]. Cronin, C. (trans.). Cambridge: Polity Press.

Hamlyn, D. W. 2005. "epistemology, history of". In *The Oxford Companion to Philosophy*[Z][OL]. Oxford University Press. *Oxford Reference Online*. Oxford

University Press. Manchester University. 17 February 2007 http://www. oxfordreference.com/views/ENTRY.html?subview=Main&entry=t116.e762;

Hartmann, R.R.K. 2006. An International Encyclopedia of Translation Studies (review) [J]. *Target*, Vol. 18, No.1, 177–198.

Hatim & Mason. 1997. *The Translator as Communicator*[M]. London and New York: Routledge.

Hermans, T. 1997. Translation As Institution[A]. in Snell-Hornby, Jettmarova & Kaindl (eds). *Translation as Intercultural Communication: Selected papers from the EST Congress - Prague 1995*[C]. Amsterdam / Philadelphia: John Benjamins Publishing Co.

Hermans, T. 2004. *Translation in Systems: Descriptive and System-oriented Approaches Explained*[M]. Shanghai: Shanghai Foreign Language Education Press.

Hermans, T. 2007. Literary Translation[A]. in Kuhiwczak & Littau (eds). *.A Companion to Translation Studies*[C]. Clevedon / Buffalo / Toronto: Multilingual Matters Ltd.

Holmes, J. 1988. *Translated: Papers on Literary Translation and Translation Studies*[C]. Amsterdam: Rodopi.

Honig, H. G.. 1998. Position, Power and Practice: Functionalist Approaches and Translation Quality Assessment[A]. in Schaffner, C.(ed.). *Translation and Quality*[C]. Clevedon: Multilingua Matters Ltd.

House & Howe. 1999. *Values in Evaluation and Social Research*[M]. Thousand Oaks: Sage Publications, Inc.

House, J. 1981. *A model for translation quality assessment* (2nd ed.) [M]. Tubingen: Narr.

House, J. 1997. *Translation Quality Assessment: A Model Revisited*[M]. Tubingen: Narr.

Huang Long. 1988. *Translatology*[M].Nanjing: Jiangsu Education Press.

Huang, Yunte. 2002. *Transpacific Displacement: Ethnography, Translation and Intertextual Travel in Twentieth-Century American Literature*[M]. Berlekey & Los Angeles: University of California Press.

Hymes, D. 1962. The ethnography of speaking[A]. in Gladwin & Sturtevant (eds.). *Anthropology and human behavior*[C]. Washington, DC: Anthropological Society of Washington, 13-53.

Hymes, D.1974. *Foundations in Sociolinguistics: An Ethnographic Approach*[M].

Philadelphia: University of Pennsylvania Press.

Ingarden, R. 1985. Artistic and Aesthetic Values[A]. in McCormick, P. J. (ed.). *Selected Papers in Aesthetics*[C]. Washington DC. : The Catholic University of America Press.

Janaway, C. 2005. Value, aesthetic. in *The Oxford Companion to Philosophy*[Z] [OL]. Oxford University Press. *Oxford Reference Online*. Oxford University Press. Manchester University. 17 February 2007 <http://www.oxfordreference. com/views/ENTRY.html?subview=Main&entry=t116.e2619>

Jin Di & Nida, E. 1984. *On Translation*[M]. Beijing: China Translation and Publishing Corporation.

Kaindl, K., W. Kolb & D. Schlager (eds). 2021. *Literary Translation Studies*[C]. Amsterdam: John Benjamins.

Ke Ping. 1999. *Contrastive Linguistics*[M]. Nanjing: Nanjing Normal University Press.

Kearney, R. 2006. Introduction: Ricoeur's philosophy of translation. in *On Translation*[M]. Brennan, E. (trans.). London and New York: Routledge.

Ketkar, S. Literary Translation: Recent Theoretical Developments. http://www. translationdirectory.com/article301. htm

Kolak, D. (ed.). 2002. *Lovers of Wisdom: An Introduction to Philosophy with Integrated Readings*. Beijing: Peking University Press

Kovesi, J. 1998. Values and Evaluations: Essays on Ethics and Ideology. New York: Peter Lang Publishing Inc.

Kuhn, T. 1970. *The Structure of Scientific Revolutions* (2ed ed.) [M]. Chicago: University of Chicago Press.

Lefevere, A. 1978. Translation: The Focus of the Growth of Literary Knowledge[A]. in Holmes, Lambert & Van den Broeck (eds). *Literature and Translation: new perspectives in literary studies with a basic bibliography of books on translation studies*[C]. Leuven: Acco.

Lefevere, A. 2004. *Translation, Rewriting and theManipulation of Literary Fame*[M]. Shanghai: Shanghai Foreign Language Education Press.

Lefevere, A. 2004. *Translation/History/Culture: A Sourcebook*[M]. Shanghai: Shanghai Foreign Language Education Press.

Leonard, F. 1958. Translation: An Introduction[A]. in Booth, A. D. (ed.). *Aspects of Translation: Studies in Communication 2*[C]. London: Seeker and Warburg.

Levinson, J. (ed.). 2005. *The Oxford Companion to Philosophy*[Z] [OL]. Oxford

University Press. *Oxford Reference Online*. Oxford University Press. Manchester University. 17 February 2007 http://www.oxfordreference.com/views/ENTRY. html?subview=Main&entry=t116.e808

Li Yunxing. 2001. Translation Evaluation in a Systemic Perspective[J]. *Perspectives*, Vol.9:1 http://tscn.tongtu.net/ 2002-11-3

Littelejohn & Foss. 2005. *Theories of human communication*[M]. Belmont, CA: Wadsworth Publishing Company.

Liu ching-chih et al. (eds). 1997. *The Question of Reception: Martial Arts. Fiction in English Translation*[C]. Hong Kong: Centre for Literature and Translation. Lingnan College.

Liu Zhongde, 1991. *Ten Lectures on Literary Translation*[M]. Beijing: China Translation & Publishing Corporation

Low, G. 2002. Evaluating translations of surrealist poetry[J]. *Target*, 14:1, 1–41.

Maier, C. 2004. Reviewing and criticism. in Baker, M. (ed.). *Routledge Encyclopedia of Translation Studies*[Z]. Shanghai: Shanghai Foreign Language Education Press.

Matarasso, F. 1996. *Defining Values: Evaluating Arts Programmes*[M]. Nottingham: COMEDIA.

Meehan, E. J. 1969. *Value Judgement and Social Science: Structure and Processes*[M]. Georgetown: THE DORSEY PRESS.

Munday, J. 2001. *Introducing Translation Studies: Theories and Applications* (1st edition) [M]. London and New York: Routledge.

Munday, Pinto & Blakesley. 2022. *Introducing Translation Studies: Theories and Applications* (fifth edition) [M]. London and New York: Routledge.

Newmark, P. 1991. *About Translation*[M]. Clecedon: Multilingual Matters.

Newmark, P. 2001. *A Textbook of Translation*[M]. Shanghai: Shanghai Foreign Language Education Press.

Newmark, P. 2004. Non-literary in the Light of Literary Translation[J]. *The Journal of Specialised Translation*, Issue 1, 8-13.

Nida & Taber. 2004. *The Theory and Practice of Translation*[M]. Shanghai: Shanghai Foreign Language and Education Press.

Nord, C. 1991. *Text Analysis in Transaliton Theory, Methodology, and Didactic Application of a Model for Translaiton-oriented Text Analysis*[M]. Nord & Sparrow (trans.). Amsterdam: Rodopi.

Nord, C. 2001. *Translating as a Purposeful Activity: Functionalist Approaches*

Explained[M]. Shanghai: Shanghai Foreign Language and Education Press.

Norkus, Z. 1994. Axiology: Classical and Modern[A]. *Personal Freedom and National Resurgence: Lithunian Philosophical Studies, I*[C]. Bucharest: METEOPOL Publishing and Printing Company.

Olsen & Pettersson. 2005. *Text and Experience: New Analytic and Pragmatic Approaches to the Study of Literature*[M]. Hampshire / New York: Palgrave MacmiIlan.

Outhwaite, D. W. (ed.). 1996. *The Habermas Reader*[M]. Cambridge: Polity

Picken, C. (ed.). 1983. *The Translator's Handbook*[C]. London: Aslib.

Popper, K. 1972. *Objective Knowledge: An Evolutionary Approach*[M]. Oxford: Clarendon Press.

Popper, K. 1978. *Three Worlds*[OL]. The Tanner Lectures on Human Values delivered at The University of Michigan April 7, 1978. http://www.tannerlectures.utah.edu/lectures/documents/popper80.pdf)

Pym, A. 1992. *Translation and Text Transfer: An Essay on the Principles of Intercultural Communication*[M]. New York: Peter Lang.

Pym, A. 1995. Doubts about deconstruction as a general theory of translation. *TradTerm (São Paulo)* [J] [OL]. (2), 11-18. http://www.tinet.cat/~apym/on-line/research_methods/decon.html

Pym, A. 2003. Translational ethics and electronic technologies [OL]. http://www.tinet.cat/~apym/on-line/translation/lisbon_ethics.pdf.

Pym, A. 2007. Philosophy and Translation[A]. in Kuhiwczak & Littau (eds). *A Companion toTranslation Studies*[C]. Clevedon / Buffalo / Toronto: Multilingual Matters Ltd.

Raila, H. 2009. Fields, Networks and Finnish prose: A Comparison of Bourdieusian Field Theory and Actor-Network Theory in Translation Sociology[A] [OL]. in CROM, D. D. (ed.). *Selected Papers of the CETRA Research Seminar in Translation Studies 2008*[C]. http://www.kuleuven.be/cetra/papers/papers.html

Reiss, K. 2004. *Translation Criticism: The Potentials & Limitations*[M]. Manchester: St. Jerome Publishing.

Rhodes, E. F. (trans.). 2000. *Translation Criticism: The Potentials and Limitations*[M]. Manchester : St. Jerome Publishing.

Ricoeur, P. 2006. *On Translation*[M]. Eileen Brennan (trans.). London and New York: Routledge.

Robinson，D. 1997. *Translation and Empire：Postcolonial Theories Explained*[M].

Manchester: St. Jerome.

Rose, M. G. 1997. *Translation and Literary Criticism: Translation as Analysis*[M]. Manchester: St. Jerome Publishing.

Rozov, N. S. 1998. *Values in the Problematic World: Philosophical Foundations and Social Applications of Constructive Axiology*[OL]. Novosibirsk: Novosibirsk State University. http://www.nsu.ru/filf/rozov/publ/val/summary.htm

Sager, C. 2000. Katharina Rei β : Translation Criticism: The Potentials and Limitations (review) [J]. *The Translator*, Vol. 6. No.2.

Sager, J. C. 1983. Quality and standards—the evaluation of translations[A]. in Picken, C. (ed.). *The Translation's Handbook*[C]. London: Aslib.

Sager, J. C. 1998. What Distinguishes Major Types of Translation? [J]. *The Translator*, Vol. 4, No. 1, 69-89.

Schaffner & Adab. 2001. The Idea of the Hybrid Text in Translation Revisited[J]. *Across Languages and Cultures*. 2(2), 277-302

Schaffner, C. (ed.). 1998. *Translation and Quality*[C]. Clevedon: Multilingua Matters Ltd.

Scott & Marshall. (eds.). 2005. *A Dictionary of Sociology*[Z] [OL]. Oxford University Press. *Oxford Reference Online*. Oxford University Press. Manchester University. 16 February 2007 http://www.oxfordreference.com/views/ENTRY.html?subview=Main&entry=t88.e1913

Scriven, M. 1991. *Evaluation thesaurus* (4th ed.) [M]. Newbury Park, CA: Sage Publications.

Selden, Widdowson & Brooker. 2004. *A Reader's Guide to Contemporary Literary Theory*[M]. Beijing: Foreign Language Teaching and Research Press.

Shuttleworth & Cowie. 2004. *Dictionary of Translation Studies*[Z]. Shanghai: Shanghai Foreign Language and Education Press.

Simeoni, D. 1998. The Pivotal Status of the Translator's Habitus[J]. *Target* 10 (1): 1-39.

Simon. S. 1996. *Gender in Translation: Cultural Identity and the Politics of Transmission*[M]. London and New York: Routeledge.

Singh, A. K. (ed.). 1996. *Translation: Its Theory and Practice*. New Delhi: Creative Books.

Snell-Hornby, M. 2001. *Translation Studies: An Integrated Approach*[M]. Shanghai: Shanghai Foreign Language and Education Press.

Snell-Hornby, M. 2006. *The Turns of Translation Studies: New Paradigms or Shifting*

Viewpoints? [M]. Amsterdam/ Philadelphia: John Benjamins Publishing Co.

Spolsky, B. 2000. *Sociolinguistics*[M]. Shanghai: Shanghai Foreign Language Education Press.

Stufflebeam & Shinkfield. 1985. *Systematic Evaluation: A Self-Instructional Guide to Theory and Practice*[M]. Norwell: Kluwer-Nijhoff Publishing.

Toury, G. 2001. *Descriptive Translation Studies and Beyond*[M]. Shanghai: Shanghai Foreign Language Education Press.

Van den Broeck, R. 1978. The Concept of Equivalence[A]. in Holmes, Lambert & Van den Broeck (eds.). *Translation Theory: Some Critical Reflections in Literature and Translation: New Perspectives in Literary Studies*[C]. Lerven: ACCO.

Van den Broeck, R.1985. Second Thought on Translation Criticism: A Model of its Analytic Function[A]. in Hermans, T. (ed.). *The Manipulation of Literature: Studies in Literary Translation*[C]. New York: St. Martin's Press.

Venuti, L. (ed.). 2000. *The Translation Studies Reader* (2nd ed.)[C]. London and New York: Routledge.

Venuti, L. 1998. *The Scandals of Translation*[M]. London: Routledge.

Williams & Chesterman. 2004. *The Map: A Beginner's Guide to Doing Research in Translation Studies*[M]. Shanghai: Shanghai Foreign Language and Education Press.

Williams, M. 2001. The Application of Argumentation Theory to Translation Quality Assessment[J]. *Meta*, Vol. 46, No. 2, 326-344.

Williams, M. 2004. *Translation Quality Assessment: An Argumentation-Centred Approach*[M]. Ottawa: University of Ottawa Press.

Wilss, W. 2001. *The Science of Translation: Problems and Methods*[M]. Shanghai: Shanghai Foreign Language Education Press.

Wisker, G. 2007. *Key Concept in Postcolonial Literature*[M]. Houndmills: Palgrave Macmillan.

Yannakopoulou, Vasso. 2008. Norms and Translatorial Habitus: in Angelos Vlahos' Greek Translation of Hamlet[A]. in BOULOGNE, P. (ed.). *Translation and Its Others: Selected Papers of the CETRA Research Seminar in Translation Studies 2007*[C][OL]. http://www.kuleuven.be/cetra/papers/papers.html

Yeh, M. 1995. On English Translation of Modern Chinese Poetry—A Critical Survey (1936-1990) [A]. in Eugene Eoyang and Lin Yao-fu. (eds.). *Translating Chinese Literature*[C]. Bloomington & Indianapolis: Indiana University Press.

Zhang Zhongzai. 2000. *Selected Readings in Classical Western Critical Theory*[M]. Beijing: Foreign Language Teaching and Research Press.

Zhu Gang. 2001. *Twentieth Century Western Critical Theories*[M]. Shanghai: Shanghai Foreign Language Education Press.

Zilahy, S. P. 1963. Quality in Translation[A]. in Cary & Jumplet (eds.). *Quality in Translation: Proceedings of the IIIrd Congress of the International Federation of Translation (FIT)* [C]. New York: The Macmillan Company.

Zlateva & Lefevere. 1993. *Translation as Social Action: Russian and Bulgarian Perspectives*[M]. London and New York: Routledge.

Cai Xinle. 2005. *An Ontological Study of Translation* [M]. Shanghai: Shanghai Translation Publishing House.

Chen Fukang. 1992. *A History of Translation Theory in China*[M]. Shanghai: Shanghai Foreign Language Education Press.

Chen Hongwei. 2002.Artistic Accomplishments of the English Version of KONG Yi —ji Viewed from Fictional Aesthetics [J]. *Journal of Foreign Languages*, (2), 62-68.

Chen Ming. 2005. The Historical Starting Point of Axiology Aesthetics[J]. *Journal of Hainan Normal University*, (4), 118-121.

Chen Xiaolong. 2005. From General Epistemology to the Doctrine of Wisdom—A Concurrent Study on the Essential Spirit of Feng Qi's Philosophy[J]. *Journal of East China Normal University*, (2),9-14.

Chen Xinhan. 1994. On the Mechanism of Social Evaluation [J]. *Journal of Humanities*, (1), 18-23.

Chen Xinhan. 1997. *On Social Evaluation*[M].Shanghai: Shanghai AcademyofSocial Sciences Press.

Chen Xinhan. 2000. My View on the Study of Some Issues of Evaluation [J]. *Tianjin Social Sciences*, (2), 31-35.

Chen Zhen. 2008. Moral Relativism and Moral Objectivity[J]. *Academic Monthly*, (12), 40-50.

Cheng Aihua. 2002. Translation Criticism: Dilemma and Choice[J]. *Journal of Shandong Teachers University*, (6), 70-71.

Dong Qiusi. 1950. The Criteria and Focuses of Translation Criticism [J]. *Chinese Translators Journal*, (4), 2-4.

Du Jianhui. 1998. *Introduction to Translation Studies*[M]. Beijing: The Ethnic Publishing House.

Fan Cunzhong. 1985. *Translation Theories and Techniques* [M]. Beijing: China Translation and Publishing Corporation.

Fan Shouyi. 1994. Fuzzy Mathematics and Translation Criticism [A]. Yang Zijian & Liu Xueyun (eds). *New Perceptions of Translation*[C]. Wuhan: Hubei Education Press.

Editorial Board of *Chinese Translators Journal* (ed). 1984. *Collected Papers on Translation Studies:1894—1948*[C]. Beijing: Foreign Language Teaching and Research Press.

Editorial Board of *Chinese Translators Journal* (ed). 1984. *Collected Papers on Translation Studies: 1949—1983*[C]. Beijing: Foreign Language Teaching and Research Press.

Fang Mengzhi. 1999. *New Perspectives of Translation and Practice* [M]. Tsingtao: Tsingtao Publishing House.

Fang Mengzhi. 2004. *A Dictionary of Translation Studies*[Z]. Shanghai: Shanghai Foreign Language Education Press.

Fang Wentao. 1999. Thoughts on Philosophy at the Turn of the Century: Comments on *Communicative Practice and Intersubjectivity*[J].*Jianghai Academic Journal*, (4), 189-190.

Fang Yongquan. 2007.Axiological(Aesthetics) and Education[OL]. http://web.edu. ntnu.edu.tw/~ycfang/_document/sylllabus7(eduph).doc.)

Feng Ping & Chen Lichun. 2003. Turn from Ontology to Epistemology in Axiolgy— A Study on Urban's Theory of Valuation [J]. *Journal of Fudan University*, (5), 65-70.

Feng Ping. 1995. *On Evaluation* [M]. Beijing: Oriental Publishing House.

Feng Ping. 2006. The Verifiability of Value-Judgment:John Dewey' s Criticism on the Anti-Value Theory of Logical Positivism [J]. *Journal of Fudan University*, (5), 112-119.

Feng Qinghua. 1997. *A Practical Coursebook of Translation*[M]. Shanghai: Shanghai Foreign Language Education Press.

Fu Daobin & Yu Fu. 2002. *What is Literature?* [M]. Beijing: Peking University Press.

Fu Jingmin & Zhang Hong.2020，Towards Constructing A Viable Translation Criticism Discourse System[J]，*Shanghai Journal of Translators*（2），1-6.

Fu Xiaoping. 2005. "Newly Published Quality Translations Are in Bad Need!". *Literature Forum*, Mar. 17, 2005.

Gu Zhengkun. 2003. *China and West: Comparative Poetics and Translatology* [M]. Beijing: Tsinghua University Press.

Hai Fang. 2003. Statistics and Analysis of Domestication and Foreignization [J]. *Foreign Language Research*, (1), 99-103.

Han Dan. 2009. A Defence for Relativist Criticism[J]. *Theoretical Investigation*, (3), 161-165.

Han Mingdai. 1985. On Equal Value Translation [J]. *Shandong Foreign Language Teaching*，(1), 51-53.

Han Shuqin.2021.An Overview of Domestic Translation Criticism Study:（2011-2021）[J]. *Foreign Language and Translation*,(4):46-50.

He Haibing & Qin Hongyi. 2008. Studies on Social Evaluation: Its Progress, Problems and Wayout[J]. *Social Scientist*, (4), 132-134.

He Lin. 1984. On Translation[A]. *Collected Papers on Translation Studies*:1894-1948[C]. Beijing: Foreign Language Teaching and Research Press.

Huang Kaifeng. 2001. *Aesthetics in Light of Axiology*[M]. Shanghai：Xuelin Publishing House.

Huang Shuquan. 2001. *New Perceptions on Literary Criticis*m[M]. Hefei：Anhui University Press.

Hu Gengshen. 2013. *Eco-Translatology: Construction & Interpretation* [M].Beijing：Commercial Press.

Hu Gengshen. 2019. Thoughts on Studies of "Eco-Translatology and Eco-Civilization Construction"[J]. *Journal of PLA University of Foreign Languages*，（2）：125-131.

Hu Gengshen. 2021. On Creative Initiatives and Its Going Global of Eco-translatology [J]. *Journal of Zhejiang University*（*Humanities and Social Sciences*）,(1): 174-186

Hu Gengshen & Wang Yuan. 2021. Paradigm of Eco-translatology: Location, Connotations and Characteristics[J]. *Foreign Language Education*，（6）：1-6.

Hu Kaibao.2011.*Introduction to Corpus-based Translation Studies* [M].Shanghai：Shanghai Jiaotong University Press.

Hu Kaibao.2018.*Introduction to Corpus-based Critical Translation Studies* [M]. Beijing：Higher Education Press.

Hu Tingshu.2017.Transformation of translation paradigms: A Philosophical Perspective [J]. *Journal of Xi'an International Studies University*，（1）：115-120.

Huang Qiongying. 2002. Translation Criticism in the Past Ten Years[J].Journal of Foreign Language College,Shandong Normal University,(4),69-72.

Huang Zhonglian. 2000. *Essence of Translation*[M]. Wuhan: Central China Normal University Press.

Huang Zhonglian. 2013. *Criticism on Translation Studies*[M]. Beijing: National Desense Industry Press.

Huang Zhonglian & li Zhenglin.2015.Thoughts on Translation Criticism from the Perspective of Semiotics[J]. *Foreign Language Education*, (4): 95-97+113.

Jiang Qiuxia.2002. *Aesthetic Progression in Literary Translation:Image-G Actualization* [M]. Beijing: Commercial Press.

Jiang Zhiwen & Wen Jun. 1999. *On Translation Criticism*[C]. Chongqing: Chongqing University Press.

Jiao Juyin. 1950. On Translation Criticism [J]. *Chinese Translators Journal*, (6), 6-9.

Jin Di. 1986. On Translation of Equivalent Effect [J]. *Foreign Language Teaching and Research*, (6), 6-14.

Jin Di. 1998. *A Study on Translation of Equivalent Effect* [M]. Beijing: China Translation and Publishing Corporation.

Jin Shenghua. 1997. *Eighty Essays on Translation*[M]. Beijing: China Translation and Publishing Corporation.

Ke Ping. 1993. *A Textbook of Translation Between E-C and C-E*[M]. Beijing: Peking University Press.

Lai Qinfang. 2006. Reconsideration of Liu Xie's Wen-Zhi Theoru[J]. *Jianghuai Tribune*, (1), 148-154.

Lan Hongjun. 2020. Task of Translation Criticism—To Rebuild the Discourse Power of TC[J]. *Foreign Language Education*,(3):84-88.

Li Deshun. 2004. *New Axiology*[M]. Kunming: Yunnan People's Press.

Li Guohua. 1999. *The Science of Literary Criticism*[M]. Shijiazhuang: Hebei University Press.

Li Jinshu, 2020. A Four-dimensional Approach to Writing a Period-specific History of Translation Criticism[J]. *Chinese Translators Journal*, (6): 5-12。

Li Lianke. 2003. *Introduction to Philosophy of Axiology* [M]. Beijing: Commercial Press.

Li Ming. 2006. *Translation Criticism and Appreciation* [M]. Wuhan: Wuhan University Press.

Li Xiaomin & Yang Zijian. 2003. Rethinking the Criteria for Translation Criticism [J].

Shanghai Journal of Translators for Science and Technology，(3), 17-20.

Li Zhengshuan. 2004. Faithful Equivalence: An Important Principle for Translation of Chinese Poems into English[J]. *Foreign Languages and Their Teaching*，（8）:36-40.

Li Zhengshuan & Yan Yunxia. 2020. Xu Yuanchong's Translation Thoughts: Contribution to and Implication for China-to-foreign Discourse System in Literature[J]. *Journal of Xi'an International Studies University*，(1): 93-98.

Liao Qiyi. 2000. *Studies on Contemporary Western Translation Theories* [M]. Nanjing：Translations Publishing House.

Liao Qiyi. 2020. *Studies on Discourse of Translation Criticism of the 20ᵗʰ Century in China*[M]. Beijing: Peking University Press.

Lin Huangtian. 1997. *A Dictionary of Translation in China*[Z]. Wuhan：Hubei Education Press.

Ling Chenguang. 2001. *Contemporary Literary Criticism*[M]. Jinan：Shandong University Press.

Liu Huawen.2011. Three Chinese Classical Approaches to Translation Criticism[J]. *Foreign Languages Research*, （5）：81-85+112.

Liu Junping. 2019. *A General History of Western Translation Theory*（2ed edition）[M]. Wuhan：Wuhan University Press.

Liu Miqing. 1990. *Modern Translation Theory*[M]. Nanchang：Jiangxi Education Press.

Liu Miqing. 2005. *Introduction to Aesthetics of Translation*[M]. Beijing：China Translation and Publishing Corporation.

Liu Miqing. 2005. *A Comparative Study of Chinese and Western Translation Theories* [M]. Beijing：China Translation and Publishing Corporation.

Liu Xingfeng & Wang Hong. 2016. Shifts, Problems and Countermeasures of Translation Studies[J]. *Foreign Languages Research*, (2) : 87－91.

Liu Yunhong.2015. *Studies on Translation Criticism*[M].Nanjing：Nanjing University Press.

Liu Yunhong & Xu Jun (eds).2015. *Studies on Translation Criticism: Theories and Methods* by [C]. Nanjing：Nanjing University Press.

Liu Yunhong & Xu Jun. 2017. The Location and Values of Translation[J]. *Chinese Translators Journal*, (06): 54-61.

Liu Yunhong.2018，Theoretical Studies and Practice of Translation Criticism in the New Era[J]. *Chinese Translators Journal*, （6）：15-17.

Liu Yunhong (ed).2020.*Criticism of Criticism: Construction and Reflection of Theories of Translation Criticism*[C]. Nanjing：Nanjing University Press.

Liu Zequan & Zhang Bing. 2012. An Overview of Domestic Studies on Translation Quality Assessment[J]. *Journal of Yanshan University (Philosophy and Social Science Edition)*，（3）：96-100.

Liu Zhongde. 1991.*Ten Lectures on Literary Translation*[M]. Beijing：China Translation and Publishing Corporation.

Liu Zhongde. 2002. *Studies on Western Translation Theories* [M]. Beijing：China Translation and Publishing Corporation.

Luo Xuanmin. 2006. Ideology and Literary Translation ———A Brief Discussion on LIANG Qi-chao's Translation Practice ［J］. Journal of Tsinghua University(Philosophy and Social Sciences), (1):46-52.

Luo Xinzhang. 1984. *A Collection of Essays on Translation*[C]. Beijing：Commercial Press.

Lv Jun & Hou Xiangqun. 2009. *An Introduction to the Science of Translation Criticism* [M]. Shanghai: Shanghai Foreign Language Education Press.

Lv Jun & Hou Xiangqun. 2010. Paradigm Shift or Perspective Switch: A Response to Prof. Xie Tianzhen [J]. *Chinese Translators Journal*, (1)，41-45

Lv Jun & Hou Xiangqun. 2001. *A Coursebook of English-Chinese Translation*[M]. Shanghai: Shanghai Foreign Language Education Press.

Lv Jun & Hou Xiangqun. 2006. *Translatology—A Constructivist Perspective of Translation Study* [M]. Shanghai: Shanghai Foreign Language Education Press.

Lv Jun. 2000. Linguistic Turn in Philosophy and Translation Studies[J]. *Journal of Foreign Languages*.（5）

Lv Jun. 2001. A Retrospect and Prospect of Translation Studies in China [J]. *Chinese Translators Journal*，(6), 8-11.

Lv Jun. 2002a. Literary Translation:A Special Kind of Communicative Action [J]. *Journal of PLA University of Foreign Languages*, (1), 63-66.

Lv Jun. 2002b. Translation studies: from theory of text to theory of power and discourse [J]. *Journal of Sichuan International Studies University*, (1),106-109.

Lv Jun. 2002c. Translation Criterion in the Post-Modernist Cultural Context[J]. *Foreign Languages and Their Teaching*, (3), 41-45.

Lv Jun. 2004. Xu Jun's *On Translation*: A Book on Translation Studies Worth of Careful Reading [J]. *Foreign Languages and Their Teaching*, (4), 61-64.

Lv Jun. 2006. Axiology and the Science of Translation Criticism [J]. *Journal of*

Foreign Languages, (1),52-59.

Lv Jun. 2007a. The Crisis of Translation Criticism and the Science of Translation Criticism[J]. *Foreign Language Research*, (1),125-130.

Lv Jun. 2007b. An Axiological Reflection on the Criteria of Translation Criticism[J]. *Shanghai Journal of Translators*, (1)，1-6.

Lv Jun. 2007c. The Multiplicity of Translation Criterion and the Objectivity of Evaluation [J]. *Journal of Foreign Languages*, (2), 67-73

Lv Jun. 2007d. *Selected Papers on Translation Studies by Lv Jun*[M]. Shanghai: Fudan University Press.

Ma Hongjun. 2000. *Random Talks on Translation Criticism*[M]. Beijing：China Translation and Publishing Corporation.

Ma Junfeng. 1999. Several Theoretical Questions about Evaluation Studies [J]. *Theory and Modernization*, (12), 4-8.

Ma Junfeng. 1994. *Studies on Evaluation Activity*[M]. Beijing：China Renmin University Press.

Ma Zuyi. 1984. *A Brief History of Translation in China*[M]. Beijing：China Translation and Publishing Corporation.

Min Ze & Dang Shengyuan. 1999. *Value of Literary Works* [M]. Beijing：Social Sciences Academic Press.

Mu Lei. 2007. Definition and Location of Translation Test[J]. *Foreign Language Education*, (1), 82-86.

Peng Zhen. 1997. Criticism of Literary Translation: Structure and Function [J]. *Journal of Peking University(Special issue of Foreign Languages and Literature)*.

Qian Mu. 2005. *New Interpretations of the Analects of Confucius*[M]. Shanghai: Joint Publishing.

Ren Ping. 2000. A Study on the Viewpoint of Communicative Practice[J]. *Seeking Truth*, (3), 13-18.

Shen Yuping (ed). 2002. *Selected Western Translation Theories* [M]. Beijing: Foreign Language Teaching and Research Press.

Shi Fuwei. 2006. Significance of Distinguishing Value Standard from Evaluation Standard [J]. *Journal of Party College of Sichuan Province Committee of CCP*, (2), 99-101.

Si Xianzhu. 2004. On the Model for Translation Quality Assessment in Light of Functional Linguistics [J]. *Foreign Language Education*, (4), 45-50.

Si Xianzhu. 2006. Revisiting the Translation Criteria in Light of Functional

Linguistics [J]. *Foreign Language Education*, (2) 63-67)

Si Xianzhu. 2008. Reconsideration on the Model for Translation Quality Assessment in Light of Functional Linguistics [J]. *Chinese Translators Journal*,(2), 57-60.

Si Xianzhu.2007.*Translation Studies: A Functional Linguistics Approach— Constructing a Translation Quality Assessment Model* [M]. Beijing: Peking University Press.

Su Fuzhong. 2001. On Assessment and its Criteria[J]. *Journal of Jinan University*, (6), 11-15.

Sun Yingchun. 2003. A Study on the "Plural Complementarism of Translation Standard" [J]. *Foreign Languages and Their Teaching*, (8), 43-45.

Sun Zhili. 1996. *Introduction to Translation of British and American Literature: 1949-1966* [M]. Nanjing: Translations Press.

Sun Zhili. 1999.Translation Criticism in the New Period [J]. *Chinese Translators Journal*, (3), 2-6.

Tan Zaixi & Nida. 1987. Five approaches to translation[J]. *Foreign Language Teaching and Research*, (1): 24-30.

Tan Zaixi. 2005. *Translatology*[M]. Wuhan: Hubei Education Press.

Tan Zaixi. 2007. The Absolute and Relative Nature of Translation[J]. *Journal of Guangdong University of Foreign Studies*, (1), 5-9.

Tang Jun.2005. Theoretical Thinking on Translation Criticism[J]. *Minzu Tribune*, (6), 58-59.

Wang Shunning. 2002. Basic Questions of Nietzsche's Aesthetics [J]. *Philosophical Research*, (4), 61-67.

Wang Dongfeng.2004.The Deconstruction of "Fidelity" and the Demythologization of Translation[J]. *Chinese Translators Journal*, (6), 3-9.

Wang Hongtao. 2016. Critical Reflections on Socio-Translation Studies[J]. *Chinese Translators Journal*, (4):6-13.

Wang Enmian. 1999. On Translation Criticism in China [J]. *Chinese Translators Journal*, (4), 7-10.

Wang Enke. Study on the Subject of Translation Criticism in Light of Axiology [J]. *Foreign Languages Research*, 2020(2):70-75+90.

Wang Ning.2021.Eco-translatology: Rise of A Humanity Paradigm[J]. *Foreign Language Education*, (6):7-11.

Wang Fulin. 1997. *The Analects of Confucius（annotation and translation）* [M]. Beijing: World Publishing Corporation.

Wang Haiming. 2004. Ethical Relativism and Ethical Absolutism [J]. *Sixiang Zhanxian*, (2): 25-29.

Wang Hong.2014. A probe into the English translation of The Peony Pavilion[J]. *Foreign Studies*，(1): 84-92.

Wang Hongyin. 2001. *50 Poems In A Dream Of Red Mansions: A Comparative Study Of Two English Versions* [M]. Xi'an: Shanxi Normal University Press.

Wang Hongyin. 2006. *On the Criticism of Literary Translatio*n [M]. Shanghai: Shanghai Foreign Language Education Press.

Wang Kefei. 1997. On the Nature of Translation[J]. *Foreign Languages and Their Teaching*, (4) ,47-50.

Wang Kefei.2012.*Approaches to Corpus-based Translation Studies* [M]. Shanghai: Shanghai Jiaotong University Press.

Wang Shuhuai.2020. Affect Appraisal in Fictional Translation Criticism—Taking Zhufu as an Examole[J]. *Foreign Language Research*, （5）: 86-92.

Wang Tianming. 1989. On Equivalence in Literary Translation[J]. *Modern Foreign Languages*, (4), 20-27.

Wang Yichuan(ed). 2009. *A Textbook of Western Literary Criticism*[M]. Beijing: Peking University Press.

Wang Yuliang. 2000. New Perception on the Scientificity of Value Standard [J]. *Journal of Xi'an Politics Institute*,(4), 80-82.

Wang Yuliang. 2006. On Deng Xiaoping's Practice-oriented Axiological Thought [J]. *New Horizons from Tianfu*, (1), 13-22.

Wen Xiuying. 2007. Translation Criticism: From Theory to Practice [M]. Tianjin: Nankai University Press.

Wen Jun & Liu Ping. 2006. Translation Criticism in the Past 50 Years: Retrospective and Perspective [J]. *Gansu Social Sciences*, (2), 38-43.

Wen Jun. 2000. Translation Criticism: Classification,Function, Process and Criteria[J]. *Journal of Chongqing University(Social Scirnces Edition)*, (1) , 65-68.

Wen Jun. 2006. *Introduction to Scientific Translation Criticism* [M]. Beijing: China Translation and Publishing Corporation.

Wen Jun (ed). 2006. *A Hundred Year of Translation Criticism in China* [M]. Beijing: Beihang University Press.

Wu Xinxiang & Li Hong'an. 1990. *On Equivalent Translation* [M]. Nanchang: Jiangxi Education Press.

Wu Xinxiang & Li Hong'an. 1984. A Tentative Study on Equal Value Transformations[J]. *Foreign Language Teaching and Research*, (3), 1-10.

Xia Zhaohui & Cao Hejian. 2003. Quantitative Evaluation of Stylistic Translational Equivalence[J]. *Journal of Hunan University（Social Sciences）*, (1), 84-87.

Xiao Xinfa. 2004. Appraise the Theory of Key Element[J]. *Wuhan University Journal （Humanity Sciences）*, (5), 523-528.

Xiao Weiqing.2010. Studies on Models of Translation Criticism[M]. Shanghai: Shanghai Foreign Language Education Press.

Xu Jun (ed). 2001. *Theory and Practice of Literary Translation: Dialogues Recorded* [M]. Nanjing：Translations Press.

Xu Jun and Gao Fang. 2006. Internet and literary translation criticism[J]. *Foreign Language Teaching and Research*, (3)，216-220.

Xu Jun and Mu Lei. 2009. Translation Studies in the Past Three Decades (1978 -2007)[J]. *Journal of Foreign Languages*, (1)，77-87.

Xu Jun, Yuan Xiaoyi. 2001. *ContemporaryTranslation Studies in France*[M]. Wuhan：Hubei Education Press.

Xu Jun. 1992. *Studies on Criticism of Literary Translation* [M]. Nanjing：Translations Publishing House.

Xu Jun. 2003. *On Translation*[M]. Wuhan：Hubei Education Press.

Xu Jun. 2005. Translation Crisis and Absence of Criticism[J]. *China BookReview*, (9), 12-15.

Xu Yuanchong. 1984. *The Art of Translation*[M]. Beijing：China Translation and Publishing Corporation.

Xu Yuanchong. 2000. New Translation Theory in the New Century[J]. *Chinese Translators Journal*，(3), 2-6.

Xu Yuanchong. 2002. Literary Translation and Translation of Science[J]. *Shanghai Journal of Translators for Science and Technology*, (4), 1-4.

Xu Yuanchong. 2003. Three Questions for A Literary Translator[J]. *Chinese Translators Journal*，(4), 30-33.

Yang Guorong. 2006. On Feng Qi's Epistemology in the Broader Sense[J].*History of Chinese Phikosophy*, (1), 103-110.

Yang Xiaorong. 2001. Foundation of Criteria for Translation: Condition[J]. *Journal of Foreign Languages*, (4), 70-76.

Yang Xiaorong. 2005. *Introduction to Translation Criticism* [M]. Beijing：China Translation and Publishing Corporation.

Yang Yitang. 2009. Why We Still Sacrifice Confucious Today?[OL]. http://www.jnnews.tv/kongzi/2009-09/08/cms28358article.shtml

Yang Zijian & Liu Xueyun (eds). 1994. *New Perceptions of Translation*[C]. Wuhan: Hubei Education Press.

Yang Zijian. 2006. Comments on Translation Criticism: Preface of *On the Criticism of Literary Translation*[J]. *Journal of PLA University of Foreign Languages*, (1), 52-54.

Yi Zhongtian. 2008. Interview with Yi Zhongtian by *Jiefang Daily* [OL]. 2008-11-19. http://blog.sina.com.cn/s/blog_476e068a0100b2o6.html)

Yu Guangzhong. 2002. *Yu Guangzhong on Translation*[M]. Beijing: China Translation and Publishing Corporation.

Yu Zhenhua. 2007. Two Approaches to Expand Epistemology [J].*Journal of East China Normal University*, (2), 1-8.

Zhang Boran & Xu Jun (eds). 2002. *Translation Studies Facing the New Century* [C]. Beijing: Commercial Press.

Zhang Jin. 1987. *Principles of Literary Translation*[M]. Kaifeng: Henan University Press.

Zhang Mi. 2021. The Name and Nature of Translation Criticism Studies: An Interview with Prof. Juliane House[J]. *Journal of Yanshan University(Philosophy and Social Science)*, （3）: 91-95.

Zhang Peiji et al. 1986. *A Coursebook of English-Chinese Translation* [M]. Shanghai: Shanghai Foreign Language Education Press.

Zhang Xianghao & Chen Yi. 2009. Revisiting Wang Yangming's Theory of Mind[J]. *Journal of Southeast University (Philosophy and Social Science)*, (2), 70-72.

Zhang Xu. 2002. On the Internet Translated Literature[J].*Comparative Literature in China*, (2), 16-22.

Zhang Yanqin. 2007. Literary Translation in the Age of Internet and Diversity of Reader's Role [J]. *Journal of Guangdong University of Foreign Studies*, (6), 15-19.

Zhang Zhiqiang. 1998. Informational Adequacy and Cultural Transplant[J]. *Shanghai Journal of Translators for Science and Technology*, (4), 28-30.

Zhang Zhiqiang. 2006. Views on Translation and Translation Teaching[J]. *Shanghai Journal of Translators*, (3), 40-43.

Zhang Zhiqiang. 2008. Analysis of Contextual Features, Translation and Translation Criticism [J]. *Translations*, (3), 205-209.

Zhang Zhiqiang & Yang Ningwei.2021.Achievements, Problems and Methods in Current Studies on Translation of Chinese Classics[J].*Foreign Languages and Translation*，（4）:19-25.

Zhang Zhizhong．2015.*An Aesthetic Study on Poetry Translation*[M]. Beijing：Commercial Press.

Zhao Dunhua. 2006. *Zhao Dunhua on Popper* [M]. Beijing: Peking University Press.

Zheng Hailing. 1999. New Criterion for Translation: Harmony[J]. *Chinese Translators Journal*, (4), 2-6.

Zheng Hailing. 2000. *Literary Translatology*[M]. Zhengzhou：Wenxin Publishing House.

China Translation and Publishing Corporation (ed). 1983. *Collected Papers on Translation Theories and Techniques* [C]. Beijing：China Translation and Publishing Corporation.

Zhou Jingshan. 2003. *Literary Criticism of "Chuang Zao She": from the Art-oriented to the Politics-oriented* [D]. Doctorial Dissertation of Fudan University.

Zhou Lingshun.2014a. *Translator Behavior Criticism: A Theoretical Framework* [M]. Beijing：Commercial Press.

Zhou Lingshun.2014b. *Translator Behavior Criticism: An Approach Explored* [M]. Beijing：Commercial Press.

Zhou Lingshun.2019. New Trend of Translation Criticism[N].*Social Sciences Post*,2019-8-1-005.

Zhou Lingshun & Zhou Yike.2020. What Criteria Are Needed for Translation Criticism?—Establishment of A Model for Translator Behavior Criticism[J]. *Foreign Languages and Their Teaching*, （5）:107-117+138.

Zhou Yi & Luo Ping. 1999. *A Critical View on Translation*[M]. Wuhan：Hubei Education Press.

Zhou Zhaoxiang. 1998. *Translation and Life*[M]. Beijing：China Translation and Publishing Corporation.

Zhou Zhaoxiang. Translation in the 21 century: value for money[OL]. http://www.simonchou.hk/Chinese_GB/index.htm

Zhu Chunshen. 2008. *Words, Texts, Poetics: New Perspectives on Translation*[M]. Nanjing：Translations Press.

Zhu Liyuan. 1997. *Contemporary Western Literary Theories*[M]. Shanghai：East China Normal University Press.

Zhu Wanjin. 1992. *Introduction to Sociolinguistics*[M]. Changsha: Hunan Education

Press.

http://en. Wikipedia.org/wiki/Paradigm

http://en.wikipedia.org/wiki/Hermeneutics

http://www.evaluationwiki.org/index.php/Evaluation_Definition:_What_is_
    Evaluation%3F

http://www.fit-europe.org/vault/deont/CODE_PROF_PRACTICE.pdf

http://www.fit-ift.org/en/charter.php

http://www.newworldencyclopedia.org/entry/Hans-Georg_Gadamer

http://www.religioustolerance.org/parliame.htm

Acknowledgments

At the completion of this book, We would like to express our heartfelt appreciation to those who have helped us during the program in one way or another.

First, we are particularly indebted to Professor Lv Jun at Nanjing Normal University for his insightful understandings of Translation Studies, especially in the field of translation criticism.

We then extend our heartfelt thanks to Prof. Zhang Boran of Nanjing University, Prof. Xin Bin of Nanjing Normal University, Prof. Liu Junping of Wuhan University, Prof. Cai Xinle of Shenzhen University, Prof. Wang Hong of Suzhou University, Prof. Yang Xiaorong of Nanjing Guoguan University, Prof. Ke Ping of Nanjing University for their precious suggestions on the book.

Our gratitude also goes to Prof. Mona Baker, Dr. James St. Andre, Dr. Siobhan Brownlie, Dr. Maeve Olohan of the Center for Translation and Intercultural Studies at the University of Manchester where one of the authors, Zhang Zhiqiang was once a visiting scholar with Prof. Mona Baker acting as his host supervisor. And he will never forget the librarians at The University of Manchester who offered a lot of help for the books in and out of the University libraries. Moreover, he would like to thank Juliane House with whom he had a discussion about translation criticism during his visit at The University of Manchester.

Sincere thanks go also to Dell Hymes, Lawrence Venuti, Gideon Toury etc. who offered timely reply to our questions via emails.

Furthermore, we would like to express our heartfelt thanks to our colleagues of the Faculty of International Studies, Henan Normal University where we are working, for their warm-hearted help and support.

Last but not least, we are greatly indebted to our families, for their unremitting love, support and encouragement all the time.